RISE OF THE RANGER

THE ECHOES SAGA: BOOK ONE

PHILIP C. QUAINTRELL

Copyright © 2017 by Philip C. Quaintrell
First edition published 2017.

Cover Illustration by Chris McGrath
Book design by BodiDog Design
Edited by David Bradley

ISBN: 978-1-916610-00-2 (paperback)
ASIN: B072BL3C3C (ebook)

Published by Quaintrell Publishings

For my Dad. I wouldn't be a geek without you...

ALSO BY PHILIP C. QUAINTRELL

GRIMWHAL

BHAN DORAL

KHALDARIM

DHENAHEIM

THE WHISTLING MOU

SILVYR HALL

THE VENGORAN MOUNTAINS

THE KING'S LAKE

NAMDHOR

HYNDAERN

SKYSTEAD

THE WHITE VALE

ILLIA

NIMDUHN

WOOD VALE

KELP TOWN

THE KING'S INN

IKIRITH

GREY STONE

THE EVERMOORE

SNOWFELL

BLEAK

THE NORD

LIRIAN

CARSTANE

THE WILD MOORES

ELETHIAH

VANGARTH

WHI TO

QAMNARAN

THE NARROWS

WEST FELLION

THE MOONLIT PLAIN

ILYTHYRA

GA

LAKE NUBIA

NALL

AMEERASKA

TREGARAN

THE ARID LAND

THE HOX

THE OLD GARDEN

KARATH

SYLA'S GATE

SYLA'S GATE

THE UNDYING MOUNTAINS

ITHILIA

LAKE RANDI

THE BLACK LAKE

DRAMATIS PERSONAE

Abigail Rose
A human mage and student of Korkanath.

Adellum Bövö
A general and member of the Hand of Valanis.

Adilandra Sevari
The elven queen of Elandril and mother of Reyna.

Alidyr Yalathanil
An elf and master of Nightfall.

Asher
A human ranger and previous member of Nightfall.

Darius Devale
A human knight of the Graycoat order.

～

Elaith Nevandar
A human knight-in-training of the Graycoat order.

Faros Kalvanak
Boy Emperor of Karath and Lord of The Arid Lands.

Faylen Haldör
An elf and mentor to Reyna Sevari.

Gal Tion
The first human king of Illian, a thousand years ago.

Galanör Reveeri
An elven warrior.

Galkarus Vod
A human mage in the court of King Rengar.

Gideon Thorn
A human mage and student at Korkanath.

Gregorn Orvish
King of Grey Stone and Lord of The Ice Vales.

Hyvark
High priest and advisor to The Goddess.

Isabella Harg
Queen of Lirian and Lady of Felgarn.

Krenorak
A Darkakin warrior.

∾

Lord Marshal Horvarth
Head of the Graycoats.

Merkaris Tion
King of Namdhor and Lord of Orith.

Mörygan Mörgö
An elf and advisor to Princess Reyna Sevari.

Nakir Galvörd
A general and member of the Hand of Valanis.

Nasta Nal-Aket
The Father of Nightfall.

Nathaniel Galfrey
A human knight and member of the Graycoats.

Ned Fennick
A human knight and member of the Graycoats.

Rengar Marek
King of Velia and Lord of Alborn.

Reyna Sevari
An elven princess.

Ro Dosarn
A human assassin and a member of Nightfall.

Samandriel Zathya
A general and member of the Hand of Valanis.

Thallan Tassariön
A general and member of the Hand of Valanis.

The Goddess
The queen of the Darkakin.

Tobin Galfrey
Previous Graycoat and late father of Nathaniel Galfrey.

Tyberius Gray
The founder of the Graycoats.

Valanis
The dark elf and self-proclaimed herald of the gods.

THE
ECHOES OF FATE
THE PROPHECY

These Favoured elves fall and lose their way, as man's anger devours all dragons' fire. The immortal man is set to rise, bringing the dark one closer to his most dangerous desire.

Paldora's celestial gem graces the daylight, and in its beauty ordains calamity. Only alliance and trust between two shores offers an intimation of hope and a glimpse of eternity.

Children of fire and flame offer great promise, but only one perceives the time we will fall. As the Gods recast their fortune and power, one will suffer the burden of destiny for all.

- Nalana Sevari

PROLOGUE

T he sound of men dying in battle wasn't unknown to Asher. In the past, he had remained hidden, while his father and brothers had fought against rival clans in The Wild Moores.

The boy had heard the sound of their weapons clash and the noises men made when they died. But he had never heard the sounds that drifted through the open window now, carried in the wake of a hundred war horns. When the elves went into battle, it could not be called a conflict or a skirmish, as it was with the human tribes, but was in fact given another name that was new to Asher.

The elves called it a war...

The cries of the two armies were drowned out by the ominous beating of heavy wings that thundered overhead, delivering deaths by the hundreds across the battlefield below - their fiery breath igniting the sky. The battle outside had spread, breaching Elethiah's great walls and drawing ever closer, the clash of steel against steel echoing through its stone corridors.

Asher dared to steal a glance over the window ledge, only to be terrified by the hulking shadow that flew across the moon, eclipsing its glow with bat-like wings. The boy quickly ducked, hugging the cold stone and scrambling for the safety of the large wooden table in the centre of the room. His nine-year-old body was too gangly for his young mind to control, and he barely registered the pain as his head bumped into the table leg. Asher's heart pounded in his chest at the sound of a roar no man could rightfully stand against. The great flying beasts went by another name that was new to the young boy, and the word felt strange in his mouth. The elves called them dragons!

The door to his right burst open in a splintering of wood, accompanied by the familiar song of swords colliding with incredible speed. From his sheltered vantage, Asher could only see a pair of armoured legs stagger into the room, crashing into the table, as another pair of legs followed him in, clad in a flowing white dress that danced around their foe. The laboured breaths of a man and a woman were matched by the slash and parry of their swords. The armoured legs jumped onto the table as metal scraped against the smooth wood, knocking over Asher's glass and the jug of water, before finally landing on the other side. Water washed over the parchments covering the table and poured over the edge, splashing the boy's hands and face.

The white dress dashed over the table, making no sound at all. Something softer than a sword struck the armoured man and sent him stumbling into a bookshelf. The white dress dropped to the floor once more and met its attacker with a flurry of swords and sparks.

The conflict came to a swift end as one of the swords hit the floor with a loud clatter, and hot red blood spattered against the stone. The armoured feet faltered, until a pair of knees fell to the floor, under the crumpling body of a dark-haired elf. Blood rushed from his throat and mixed with the water, slithering ever closer to where the boy knelt. Asher gasped, trying to crawl backward as the blood moved like a snake towards him.

"Asher!" The white dress wrinkled as the beautiful face of a blonde elf appeared under the table top. Her fair features were

2

marred with concern at the sight of him. Droplets of blood were streaked across her cheeks and golden hair, though they did nothing to reduce her beauty.

With one strong hand, she pulled him out from under the table, careful not to drag him through the blood. She steadied him by the shoulders and quickly checked him over for any injuries, her soft hands gliding over his skin.

"I'm fine." Asher gently reached for her hands and pushed them away.

The boy was always ashamed of his ragged human appearance in the company of such magnificent creatures. His dirty clothes and unwashed skin made him stand out even more than usual next to her perfect complexion and exquisite clothes.

"We need to find your father and brother. You need to get back to The Wild Moores as fast as possible. You will be safer there."

That statement alone was proof of their dire situation. If The Wild Moores were safer than Elethiah, he hated to imagine what was going on beyond this room.

"I don't want to leave you, Nalana..." Asher looked into her crystal blue eyes and knew she would insist.

Nalana was the mother he'd never had and cared for him in a way his father and the rest of his clan never could. She had spent years teaching him the elven language, and countless days had been devoted to helping him read and write. He was the first of many Outlanders the elves planned to take in and teach to be civilised. After just four years of her tutelage, Asher knew he was already smarter than most of his clan, if not the strongest.

"There's no time, young one. You remember what I told you, about Valanis?"

Of course he remembered. Valanis was the tyrannical elf, set on ravaging the whole of Illian like a hungry plague of locusts. His name seemed to strike fear into the hearts of every elf in Elethiah. Asher's father had told him to leave elven troubles to elves, but Elethiah stood on the edge of The Wild Moores, and it seemed Valanis had brought his madness to the Outlanders' home too.

"His army attacks without fear of death. I don't know how long our forces and the dragons can keep them at bay. The eastern wall is already breached and they are swarming the city." Nalana nodded to the dead body behind him. "I will get you as far as the kitchens. Do you remember the door I showed you, our secret door?" He nodded absently, looking past her to the sound of fighting. "Take your family through there and run as fast as you can. Are you ready?"

Nalana took his hand and picked up her curved blade off the table. Asher had never seen her wield a sword before. It was hard to fathom that someone so delicate and gentle could be so deadly. The boy couldn't take his eyes off the sword and its unique shine, as the Outlander had never seen a sword as ornate and well-crafted as this. His own people could do no better than blunt axes and weak spears. The flat of the blade was engraved with runes he had yet to learn, and he once again felt the hunger for knowledge that Nalana had awoken in him.

They made their way through the halls and adjoining rooms as quickly and quietly as they could, Asher by comparison to Nalana sounding like a team of Centaurs. When eventually the choice of direction arose, left or right, Nalana hesitated. Asher had just enough fear to extinguish his excitement at the path the elf chose. They soon passed under a large wooden arch that led into Elethiah's grand library, a forbidden place. The race of men was not granted access to the ancient tomes of the elves, for fear of the books being mishandled.

It was everything he imagined and more as the room opened up into a tall oval shape, covered in wall-to-wall books, and with walkways connected by spiral staircases. Every corner was illuminated by a soft glow, emanating from yellow orbs that floated between the shelves. The orbs were a simple creation for any elf with a basic understanding of magic. It was an understanding Asher was decades away from grasping. Long tables of red-brown wood filled the space between the archway and the double doors on the other side. Asher knew that the library offered a shortcut through the main palace and had always hated taking the longer route to reach Nalana's teaching room.

Without warning, the doors were violently thrust open as four elves in dark armour and shadowy cloaks strode into the room.

Nalana pushed Asher back, putting herself instinctively in front of him while raising her sword. "Stay back, Asher."

He did as he was told and clung to the wooden arch at his back.

Nalana calmly walked around the long table and closed the gap between her and the dark elves. Their movements were hard for Asher to keep track of as they advanced on her with great speed, each of their swords angled to remove a limb. Nalana's grace and precision were unparalleled by the dark elves, and she deflected two of the strikes whilst narrowly dodging the others. Metal rang against metal in every direction as the fighters danced across the table top. Nalana looked a true warrior, using her hands and feet to push the dark elves back, whilst knocking a short-haired elf off the table with a strong backhand from her sword.

"Nalana!" Her younger brother, Elym, charged into the library with his dark hair flowing out behind him.

Elym deftly flipped onto the table and charged in with his double-ended spear. Nalana cut down the tallest of their attackers, removing his head and the hand of another elf in one blow. Elym took the advantage and impaled the one-handed elf with his spear, twisting his own body to avoid the blade of the third attacker. Asher watched as the back-handed dark elf rose from the floor, ready to swipe Nalana's legs out. To protect his teacher, the Outlander reacted without thinking and pulled a leather-bound book off the nearest shelf and threw it into the dark elf's face. The surprise blow was all Nalana needed to drop to one knee and drive her blade straight down into the elf's head, burying it deep into his body.

Elym's sudden cry of pain pierced the library, as his blood splattered against the wood. Nalana spun on the ball of her foot and whipped her sword across the final dark elf's chest, slicing through the armour and splitting his ribcage. Nalana paid him no heed as he toppled off the table, instead rushing to the aid of her brother. Asher had met Elym several times over the years, but the young elf had never quite agreed with teaching the wild humans, who had arrived from lands unknown to the elves.

Asher ran to the table, making a wide circle around the dead elves. Nalana held Elym in her arms as blood slowly poured from a gash across his gut. He groaned in pain and clung tightly to his sister.

"I have seen worse little brother..."

"We don't have time." Elym's words came through gritted teeth. "I came from the Hall of Life." The young elf reached into his tunic and tugged at the silver chain around his neck. He presented Nalana with a rugged, black crystal the size of his little finger. "Valanis is here. They're preparing to cast the Amber Spell..." He placed the crystal in the palm of her hand. "He's already killed the king and Lady Syla. We need to keep it safe, Nalana."

She remained silent; staring at the necklace with an expression Asher couldn't read. Elym's pain-filled cry, however, brought her out of the reverie soon enough. Nalana looked from her brother to Asher, gripping the crystal until her knuckles whitened.

"Asher..." Nalana called him closer. "I will stay with Elym. You need to find your family and make for The Wild Moores. Stop for nothing." Nalana rested her brother's head on her knee and quickly looped the necklace over Asher's head. "Take this and hide it deep in the forest. I will come for you when the battle is over." Asher stared at the crystal sitting in the middle of his chest before Nalana tucked it into his ragged top. "Run, Asher!"

With a lasting look at the siblings, he ran for the door.

Asher made for the kitchens, calling his father and brother as he did. Fighting had broken out across the palace, forcing him to search for new ways through the stone corridors.

"Asher!" His father's voice echoed down the hall. Typically, they were already hiding around the kitchens, always looking for food to take back to The Wild Moores. "Where have you been? We were about to leave without you!"

Such were the ways of his people. You either help the clan or you get left behind.

His older brother looked truly scared, clearly having witnessed the elves in combat or one of the winged beasts that swarmed above the city. Asher's father was sweating, no doubt fearful for his own survival while being slowed by his sons.

"This way, follow me!" Asher led them through the kitchens and down into an old tunnel, long abandoned in favour of newer refurbishments.

His brother and father ran on ahead, while Asher closed the kitchen hatch behind them. Their splashing was easy to follow once Asher jumped off the last rung. At the end of the tunnel was an old wooden door that allowed a small grid of moonlight to illuminate the wet ground and moss-covered walls.

"He'll never make it!" His brother's voice echoed through the tunnel as the pair ran full pelt through the doorway.

Their doubt in Asher's ability to survive only spurred him on to run faster.

Both his father and brother ran into The Moonlit Plains, heading straight for The Wild Moores as if the dragons themselves were at their heels. Neither looked back to check on Asher.

Before reaching the door, Asher heard one last roar, this time from somewhere deep inside the palace. He didn't stop, but rather pressed on as fast as his legs would take him. The green fields, which glowed under the moonlight, came into view beyond the door. His father and brother ran for cover under the canopy of a large oak tree.

"Keep running!" his father shouted.

Asher's chest burned, desperate for breath, as he ran for the moonlight. The black crystal around his neck pulled at his attention when it floated out in front of him, still tethered to his neck. The unexplainable occurrence didn't stop him from running through the threshold with all haste.

Asher ran through and felt the cool night air suddenly transform into warmth, as blinding light erupted from all around. Dropping into the field, Asher covered his head, fearing the hot fury of what was surely a dragon's breath. An eternity went by as he waited for the inevitable pain and darkness of death to take him. But when death should have claimed him, Asher instead heard the squawk of a bird overhead and the warmth on his back was nothing but pleasant.

The Outlander opened his eyes to a world he didn't recognise.

A midday sun beat down on a field of overgrown, faded yellow grass. Asher stood up in a daze, his ankles deep in bog water where it had moments ago been hard ground and short green grass. He took a breath, slowly turning to survey his bizarre surroundings. The city of Elethiah remained behind him, where it should be, but as a shadow of its former glory. The stone had darkened and become overgrown with weeds and thick roots, which crawled up the great walls. To his left, were the remains of a demolished tower, lying in ruin where it had fallen. The oak tree, where his father and brother had taken shelter, was gone, a broken rotten stump in its place and his family nowhere in sight.

Beyond the stump, he could still see The Wild Moores in the distance. The forest was over five hundred miles from north to south with incredible depth. Asher gasped for breath, unbelieving of his new reality. Where had the night gone? Where had Valanis's forces and the dragons gone? Where was his family? He cried for his father and his brother, screaming at the top of his voice.

The reply came not from his father or brother, but from the howl of a creature he had never heard before. Asher ducked into a patch of long grass, seeing dark shapes moving through the strands, crouched low to hide their true form. Something slipped out of his shirt and he held it in front of him.

The black crystal...

He didn't have time to think about it before the howls came again, much closer this time. He dropped the crystal back into his shirt and ran for the forest that lay sprawled before him. His clan was surely in there somewhere and they would protect him. The rapid padding of many heavy feet came from behind, but he had no idea of their number.

It wasn't long, however, before he realised the forest was simply too far away. The Outlander would never make it before the predators caught him. Changing course, Asher ran for the collection of large rocks dug into the small hillside on his left. Maybe he could lose them in there.

By the time Asher reached the first rock, he was exhausted. He fell to the grass and crawled further into the outcropping. Rolling onto his back, he saw a lumbering creature climb the rock at his feet and stretch to its full height. Dark green scales covered its sloping leathery head, with two thick arms reaching down to its knees and ending in pointed fingers of sharp bone. Its face was closer to that of a lizard, with several rows of razor-sharp teeth. A screeching howl preceded five more, who appeared from behind the other stones, licking their maws with long slimy tongues.

The first creature jumped off the rock, blocking out the sun as it came to land on top of him - only it never did land, at least not alive. The beast had been struck in the face by an arrow, mid-air. Looking up from his back, Asher glimpsed a stranger charge over his head and dive into the fray, with a short-sword in one hand and a bow in the other. The beasts leaped at their new prey, only to have their limbs removed with every slash of the stranger's sword. His movements were similar to that of an elf but Asher could also see the differences; this was a man.

The fight was over in seconds and the stranger was standing amid a heap of diced monsters.

The stranger turned to Asher, his sword shining under the sun. He wore dark leather armour, engraved with unusual, intricate patterns, and a grey cloak which spread out across the ground, collecting mud. Perhaps the strangest element of his appearance was the red blindfold he wore. He had apparently defeated those beasts without his sight. The stranger proceeded to remove the red cloth from his face, revealing shadowed, brown eyes and curly black hair.

"Gobbers," the stranger stated flatly, wiping the blood off his sword with the edge of his cloak.

Asher had heard Nalana speak of such creatures and was thankful for surviving the encounter.

"And who might you be?" the stranger asked.

Asher's eyes searched the plains for his father once more. "I am... Asher," he stuttered.

"Is that a statement or a question, boy?" The stranger flicked his bow in the air, activating a series of mechanisms and cogs built into the wood. A moment later the bow had folded into itself, before the stranger placed it out of sight, under his cloak.

Had Asher not been too stunned by the events of the past few minutes, he would have marvelled at the bow's construction.

"My name is Asher," he replied more boldly, standing up and wiping the dirty water from his face.

The stranger regarded him curiously. "Is that it? Just Asher? Well, this is no place for a boy to wander; between the swamps of Elethiah and The Wild Moores... You must have a talent for survival." His voice had a foreign twang to it that Asher couldn't place.

The boy nodded absently, trying to make sense of the stranger's words. From here, Asher could see what remained of Elethiah. Its beautiful spires and domed towers were gone, with nothing but decay hanging over the entire land. It was more akin to a swamp now, the splendid Moonlit Plains nothing but a memory. He wrapped his hands around his arms feeling the cold against his wet skin.

The stranger announced, "I am Nasta Nal-Aket, of Nightfall..."

Asher remained silent, unaware of the man's significance or the place he was from.

"Have you never heard of it, boy?"

Asher shook his head slowly.

"I am a spectre, an Arakesh," he stated proudly.

Asher's face dropped at the sound of the elvish word; he knew that word.

"I am an assassin," Nasta Nal-Aket confirmed.

Asher stood his ground, as his father had taught him when facing a bear.

"If I had to guess from your appearance, I would say you're an Outlander."

Asher became self-conscious of the black tattoo, outlining a wolf's fang, below his left eye, signifying he was from a clan of hunters.

"I didn't think your kind strayed beyond The Wild Moores these days. What are you doing out here?" The assassin tucked his blindfold into his belt, letting it hang loosely in the breeze.

Asher noted the assassin steal a look at Elethiah, but he appeared physically disturbed by the landmark and walked further into the hillside as if to gain more distance.

The Outlander looked up at the sun and knew it should be the moon that greeted him. "I was..." Asher didn't know how to explain it. "The elves were fighting and..." He could only look at the ruins of Elethiah.

Nasta looked from the ruins to Asher in puzzlement. "Elves? Are you talking about The Dark War?"

Asher didn't know anything of a Dark War and began to look round for his family once more. They wouldn't be out there looking for him, he had fallen behind. He was alone.

"And what would a young Outlander know of a battle over a thousand years past?"

The gravity of Asher's situation drained the blood from his head, blurring his vision. "A thousand years..?" He spun in every direction, desperate to find something, anything familiar. The landscape began to blur when the colours of the world faded and his vision narrowed. The ground rose up to greet him and the darkness swallowed him whole.

PART ONE

CHAPTER I
A RANGER'S LIFE

Forty years later...

The forest began to close in, the canopy gathering until only the narrowest shafts of golden light illuminated the ground. The smell of damp wood and old moss had taken over the aroma of pine and sweet-scented flowers, the air now becoming stale and cool.

Asher had followed the tracks through The Evermoore for over six miles from the border of Whistle Town. However, the effects of the dark magic were just as easy to follow, with the life of the great wood decaying under the dark magic's insidious will.

Asher was careful to step over and between the fallen branches to hide his approach. Looking back, he could no longer discern his horse, Hector, the thoroughbred's black coat impossible to see through the mile of trees that separated them. He hated leaving his only companion behind but felt Hector would most certainly give him away, especially with his prey's senses. Asher had followed the human tracks but was more than aware of the giant paw prints which accompanied his target. The occupants of Whistle Town had seen those same tracks and immediately sought his unique expertise.

His measured approach did nothing to slow down the hunt, however. After decades of honing his every muscle and senses, under the tutelage of the most dangerous men and women in Verda, this was just another stroll through the woods. Asher continued on with the knowledge that he was the scariest thing in The Evermoore right now.

After another mile, Asher noticed the absence of wildlife around him. The ground remained undisturbed, but the sound of the birds faded until an eerie silence settled on the forest. The ranger pulled in his thick green cloak to avoid snagging it, as he climbed over a fallen log, pausing to run his hand over the three claw marks streaked across the wood. They were big. He tugged at a piece of fur caught in the splinters, holding it close under his nose. There was no mistaking the scent of a wolf, regardless of how mutated it was by the dark magic controlling it.

The drop from the log was short, but Asher continued his stealthy approach by slipping a hand under his cloak and supporting the quiver on his back. The arrows made no sound as his feet sank into the mud.

He pushed on, crouching routinely to check the tracks beneath the rotting plants. It wasn't long before the familiar smell of death reached his nostrils. Asher instinctively rested his left hand on the hilt of his sword, sheathed on his hip. His fingers wrapped around the two-handed grip until the spikes on the rounded pommel dug into his glove. A moment's consideration made him re-evaluate his approach and he released the handle, instead reaching for the rune sword on his back. The sound of the metal sliding out of the sheath was comforting, having been heard every day for as long as he could remember. The feelings associated with the sound had slowly grown from the fear of combat to the knowledge of his success.

The few beams of light that pierced the canopy reflected off the short-sword, accentuating the runes that ran the length of the blade.

The runes were an ancient script that predated the elves and was known to only a few across the whole of Verda. The ancient form of spellcasting imbued the rune sword with incredible durability and an edge sharp enough to cut through a Griffin's hide. Without them, Asher's job would be made that much harder.

The ranger hefted the weight in one hand, feeling the perfect equilibrium in the balance between the blade and the hilt. With the length of the blade being just shorter than his arm, it was easily manoeuvred as he twirled it in his hand. The sword was hourglass shaped and made from pure silvyr, the strongest and most expensive mineral in all of Verda. It had been forged by Danagarr, the greatest blacksmith in Illian. He was also a very short-tempered dwarf when he wasn't tending to his forge and anvil, but Asher was lucky enough to have the blacksmith in his debt, after an unfortunate incident with a Mountain Troll.

The point of his blade led Asher into a small clearing, devoid of light. The smell would be unbearable to most, but the old ranger thought nothing of it, more concerned with the creature that created such a foul stench of dead flesh and shit. Asher could feel the weight in the air as if a sixth sense was telling him there was something wrong with his environment, something unnatural. The dark magic was coalescing in the opening before him, the epicentre of the forest's infection.

He had found his prey.

Asher pulled tight on his fingerless glove to uncover the shard of black crystal, set into the silver ring on his right index finger. The fragment of the gem was his oldest possession and, though only a shard of the whole, still connected him to the magical world. This connection had always come naturally to him, for as long as he could remember. Despite the fog of his childhood memories, there was a part of him that recognised the dark crystal was responsible for his sensitivity to magic.

The ranger held up his hand and felt the familiar tingle in his fingertips. A ball of soft light was birthed in his palm before floating away, over his head. As the orb grew in height, so too did its intensity, until the gruesome scene was clear to see. Half-eaten bodies of men and women were strewn across the bloodied ground. Some were fresh kills with horrified expressions covered in buzzing flies, while others appeared to be skeletal and utterly decomposed. No single body was intact. Asher hesitated with his next step. It was impossible to walk through the clearing without stepping on a stray bone, some of which remained hidden beneath torn clothing.

The trees had grown tall, producing what looked from the ground to be a tower of darkness, every branch and trunk fused together. The orb found its resting place at twenty feet, revealing the disturbing sight of a large, hairy spindle-like leg, retreating higher into the darkness above. It seemed the wolf wasn't the only creature affected by the magic.

"You're either very brave or very stupid..." The nasal voice came from the shadows in front of Asher, where the floating orb was unable to cast any light on the source. "You must be the hunter."

Asher gripped his sword tighter when the shadow took form in front of him. The hulking body rose to its feet, all four of them. The giant wolf quivered, shaking its black fur as it ran its tongue over teeth dulled with old blood. A low growl rumbled from deep inside its throat, while golden eyes bored into Asher with deadly intent.

The scrawny figure that emerged from behind the wolf was every bit as pathetic as his voice suggested. Bloodied rags drowned the haggard man, his balding head covered in wrinkles and liver spots. There was something about his eyes, however, a spark that Asher could only describe as youth.

"I bet those fools in Whistle Town sent you in here to kill a Werewolf!" The scrawny man chuckled as he made a slow circle around the edge of the tree line, while the wolf moved off in the opposite direction.

Asher's voice was gruff from disuse. "That's not a Werewolf. Just a sick animal you've tormented."

"I'm afraid there's more sickness in these woods than you know, Ranger."

The sound of a dozen legs crawling over wood echoed from above.

Asher took greater note of the long staff supporting the man and began to put the pieces together. The staff was taller than either of them and adorned with a head of antlers. Somewhere inside that staff would be a crystal no doubt, fixed into the wood and harnessing the true strength of the magic the pathetic man tried to control. Judging from his complexion, Asher could see how that control had taken its toll on what had most likely been a young man.

"You don't talk much," the scrawny man observed. "I thought there would be some righteous speech. I've heard the last words and dying pleas of many a folk these past months." A black tongue made a quick dash over his cracked lips.

Asher's free hand found its way to the strip of dirty red cloth that hung from his belt, as it always did in times like this. He thought not only of the power it would grant him but the comfort too, as it slipped over his eyes. He let it go, confident in his abilities as well as his prediction of the darkness that was about to fall over him. The ranger had no greater ally than the dark.

The giant wolf continued to stalk round to his left, while the scrawny man closed the gap on his right. The crawling overhead grew closer. They were boxing him in with no communication required to organise their attack. The staff was the key, it had to be.

"Like my staff, do you?" The scrawny man had taken notice of Asher's lingering gaze. "Found it on the back of a merchant's cart. He had no idea what he carried but I could feel its power. It called to me. It needed me!"

Asher had seen infectious relics before and cared little for where this one came from. The ranger took a long breath. He had seen more bloodshed, and caused much of it himself, than most men would in their lifetime. The wolf and whatever else lived in the nest would have to die, but if there was a chance this young man could atone for his crimes, then shouldn't Asher give him the opportunity?

"The folk of Whistle Town want the matter resolved and the beastie dead." Asher glanced at the growling wolf. "Hand over that staff and walk away. Use whatever years it hasn't taken from you and do something good with it."

"Stupid old fool, aren't you. Why would I give up my power, Ranger?" The scrawny man had come to a stop, just beyond a sword's reach.

"Because I'll kill the wolf and take the staff if you don't."

The scrawny man laughed hoarsely. "But in the dark, you're just prey..."

The silent signal had been given. The underbelly of a giant spider was momentarily visible before the weight of its body flew through the air, dissolving the orb of light. Asher was submerged in pitch black and surrounded by monsters. Dozens of legs scurried down the twisted oaks while the wolf leaped for his throat, its mouth easily capable of encompassing his entire head.

The Nightseye elixir, which would forever course through his veins, came to life. The darkness brought clarity to his mind, granting him new vision. Asher sidestepped the wolf, feeling the position of every creature as they closed in. The smell of the wolf was instantly increased as it passed him by, mingling with the acrid aroma of the spiders and rotten flesh displaced beneath their feet. He had once found the attack on his senses nauseating, but now he welcomed it. Asher could hear the heartbeat of every beast, the scrawny man included, thumping like thunder in his ears. He kept his mouth shut to try to avoid tasting the blood and shit in the air.

Every muscle responded with decades of memory in the art of dealing out death. He pointed his sword forward, impaling the first spider to make a move. It squealed in a moment of agony before death claimed it. Asher continued his attack, trained never to give an inch. He flung the spider off the end of his sword, throwing it into the oncoming wolf. A small yelp from the beast confirmed the collision, as Asher pivoted on one foot, just in time to bring his sword down on the next spider, the blade cutting through two hardened legs and a torso. Without stopping, he thrust his left leg into another spider, pinning it to the nearest tree while swinging the sword to his side, slicing through two more spiders at once. The arachnid beneath his boot wriggled and squirmed to get free, but soon succumbed to death at the point of a sword.

The scrawny man laughed at the spectacle, despite his own lack of vision. "You're lasting longer than most!"

Asher could smell the raw flesh on his breath.

The wolf came for him then. Asher deftly pivoted again. He felt the impact in the air as the beast head-butted the tree, its anger rising. Four quick movements of his sword brought an end to the lives of three more spiders, their pungent blood spoiling the air.

Asher heard the lips of the scrawny man part, but no words left his mouth. He had obviously noticed the lack of spindly legs hurrying across the bone-littered ground.

The wolf's claws dug into the mud, the sound exaggerated to Asher's ears. He stood his ground, steadying his breathing while replacing his rune sword and unsheathing the double-handed broadsword. He gripped the hilt with both hands, feeling the balance of the blade.

The wolf charged with a snap of its jaws, leaping high into the air. Asher dropped to one knee and buried the base of the spiked pommel into the ground, the blade pointed to the hidden sky. He braced his arms as the full weight of the wolf landed on the point of the sword. The blade, thick with blood, had entered through the mouth and come out through the top of the wolf's head, killing it instantly.

Asher turned the beast over and placed one boot on the creature's chest as he pulled the sword free. He could feel it lying there, lifeless in the dark, a beautiful animal twisted by the malevolent will of the scrawny man.

There would be no atoning for him now.

With his free hand held high, another orb of light formed in Asher's hand and took flight, illuminating the massacre. The scrawny man looked about in fright and no small amount of shock.

"It's... it's not possible." His eyes finally fell on Asher. "What are you?" The scrawny man was defenceless without his creatures, appearing more pathetic than before. "I just wanted them to notice me..."

Asher had nothing to say. The ranger side-stepped and spun on the spot, his sword a blur as it cut through the staff and beyond, into the man's face, where it separated everything above his nose.

With the staff broken, the dark magic would lose its grip on the area, allowing the trees to return to their original splendour in time. Had the magical infection been allowed to grow any further, it would have caught the attention of the woodland folk of Felgarn and the kingdom of Lirian.

A greedy part of Asher wished he had allowed the infection to grow; the queen of Lirian would have paid a larger sum for his skills than the governor of Whistle Town. Asher noticed the slaughtered body of a child and tried to forget he had ever entertained the thought.

Thinking of his intended reward, he regarded the remains of the scrawny man. The governor would have a hard time believing the pathetic corpse, of what appeared to be an old man, to be the cause of so many deaths, especially when they already believed a great beast was the menace. Asher hefted the broadsword one last time to bring the blade down on the wolf's neck, cleaving the head from its body.

CHAPTER 2
A KING'S ORDER

The sun was setting low in the west, the tips of The Evermoore taking on an orange hue as storm clouds moved in from the east. Nathaniel Galfrey twisted on his horse, looking back at the land he had covered over the last four days. The sanctuary of West Fellion was well beyond the horizon, its high walls a comfort he wouldn't see for many months, though, in truth, he preferred his life on the road, serving out the justice as his order had been charged with almost a thousand years ago.

The dull visage of Whistle Town lay sprawled before him in all its antiquated glory. As an original human settlement, it had no elven structures, leaving it free of their elegant architecture and grandeur. It was also the poorest town in all of Alborn, an otherwise rich region of Illian.

A heavy sigh from his left reminded Nathaniel that he wasn't alone on this particular edict. He turned to see his new ward, Elaith, looking as sullen as ever. It had been a long four days in the company of the eighteen-year-old girl. Unlike Nathaniel, she had not volunteered to be trained as a Graycoat but was instead taken in as an orphan over a decade ago. Elaith's olive skin was a testament to her previous life in Ameeraska, in the southern region of The Arid Lands. It was not an easy place to survive as an orphan on the street.

"My first mandate outside of West Fellion and I end up in this shit-tip..." She wore her large leather coat the same as any other Graycoat, only it still shone with a mere five days of life, unlike Nathaniel's which had taken on a lighter tone of brown after years of wear.

The coats were their badge of identification when travelling across Illian, known in all the regions of the realm by their specific tailoring. The coat was buttoned tight across the torso, ending just above the waist, where it billowed with two flaps that reached to the ankle. Nathaniel wore his sword belt within the flowing coat, whereas Elaith had started wearing hers over the top, since she had been presented with it upon their departure, four days ago. He had to admit, she wore it well.

They had identical bows and quivers slung across their backs. Nathaniel enjoyed the weight of it, comforted by the bow's presence. He had more skill than any Graycoat when it came to archery, though the order was loath to admit it. He cast away the thoughts of prejudice he had lived under, trying not to dwell on the order's opinions of him.

"Whistle Town has its... charms," he lied.

"We couldn't have been charged with hunting Trolls in Vengora, or patrolling The Ice Vales for bandits?" Elaith continued.

Nathaniel had endured four days of the whining. "The beasts that lurk in Vengora are not to be challenged lightly. Take it from someone who's actually passed through those mountains and has the scars."

"You're from Longdale, right, in The Iron Valley?" Elaith's tone implied a lack of knowledge regarding Nathaniel's past, despite the fact that there wasn't a Graycoat alive who didn't know about him. Like other wards before, she was prying for more information about the order's ugly duckling.

"And The Ice Vales would come as a shock to someone from

Ameeraska," Nathaniel continued without answering the question. "It lives up to its name."

Elaith sighed, the bait untouched. "But Whistle Town...? Alec and Bjorn were taken to The Narrows to destroy a nest of Sandstalkers. That's right on the edge of The Wild Moores!"

"Then consider yourself lucky. This is your final test to keep that coat. All we have to do is escort one man to Velia. Alec and Bjorn will be lucky to return at all from The Narrows!" Nathaniel flinched at his own words; he shouldn't have said that. Elaith had been training with them since she was eight years old. A moment of awkward silence passed between them. "I'm sure they'll be fine though, for masters Vayga and Selena accompany them, veterans each."

"So who is this man we're to escort?" The whining teenager was now replaced with what sounded like a professional Graycoat.

Happy with Elaith's change in subject, Nathaniel explained. "I don't have all the details, but this mission came directly from Lord Marshal Horvarth." That particular detail perked Elaith's interest, as it had Nathaniel's when the orders were handed down from the commander of West Fellion. "Our man in Whistle Town's sector house sent word that this individual has been temporarily hired by the governor. Our window of opportunity is small. We are to escort him to Velia, where brother Devale will take custody."

"So this man is to be our prisoner?" Elaith asked.

"I would imagine so, and possibly a dangerous one at that if Darius Devale is to take charge of him, though why he is needed in Velia I couldn't say." Nathaniel did his best to hide the fact that they were simple delivery boys for the Graycoats' most accomplished warrior. The danger posed by the mystery man, however, was of little concern to him. Nathaniel Galfrey was sure he had seen the worst the world had to offer.

The rain was falling hard by the time the Graycoats entered the muddy streets of Whistle Town. Nathaniel dug his heels in, spurring his horse on to reach shelter as fast as possible. Elaith's short spiky hair was flattened against her scalp, though it did nothing to ruin his own shaved hair. The streets cleared quickly, as people sought cover in the nearby buildings, while the market stalls sat empty having already been cleared before the rain fell.

Water poured out of the gutters, under the thatched roofs, creating small rivers in the mud. Looking on, Elaith appeared to be unable to change her expression of disdain. Lanterns were ignited throughout the town, bringing a soft, yellow glow to the windows. Smoke struggled to defy the rain and rise from almost every house and inn.

Nathaniel led them through the streets to the sector house in the north-east corner, a crooked and decrepit looking building with old wooden beams cutting across the white exterior.

They herded the horses into the small stable, adjacent to the sector house, and knocked heavily on the dark door. Turning up their collars did little to keep out the cold rain, as they waited for the door to open. They were greeted by a young teenage boy with curly ginger hair and a face full of freckles.

"They're here, Master Bail!" the boy shouted back into the house. Their coats were always the giveaway.

Nathaniel stepped past the boy without a word, thankful for the heat emanating from within. The interior was just as unkempt as the exterior, with used plates and cups strewn haphazardly across every surface, books stacked to ridiculous heights and dirty scrolls littering the floor. The few candles that had been laid out failed to illuminate the dark corners and winding staircase.

"Welcome, Brother Galfrey." Master Bail remained seated behind his long table, wine-cup in hand. Had it been any other Graycoat at his door, Nathaniel was sure the master would have stood and greeted him with respect.

Bail was a shadow of his former self: once a young and ambitious

Graycoat, before a Ghoul tore out his calf and disfigured his face. In his late fifties, he was now bound to these four walls, crippled and useless as a travelling Graycoat - good only for managing a sector house. His girth prevented him from wearing his coat, instead favouring a large black cloak lined with fur. His facial scars kept his hairline high, on the left side of his scalp, in long, grey scraggy knots.

"Master Bail," Nathaniel gritted his teeth and gave a curt nod. "This is Elaith Nevandar; she is taking her final trial."

Elaith ran a gloved hand through her hair in an attempt to look more presentable.

Bail turned to the young boy. "Well don't just stand there, boy, bring food and water!" He hurried off into a room behind the table. Bail winced at the clatter of pots and pans created by the clumsy teenager. "I have to say, I'm surprised Lord Marshal Horvarth sent you for this mission. I thought they just let you loose on the land and left you to it."

Nathaniel's leather glove creaked as his grip tightened around the hilt of his sword. He glanced at Elaith who did her best not to react to Bail's comment.

"It's a simple escort job. I'll be off the beaten track before the week's end. Remind me. Where will you be, Master Bail?" Nathaniel noticed the hint of a smirk on Elaith's face but maintained his own stony expression.

Bail's eye twitched as he looked from one Graycoat to the other. "You obviously don't understand the gravity of your mission, Brother Galfrey." The old Graycoat opened the top drawer of his desk and removed a tightly bound scroll. He continued to roll out the parchment until Nathaniel noticed the wax seal of Lord Marshal Horvarth at the bottom.

"You are a small cog with a very important job. I can only hope that you're up to the task. The order has been commissioned by King Rengar of Velia. We are to bring before him the ranger known as, *Asher...*"

Bail's words hung in the air, filling the room with silence as if it were a physical being. Nathaniel was sure the old man must have misspoken. The red-headed boy returned from the kitchen with two plates of bread and dried fish. He looked at them all in turn, clearly wondering why nobody spoke in his presence, before Bail waved him away.

"We are to deliver Asher to King Rengar?" Nathaniel couldn't take his eyes off the scroll.

"Eh, no. You are to deliver him to Brother Darius Devale. He will present Asher to the king." Bail began to break off strips of fish and drop them unceremoniously into his mouth.

Elaith's expression crumpled in confusion. "Who is—"

"Where is he now?" Nathaniel interrupted.

Bail's reply came through mouthfuls of fish and bread. "He has a room at the Green Hag. Paid for one more night."

"How accurate are your sources?" Nathaniel probed, doubtful of Bail's information.

Bail stopped eating. "He accepted a job five days ago to rid the town of whatever beast was hunting on the edge of The Evermoore. After questioning several townsfolk, he set out into the forest and returned this very afternoon with the head of a giant wolf. He presented the kill to the governor and accepted his coin willingly. My latest report came not one hour past, stating that the ranger was happily spending his reward on the Green Hag's famous golden ale."

Bail gave Nathaniel a look just begging to be challenged. He might be useless to the order in the field now, but his network of spies could not be questioned in their efficiency.

Nathaniel stroked the stubble that had grown over the last four days. "Why wasn't this beast handled by the order?" He wanted as many facts as possible.

"I put the request in for assistance a month ago, but no other Graycoats were available." Bail continued to stuff his face.

"Well, at least you kept the sector house in order..." Nathaniel glanced at the filth beneath his boot and, before Bail could protest, continued, "What does King Rengar want with him?"

"A king's wants are not for us mere mortals to know." Bail downed his cup of wine greedily. "He has asked for the Graycoats' assistance, and Lord Marshal Horvarth has answered. Illian may not be under one banner anymore, but we are still servants to the realm and its leaders, are we not?"

Nathaniel could only wish that he had lived in such times. It was almost a millennium past when all of Illian was ruled by the one king, Gal Tion. After the elves left for the shores of Ayda, in the east, King Tion unified the land under his banner with the help of Lord Tyberius Gray, the original patron of the Graycoats. They had been simpler times, when the Graycoats patrolled the land as knights, with the authority of the king, dealing out justice and slaying the horrors that preyed on the weak.

Now, they were living on handouts from the royal families, though Dragorn, the island nation between Illian and Ayda, didn't pay for their continued service to the land since they claimed not to need it.

West Fellion was inhabited by orphans and occasional volunteers now. Under King Tion's rule, their ranks had reportedly swelled under the number of volunteers that flocked from across the realm. Those days were long gone.

With the six kingdoms that now shared Illian, Nathaniel was forced to live in a world of politics, where the knights of West Fellion were more akin to peacekeepers between the greedy kings and queens, each with their own agendas and need for more power.

"Is he alone?" Nathaniel asked.

"He is. If you are to believe the rumours, he always travels alone." Bail poured himself another cup of wine.

"It's not the rumours that concern me..."

Bail nodded in agreement, though Elaith continued to look puzzled. "I will have a raven sent to Velia, notifying Brother Devale of your presence. He will expect you in no more than three days."

Nathaniel took a moment to consider his options. This was not going to be easy, if possible at all, especially with a fresh-faced Graycoat at his side and no reinforcements. Either Lord Marshal Horvarth had great confidence in his ability to fulfil this task, or he was simply hoping it would be the mission that finally rid the order of their black mark. Nathaniel assumed it was the latter.

"Get word to your man watching him. Tell him to wait for us outside the Green Hag and show us in through the back. I want to lay eyes on Asher before he sees us. Surprise is going to be our greatest weapon."

One look from Master Bail sent the boy sprinting back into the kitchen and out through an unseen door. "Your orders, Brother Galfrey." Bail handed the signed parchment to Nathaniel. "Try not to get yourself killed, eh?"

"I didn't think you cared?"

"I was talking to *her*." Bail eyed Elaith as they turned to leave.

The rain had reduced to a light drizzle when Nathaniel and Elaith found the Green Hag. As requested, Bail's man was waiting under the shelter of a balcony, outside the inn. Elaith had questioned Nathaniel for most of the walk over, giving up when she realised her mentor was in a completely different world. He had trapped every kind of animal and most forms of beast in his time, but he couldn't fathom how he was going to capture this monster.

Bail's man showed them in through the back door and discreetly ushered them into a dimly-lit booth. From their position, Nathaniel could see most of the tables and the entire length of the bar. His target was easy to identify amidst the everyday rabble of the townsfolk.

Asher was older than Nathaniel remembered, with greying hair to his shoulders, the front tucked back into a small ponytail on the crown of his head. His face remained hidden for the time, as the ranger sat on a stool, hunched over the bar with an empty plate and a tin mug, frothing with ale. He wore a muddied, long green cloak with a short-sword slung across his back, tightly packed against a stuffed quiver. As an archer, Nathaniel noticed the absence of a bow, though he certainly noticed the second sword that hung at his hip, with a spiked ball for a pommel.

Nathaniel could see the frustration on Elaith's face and decided to elaborate now that he knew for sure that Asher was indeed his target.

"This ranger is no ordinary man." He spoke in hushed tones despite the din. "In all your years to come, you can only hope to never again come across an individual as uniquely skilled as this man."

"Why? Because he's a *ranger*? That just means he knows his way around a sword. So do we." Elaith's hand went to the hilt on her hip.

"Before he took to his life on the road, he lived a far darker one. I first encountered him fourteen years ago, on my first trial as a Graycoat, as you are now. I watched him cut through six Graycoats before assassinating the High Priest of Wood Vale. And he did it all with his eyes closed..."

Elaith's face lit up as she looked on in amazement at the grey-haired man, sitting ten metres away. "Arakesh..." she whispered.

"He is a student of Nightfall, an assassin of the highest order. He is not to be underestimated." Nathaniel was assessing the space between Asher and himself, counting the people in the way and estimating the time it would take him to notch an arrow. The ranger downed his drink and ordered another with the flick of his finger.

"I thought Nightfall was a myth, something the older masters used to give the freshers nightmares." Elaith tried to stop staring at the ranger but appeared to have lost control of her eyes.

"We only wish it was a myth. Nightfall has been churning out assassins for as long as West Fellion has been churning out Gray-coats. They are the order's sworn enemy, though our hierarchy prefers to ignore them since we can do nothing about them. For centuries we have searched for Nightfall and its deadly inhabitants, but to no avail. Asher here is the first Arakesh we actually know about - the others are just shades."

Elaith suddenly appeared more excited about her boring assignment. "So Asher could give us the location of Nightfall?"

"Knowing he exists doesn't make him any easier a prize. Since he left Nightfall, our order has tried several times to capture him." Nathaniel gave the ranger's back a hard look, noting the barkeeper set down another tankard of ale. "I don't suppose you lose those particular skills..."

"Why did he leave Nightfall?" Elaith was hungry for information now.

"Nobody knows. That's the problem; he's too much of a mystery. A couple of years after I came across him, he suddenly showed up in Lirian, in the heart of The Evermoore. He killed two of his own, stopping a plot to assassinate Queen Isabella. It made him famous overnight. It was also the first time in decades anyone had actually laid eyes on the bodies of two Arakesh.

"After that he showed up here and there, presenting himself as a ranger. There were rumours that he became Nightfall's biggest target after Lirian. But like everything concerning that wretched place, it's just rumours."

"What would King Rengar want with him?"

"I have no idea. Our main concern is getting him there. He won't come with a pair of Graycoats willingly." Nathaniel took a moment to consider his plan. "Here's what we're going to do. You walk up to him one side, me the other. Don't draw your sword until you're right at his side. Before he stands, we'll remove his weapons - all of them. We can't leave him with a single blade. Then we walk him back to the sector house and wait until first light before setting off. We'll have to bind him and tie him to his horse..." Nathaniel did a poor a job of hiding his lack of confidence. In truth, he wasn't sure they would even get past drawing their swords.

A nod from Elaith was her only agreement, trusting in Nathaniel's experience. They both stood as one and moved between the tables, weaving their way to the bar. It felt as if a hundred miles separated them as they approached their target. They were so close now that the ranger's pungent odour of sweat and alcohol permeated the area around him. Nathaniel's hand went to his hilt, ready to draw it with all his speed.

Asher's hand fell to the bar, along with his empty tankard, before his head followed suit and rolled off the counter, taking his body with it to the floor. The ranger collapsed on his back with the stool awkwardly strewn between his legs.

Nathaniel half drew his sword with the sudden movement but now stood looking down at the unconscious man with shock and elation.

"Well, that was easy..." Elaith sheathed her sword and bent down to inspect the ranger.

"Nothing to see here; Graycoat business." Nathaniel flicked his wrist to encourage the patrons to continue with their merriment and drink.

They crouched down to better inspect Asher's sleeping form. The ranger's face hadn't changed much in the decade: a few wrinkles around the eyes, a new scar across his cheek to accompany the vertical cut beneath his right eye. Thick, greying stubble lined his sun-beaten cheeks, drawing Nathaniel to the black fang tattoo beneath his left eye. Tattoos like that were common among the Outlanders and Nathaniel had always wondered what the connection was between them and the old assassin.

"What do we do now?" Elaith asked.

"Change of plan." Nathaniel stood and turned to the barkeep. "I'm going to need a room for the night, and I need to know which room belongs to this man." The barkeep nodded gravely and disappeared to retrieve another room key. "Search him for weapons and leave them behind the bar. We can pick them up in the morning."

"We're to stay here? With him?"

"Well, *I'm* not carrying him back to the sector house. We can take it in turns to guard him."

Nathaniel removed Asher's sword belt and the concealed knives, sheathed on his thigh. Elaith unbuckled the strap across his chest and they rolled him over to remove the quiver and short-sword. Nathaniel took a moment to look at the sword, drawing it from its sheath of basilisk hide. The blade was exquisite, with an hourglass shape and ancient runes carved up the spine. The Graycoat tapped the flat of the blade and listened for the resounding hum.

"What is it?" Elaith was busy removing more concealed knives.

Nathaniel walked to the nearest window and held the sword out, allowing the sliver of moonlight breaking through the clouds to shine down on the exotic metal. In the light of the moon, the sword sparkled as if inlaid with diamonds.

"Silvyr..." He stepped aside to show Elaith, whose eyes lit up. "They say only a few pounds of this exists beyond Dhenaheim." Nathaniel returned to the prone form and sheathed the sword.

"Dhenaheim! You mean the land of the dwarves?" Elaith's hand hesitated over the hilt.

"They mine it from a crater about a hundred miles beyond Vengora, in the north of Illian. The dwarves don't like trading with it beyond their own people. It's said that they use it themselves to forge their weapons and shields, giving them the advantage in any battle."

"So how did he come by an entire sword made of the stuff? Do you think he killed a dwarf for it?"

Nathaniel noticed the increase in attention from the surrounding patrons. "I don't know and I don't care. Let's get him upstairs."

Elaith lifted up the quiver and Nathaniel spotted the unusual contraption hooked onto it. If he wasn't mistaken it was some kind of bow, or at least parts for a bow. He promised himself to look at it tomorrow after they had tied Asher to his horse.

CHAPTER 3
A LONG WAY FROM HOME

The sun had set over Dragorn, and the great pyres had come to life atop the mountainous walls that protected the island nation. At nearly fifty miles across, the city was hard to navigate through its maze of districts, tight alleyways and labyrinth-like temples. The hum created by its thousands of denizens never ceased, even into the night. This proximity and noise were considered a regular way of life for Dragornians, a people often noted for their love of enclosed spaces.

For an elf... it was hell.

Galanör inhaled a deep breath and held it as he passed through the outskirts of the city, composed mostly of farmland, though still within the protected boundaries of the high walls.

He pulled his hood lower and wrapped his blue cloak tightly around his arms, as he exited through the main gate. The guards paid him no heed, always more concerned with citizens coming than going.

The sea air was glorious and refreshing. The elf breathed deeply, trying his best to forget the pungent odours and scents given off by every human. Galanör's elvish nose and ears were far too sensitive for such a place, forcing his kin and himself to ingest several potions a day, in an attempt to keep the nausea at bay.

The path from the main gate sloped down to the crescent moon-shaped port, where hundreds of boats and ships rested in the harbour. The water's edge was lined with warehouses and their own private guards, keeping watch over the legal and illegal goods that ferried between Dragorn and the rest of Illian. Nothing travelled east of the island, to Ayda, where the sun rose and the elves called home.

After several minutes of walking along the harbour, Galanör left the light of the port, continuing along the shoreline, with the moon-light his only guide. The beach soon gave way to a rocky terrain as the island rose up on his right, the base of the wall now a hundred feet above sea level.

Confident that he was alone, Galanör stretched out his arm and conjured a ball of light the size of his palm. The glowing orb floated in front of him, highlighting the safest path around the island.

After almost an hour of navigating the sharp rocks and small pools, Galanör came to a break in the shoreline, where the sea separated the two halves of the land, as a river would. He waded through until the water came up to his knees, leaving his long cloak to float behind him. The ocean continued into the island on his right, where it entered a deep jagged cave that ran beneath Dragorn.

Galanör ignored the cave and turned to the sea, commanding the orb to rise higher, so his eyes could adjust to the darkness beyond the water's edge.

The Adean was laid out before him, a vast ocean that separated Illian from Ayda, his homeland in the east. It was a fact that Galanör was only too thankful for, having observed the humans for the first time in their own environment. Everywhere humans went, they twisted the world to fit around them, forcing the land to pay tribute to their superiority.

Galanör couldn't fathom why his people had abandoned Illian a thousand years ago. They should have stayed and put mankind in their place, beneath the immortals. Elves were stronger, faster and far wiser with their long lives. Every elf was born with a natural connection to the world that made the manipulation of magic as easy as breathing. They had no need of wands or staffs to direct their will, though the use of crystals were used by both for harnessing greater wells of magic.

Galanör's first order would have been to stop them breeding like rabbits. Maybe then the dragons would still be around.

The waves crashed against the rocks with more force, bringing Galanör's attention to the distant storm. The thunderous clouds stretched for hundreds of miles, from Velia, the coastal city on the very edge of Illian, to the shores of The Amara Forest in Ayda, in the east.

There was something unnatural about the storm, something that made the hairs on his neck stand on end. The extra sense that attuned him to magic told him the black clouds were the will of some darker spell caster. Either way, it had disrupted an integral part of his plan, leaving him with only one choice.

The satchel on his hip was light, filled only with the ingredients he required for such an occasion. He had spent the last two days gathering the necessary parts after his conversation with Mörygan, a far older and wiser elf than he. The feeling Galanör was getting from the storm, coupled with Mörygan's news, was unsettling.

"The storm is unyielding, Galanör," Mörygan had said. Both elves had sat crossed-legged, each with a small black orb cupped in their hands and held tight to the chest. Despite the hundreds of miles between them, the orbs connected the elves' minds in a reality between the fabric of the known world. "The oldest amongst us have tried to calm it, but to no end. We have sent word to King Rengar's court. We will be arriving higher up the coast, in the mouth of The Unmar. If we head for Velia now, it will take us through the storm..."

It had made sense to Galanör, who had spent years studying the map of Verda. The Opal Coast of Ayda, in the east, and The Shining Coast of Illian, in the west, were closer in the north, as the two lands came together, similar to that of an arrowhead that never quite met.

"That will add days to your journey, not to mention the added peril of travelling south to Velia on foot." Galanör had struggled to hide the concern in his voice, made only harder by witnessing first-hand the cruelty of human nature amidst the alleys of Dragorn.

"Fear not, Galanör. The princess will be safe with Faylen and myself. No doubt King Rengar will send an escort to meet us." Mörygan's image had been fleeting in the shadow realm. To one another, the elves had appeared to be made from smoke.

"I fear the storm has undone our plans here as well, Mörygan. Until The Adean settles, no captain will take his supply boats north, to Korkanath."

"I trust you will find another way to achieve your goal," Mörygan had replied.

"I have already set another plan in motion. We will reach Korkanath, you have my word." Galanör had felt a presence in the real world and knew another elf had entered the room where he sat.

"I believe you have already given such a word to our king, and he a word to you." Mörygan's words dripped with arrogance. He was part of the inner circle and had therefore been privy to the pact made between Galanör and the lord of elven kind.

"Indeed..." Galanör guarded his reply.

After their return to reality, Galanör had relayed the news to the rest of his team and set about bringing his new plan to fruition.

He now stood up to his knees in the cold Adean, while the sea breeze blew his hood back, revealing his long brown hair, tied into a tight knot at the back of his head. Galanör removed the first item from his satchel, a stalk from the Varlano plant that grows along most shorelines on every continent in Verda. The elf crumpled the stiff leaves and dropped them into the water in a semi-circle around his body.

Moving quickly, before the current washed them away, he doused a small helping of oil over the top of the leaves. The elf continued the ritual by popping the cork on a glass vial and pouring a dark liquid amidst the leaves and oil. He wrinkled his nose at the smell of the blood and tried not to dwell on how Adamar had acquired the sample from a child. Galanör knew the large elf had mentioned a local brothel from which he could source the ingredients - as Adamar had put it - but it still didn't bear thinking about.

With a flick of his wrist, Galanör conjured a flame that spread across the oil and set the leaves and blood on fire. Using the ancient language, he called out to the sea and waited.

Galanör looked up at the moon, which had moved a hand's length in the sky since his call to the sea. He tried to remind himself that, as an elf, he was expected to possess a certain amount of patience, though in this moment it eluded him.

The orb of light had long since extinguished, along with the fire. Galanör stood in darkness, his eyes now fully adjusted to the light of the moon.

A small splash that wasn't in time with the waves caught his attention, and his keen ears narrowed the sound to an outcropping of rocks on his left.

With an outstretched hand, Galanör produced another ball of light and commanded it to float higher and farther out to sea. There was another splash, this time to his right, where he caught a glimpse of a large fishtail sinking below the water's surface.

Galanör resisted the urge to call out and state his business as being peaceful. Some of his earliest lessons as a child had covered the mysteries of the ocean and its ancient Mer-folk, even if it was a memory from four centuries ago. He knew to stand his ground after summoning a Mer-man, to remain silent and allow them the first word. Any hint of disrespect would end with a watery death for the elf.

The ocean became eerily still, as even the waves ceased to crash against the rocks. Galanör kept his arms at his sides, his hands easy to see, as the gloom gave way to one of the oldest creatures in existence.

The Mer-man slid from the water, breaking the surface without a sound as if some unseen force was pushing it up. Of course, Galanör knew that a powerful tail was coiled beneath the Mer-man, its fin breaking the water's edge twenty-feet out to sea and shining brilliant silver in the moonlight. The dark scales changed at the navel, becoming more akin to human flesh, while the fish-like scales faded. The skin was a beautiful mixture of red and gold, highlighted by the glowing orb above them.

Long, pointed fingers glided at its sides with translucent webbing between every digit. The Mer-man's chest was as chiselled as any statue of the gods, every muscle evolved to enhance their speed and agility at swimming. Small spikes protruded from the skin in a perfect row, straight up the middle of the Mer-man's body, stopping at the chin.

Galanör spotted three gills on each side of the neck before they closed off completely, and the creature inhaled a deep breath through a nose devoid of cartilage.

"You dare to summon me, ape?" Its voice came out in a rasp as if multiple membranes were opening and closing rapidly inside its throat. It was entirely possible that this was the first time in hundreds of years that the Mer-man had even used its vocal cords in such a way.

Galanör was frozen in a moment of shock, having only ever glimpsed their kind as a child. Its wide-set jaw of razor sharp teeth rose up into a head with eyes as bottomless as the ocean itself. Though larger than his own eyes, Galanör couldn't help but be drawn into them. From its head sprouted long tendrils of what could only be described as seaweed, though the elf was sure it was a different substance altogether.

"Speak man-thing!" The Mer-man rose higher into the air and another coil of its tail pierced the surface.

"Forgive me. I am not as I appear. But you must use more than your eyes to see it..." Galanör lifted his head slightly.

The Mer-man moved with lightning speed until its upper body was level with Galanör's, their faces only inches apart. Two small nostrils expanded on the sea creature's face and its head tilted in the manner of a curious dog. Without the definition, it was hard for Galanör to tell where the creature's eyes were looking, though the elf was sure it had taken a moment to observe his rounded ears.

"I thought you stank of magic..." The Mer-man retreated to a more comfortable distance, but it did nothing to remove the odour of fish.

Galanör curved his finger over the top of his ear, "'Tis only an illusion, to conceal my identity amongst the humans."

"There is an accord between our people, elfling. A peace. Why have you summoned me, and on shores that are not your own, no less?" The Mer-man's rasping voice got better with every word.

"I have need of your people."

"Need?" the Mer-man echoed. "The arrogance of your kind. You draw my people out with your spells and younglings' blood, yet I see no children for us, and I fail to see what you have to offer for our assistance, little elf."

Galanör took the insult in his stride. Starting a fight with an unknown amount of Mer-folk was a suicidal idea. He thought of his mother and father and applied a more diplomatic tone.

"Forgive my rudeness. I forget myself, for my need is great. My name is Galanör of house Reveeri. I am on an important errand on behalf of the Lord of Elves. In exchange for this assistance, you but name it and I shall supply it. You have my word..."

The Mer-man was silent, considering the elf's words. "You could not say my name if you tried elfling, so do not think me rude for withholding it. Our demand will be equal to the task required of us. Before I can ask anything of you, you must first state what you need from us."

Galanör had already considered his words on the matter. Their mission had to remain a secret at all costs; there was no telling what alliances had been made beyond Ayda. He was confident that the Mer-folk were part of no other alliance, but the lives dependent on the mission's secrecy were more than just his own.

"Five others and I need to reach the shores of Korkanath. Our reason is our own." The elf bowed at the end of his request.

The Mer-man gave a sharp laugh. "It has never failed to amuse how the sky can affect your kind in traversing the seas." The creature looked away for a moment, before returning its abyss-like stare. "Let your reason be your own. The fact still remains that your kind would not survive such a swim. Your lungs are too small and your bodies too frail. You could not fathom our speed..."

"Leave that to us," Galanör replied.

"Hmm, more magic. So be it, elfling. But be warned, from here to Korkanath you will not see the sky. My kind does not break the surface within ten leagues of that island. I don't need to tell you what protects it, I hope?" A wicked smile crept across the Mer-man's face.

Galanör considered the very reason for his mission and knew well that he didn't need educating on the island's protector.

"What is your price?"

A forked tongue slithered out of the Mer-man's mouth and tasted the air. "Six of you mean six of us. We require a child each..."

Galanör's mouth opened, but he failed to find the words. He didn't much care for human children, but innocence was innocence. "Kidnapping six children isn't easy, even in a city as large as Dragorn. The mission relies on our being here to remain a secret and, forgive the pun, it will make waves."

"Then our talking has been for naught, Galanör of house Reveeri." The Mer-man began to sink back into The Adean.

"Wait!" Galanör called. The Mer-man paused before facing the elf again. "I can get you three children." Galanör knew that with those words, a part of him had died.

"Then perhaps we should take only three of you to Korkanath..."

"Any more and we risk revealing ourselves. That would put my lord's errand in peril." Galanör hoped the reminder of who sent them to Dragorn would be enough to convince the Mer-man. It was not wise to cross the Lord of Elves, even for a Mer-man. "Three children and anything else you wish."

The Mer-man puffed out its impressive chest and half turned back to the open sea. The elf's sharp ears picked up the faint sound of whispering but he couldn't define the words coming from the ocean.

"Very well, elfling. Three children it is, but you must also bring two women, as beautiful as you can find. Is your word your bond?"

Galanör considered his limited options. "It is."

With that, the Mer-man turned to the sea and dived back into the comfort of its embrace. In that same moment, the waves returned with a crash and the current resumed its flow into the cave behind Galanör. He was alone.

When the sun finally rose, it struggled to pierce the grey storm clouds, their heaving mass now looming over Dragorn. Galanör sat crossed-legged on the wooden floor, watching the sullen clouds through the window of the dirty apartment the elves had rented since their arrival on the island. The storm reminded him of a hungry god, come to devour all of Verda. Perhaps Atilan himself, the king of the gods, was finally preparing to undo all his work. The thought made Galanör chuckle to himself; as if the gods could ever exist, he thought.

The elves had lost their faith long before Galanör was born, handing their superstitions over to the humans. When mankind emerged from The Wild Moores, Galanör's ancestors made the mistake of teaching the humans all they knew, with the hapless race taking on the elves' love of the gods as if they were their own. Galanör couldn't imagine believing in a god now, in this day and age, especially after the so-called deities were the reason for so many elven deaths.

If only Galanör had been alive during The Dark War, he thought, he could have proven his worth by slaying the mad elf, Valanis, the self-proclaimed herald of the gods.

A single ray of sunshine defied the storm and broke through to illuminate Galanör's window. He closed his eyes and soaked up the ray as he thought of home and wished he could be back there.

The shining city of Elandril was six hundred miles from where he currently sat, in the north of Ayda, to the east. Its beautiful spires and glistening pools were far from reach now. He was tempted to pick up the diviner orb and speak to his father. No, not his father - Galanör wanted to speak with his mother or even his sister. His father would no doubt be counselling their lord, making further promises on Galanör's behalf in order to elevate his own position.

He just wanted to see the forest again. The Amara's gigantic trees and the chance for adventure called to him across The Adean, calling him home. His father's words rang clear in his mind.

"All of Verda is ours by right, Galanör. Illian was our home before the humans crawled out of the mud, and so it shall be again..."

If the humans had transformed Illian into anything like Dragorn, then it wouldn't be worth claiming back.

The human stench wafted through the open window with the usual buzz of the waking city. Galanör heard the stall owners shouting their prices across the crowds, while jesters made fools of themselves for coins on the roadside. Their chosen district was a poor one, packed with the many vices that man fell prone to. Even at this early hour, Galanör could hear women calling from the doorways and windows of their brothels, while other stragglers staggered out of taverns that never closed, easy prey for the many thieves that never slept.

The creaky door opened behind him and the sweet smell of Lyra filled the room. She came to her knees behind him, bringing her face close to his own as she swept aside his long brown hair. Her soft fingers gently caressed the skin on his neck and he felt her warm breath on his cheek.

"Have you not slept?" Even her voice was melodic to his ears.

"Their price is steep..." Galanör looked at his boots in the corner, still damp and matted in sand. "Their desire for child flesh is no myth; they hunger for more than just their blood."

"We will meet their price, whatever it is. The mission demands it." Lyra's unflinching resolve to see their lord's errand through was one of the reasons she had been picked for it. She was beautiful but deadly.

Like most elves after The Dark War, Lyra's life was a shadow of their former ways. No longer did they spend hours singing to the trees or writing poetry and creating magnificent works of art. The war had made them brutal and harsh. They had examined their own immortality and recognized their superiority over the world. Their mistake, a shame that had passed down the generations, had been leaving Illian to the humans and the dragons to their demise.

It seemed childish now to recognize the gods when they themselves were gods to all other creatures, man included. Despite them being his thoughts, Galanör could hear his father's words behind them, always colouring his view.

"We have to find three children and two women."

"What do the Mer-folk want with two human women?" Lyra asked.

"There are legends that the Mer-folk can walk on land, given a good enough reason. I read as a child that they occasionally mate with the females in order to produce a half-breed. These half-breeds have an unwavering loyalty to their ocean brethren and become spies for them, so the stories go. It seems even the Mer-folk like to keep a close eye on human affairs."

Galanör imagined the half-breeds to have incredible advantages over the humans, possibly even the elves. There was no telling how it might affect their lifespan, but it would certainly enhance their strength and senses, not to mention their unique set of lungs.

Lyra's hand slipped under his shirt, tracing the edges of his muscles. "Adamar never came back last night. He's quite taken with these brothels, though how he can stand their smell I'll never know."

"I'll speak to him when he comes back."

"Leave him to his fun..." Her hands moved ever south.

"He needs to be careful. The women are lucky his strength hasn't crushed them, let alone his stamina tiring them all to death." There wasn't much known about mating between the species, but sex with an elf posed certain dangers for the weaker humans. "I'll send Naiveen to retrieve him. We need to be ready and there's still much to do."

Lyra pressed against him so he could feel her breasts on his back while her teeth nibbled on his ear, her breath causing his hair to tingle along his neck. She moved round to sit on his lap and fold her legs around his waist. Galanör couldn't help his hands as they naturally found the curves of her body.

"Deal with him later..." she whispered seductively.

Galanör looked up to meet her lips. Her black hair fell in ringlets down to the middle of her back. Her face was typical of an elf, with her soft milky skin, perfectly symmetrical cheeks and sparkling eyes, which shone a brilliant blue, while her luscious lips were complemented by a cute, upturned nose.

How could something so beautiful be so deadly? Galanör had seen Lyra train in The Wynnter Forest, south of Elandril, and knew her skill with a sword and bow was hard matched. Her lack of interest in handing over the children to the Mer-folk was also testament of the elven ego, now common amongst their people.

Galanör thought of his own hesitation in handing over the children and wondered if there was something wrong with him. That was before Lyra stood up and slipped off her negligee, revealing her warrior's physique and pale breasts. She provocatively crawled onto the bed behind her and beckoned him with a finger.

"You *know* I am promised to another." Galanör only mentioned it because he knew how much it aroused her.

"That's what makes it more fun..."

Galanör woke to the sound of talking coming from the main living room. Lyra woke with him, her ears picking out the same words as him, no doubt. Adamar was back.

"I had to pay for three of them last night!" Adamar's boast was disguised as a complaint. "They kept tiring! These humans have no stamina..." He stopped talking as Galanör and Lyra entered the room.

Adamar was the tallest elf Galanör had ever seen, the widest too. His physique was well muscled beyond that of any other of their kind, and his size was matched only by his violent nature in combat, saying nothing of his libido. Adamar maintained two parallel braids of light brown hair on each side of his bald head, another diversion from most elves, who preferred long natural hair.

"You realise the coin we brought to this island is limited and wasn't meant to be wasted on whores and harlots?" Galanör took note of the others, all wearing their cloaks. They had obviously returned from some errand, likely made up, to get them out of the cramped apartment while Lyra and he started the day in their own way.

"What's an elf to do?" Adamar threw his hands in the air. "You have Lyra, Naiveen isn't interested in anything of the male variety and these two are content to simply sit!" He nodded at Ailas and Eliön, sitting in the corner.

"This elf is to take orders and not endanger the lives of his companions!" Galanör fumed. "Your ears...?" Adamar touched the pointed tip of his right ear. "When did you last cast an illusion?" A hint of anger had crept into Galanör's voice.

Adamar tried to shrug it off. "Humans haven't seen an elf in a thousand years. They probably wouldn't recognize one from a pair of pointed ears! I had my hood up the whole way—"

His excuse was cut off when Galanör sprang with the reflexes of a cat and jumped within arm's reach of the larger elf. His hand lashed out, as fast as any whip, and caught Adamar in the throat, before another lightning punch with his other hand connected with Adamar's kidney. Galanör followed the punches up with a swift kick to the inside of his knee, taking care to drop the large elf without actually breaking anything.

With one hand over his sore throat, Adamar looked up at Galanör, supported on his one good knee. Galanör appeared perfectly calm, with his breathing controlled; it looked as if the elf had never moved.

Adamar averted his gaze and knew well enough not to press the matter. If he rose so soon, Galanör would put him back down with annoying ease. Despite their difference in size, it could not be contested as to who was the better fighter.

Galanör turned back to the group, his leadership reaffirmed. "I have secured our passage to Korkanath." He locked eyes with Lyra. "But the price cannot be met in coins..."

CHAPTER 4
AN UNLIKELY TRUCE

Asher opened his eyes to the light of dawn, having pretended to sleep for several hours. From the lack of movement outside his door, the ranger had surmised that the young Graycoat had fallen asleep a couple of hours ago.

Not long after they dumped him on the bed, he had heard the knights discuss taking it in turns to stand guard. For the first few hours, his room had been watched by the older Graycoat, who was far more seasoned, if his equipment and clothing were anything to go by. Asher had decided it best to wait until the runt was watching his door before making his move.

Putting his old skills to use, Asher opened the door, careful not to make a sound. The young girl was drooling, slumped in a chair, opposite his room on the landing of the inn. He glanced at the door to his right, where the older knight slept, his snores audible through the walls; he only wished he could stay to see their faces when they awoke.

Asher made his way downstairs, avoiding the steps he already knew to be creaky. The innkeeper was busy behind the bar, preparing for the day to come. Upon sighting the ranger, the portly man's jaw dropped an inch, surprised to see him free of his Graycoat escort. Asher spotted his swords and quiver behind the bar, along with his folded bow, one of the few items he still possessed from his previous career.

The thought alone was enough to make him subconsciously reach for the red cloth, hanging from his belt, and rub the old material between his fingers.

"That should settle my bill." Asher dropped a small bag of coins onto the counter. "And this is for my gear, and as much time as you can give me." He proceeded to drop another sack of coins onto the table. The innkeeper's mouth twisted as he considered the bribe, before expressing a friendlier face and nodding politely.

A cold air and soggy mud greeted the ranger outside the Green Hag. Dark clouds hung overhead, stretching to the east as far as the eye could see. Hector stamped his feet when Asher entered the stables, across the street from the inn.

"Easy boy, the lightning wasn't that bad, was it? We'll soon be on the road again." He stroked the horse's chestnut neck and gave him a hearty pat across the ribs.

Asher threw his cloak over the saddle and reattached his sword belt and sheath, checking all the small blades that rested in the small of his back. When the quiver and bow sat comfortably on his back, nestled close to his rune blade, he donned his long, green cloak again.

With one foot in the stirrup, he felt the urgency in his bladder; he had after all drunk a considerable amount of golden ale in order to fool the Graycoats. Thanks to potions he had been force-fed as a teenager, alcohol was as effective as water when dulling his senses. Of course, the potions did nothing for his bladder.

"Hold that thought." Asher walked into the alley behind the stables and relieved himself of the longest piss of his life. A gasp of shock to his right brought the old ranger some embarrassment. "Morning, Miss..." he said casually. Another gasp saw the young woman hurry out of the alley and into a side door, to the local bakery. He managed a quick shake as the commotion grew on the other side of the bakery door.

"Time to put Whistle Town behind us, Hector." Asher jumped onto the horse and made a quick check of the saddlebags either side, a distraction from the ache he was beginning to feel in his knees. Hector let out a sharp breath through his nostrils. "Who are you calling old?"

The horse left the stables at a canter when the owner of the bakery came out of the side door to inspect the alley. The baker's angry demeanour quickly faded upon seeing Asher atop his horse, though it was more likely the sight of his swords that calmed the man. The colour began to drain from his face as he tried to make his return to the shop appear natural. The baker even shot the ranger a quick smile and a nod of the head.

Asher steered the horse east, towards Velia and The Shining Coast. The Green Hag was as quiet as a mouse in the early dawn. Thankfully, nobody was visiting the tavern at such an early time, and the innkeeper's bribe should give him a two-hour head start at least. The ranger thought of the young Graycoat, asleep outside his door, and couldn't help feeling a little sorry for her. That feeling only lasted a moment. Asher trotted all the way to Whistle Town's outskirts, smiling from ear to ear.

"You incompetent half-wit!" Nathaniel thundered down the creaky staircase of the Green Hag.

"It was an accident!" Elaith's olive skin turned a deep shade of pink beneath her cheeks.

Nathaniel immediately noticed the absence of the innkeeper and Asher's weapons. The Graycoat decided to check the other side of the bar in case there was a dead body to be claimed. He frowned at the sight of an empty bar without a single drop of blood - no doubt the innkeeper's purse had grown fat upon Asher's departure.

Nathaniel slammed the bar with his fist and cursed the absent innkeeper.

A light drizzle fell from the dark clouds that concealed the sun, though dawn was a few hours past now. They made for the stables and cursed again. Asher's horse was gone and there was no way of telling which way he had left with so many tracks pressed into the muddy road.

The main road from Whistle Town headed east, over the banks of The Unmar and continued on until it met The Selk Road. From there, it was another day's ride to Velia, though the ranger could go north or south from the road. It was also possible that Asher was following the unbeaten path along The Unmar, heading upstream and into the heart of The Evermoore. It was highly unlikely that the ranger would head south of The Unmar, however, for that would take him too close to West Fellion, a place Asher would surely avoid at all costs.

"Shit!" Nathaniel cried. He strode from the stables in a desperate search for any trace of the old assassin.

The streets were already filling up as the town came to life. Children ran past in fits of laughter, paying no attention to the bad weather or horse and carts that moved through the streets. Nathaniel ignored the occasional stares, curious to see two Gray-coats, and in apparent distress at that.

"He couldn't have gotten far." Elaith turned this way and that in the hope of glimpsing his green cloak.

"He could be anywhere by now. He was trained to be a ghost, remember? He could be halfway to Lirian in The Evermoore, or even just sat in another tavern across town." Nathaniel sighed, defeated. The whole mission had gone from bad to worse in a single night. "Where are *you* going?" he asked Elaith, who was walking away from the stables.

"I'm hungry!" Elaith entered the bakery next door.

Nathaniel opened his mouth but failed to find the insult to match his annoyance. "This is why I work alone..." he muttered to himself.

The mention of food brought his hunger to the surface, and the smell coming from the bakery was hard to ignore.

A minute later Elaith returned with a triumphant smile and a bag of delicious smelling pastries. "He headed east, out of town." The young Graycoat tossed the bag at Nathaniel.

"And you know this, how?" Nathaniel quickly removed the pastry and devoured it in two easy bites.

"By asking for directions..." Elaith jumped onto her mount with no lack of superiority displayed across her face. "If we ride out now, we might catch him at the crossing. I'd bet my wage he's heading for another town, Palios or Galosha perhaps. He would travel via The Selk Road for either."

Nathaniel was impressed, though he tried to hide it, still annoyed with the girl for letting Asher escape in the first place. He mounted his own steed, a large black horse from Calmardra, in The Arid Lands in the south of Illian. The Calmardras bred the fastest horses in all of Illian, and West Fellion paid for a constant supply for its knights.

"We'll have to ride hard if we're to catch him at the crossing." Nathaniel adjusted the bow and quiver on his back, as the horses trotted out of the stables.

"Is there any other way for a Graycoat to ride?" Elaith asked with a wicked smile.

"Perhaps there's hope for you yet." Nathaniel spurred his horse into a trot that quickly became a gallop.

His cry warned the people to move aside, as well as to motivate the horse. After a few angry looks and curses from the townsfolk, the Graycoats departed Whistle Town with unmatchable speed.

The sun was beginning to set by the time the sound of The Unmar could be heard across the plains. Nathaniel and Elaith had ridden all day, proving their horses' legendary speed and stamina to be true. After passing through a small ravine, the land began to level out again, with great fields of green and yellow turning orange in the sunset. Velia, however, was still too far from sight.

Before reaching the bridge, the Graycoats rode past a small caravan of merchants, their wagons overfilled with goods to sell in Whistle Town. Everything from pots and pans to a variety of vegetables and colourful clothing poked out from under the white tarp that strained to contain it all.

Nathaniel pricked his ears at the hushed conversation between the two men sitting at the front of the cart, in the lead wagon. "He looked to be a dangerous sort..." one remarked.

The Graycoat dared to hope and dug his heels into the horse's flank, pushing for one last burst of energy. The great horse managed a modest trot, putting the dust of the caravan behind him. Barden Bridge stood strong in the fast flowing river, with its grey stone arching in three places across The Unmar. Small pyres lined the edges of the bridge and had yet to be lit in the dying light.

The details of the old bridge were overshadowed by the presence of a small troop of Velian soldiers, notable by their quilted red hauberks with chainmail sleeves and long spears. The right breast of every hauberk was adorned with a dark blue wolf's head, howling into the air.

Nathaniel took note of the horses and tents set up on the other side of the river. These guards had clearly been ordered to patrol the bridge, but only on the western side. They were only concerned with people heading east, towards Velia. Nathaniel couldn't fathom why - he had never seen the king's soldiers on Barden Bridge before.

"Nathaniel..." Elaith had spotted Asher too.

The old ranger stood next to his horse in what looked to be a heated conversation with the soldiers.

"Do as I do, and no sudden movements. If you draw your sword prematurely, he may react instinctively and you'll lose an arm. This can work in our favour and, if done right, without bloodshed." Nathaniel slid from his horse and walked up, behind Asher.

"I need to cross this bridge..." The ranger's voice was rough.

"So you've said, but no pass or seal of approval means you don't step one foot on this bridge," the bald sergeant replied, hiding little of his contempt for the man before him.

"You just let that caravan through." Asher sounded aggravated and Nathaniel wondered how long he had been standing there.

"They were heading to Whistle Town. I don't give two shits what goes on there! My concern is why you wanna' go to Velia." Four more soldiers had walked over to bolster the bald one.

"The king wishes to see me."

Asher's reply stumped Nathaniel. How could the ranger possibly know that? And why would he go willingly?

"And I *wish* my old lady's tits were bigger, but wishes aren't gonna' get you over this 'ere bridge!" That drew a chorus of laughter from the other soldiers.

"I'm crossing this bridge before dusk..." Asher's hand rested on the pommel of his broadsword. "One way or another, boys..."

The soldiers' faces dropped at the obvious threat. As one, they all reached for their swords or adjusted their spears.

Nathaniel pushed past the ranger to stand between him and the soldiers. "This man is in our custody." All eyes fell on Nathaniel. "We are to escort him to Velia with all haste, at the king's behest."

The soldiers looked at one another, dumbfounded, while the bald sergeant kept his gaze fixed on Nathaniel. Asher made no move against them, while the sergeant scrutinized the odd pair.

"What's this have to do with Graycoats?" the bald man spat.

"He is our... prisoner. We are to—"

"He doesn't look like a prisoner!" one of the other guards stated.

"Your *prisoner* has been talking at me for some time, Graycoat. Yet you only appear now." The sergeant looked Asher up and down. "And your prisoner is armed to the teeth it seems." The sergeant flashed a smug grin, devoid of many teeth.

Nathaniel hesitated with his answer, knowing a fight wouldn't end well for the soldiers, and would ultimately pit him and Elaith against Asher.

"This is all you need to know, Sergeant." Nathaniel retrieved the rolled up parchment from inside his coat and thrust it into the soldier's chest.

The sergeant unravelled the scroll and scrunched up his face, as he attempted to read the elegant calligraphy.

Nathaniel realised that there was a chance the sergeant couldn't read. "If you observe the seal at the bottom of the scroll, you'll recognise the mark of Lord Marshal Horvarth of West Fellion. The letter clearly states that we are on an errand for the king, *your* king."

The sergeant handed the scroll back and begrudgingly stepped aside, sweeping his men with an outstretched arm. "On your way." The other soldiers continued their excellent impressions of being confused.

The three unusual companions mounted their horses and crossed the bridge unfettered. Nathaniel glanced from Elaith to Asher, unsure what to say as to the ranger's cooperation. The sound of the river and the horses' hooves on stone was the only noise to be heard for some time. They continued over the rise in silence, The Unmar behind them, glistening in the sunset.

Nathaniel commanded his horse to trot ahead and cut off Asher's own steed. The ranger stopped without a fuss and gave the Graycoat a hard look and an unreadable expression. Nathaniel felt an uneasy feeling creep into his stomach and knew it was fear.

It had been a long time since the primal spasm had dominated his emotions. The Graycoat tried to remind himself of all the monsters and murderous men he had faced and cut down. This was just another man. *A man.* There were no claws or powerful jaws filled with razor sharp teeth coming at him. In fact, the man before him was older and no doubt slower, feeling the weight of his life in service to the Arakesh.

"I cannot present you to the king with all those weapons." Nathaniel gripped the hilt of his sword but kept it sheathed.

"Then it's a good thing you're not the one to present me to the king. I believe that *honour* falls to Darius Devale, does it not?" Asher raised a cocky eyebrow.

Nathaniel guarded his expression, whereas Elaith appeared in complete shock. The Graycoat adjusted his seating and lifted his head, trying to remain composed and in control. "How do you know that?" He kept his voice even.

"I knew you were coming for me before *you* did..." Asher waited expectantly for an introduction that Nathaniel wasn't inclined to give. "Master Bail's spies were about as subtle as a Hydra in heat," he continued, "to say nothing of his shoddy locks."

Nathaniel was building a profile of the ranger with every new detail. It was clear that Asher had followed his own tail back to the sector house, and not only broken in, but read the letter from West Fellion, and left again without so much as a trace. It was another reminder that the ageing man before him was a highly trained assassin and not just some ranger of the wilds.

"So you're willingly going to present yourself to the king?" Elaith came up beside Asher on her horse, well within reach of a killing blow.

Nathaniel rolled his eyes at the danger the young girl put herself in.

"I live from job to job..."

"...Elaith, Elaith Nevandar," she eagerly replied.

Nathaniel visibly sagged in his saddle, unbelieving of his ward.

"*Elaith*." Asher smiled pleasantly. "I live from job to job, and a king's job sounds rewarding." The ranger turned back to Nathaniel, apparently happy to wait for the Graycoat.

"Well..." Nathaniel looked away uncomfortably. This was not going the way he expected. "It seems we are both going the same way, and you won't get within five hundred yards of King Rengar without an escort, prisoner or not. Perhaps you should allow us to hand you over to Darius Devale and he can make the proper introductions?"

Asher looked to the horizon for a moment. "Why not? We'd be

doing each other a favour then." The ranger tapped his heels against the horse to get it moving again. "Velia is three days' ride from here, maybe two if there aren't too many more of those checkpoints." He flicked his head back to the direction of Barden Bridge.

Nathaniel moved his horse out of the way, eyeing the ranger with new intrigue. He had expected a violent man, devoid of manners or rationale, whose only impulse was to kill.

"Are the checkpoints unusual?" Elaith asked.

"You *are* new." Asher was already trotting off into the distance.

The Graycoats brought their horses up behind the ranger's. "You should know this already." Nathaniel allowed some of his previous annoyance with the girl to be heard in his tone.

"Geography was boring - almost as boring as Master Golth's monotonous—"

"Show respect; remember you're still trying to *earn* that coat." Nathaniel took a moment to allow the irritation to drain away, recalling his role of mentor. "King Rengar rules the region of Alborn from his throne in Velia. It's the largest city in Alborn and home to Direport, the largest harbour in Illian. There is relative peace between the regions right now, or at least I thought there was. I haven't seen checkpoints in these parts for years."

"Do you think it has anything to do with the king wanting to see Asher?" Elaith lowered her voice.

"I can't imagine they're connected."

"And I would say the girl has more insight than *you*!" Asher shouted over his shoulder.

Nathaniel bit back his retort. "You think highly of yourself, Ranger!" Asher had no reply. "We should think about making camp, the sun is setting." Nathaniel changed the subject, seeing the stars appear on the far horizon.

"There's at least another hour, yet." Asher pressed on.

"We can't all see in the dark, remember?" the Graycoat added defiantly. Despite only seeing the back of his head, Nathaniel was sure the ranger was smiling.

CHAPTER 5
THE MASTERS OF LIES

The waves slammed into the ship with no rhythm at all, as the storm churned the surface of The Adean. Even on the outskirts of the furious clouds, the sea was thrown into fits and the wind whipped into a frenzy.

Reyna's alchemy was constantly interrupted by the rogue waves determined to capsize and deliver them to the depths. The young elf did everything she could to steady herself, while her arms dashed out across the table to catch rolling vials and herbal ingredients that slid from left to right.

"Argh!" A bottle of sap oil came loose from its rack and tumbled off the edge of the table.

There was no sound of glass shattering on the floor but, instead, the blue vial rose through the air. "You need to work on your magical reflexes." Faylen had her teaching voice on, as her hand guided the floating vial of oil back into the rack.

"It's this constant motion!" Reyna replied. "Elves were made for land, not the sea. Give me fields and forests or even mountains over this..." She covered her mouth feeling the nausea rising in her gut. "Why couldn't we use a portal?"

"To cross The Adean in a single step takes more magic than even our kind possess. Besides, we don't want the humans to know we have knowledge of such magic. Have you taken any more Seabreath?" Faylen seemed to almost glide to the table, where she deftly put the ingredients together, before adding the sap oil and placing it inside the flask on the tripod. The liquid bubbled as the candle beneath heated the various parts into a drinkable potion.

Reyna tried to distract herself by sprinkling Redandon herbs into the marble mortar and grinding them with the pestle. "I'm trying to make enough for the three of us, but everything is taking twice as long with this ridiculous weather!"

The princess accepted the vial from Faylen and downed the Seabreath in one. The warm liquid began to take effect almost immediately, relieving Reyna of her seasickness and leaving her with a tingling sensation in the back of her throat.

Faylen demonstrated her centuries of magical experience and levitated the ingredients and equipment across the table with ease. Everything came together perfectly until the flask was filled with enough Seabreath for two days' worth of consumption. After the potion had cooled, the flask floated into the air and the dark blue liquid was poured into multiple empty vials until finally each was fitted with a small cork. Faylen took two and placed them within her long purple robe, as all the moving parts came to settle once more on the table.

"I'll take one for Mörygan as well." Faylen turned for the door, heading back to the ladder that connected to the top deck.

"How is he faring?" Reyna felt she could actually stand up now. She gathered the alchemy equipment and quickly packed it all away into the chest on the floor.

"He has spent many a year sailing on The Crystal Sea, long before either of us were born; he will be fine. You, on the other hand, still have much to learn. You should continue to practise magic. You favour the sword and bow over anything else, but magic is the real strength of our people - always remember that. Among other things, it is our greatest advantage over the humans, and will serve you better than any piece of steel."

Faylen's dark eyes appeared lifeless in the shadow of the candle-light. Of course, Reyna knew her guardian's eyes to be full of life and beauty. Faylen had been with her since she was born, tending to her every need as well as her education and training, while Reyna's father, the Lord of Elves, made plans for the future of their entire race. Faylen was her mother and father.

Reyna looked to the white owl, sitting on his perch in the corner of the room, and tried to push away thoughts of her real mother. "Ölli's wings will get cramped if we stay on this boat much longer." Reyna wanted to change the subject from talks of their inevitable plan.

"You are still uncomfortable with your father's strategy." Faylen wasn't asking.

Reyna had come to love and hate that her guardian could always read her like a book. "I'm uncomfortable moving against a people I've never even met. Humans are just stories from an old book to me."

Faylen walked over to Ölli's perch and stroked the owl's wing. "I too have never seen Illian's shores." The elf took on a serious tone. "But there are many who still remember their barbarism and greed, their lust for dominance and power over all life. Unlike your mother and father, *my* parents didn't witness The Dark War, but they did witness the war man waged against the dragons. They drove the oldest and noblest of creatures to the brink of extinction for naught but wealth."

"I know, I can recall the stories you told me word for word, but that's all they are to me, *stories*. Even the dragons are just paintings on a wall."

"We will soon bring those stories to life. You have a great part to play in freeing this world, Reyna." Faylen held the princess close, tucking Reyna's blonde hair behind her shoulders. "And I will be there, by your side, every step of the way." She placed a gentle kiss on her forehead. "Now practise…"

~

Faylen fastened her robe tight around her waist, as she stepped onto the first rung. The rain came through the hatch, creating puddles under the ladder and making the rungs slippery.

Lavo Weis.

As the ancient words formed in her mind, the rain flowed over and around her body, keeping her dry.

From the top deck, the ship appeared to move like a seesaw from stern to bow. The white sails were taut in their rigging, full with the ferocious winds. The elf walked across the decking, towards the platform at the bow of the ship, pausing briefly to observe the storm off the port side. Everything to the south was blanketed by the dark clouds and relentless rain. Looking starboard, to the north, Faylen could see stars twinkling on the horizon, free of the storm.

"A beautiful night in Dhenaheim, it seems," Mörygan announced from the platform above her. He didn't have to shout over the wind and rain, with Faylen's sensitive ears easily picking up his every word.

"Yes. A pity it's wasted on a race that prefers to live underground…" she replied, referring to the reclusive dwarves.

Mörygan stood as a sentinel behind the wheel of the ship. Faylen could feel the magical will he exerted across the various rigging, as well as the barrier he had erected around himself, just as she had done. What should have taken the skills of a dozen sailors was being performed by Mörygan alone. He directed the wind into the sails and telekinetically manipulated the rigging and sheets, pushing the ship on with as much magical assistance as he could muster.

His shoulder-length black hair was tied in a ponytail that met his long, black and blue robes. Many of his fingers were adorned with rings that harnessed wells of magic inside their crystals.

"Reyna has made more Seabreath for us." Faylen offered the vial, but Mörygan didn't take it.

"You mean you have made more Seabreath?" Mörygan raised an eyebrow. "She is yet to make a single batch that has the desired effect."

Faylen could hear the criticism in his voice and it made her blood boil. "She is *trying*, Mörygan."

"She is twenty-seven years of age. Her years of trying should be behind her." An almost imperceptible nod of his head was all he gave in his efforts to steer the ship farther north, away from the storm.

"Her magic is coming along." Faylen looked out to sea, not wanting to make eye contact. "She has accomplished more than I did at her age."

"We both know that's a lie," Mörygan countered. "Her magical abilities might put her ahead of any human, but she is still a child of the arts by our reckoning." His cold, grey eyes rested on Faylen. "We all have an important task to undertake. But never forget that it is just us out here. When that line is finally crossed, we three will be well and truly stuck behind enemy lines. We will have to rely on each other's strengths if we are to see the new dawn."

Faylen sighed. "Couldn't we have brought someone else? We could have just told them I was the princess."

"The humans are the masters of lies. We couldn't take the chance. Besides, this is an opportunity for Reyna. She might even redeem her mother's cowardice."

The irony of who the real liars were wasn't lost on Faylen, but her focus was required on not rising to Mörygan's comment. Had it been anyone else, she would have challenged them right there and then, but there was a reason Mörygan never carried a sword - he didn't need one. Instead, Faylen settled with giving him a glare that would kill most elves.

"Come now," he continued. "You and I both know Adilandra will never return, along with the others that followed her on that pointless pilgrimage."

Movement on the port side of the ship caught their attention. Ölli sat on the railing, watching them with his large black eyes. The rain moved around the bird as it did them, and Faylen immediately looked around for any sign of Reyna on the deck. The princess had obviously put the spell on the owl, to allow him some time in the air, but Faylen was more concerned with anything Reyna might have overheard.

"I would be more concerned with *us* returning..."

CHAPTER 6
THE HUNTED

In the void between realities, Adilandra watched Faylen and Mörygan through the eyes of Ölli, the white owl. The animal's keen eyes and ears were the perfect way to watch over her daughter. The elf couldn't feel her own body or the environment in which she sat, but she could smell The Adean and hear its mighty waves rage over a thousand miles away.

She trusted Faylen with Reyna's life, but it churned her stomach to think of Mörygan Mörgö as one of her guardians. He wasn't an elf to be trusted in Adilandra's opinion: in fact, the entire Mörgö family wasn't to be trusted.

During The Dark War, more than one in their bloodline had been tried and found guilty of sympathising and spying for Valanis. She had always found it hard to believe that her husband had allowed the Mörgös to claw their way back up the hierarchy.

"Adilandra!" Her name was called from the ether by a familiar voice, full of fear.

The elf released the owl from her spell and allowed her consciousness to be pulled back into her own mind. Her eyes reverted back to her normal shade of blue, having appeared completely black for her time possessing Ölli.

As her mind snapped back, so too did her body's senses, informing her of the damp jungle ground on which she sat, and the close humid atmosphere that clung to her body like a parasite.

"Adilandra, they've found us!" She followed the hand on her shoulder to the terrified face of Fallön. "The Darkakin have found us. We have to go, now!" The scar that ran from his forehead down to his right eye crinkled under an expression of desperation.

In the distance, her elvish ears picked up the sound of barking dogs and rustling trees, as the band of human savages closed in. Fallön helped Adilandra up and passed her the large pack that she immediately slung over her back. Over the last four years, her body had become accustomed to its bulk and weight. To her left, Ederön and Lörvana hefted their own packs and ran further into the jungle, away from the barking dogs.

Close behind them, Adilandra and Fallön rushed through the giant leaves that hung limply from low branches. Their superior speed gave them the advantage over the humans, but in the jungle, it only proved to work against the elves. Ederön fell over a root in front of them and skidded across the ground.

"Keep going!" Adilandra shouted to Fallön and Lörvana. She quickly knelt down to help Ederön up, abandoning the small book that slipped from his pack.

The barking was soon accompanied by the rapid patter of paws. They had let the dogs go. Adilandra and Ederön met each other's eyes briefly, before turning to run as fast as possible. The fear of what was coming pushed them past logical thought and the danger their speed presented. They soon caught up with Fallön and Lörvana who were cutting their way through a thicket of plants. Their elvish swords appeared dull under the jungle canopy, though Adilandra could still make out the ornate runes that decorated each blade.

"This is too slow!" Ederön looked back at the way they had come. They could all hear the Banshee-like cries from the Darkakin in the distance. Adilandra could see the fear on all of their faces, the desperation that had robbed them of hope years ago.

"We have to go up!" Adilandra deftly hopped from one tree to another, gaining height as she did, until the elf was almost at canopy level. The others followed her, as they always had, and jumped up the nearest tree, moving from one to the next.

When the ground cleared, all four elves found their way down and continued to run for their lives. If the Darkakin caught them... Adilandra knew it was better to die fighting them than to be taken prisoner.

They ran for another hour, when the first glimpses of dawn could be seen piercing the canopy. The hunters had lost their tracks in the trees and had no doubt been slowed by the ever increasing thickness of the jungle. The elves stopped to catch their breath, some leaning against a tree, others simply falling to the ground in exhaustion.

"They've been hunting us for seven months..." Lörvana slid down to the ground, her auburn hair matted around her face in sweat. "What evil drives them so?"

"What do you expect?" Ederön nursed his sore knee. "They are human, after all. Wickedness is the foundation of their nature. They know no other way."

Adilandra winced at Ederön's tone. Ever since they encountered the Darkakin, two years ago, his hate for humanity had festered and grown. It was becoming harder to disagree with him though; the Darkakin had killed five of their expedition and captured two alive.

Adilandra didn't like to think about the two captives. After five months of tracking them down, one was still missing; sold to another tribe, never to be found, and the other had been publicly tortured to death in one of the bigger camps. The four of them had been forced to watch, no match against a whole mob of Darkakin. After four years, they were the only ones left to continue with their self-appointed mission into the uncharted lands, in the south of Ayda.

"They are the worst of mankind, but do not blanket their whole race with your hate, Ederön." It was Fallön who still had the strength to speak up.

Adilandra looked at him fondly and knew she couldn't have reached this far without his support.

"Hate is what turned our own kind from the path," he continued. "We few must remember what it is to be an elf. For too long have we plotted against the humans, against all of Illian. The humans lost their way because we let them. The gods charged us with teaching them and we abandoned them when they needed our wisdom most.

"So many elves blame the humans for what they did to the dragons, but the fault lies with us. Had we stayed in Illian we could have prevented The Dragon War and kept the peace. More than that, we could have ensured that Valanis remained locked away inside Elethiah, *forever*. Now we're half a world away, grasping at hope..."

Adilandra could hear the strength of his convictions faltering in him. Their bleak surroundings and dire situation were enough to rid any elf of hope, especially when they had seen all of their friends and lovers cut down by savages.

"Just out of curiosity," Lörvana asked through laboured breaths, "how many of those speeches do you have stored away?" The group smiled for the first time in days and relaxed for a moment.

"I don't care what you say, Fallön." Ederön had finished the healing spell on his knee. "We cannot be blamed for the Darkakin. They came out of The Wild Moores that twisted."

Fallön traced the edge of the scar across his face. "I can't argue with that."

They looked to Adilandra, as they had when they first came across the Darkakin. She was the only one old enough to remember the humans when they first emerged from unknown lands. Despite the millennia of time that lay between now and then, the elf still recalled the bloody battles that took place.

Some of the human tribes had been happy to be taken in by the elves, eager to learn more about the world and their place in it. But there were many who came out of The Wild Moores hungry for war

68

with the first thing they saw. Having just pulled through the biggest war in elven history, against Valanis, the elven nation was tired of fighting and killing and barely managed to push the Darkakin back, driving them south of The Arid Lands.

In the centuries left to themselves, the Darkakin had swelled in size, growing into an empire that spanned a continent. The evil humans had found land that connected Illian to Ayda, west to east, and spread across Verda like a disease, conquering everything in their path. Since arriving in their land, the elves had heard rumours of The Goddess that apparently ruled the Darkakin. Whoever this woman was, Adilandra couldn't imagine what it would take to govern such a people.

"We should just be thankful they are content with the southern lands." Adilandra didn't want to recall the past in all its bloody detail.

"I can't believe they even found a way into Ayda." Lörvana removed some bread from her pack and shared it out. "How did we not know there was land between the two continents?"

"We've never travelled south of The Lifeless Isles before." Ederön was clearly upset that they were the first to have done so. Adilandra could feel the anger bubbling over in Ederön, as it always did after a close encounter with the Darkakin. "This is a fool's errand!" He always started the same way. "We've been journeying south for four years with nothing but blood to show for it. As if crossing The Flat Wastes wasn't hard enough, we've found nothing but legends and drawings on cave walls since we set out. I'm just saying what we've all been thinking. We will never find the last of the dragons..."

Adilandra moved to sit next to Ederön and took his hand in hers. "Have faith, Ederön. I just need a little more strength to see our journey through. We're close now, I can feel it. You were only a child when the dragons left The Lifeless Isles, but I remember it as though it were yesterday. When all was lost, Rainael the emerald star gathered the last of her kind and flew east. We followed them to Ayda soon after, and from there I watched them leave Mount Garganafan, travelling south. The legends and drawings simply prove that they came this way.

The Darkakin were scattered across Illian as tribes back then. They could not bring down the dragons. They're here somewhere." Adilandra could see the doubt that still lingered on Ederön's face. "Think of the prophecy. Feel Nalana's words in your bones and you will know them to be true. We don't have the time my husband thinks we do - his plan will take years, maybe centuries to bear fruition. Valanis *will* be freed before then. I *know* it. If Valanis breaks free of the Amber Spell he will consume the world. Finding Rainael and the others is our only chance..."

Ederön squeezed her hand and managed a faint smile. "We will not let the world fall into ruin."

A snapping twig was the only sound that preceded the twang of a bow and an arrow driving into Ederön's ribs. Adilandra felt the force of the impact in Ederön's hand, as he clenched and screamed with pain. The trees around them exploded into chaos with a dozen Darkakin bursting from the jungle. Their bodies were decorated from head to toe in tribal tattoos and white paint smeared across their faces. If they weren't bald they had black hair matted into long dreadlocks. The bones of smaller animals, as well as humans, decorated their primitive armour like spikes, while other bones pierced their skin, decoratively.

The elves drew their swords and staggered into the middle of the opening, ready to fight back-to-back. The Darkakin hunters wore loose wooden armour that exposed most of their body. Having fought them before, Adilandra knew the Darkakin weren't trained to be defensive fighters - their style was pure aggression. The humans attacked furiously with serrated spears and swords, moving like wild cats and jumping into the elves' protective circle.

Adilandra deflected a spear and cut off another's arm in the process, before ducking under a slicing sword attack. Fallön and Lörvana danced around each other, cutting down two Darkakin with perfect symmetry.

"No!" Adilandra caught sight of two more Darkakin coming from the jungle and dragging Ederön away. He was too weak to fight them off with the arrow protruding from his ribs.

Lörvana screamed to Adilandra's right, with an arrow in her leg and several cuts across her body. The largest of the Darkakin band strode through and clubbed Lörvana across the face with the end of his mace. The elf dropped to the ground in silence.

Fallön, enraged, charged at the large human with his sword held high. Adilandra could see Fallön's surroundings better than he could and knew the elf would never get close enough to strike. Four Darkakin tackled him to the ground and beat him until he stopped moving.

Adilandra deflected two more attacks and killed another with a clean slice, separating the wild woman's torso from her legs. The elf stood, exhausted in the jungle heat and bleeding from various points across her body. She was surrounded by savages eager to rip her to pieces. They slowly closed in with the big one in the lead. Adilandra took a deep breath and gripped her sword with both hands. The only sound was the blood rushing through her ears.

She wasn't going to die here.

"I have to save us... I have to save us all." The words barely left her lips she was so tired.

The large one smiled cruelly, revealing his filthy teeth, sharpened to points. Before Adilandra could take her next breath, she was assaulted from behind. The pain in the back of her head was fleeting compared to the speed with which she lost consciousness.

CHAPTER 7
KORKANATH

The ageing auditorium was the oldest structure within Korkanath's grounds. The stone floor had been transferred slab for slab from King Tion's own fortress in Namdhor, centuries ago, where the first king had been taught by the earliest mages. The dark red surface was engraved with traditional training circles that overlapped and grew in size from the epicentre, each lined in ancient runes and elvish words.

With no windows, the auditorium was illuminated by dozens of floating orbs that rested inside the domed ceiling, bringing to light the encircling sculpture that depicted the final battle of The Dragon War.

Gideon Thorn stood in the centre of the large room and scrutinised the portraits of the Magikars that lined the walls. Each wizard had ruled Korkanath through the ages, passing on their wisdom, counselling kings and queens and experimenting with new magic.

Of course, all Gideon took from the paintings was an ensemble of old men with bushy white beards and ridiculous hats. They had sat in their comfy chairs behind Korkanath's high walls and grown fat off the work of other mages, sent out into the world to do nothing but please and serve the rich. Gideon refused to follow their example. He had his sights set on a life of adventure and mystery, with matters of life and death an everyday occurrence.

The ruckus on the other side of the double doors grew louder, as dozens of feet ascended the stairwell. Gideon's best friend, Abigail Rose, led the class of third years into the room, instructing them to line the auditorium's circular edge.

Her welcoming smile always put him at ease, not that he wasn't used to teaching the younger classes by now. For the last three years, the teachers of Korkanath had called on him to assist them with classes, as well as tutoring small groups on his own, though today was new, even for Gideon.

The young teenagers milled around the edges, sticking with their friends and whispering about Gideon's presence. As third years they all wore the same red robes with wide hoods down to their waists.

Gideon remembered his third year well. As a thirteen-year-old mage-to-be, he had been so excited to finally pick his wand or staff. The boys and girls around him now were only five months away from choosing the instrument of magic that would stay with them for the rest of their lives.

"I know you were all expecting to be taught by Master Banthora this morning." Gideon's words silenced the group. "But he has accompanied the Magikar and the high council to Velia on school business. Master Banthora asked me to continue your meditation techniques today." The disappointed looks on their faces were exactly what Gideon was going for. "I know, I know, but don't forget how important it is. Meditation is the best way to harness raw magic and contain it within a crystal. You all have this test at the end of the year when you come to pick your staff or wand." He had disappointed them quite nicely. "So I thought instead of meditation, Miss Rose and I could demonstrate a few magical spells with each instrument." The mood of the class changed immediately to one of elation. "Miss Rose..."

Abigail strode into the middle of the circle, opposite Gideon.

"Thank you, Mr Thorn." Her smile betrayed her lack of surprise at Gideon's change in the lesson plan. She knew him too well.

"Miss Rose here favours a wand, as you can see." Abigail removed her wand from its leather holster around her thigh. "It has an ash coating with the feather of a Griffin infused. Its Demetrium core runs through the length of the haft. You should already know by now that Demetrium ore is extremely conducive to magic. Now..." Gideon reached over his shoulder and unclipped the small staff from its sheath on his back. When his hand gripped the middle of the staff it instantly grew outwards in both directions. "My staff has an oak finish with the hair of a centaur inlaid. If you want a compact staff like mine, then make sure you engrave the spell into the wood *before* adding the essence of any magical creature. Doing it the other way around can result in loss of eyebrows.

You should also bear in mind that if you choose a staff you will require more Demetrium for the core." Gideon walked around the edges of the group, letting them all admire the intricate artistry of his staff. The students looked on, wide-eyed, trying to make out the ancient script that spiralled the length of the wood.

Abigail muttered a spell while pointing her wand at the back of her head, creating a telekinetic effect that tied her copper hair into a ponytail. "Who here can tell me the difference between a wand and a staff?"

The teenagers shuffled in their groups until a bushy-haired girl stepped forward. "There is no difference, Miss Rose. The Demetrium core serves as an equal conduit in both instruments. The choosing of either is simply a tradition passed on from the archmages of King Tion's court." The young girl stood defiantly against her peers' obvious derision.

"Well said." Gideon took the lead again. "However, there are advantages and disadvantages to both. The wand can be concealed and easily used in confined spaces. The staff, on the other hand, can be used as a physical weapon in a tight situation and, believe me, sometimes the best option is to just hit a Gobber over the head with a strong piece of wood." His little quip had the desired effect.

"Is it true Mr Thorn that you fought off a Wold and defeated a whole nest of Gorgons in The Vrost Mountains?" an enthusiastic boy asked. The story grew with every new version Gideon heard.

"When you reach your eighth year, you will all get the chance to leave this island, accompanying a master into the field and helping them with their research or experiments. Of course, the real world doesn't have all the rules Korkanath adheres to, and real-world problems may occur. Today, Miss Rose and I are going to demonstrate a few ways to help you deal with those problems. For your benefit, we will say the spells aloud." Gideon motioned for Abigail to take her position across the room. "Anything you like..."

Abigail raised an eyebrow, with a menacing smile to match. "Vala!" A ball of molten fire exploded from the end of her wand.

"Darvuun!" Gideon braced himself, as the molten fire collided violently with a brilliant flash against his arcing blue shield.

The fire dispersed across the field and fizzled out into sparks that rained onto the ancient stone floor. With a chorus of gasps, the students took a quick step back from the magical display.

Gideon let the class settle before continuing the lesson. "Now, the ancient language is still being deciphered today by the high council and the Magikar. Every word we use, so too did the ancients. But you must not only think the ancient word but also understand its meaning and be sure to mould the spell correctly.

"Vala means fire, but the will of the caster combined with a wand or staff can change the form of the spell..." Gideon swept his staff in a semicircle and uttered the fire spell. Instead of creating a molten ball of fire, the staff erupted with a constant stream of the blazing energy. "That's called dragon's breath."

"Mr Thorn, is it true that elves don't need wands or staffs to use magic?" The girl's accent suggested she was from the north. Gideon guessed her to be from Dunwich.

"Having never met one I couldn't say for certain, but our oldest

75

tomes would suggest this to be true. I'm sure Master Sorrento has shared her theory that the elves descended from the ancients and that the key to understanding true magic lies in their blood."

"Yalai!" Abigail's spell was barely audible over the blast of ice that burst from her wand.

"Vala!" Gideon's counterspell caught the ice a metre away from his face. The opposing elements clashed mid-air, cancelling each other out in an explosion of sparks and steam. "Ebori." Gideon swung his staff around his body until his image vanished from sight. The class broke out in whispers and gasps of awe and shock.

Abigail held her wand up defensively and slowly walked around the line of students. "Mr Thorn is demonstrating the ancient word for, hidden. Mages have used it for centuries to hide and conceal their secrets, be it a relic, jewel or even a person. It does, however, take considerable concentration, causing most mages to draw on their crystals. As their will fades, so does the illusion. However…" Abigail's eyes scanned the room from side to side, "…there is a spell capable of countering Ebori." She moved her wand from left to right as she said the incantation, "Revasai…"

The ancient word for reveal made the air ripple momentarily. Gideon's lunging form emerged from the spatial distortion, his staff angled to strike Abigail in the face. The attack wasn't rehearsed, but Gideon was confident in Abigail's abilities to evade and counter. They had spent hundreds of hours sparring together while practising for their exams in their sixth and seventh years at Korkanath. Though staff casters were known for their more aggressive fighting styles, Abigail had studied almost every technique when sparring with a wand. Gideon had the scars to prove it.

"Alsa!" Her spell blinded Gideon, knocking him off balance.

Gideon felt a firm hand on his shoulder before a swift knock to the back of his leg put him on the floor. Sensing the imminent attack, he flicked his staff up and shouted, "Lavo!"

Despite his lack of vision, Gideon heard Abigail fly backward and skid across the floor. He placed his hand over his eyes and whispered,

"Hyal." The healing spell brought his sight back instantly. Rather than the expected looks of amazement and awe, Gideon was greeted by looks of horror and shock.

"Class dismissed!" The sharp instruction came from the familiar voice of Master Vorn. The third years hurried from the auditorium, making sure to avoid the master's eye.

Gideon was joined by Abigail, as he used his staff to help him stand. Master Vorn held an unyielding glare on them both. It was clear the master had never liked the quick rise of Gideon, from passing his first-year exams at the top of his class to teaching the juniors in his tenth and last year.

"I believe Master Banthora instructed you to continue their meditation techniques." Master Vorn's pale complexion was exaggerated under the white glow of the floating orbs. "Not endanger them by showing off!" His long green robes concealed the sharpened nails the master was notorious for.

"Master—"

"Silence! You are three months away from graduating to the grade of a mage. Until then, Mr Thorn, you are under my supervision. Remember, until the Magikar and the high council return, I am in charge of Korkanath. You will lead no more lessons in their absence and you will certainly keep your staff in check outside of the sparring hall. Failure to obey my commands will see you on cleaning duties for the next three months, starting with Malliath's lair." The thought of such a job gave Gideon shivers. "And you will wear your student robes from now on. You're not on some grand adventure here." Master Vorn stood aside and swept his robe dramatically, indicating the end of their conversation.

With their heads bowed, they both left the auditorium, deflated and a little angry. The third years had already disappeared by the time Gideon and Abigail walked out onto the high walls of Korkanath's perimeter. On a clear day, the thick walls of Dragorn could be seen to the south-east and even the great port city of Velia to the west. Gideon looked out onto a grey horizon with no sun in sight and rain clouds moving in from all sides.

"He has a point you know..." Abigail pulled the band from her hair and let the copper ringlets flow down to her chest.

"Not you as well?" Gideon adjusted the strap on his back to make certain the end of his staff didn't hit him in the head.

"We both know you're on track to becoming one of the best mages Korkanath has ever produced. In a few years, you could be Vorn's equal, on your way to being an archmage or even the next Magikar."

"Don't you need wrinkles and a heart condition for that job?" His humour did nothing to deter Abigail.

"You know what I mean," she continued. "You should take a little more care when addressing the masters and actually do as you're told for a change. I know you disagree with the way things are run here, but if you follow the right path you might actually be in a position to change things here for the better."

Gideon sighed. "I don't want to change things *here*. I want to change things out *there*!" He looked west, to the shores of Illian. "I want a life outside of these walls. I don't want to teach or study the old tomes, and I certainly don't want to be chained to some king or queen as a court wizard. I want to see the world, Abigail!" Gideon jumped onto the wall a little higher than his waist. "I want to see what the whole of Verda has to offer!" he shouted over the roar of the ocean below.

Abigail laughed at his dramatics. "Perhaps not a court wizard, but I can definitely see you making an excellent career as a court jester!" They both laughed together and Gideon hopped off the wall, his curly dark hair made a mess of in the growing breeze.

"I just want an adventure..." Gideon leaned against the wall and looked over Korkanath's grounds.

The high walls contained a large area filled with towers and glass domes, decorated with herb gardens and statues. Almost every tower had cobwebs of vines growing around the stonework. Beyond the northern wall, Gideon knew there to be a different kind of structure, situated at the base and dug deep into the ground. The cave was the entrance to Korkanath's underground network that had long been abandoned after the island's protector, Malliath the voiceless, had chosen the dark hole as its lair.

"And where would we start this adventure?" Abigail asked playfully.

"*We*?" Gideon looked her in the eyes and regretted it. He had always tried to stop his empathy from getting in the way when it came to Abigail but upsetting her upset him, and she wanted something he didn't, at least not yet, not while there were adventures to be had.

"Yes, *we!*" Abigail punched him in the arm. "We both know you wouldn't last a day beyond these walls without me."

Gideon laughed. "I'm inclined to agree." He could feel the probing look Abigail gave him. Gideon knew it was one of hope, that maybe this time he would confess his feelings for her after so many years. He changed the subject. "You know it's a full moon tonight..."

Abigail's gaze lingered another moment, before looking away, deflated. "You sound like one of the first years." The hope and playfulness were gone from her voice.

"Come on! Everybody knows Malliath hunts on a full moon. Do you remember in our ninth year, when that whale carcass was found on the northern shore? That was after a full moon!"

Abigail rolled her eyes. "That was almost six years ago, Gideon. He wasn't seen that night and he hasn't even been heard since. I don't think he likes to be seen..."

Gideon could hear the sadness in her voice and knew it wasn't over him anymore. "It's never sat well with you, has it?"

"I think he should have been allowed to die with the rest of his kind, not caged and enslaved for all time." Abigail sounded almost ashamed.

"Well, he had to expect it." Gideon tried to defend the choices of his ancestors, even if he didn't fully agree with them himself.

"Malliath started a war with our kind. Even the elves saw the folly in his actions. That's why they didn't help and left Illian altogether. Imprisoning Malliath may not have been the *right* thing to do but, maybe the right thing to do wasn't what was needed."

"The *right* thing is all we should ever do. And I thought you weren't paying attention to Master Harl's history lessons." The hint of a smile returned to her face.

"Don't get me wrong, most of the time I have to enchant my eyes to stay open, but if there's anything that's going to keep my attention, it's talk of dragons!"

CHAPTER 8
FIRST KILL

After a whole day of riding, with nothing but dry bread and stale water from their stores, the three unlikely companions stopped to make camp for the night. As part of her ongoing test, Nathaniel had Elaith go off in search of food for them to cook over a spit. While performing her duties as a Graycoat and her expected life on the road, she would have to spend many a night hunting game for sustenance. Theirs was an uncomfortable life, filled with violence and danger that demanded high energy only obtained from a healthy diet.

"Two squirrels and... is that a hedgehog?" Nathaniel inspected Elaith's catch with disbelief.

"I've been out there for two hours, Nathaniel! There's nothing to hunt." Elaith dropped the animals at his feet and sat by the fire, exhausted.

Nathaniel picked up the hedgehog by one of its spikes and flung it into a nearby bush. The Graycoat was careful to keep Asher in his peripheral vision at all times.

The ranger sat on the other side of the fire, patiently sharpening his broadsword. Without a word, he stood up and drove the blade into the ground. With one hand he removed the strange bow from within his cloak, and the old strip of red cloth from his belt with the other.

"And where are you going?" Nathaniel fought back the urge to stand up and block the ranger's path. Escorting Asher to Velia was his mission and, even though he was going willingly, it didn't feel right that the old assassin wasn't in chains.

"Don't worry, Graycoat, the three of us will walk through Velia's gates tomorrow night." Asher's thumb flicked a latch on the bow's handle, setting off a sequence of miniature cogs. In the blink of an eye, the bow snapped and unfolded to reveal its curving shape.

Nathaniel tried not to stare at the incredible intricacy of the weapon and its mechanical engineering - the design was unlike anything he had ever seen before. It had to be a dwarven mind behind its creation, or possibly elven, though doubtful with their long-term absence from Illian.

Asher left his sword in the ground and disappeared into the dark, beyond the firelight.

"He doesn't speak much, does he?" Elaith rolled out her blanket onto the hard ground.

"We need more firewood..." Nathaniel's comment came out as an order.

Elaith dropped her head but kept her murderous gaze to herself.

In less than an hour, Asher had returned with a small deer slung across his back. In the fierce orange glow of the fire, the ranger had been the perfect picture of an Outlander to Nathaniel. The lines around his eyes, combined with his fang tattoo, had given Asher a grim façade.

Elaith continued to struggle with the dying fire, throwing twigs into the darkness, while Asher waited with the newly skinned carcass.

"This stupid storm has made everything wet!" The young Graycoat poked at the sky with a damp branch.

"Hold this." Asher handed her the deer, before fixing the spit the way he liked it. The ranger focused his eyes on the dying fire and casually waved his hand over the top. The flames burst to life, encompassing the spit.

Nathaniel shot forward on his log. "How did you do that?" He was sure Asher wasn't concealing any wand. Even Elaith, a novice in the ways of magic, was looking at him in amazement.

Asher continued to prepare the deer without offering any explanation, leaving the Graycoats to ponder the increasing mystery of the ranger.

Not long after the deer was ready, Elaith fell asleep on her roll and Nathaniel didn't have the energy to wake her up and discipline the young woman. They should have discussed sleeping in shifts while in Asher's company. Now Nathaniel would have to stay up and wait for him to fall asleep. There was an awkward silence between the two men, the crickets and the crackling of the fire the only sound.

"My name is Nathaniel, by the way. Nathaniel Galfrey..." At least Asher would stop calling him 'Graycoat'.

Asher finished his mouthful of meat. "As in, Tobin Galfrey?"

There it was. The shadow Nathaniel would never escape. "He was my father." It was the first time in many years since he had said the words out loud.

Asher tore off another strip of meat. "I thought Graycoats were supposed to keep it in their pants?"

Was it possible the old assassin possessed a sense of humour?

"We're forbidden from starting families: no ties or vulnerabilities as the Lord Marshal calls them. Though, sex, in general, is a grey area at West Fellion..." Nathaniel stopped himself, unsure why he was talking so openly to the ranger. It was easy to forget what he really was.

"Sound's dull..." Asher continued to chew his mouthful of meat. "So old Tobin got his beak wet, huh?"

"Take a care, assassin." Nathaniel shot Asher a threatening look that he wasn't sure he could follow up with action.

"I meant no offence." Asher held up his hands. "I actually met your father once. He certainly lived up to his legend; I have a scar across my hip to prove it."

"You fought with him?" Nathaniel had never heard this story, and he had heard all the stories about his father's adventures.

"He didn't know I was an assassin at the time. I was passing as an Outlander trying to..." Asher appeared to catch himself and returned to concentrating on the meat in his hand for a moment. "...Well, Tobin Galfrey never took kindly to Outlanders, especially when they camped outside The Wild Moores."

Nathaniel looked into the fire, imagining such a battle. He wanted to know more but sensed the ranger's reluctance to even share what little information he had.

"You must hold a high position at West Fellion, the son of such a legend." Asher was watching him closely. "Ah." He had the look of an epiphany. "You're living proof that the bravest Graycoat strayed from the code, eh?"

"And what would a killer know of any code?" Nathaniel spat.

"Even the Arakesh have their code," Asher calmly replied. Nathaniel was caught off guard by the smallest of details regarding the assassins. "Let me guess; that's the most any Graycoat has ever heard about Nightfall?"

"We know plenty about your kind. You fight with two swords, traditionally short, like the one on your back. Whoever rules Nightfall is referred to as 'father' or 'mother'. And we know you can see in the dark..." Nathaniel held his tongue, not wanting to reveal all they knew.

"Is that so?" Asher had a smile on his face Nathaniel just wanted to smack.

"Well, how else could you shoot a deer under a moonless night?"

Asher held his arrogant smile and continued to eat. "Would you like to see it?" The ranger nudged the folded bow with his foot. "It's the only thing I kept."

Nathaniel noted the red cloth around Asher's belt and knew the bow wasn't the only thing he had kept. Still, the weapon was from Nightfall; that meant it was used by all Arakesh. It would make sense to use the opportunity to learn as much as possible about the enemy.

"How does it work?" Nathaniel sounded disinterested.

Asher passed it over and the Graycoat marvelled at the weapon's elegance. The upper and lower limbs were folded on a series of hinges hidden by a complex pattern of cogs. The bowstring ran through a groove that cut down the centre of the entire bow. He flicked the small latch, built into the riser, and held the weapon at arm's length as it snapped open. The bowstring was pulled taut inside the riser and the limbs until it appeared as any other bow.

"Incredible..." he whispered.

"You favour the bow," Asher stated to Nathaniel's questioning look. "Your hands..." The ranger quickly glanced over at the Graycoat's hands.

Upon examining his own hands, Nathaniel could see the markers that betrayed him as an archer and was impressed that Asher had noticed the minor details as well.

"And you favour a broadsword. Unusual for an Arakesh." The double-handed sword still stood on end, its spiked pommel gleaming in the fire.

"It fits my line of work better." Asher hesitated before continuing. "And I'm not an Arakesh anymore..."

"Does it have a name?" Nathaniel regretted his question at seeing Asher's smirking face.

"My sword?"

"Aye. I thought you ranger-types liked to do that sort of thing - you know, build a legend around your weapon..." Nathaniel did his best to sound casual.

Asher laughed to himself. "No, my sword doesn't have a name. It's a sword. I've found that the men who do that are usually overcompensating for something..." Both men looked at one another and shared a brief laugh.

Elaith was restless and rolled over under her blanket, showing them her back. Nathaniel wanted to be angry with Asher for his past life, a life devoted to murder, but found his honesty quite disarming. His mastery of eloquent speech was not mirrored by his gruff appearance and grizzly voice - which should have reflected the intelligence of, well, an Outlander.

Nathaniel readily accepted the bottle of golden ale Asher offered him. It was only after his first mouthful did he realise that the drink might be poisoned. The ranger's disarming nature was clearly one of his many weapons.

"So what does a ranger do?" Nathaniel handed the ale back.

"Same thing as you, only I get paid better." Asher's arrogant smile returned.

Nathaniel couldn't help but laugh. "I don't doubt it. Our patrols last three months. Three months on the road and all they see fit to give us are a hundred and fifty bits."

Now Asher laughed. "I was paid four hundred and seventy bits for the Whistle Town job alone!" The ranger seemed to catch himself again and reined in his moment of familiarity.

Seeing his change in mood, Nathaniel did the same, leaving another awkward silence to lie between them. The Graycoat looked up to the sky and thanked the gods the rain had abated. Thick clouds continued to roll overhead, however, promising to soak them in the morning.

"My order has been hunting you since Lirian, Asher. You revealed yourself then, put yourself out there for all of Illian to see." The ranger remained silent, focused on his food. "Why would you save Queen Isabella after spending decades assassinating people like her? Why did you leave Nightfall?" These were questions West Fellion had been asking for years.

Asher stood up suddenly and returned his sword to its sheath. "That's a story for another campfire, Galfrey." He removed his own blanket and unrolled it across the floor. "You should get some sleep - long ride tomorrow. And don't worry; you won't need to take shifts. It's like you said, I'm going to need you if I'm to actually meet the king."

Nathaniel nodded his understanding but had no intention of falling asleep until he woke Elaith up. Asher was certainly more interesting than Nathaniel had given him credit, but he trusted the ranger about as far as he could throw him.

By dusk the next day, Asher could make out the white stone of Velia's outer wall and the scattered village that lay sprawled at the city's base. The rain had hammered them since they left camp and their fingers were starting to wrinkle. Beyond Velia, the rain blocked the usual sight of The Adean and the numerous sails of the boats entering and leaving the port.

Asher pulled his hood aside to see Nathaniel and Elaith cloaked in black ponchos over their famous coats, their hoods pulled tight against the wind and rain. A flash to their left was followed by an ear-splitting thunderclap. The horses neighed, becoming hard to control when a nearby tree collapsed under its own weight and high winds.

"We should find shelter until it eases up!" Nathaniel shouted over the rain.

"It's only a couple more hours!" Asher shouted back.

Before they could argue their points anymore, Elaith steered her horse for the shelter of a rocky outcropping. The slab of rock that jutted out of the hillock acted as a shelf, with the boulders and trees creating a perfect alcove to wait out the storm. The young Graycoat jumped off her horse and struggled to remove the soaked poncho.

"Argh! I am so sick of being wet! We might as well have swum to Velia!" Her short, spiky hair was plastered to her forehead.

Asher tied Hector to a tree and pulled the sodden hood off his head. He tightened the knot in his small ponytail and wiped the water from his face. The ranger caught Nathaniel massaging his own behind in an attempt to get some feeling back into it.

"This storm isn't going to let up." Asher removed his green cloak and hung it over a small tree inside the alcove.

"We've made good time, Asher. The king demands that you be there by tomorrow. We'll finish the journey before the sun rises." Nathaniel started to gather wood for a fire.

Asher sat on a boulder, restless. He hated to be anywhere for too long; if he wasn't moving he was vulnerable. The ranger had been running for fourteen years, the Arakesh baying for his blood on one side and the Graycoats happy to torture him for information on the other. Staying on the move had been one of his earliest lessons when it came to surviving, and a little storm had never stopped him before.

"At least we can sleep for a little while." Elaith was already going for her blanket.

"Not until you go through your routines." Nathaniel dropped the sticks and gave Elaith an unyielding look.

She seethed. "Fine..." Leaving her blanket, Elaith unsheathed her one-handed sword.

Asher noted the Graycoat emblem of a sword entwined within a snake's body, the tip plunging into the animal's head, on the disc-shaped pommel of her hilt.

Elaith moved into some space, away from where Nathaniel was building the fire. She took a moment to control her breathing, before exploding into action with her sword.

The techniques were well practised, with recognisable styles all woven into one fighting form. It reminded Asher of the way he had been taught to fight; never be tied to one style, always keep your opponents off balance with a variety of techniques.

A couple of twirls with her sword overhead were definitely elven in origin. Asher had witnessed this use of elven form when confronted by Graycoats in the past. Of course, he found it easy to counter with a complete knowledge of elven fighting styles.

"How did you learn to fight like an elf?" Asher asked them both.

Elaith paused to look at Nathaniel, who in turn gave her a look to continue her training.

"I'll tell you if you tell me how you can light this fire without a wand?" Nathaniel had finished building the fire pit and was about to attempt lighting it.

Asher met the Graycoat's dark eyes but instead turned back to Elaith. The ranger didn't entirely dislike the Graycoat, but he wasn't ready to divulge all his secrets, especially one he couldn't explain himself. The fact that after nearly three days he hadn't even thought about killing Nathaniel was new to him. All of West Fellion had fallen into one category during his life, even after leaving Nightfall, and that was kill or be killed.

There was something about this Galfrey though; something that made the knight feel apart from his order, and that was something Asher could relate to. The ranger tried not to dwell on the fact that for the last fourteen years he had mostly related to his horse, Hector.

"You know at least three elven techniques." Asher slowly walked around Elaith, as she twirled and pivoted with her sword flying in every direction. "To the average fighter that would make you formidable, give you an edge. But if you ever cross swords with an Arakesh it will not be enough. Just when you should flow into the complete elven style you revert back to fighting like a human. Your form is stunted. You keep your sword in the same hand; this tells your opponent where the next attack is coming from. Don't be afraid to change hands mid-flow."

Elaith stopped and looked at Asher. "Show me." She nodded at the sword on his hip.

Asher obliged and removed his sword while taking up his position opposite Elaith. Nathaniel left the unlit fire and came to stand closer. Surprisingly he didn't try to stop them sparring, as Asher predicted he would, but he did give the ranger a warning look.

"Don't worry," Asher said. "I haven't killed one of your order in fourteen years, and I don't intend to break that streak now."

The young Graycoat held her sword in the elven form, with the blade resting on the back of her neck. Asher knew exactly what form of attack came from that particular stance and smirked at the girl, baiting her. Standing, with his sword lowered casually at his side, he waited patiently for Elaith to lunge - and lunge she did.

With reflexes he knew she wouldn't be expecting of a man his age, Asher flicked up his sword and knocked Elaith's attack wild. With her sword flung outwards, he used the flat of his blade to smack the back of her legs, followed by whipping his free hand out to catch her just above the breastbone. As planned, the Graycoat was on her back in seconds, her sword out of reach.

Nathaniel laughed. "That was just embarrassing."

Elaith picked herself up and collected her sword, pausing to shoot Nathaniel a threatening look. It was a look Asher had seen a hundred times in The Arid Lands, to the south. The young girl definitely had the southerners' temperament.

"Again!" Elaith held her sword out in front of her, in another familiar style.

As she attacked, her sword predictably rose over her head for a downwards strike. Again Asher stood with his sword lowered, but ready with his counter-attack. As her blade came down, the ranger spun on his heel, twirling his own sword to confuse her, and turned his whole body until he was behind Elaith. When her blade reached the ground, Asher's sword rested against the back of her neck.

"You're dead," the ranger stated.

They both relaxed and walked away from each other until Elaith quickly turned on Asher with her sword flipping end-over-end. She wanted to attack him again but Asher held out his hand to stop her.

"You fight as if it's a competition of skill." Asher rested his sword over his shoulder with one hand. "Fighting is about one thing; survival. You aim to kill your opponent, so showing off your skill is pointless if they're going to be dead soon. Your battle stance is a poster for your next attack. Never give anything away. Let your opponent think you're as useless as a mule in combat, then spring."

Elaith breathed out a sharp sigh, before immediately attacking again. This time she burst into action from standing still, making her first thrust unpredictable. After a very human attack, the young Graycoat broke out in a flurry of elven techniques that made Asher work to avoid the edge of her blade.

Four or five attacks later, it became obvious that Elaith had exhausted her knowledge, and possibly that of her entire order. The ranger brought his sword into his bodyline, to give him more manoeuvring room, as he spun around the girl after an exotic parry, and finished with his blade to her throat.

"You're dead."

Elaith smiled this time. "I've never seen moves like those!"

"The Arakesh are taught to fight using every style, with every weapon. Remember, your sword is an extension of you; but *you* are the weapon, not the blade. Don't be afraid to use your entire body."

Thunder echoed across the darkening sky, the trees and fields exposed in the lightning flashes. Asher turned to Nathaniel who was watching intently, no doubt hungry for more information about the assassins.

"We'll stay a few hours and see if the rain dies down." The Graycoat returned to light the fire. "Elaith, bring some of that deer over." Elaith was more than happy to have some food by a warm fire rather than continue her sword practice. "Would you mind?" Nathaniel looked from Asher to the collection of dry sticks.

Asher sat on the ground and waved his hand over the branches, setting them alight. Like every other spell he cast, the ranger only had to think about what he desired and wait for the warm tingling sensation to flow out from his ring.

The Graycoats studied him closely. They shared out the remains of the deer and relaxed in the warmth of the fire for an hour. Asher was happy for the silence while they ate. He had spoken more in the last two days than he had in the last two months. The ranger refused to admit to himself, however, that he enjoyed conversing with the Graycoats.

"I can't explain it..." Asher announced, looking at the fire, some-time later. "I've been able to use magic like that since I was a child."

"You don't require a wand or Demetrium?" Nathaniel tried to appear as disinterested as he had the previous night.

"I think I have a wand in one of my packs." The ranger looked off to his horse, beyond the fire. "Picked it up in Skystead a few years back. Very nasty dark mage if I recall..."

"What about the ancient words?" the Graycoat pressed.

"I know a few but I've never needed them." Asher absently stared at the silver ring on his finger. Without his gloves on, the shard of black crystal glistened in the light.

"You must have a bucket-load of elven blood running through your veins." Elaith stopped inspecting Asher's bow to make the comment.

"And what do you know about magic?" Nathaniel asked.

"They don't teach us magic, but they teach us *about* magic. Times have changed since you were at West Fellion," Elaith added. "Master Vintrell says that the strongest of magic casters have elven blood in their family. That means a thousand years ago, an elf and a human started your family tree."

"Master Vintrell sounds like a wise man." Asher had heard similar theories over the years, but there was no way to prove it.

"Master Vintrell wears his trousers back-to-front..." Nathaniel commented quietly. Asher stifled his laugh with the last piece of deer.

"Could your mother or father do the same?" Elaith asked eagerly.

Asher felt the usual urge to pull back and end the conversation before it went any further. Lying about his past, and his life in general, had been another lesson at Nightfall. Not every mission allowed for stealth and killing from the shadows. There were occa-sions when he had to appear as someone else for a time or gain a person's trust to reach his target or gather information. He had spent months, as part of his tests, living amongst the people in Calmardra, in The Arid Lands, learning to craft the perfect lies and manipulate conversations in his favour. But he had grown tired of that life.

"I never knew my parents; at least I don't remember them. Nightfall doesn't recruit people with family ties, like your order I believe."

"We take volunteers and orphans off the streets, the younger the better," Nathaniel said. "I volunteered at twelve. Elaith here was found on the streets of Ameeraska."

Asher looked at Elaith and saw the picture come together. She still retained that tough exterior required to survive on those streets, but her time at West Fellion had allowed for the real woman to find herself.

"I was only eight when the order came through, searching for fresh recruits," Elaith elaborated, with a long stare into the fire. "I didn't want to go but... they had nice coats," she lied. It was an obvious deflection from a truth she didn't want to share with a mentor she didn't like, and a man she probably thought of as nothing but a killer.

Asher looked at Nathaniel but he remained silent. His reasons for volunteering were his own and the ranger couldn't argue. The ranger had already told them more details about his life than anyone else.

"Perhaps the Graycoats and the Arakesh have more in common than we thought." Asher regretted his comment as soon as he saw Nathaniel's expression.

"We seek to help the people of Illian." Nathaniel increased his grip on the hilt of his sword. "We don't kill them for money. We take children off the streets and turn them into warriors for the realm. You steal children and turn them into killers and monsters."

"Are all Graycoats as sensitive as you?" Asher couldn't help himself. The Graycoat was pissing him off with his misconceptions of Nightfall, which in itself was ridiculous because Asher had grown to hate his old order more than anyone.

Nathaniel's body tensed, absorbing the insult. Asher could tell he was weighing up the potential outcomes of a fight between the two.

Elaith watched them both, clearly unsure what her role would be if it came to blows. The ranger was confident, however, in his ability to react if the Graycoat decided there had to be blood.

A twig snapped from somewhere behind Asher, where the storm raged beyond the shelter of the alcove. He berated himself for not picking up on the other sounds that he would normally have detected. Nathaniel and Elaith confirmed his fears when they both reached for their swords, their eyes looking past the ranger. He heard more branches snap and estimated at least eight men, from the different footfalls, spreading out behind him. His bow was on the other side of the fire, at Elaith's feet.

"What do we have 'ere then, boys?"

The ranger had heard words like these before and knew what followed.

Asher stood up with the others and turned to see where the offensive accent had come from. Seven bandits emerged from the dark and the ranger's instincts took over. Most were overweight and unkempt, with a collective odour that Asher should have discovered before now. He counted six swords, three axes and two bows between them all. The bows were already out with an arrow notched in both, giving them an advantage over the distance. From where he stood, Asher was too far to land a single strike against the band of criminals.

The central figure, the largest of the seven, gave the three companions a broad smile that stretched his tangled beard. As they stepped under the canopy of the rock shelf, the rainwater poured off the bandits in a collection of waterfalls.

"Can we help you?" Nathaniel asked with his sword still in its scabbard.

"Well, I should think so!" The lead bandit opened his arms, becoming theatrical. "We'll take everything ya' horses carry, probably the horses too, ya' weapons, boots and, oh, I'll take that lovely coat of ya's as well!" The other men laughed while eyeing Elaith with a different type of hunger.

Asher felt his anger rising to the surface, colliding with his years of training, which commanded him to control his emotions. His anger would only cloud his mind and stop him from making split-second decisions that would keep him alive. It was those emotions, however, that demanded he keep the mouthy one alive until last - let him see what a mistake he'd made. A clearer mind knew that killing him first would put the rest off balance though, giving him the advantage.

"We're on Graycoat business." Nathaniel lifted his sword in its scabbard, revealing an inch of the blade. "Be on your way."

Asher commended the authority Nathaniel warned them with, but he knew it wouldn't be enough.

"All I see are three o' you, and seven o' us!" The leader hefted his axe in both hands. "With the added guard on the land, it's become hard to make our way. Can't pass up easy pickings..."

Asher had heard enough; he knew where this was going. The ranger lifted his broadsword just enough in its scabbard to set the group off. Changing tack immediately, Asher released his grip on the broadsword and removed the short-sword from his back. The two arrows left their bows, as predicted, only one was heading straight for Nathaniel instead. Allowing his muscle memory to take over, the ranger deflected the arrow away from himself, tapping the side of the arrowhead at the last moment. In the same fluid motion, he lashed out, chopping the second arrow from the air, before it could end the Graycoat's life.

The cry of shock from the leader was cut short when Asher spun around and let loose his short-sword. The blade flipped end-over-end for just a second, until it impaled the leader through his open mouth, piercing the back of his head. The ranger had his broadsword free of its sheath before the big man hit the muddy ground.

Nathaniel killed the skinny one on the end with a quick-fire shot from his own bow before both he and Elaith drew their swords and leaped over the fire to join the ranger.

The bowmen had to go next. Asher's sword sliced through the

wooden bow and cut deep into the bandit holding it. The blood splattered into the eyes of the second bowman, making him pause in his attempt to notch the next arrow. The ranger moved like a dancer, spinning his sword as he moved, before plunging the tip of his blade into the man's broad chest.

With his sword buried to the hilt in the bowman, Asher let go of the blade and dashed backward, diving into a roll. By the time he jumped to his feet, his hand found the hilt of the short-sword sticking out of the leader's prone body.

The ranger's muscles knew exactly how to react, with no thought required to assist in the ending of another man's life. His free hand halted a bandit's killing blow, saving Elaith from one of her two attackers. There was no hesitation in driving the rune sword up through the bandit's jaw and continuing on, into his brain.

As the body fell to the floor, Elaith cut down her other attacker, while Nathaniel decapitated his opponent in one clean swipe of steel.

Asher stepped back and took a breath. His stamina wasn't what it used to be and his lungs felt as if they were on fire. Sheathing the rune sword on his back, the ranger moved to retrieve his broadsword, while trying to ignore the pain in his knees and back.

"Thank you..." Elaith looked at him, wide-eyed.

The ranger wasn't used to gratitude, beyond a bag of coins, and simply nodded his head in response. He looked at Nathaniel and saw himself twenty years ago. The Graycoat replaced his sword, showing no sign of exhaustion.

"Awfully close to the city for a group of bandits this size." Nathaniel kicked the leader. "A ballsy group, I'll give them that." The Graycoat laughed, all previous offences forgotten.

Asher couldn't help but smile back, Elaith's wide eyes now an amusing sight. Any fight, no matter the opponent, was an opportunity for death to claim him, and surviving seven armed criminals was still a victory.

Retrieving his broadsword from the bowman's corpse, Asher

turned and waved his hand over the fire, putting it out completely. "Storm or no storm, we should leave now."

Nathaniel nodded his agreement and placed a firm hand on Elaith's shoulder. They met each other's eyes for a brief moment, a silent conversation passing between the two. It dawned on the ranger that the young Graycoat had just taken her first life.

"Don't worry, kid, the next one will be easier." It was all Asher could think to say.

As she slowly rode away, Nathaniel shook his head at the ranger. "You give terrible advice."

Nathaniel's horse took him back into the storm, leaving Asher to reflect on his own second kill, many years ago. He wasn't shocked to realise he couldn't remember it.

The rain lashed against the side of Asher's hood, as the three companions came to a stop outside Velia's main gate. The small village at the city's base was devoid of activity, with only rats and mice darting between the various buildings and the occasional drunk making their way back from a night in the tavern.

The defensive walls of the city curved round from the main gate, where they met the ocean and formed into the great Direport. Asher inhaled deeply, in hope of smelling the salty sea air, but quickly turned his head at the foul stench of piss and shit running out of the drains and mixing with the rainwater at the bottom of Velia's thick walls.

Nathaniel rode up beside Asher. "You know what happens after we pass through those gates, don't you?"

Asher looked at the six guards sat on stools inside the shelter of the portcullis. Two of them were asleep with their heads resting against the wall, while the others played cards to one side. The ranger couldn't ignore the voice in his head that told him the quickest way to kill all six guards. When he saw weapons it was the first scenario his mind worked out, before he could move on to more civilised thoughts.

"We'll be fine."

"Oh, I know I'll be fine," Nathaniel replied. "After the king is done with you, the order will take you in for questioning. They won't ask nicely, Asher. Lord Marshal Horvarth wants a place in history, a place easily secured if he can locate Nightfall."

"That's a war he wouldn't win." Asher thought about Nightfall's defences but knew the real difficulty would be marching the Graycoats into the southern deserts of The Arid Lands.

"Win or lose, it still starts with throwing you in a dark room with West Fellion's inquisitors."

Asher couldn't help his cocky smile. "We'll see..." With that, he tapped Hector's ribs and continued towards the portcullis.

Having Graycoats by his side, the ranger was able to move through Velia with ease. Asher noted the extra guards patrolling the streets, unusual for the time of night. There was a definite absence of people as they made their way through the alleys and streets, heading into the north-west corner of the city. The ranger had never been inside the Velia sector house, but he certainly knew where it was.

"Where is everybody?" Elaith asked. They were the first words she had said since they were attacked by the bandits.

"There must be a curfew." Nathaniel looked just as confused.

After a few more minutes of weaving through mostly empty streets, the group came across the grand sector house of the Graycoats. Asher was still unable to hear the ocean over the pouring rain, but he could see several sails at the end of the street, where the port opened up.

Nathaniel banged on the green oak door and Elaith handed over the horses to their private stable hand. The door was soon answered by a Graycoat with shoulders as wide as the oak.

"We've been expecting you." The Graycoat's voice was as deep as his shoulders were wide.

Asher followed them in, surprised to feel his heart rate increasing. He really was getting old.

Keeping his breathing and heart rate in check had become second nature after his training; he usually didn't even need to think about it. But, right now, the ranger could feel his heart quicken as the door closed behind him. He had cheated death so many times and thought nothing of it, revelling in his youth with the feel of invincibility. With old scars causing pain and his joints feeling the hardship of his violent life, Asher could sense death closing in on him.

It shocked him to find that he didn't fear death, but instead feared the unremarkable life he left behind him. With no children to take pride in and no great love to mourn him, the ranger would leave nothing but a trail of bodies to speak for his life.

Nathaniel cleared his throat and woke Asher from his reverie. Standing in the centre of the large foyer was a handsome man with a long face and shoulder-length blond hair. His long coat identified him as a Graycoat, though his overall appearance told Asher he kept his gear, and indeed himself, in good condition. It was his arrogant smile that gave him away.

"Darius Devale..." Nathaniel stepped aside to properly reveal the ranger. "This is Asher, formerly of the Arakesh."

Devale lingered on Nathaniel after hearing the introduction. It was certainly the nicest thing he had said about the ranger yet.

Devale stepped forward and Asher felt his instincts alert him to the tactical advantages. The prestigious Graycoat was now within striking distance, but he could also be used as a shield or leverage to secure his escape, should he need it.

Despite everything Asher had heard about the promising Devale, he possessed nothing the others didn't. His sword was identical, if more polished, and his bow was just as unremarkable as Nathaniel's.

"You come willingly, assassin." Devale screamed confidence and control, but Asher could sense the fear bubbling under the surface. "Did you hold his hand the whole way, Nathaniel?"

Asher's fist clenched naturally at the sight of Devale's smile. The surrounding Graycoats laughed at Nathaniel's expense, only Elaith maintaining her stony expression. The ranger observed Nathaniel, expecting some sarcastic reply to put Devale in his place, but none came. The Graycoat was obviously used to this treatment and had learned to grit his teeth over the years. It wasn't hard to chart Darius Devale's career path and know that someday he would be the next Lord Marshal of West Fellion.

"We were met by a band of rogues not far from here." Nathaniel stayed professional, but locked eyes with Devale. "But it was nothing we couldn't handle." Asher could see the threat behind his eyes and wondered if Devale noticed it too.

Darius lost some of his bluster under Nathaniel's gaze. "Good. I'm sure the assassin's skills came in handy." He turned his attention on the ranger. "King Rengar wishes an audience with you. I will show you to his Grace and you will obey my every command in his presence. If I think the king's safety is compromised for a second—"

Asher took a single quick step, bringing him nose to nose with Devale. "You'll do what?" he asked.

The seven Graycoats behind Devale tensed, while two bowstrings were pulled taut, somewhere above Asher on the landing.

Devale's chiselled jaw twitched as he held back what would have been a sharp reply. His emerald eyes darted from side to side for a moment, while he calculated his next words very carefully. "Your weapons will not be permitted in the king's presence."

It was Nathaniel who spoke up. "Give them to me and I'll see them returned when the king is satisfied."

Asher instantly picked up on the confusion in the room. Devale had just lost face in front of his men, while the runt of the litter confronted the scariest thing they had ever met. Enjoying the reversal more than he expected, Asher complied with Nathaniel's request and handed over all of his weapons, a lengthy process in all.

After retreating a few steps, Devale found his voice again. "Your part in this is done, Galfrey. Take your ward and return to West

Fellion. You will receive new orders there." With a flick of his head, he commanded one of the others to take Asher's weapons away.

"But we're already here!" Nathaniel protested. "We might as well be part of the detail."

"You might be wearing his coat, but you are not Tobin Galfrey. You are of little use here..."

It was clear that Devale had a talent for striking nerves. Nathaniel's hand gripped the sheath of his sword, under the guard. Even from across the room, Asher could see his knuckles whitening, desperately trying to stop his hand from reaching for the hilt.

With a lasting look at Asher, Nathaniel turned for the door. "Elaith..." The young Graycoat obediently followed her mentor after silently mouthing good luck to the ranger.

Asher was left alone with Devale and his dogs.

Darius raised his chin. "The king is waiting."

CHAPTER 9
THE CRIMINAL ELEMENT

The wind tore through the streets of Dragorn, expelled by the great storm rolling over The Adean. Galanör's dark robes were whipped about him, standing atop one of the many flat-roofed buildings that populated the south-east quarter of the sprawling city. The building was three storeys, giving him an excellent vantage point on the winding streets and alleys below. As if he were a bird-of-prey, the elf watched the humans scurrying about in the moonlight. The tavern across the street was the hub of activity in the neighbourhood. Situated on the corner of the block, The Anvil was at the head of an intersection where five roads came together.

It wasn't hard for Galanör to find what he was looking for. His elvish eyes spotted the armed men, disguised in everyday robes, positioned on the corner of the road. Galanör had expected extra protection to be present, but that's why he had brought his own. Across the intersection, the elf could just make out Naiveen, hiding in the shadows of the adjacent roof. Ailas and Eliön were somewhere on the ground, disguised as beggars, ready to spring if he was walking into a trap. With forward planning, he had sent Adamar into

The Anvil at dusk, leaving him there to blend in with the other drunks.

"Doesn't this city ever sleep?" Lyra crouched by his side in the darkness. Her perfume was intoxicating.

"It's hard to believe what was here before they arrived." Galanör looked on the sprawling cityscape, wishing he could have seen the great island when his own people inhabited it, alongside the dragons.

"I must have read every book ever written about the Dragorn." Lyra joined him in his wistful expression, across the building tops.

Galanör had a similar childhood. "My mother told me stories of them growing up. It was said that the dragons actually allowed the Dragorn to ride them..." The elf couldn't imagine a more magnificent experience, even with Lyra standing next to him.

"You mean hold onto them while they fly," Lyra corrected. "No one rides a dragon."

Galanör knew her words to be true. The chosen elves, who called themselves Dragorn, had been allowed to live among the noblest of creatures, because of their ability to converse with the dragons in a way that could only be dreamed of by others. But living among them and speaking with them still paled in comparison to soaring above the mountains of Verda, defying the gods' will that all intelligent creatures remain enslaved to the land.

"Now we see the mockery the humans have made of their great name." Lyra continued with a look of disgust at the human architecture. "Perhaps we will see it restored, yes?"

Galanör thought of everything that would have to happen for that future to be recognised. The largest city in Verda and all its inhabitants would have to be removed, at the point of a blade no less. The elf considered that thought and realised that he was already laying the foundations for enacting that plan. He would be the catalyst that saw the end of man. That idea had weighed heavy on Galanör's mind since they left Ayda...

Galanör ignored Lyra's question and focused on the mission.

"The Trigorn's man is already inside." He was duty-bound to see the rise of the elves, even if that meant the fall of man.

"We should just kidnap the women and children. We take a great risk involving the humans. I hope this is worth it, Galanör. We don't have much coin left." Lyra perched on the edge of the roof, imitating a cat.

"Let me worry about that. All that matters is getting to Korkanath." It had proven costly to arrange this meeting, and if it went well it would only cost more.

"Your worries are mine."

Their relationship was purely physical, but Galanör could sense Lyra's other motives. She hopelessly endeavoured to show him that they were a better match than his intended. His family was among the highest in Ayda, and becoming a part of that would elevate her greatly. Unfortunately, Galanör's father felt the same thing would happen by arranging his marriage to Reyna Sevari, the daughter of their king. The Reveeris would become a part of the royal family of elves and have their place secured for all time. These plans had been set in motion years ago, and Galanör was powerless to change them. He was an instrument of his father's ambition and his lord's machinations for Illian. Nothing more.

"Be ready for anything." After four centuries scaling the giant trees of The Amara, Galanör dropped into the alley, off the main road, with ease.

Before he reached The Anvil's door, Ailas walked past him in rags and with dirt smeared across his angular face. The two never looked at one another, but Galanör caught his hushed words. "Three more inside."

Galanör had seen only two go in with the Trigorn's man; they must have sent one ahead as he had.

Inside, the tavern was an explosion of sound, as men and women, on all three floors, drank into the night. The elf moved through the drunken crowds with grace, constantly aware of his surroundings. Two men were fighting over a whore on the second level that no one seemed to care about, while Galanör noticed the four pick-pockets moving around the room, taking coin with ease. Adamar was sitting at the back, near the darkened booth where the Trigorn's man sat, waiting. The large elf had a woman straddled across his lap, laughing at Adamar's jokes. Galanör resisted the urge to curse aloud and hoped the larger elf wasn't too drunk to notice the meeting taking place next to him.

With a cursory glance, he found the two guards sitting close by, at separate tables. The third was sitting at the end of the bar, near the door. The humans were as subtle as their odour.

Galanör took his seat opposite the Trigorn's man. He had been easy to spot in his finer clothes, well-cut hair and freshly shaved face. To most in this part of the city, he was walking money, the perfect mark. But Galanör had stalked the man for many blocks to the tavern and observed the wide berth given him.

Nobody crossed the Trigorns.

Elf and man sat in silence for moment, taking one another in. Galanör had cast the spell to round his ears and put some stubble on his cheeks to make him appear more human. The human had styled hair, as black as his clothes, with cold eyes that bore witness to the Trigorn's cruelty.

Galanör had spent the last couple of days setting this meeting up and knew all about the Trigorn's man. He was called Lucas Farney, but the people of Dragorn called him The Fang, on account of the pointed tooth at the front of his mouth. When the Trigorn family had need of violence they sent Mr Farney. It didn't bode well that he had been sent to meet with Galanör, but the elf was an unknown, a fact that put the Trigorns on edge, no doubt.

"You know who I represent." Farney's voice was a rasp.

"I do."

"Then you have me at a disadvantage." This was clearly a position Mr Farney didn't like. "You don't work for one of the other families; otherwise you would have contacted my employers via the usual channels."

The Trigorn family was one of four that ruled Dragorn, with an elected member of each on the High Council that governed the island. Of course, the election was rigged with a member from each always winning the position. No one else had the money to fund a campaign and buy the votes to compete. It was the biggest difference between Dragorn and the rest of Illian. To Galanör's knowledge, there had never been a royal family on the island since humans took the land from the dragons.

"My name is Galdor Reveer. I am part of an independent organisation, one that has no interest in challenging the Trigorns, or any of the other families, I assure you. I need something your employers can acquire for me, discreetly."

Mr Farney looked away, subtly scanning the tavern. He was suspicious of Galanör. Thankfully, Adamar was currently face-deep in the cleavage of the woman on his lap.

"What is it you want, Mr Reveer?"

"In just over a week from now, I need two women, attractive women, and three children, preferably under ten years old." Galanör could hardly believe he was actually doing this, bargaining in lives. He reminded himself that their part in the plan was pivotal, and that failure could mean the end of all of Verda.

Mr Farney shifted, uncomfortably. "You're obviously not from Dragorn, Mr Reveer. You're not in The Arid Lands and this is not Karath. The Trigorn family doesn't deal in slaves. If you require women and children I can direct you to the nearest brothel."

"Your employers own the establishments that *sell* these people."

"We sell an *experience*, Mr Reveer. We don't sell *people*."

The plan was starting to unravel...

It was clear to see that Lucas Farney's position was unwavering. It angered Galanör that scum like the Trigorns could draw a line in the sand and feel righteous about it. They committed every crime imaginable, ruling their quarter of the city with an iron fist, but they decided that controlling men, women and children under threat of death wasn't slavery.

"If it's a matter of coin—"

"Keep your coin. I'm more interested in who you represent. You might not be here to challenge the families but, from the coin I hear you've been throwing around and the need for women and children, you must be seeking a stake in some territory. It doesn't matter in what corner you peddle your wares, Mr Reveer, every inch of this city is owned by one of the four. So if it's a brothel you're interested in, I suggest you seek one to buy rather than starting your own. I can schedule you a meeting with the Trigorn accountants if that's the case..."

Galanör's anger was rising. "I have no interest in whore houses, Mr Farney."

"Then what could you possibly want with two women and a few children?" The Fang's interest was piqued.

The elf could see his failure now. They would have to resort to their backup plan, which was now potentially compromised by Lucas Farney's curiosity. Eliön had already scouted the location of one of the Trigorn's brothels where they could take the humans if it came to it, but Farney's knowledge of their needs put everything in danger.

Galanör had but one choice, for Verda.

"It used to be an honour to live on this island..." the elf mused, allowing his disgust with Dragorn's current occupants to lace his words.

Lucas Farney raised an eyebrow in curiosity, but with speed beyond human reaction, Galanör whipped his arm across the table and buried his hidden knife into The Fang's eye. With his superior strength, it took little effort to ensure the blade sank into the man's head until the hilt met his eye socket. Lucas Farney was dead before he even realised his fate.

The three guards reacted as predicted, each jumping from their chairs and reaching for their swords. Adamar moved before Galanör had retrieved his own blade.

The large elf leaped up, taking the woman on his lap with him, before throwing her back into the nearest bodyguard. The impact sent the two humans tumbling across the table in a tangle of limbs and broken chairs. Proving his worth, Adamar dashed to his left and used the empty chair to give him height so he could jump clear over the three men sitting next to him. When he landed on the other side, he brought his powerful fist down on the second bodyguard, paralysing the man's solar plexus. The wind was knocked out of the human, bringing him to his knees at Adamar's feet. The elf snapped his neck without hesitation.

The bodyguard by the door lost his nerve and turned to run for help. Galanör casually threw his knife the length of the tavern, demonstrating deadly precision, and narrowly missing several patrons. The blade sank into the back of the human's neck, killing him instantly and pushing him into the closest patron, his dead weight forcing them both to the ground.

The last bodyguard pushed Adamar's woman off and stood with his sword ready. He advanced quickly on Galanör with a strike intended to remove the elf's head. To Galanör, the man might as well have been moving through treacle. The elf ducked under the swing and popped up at the man's right side, where he promptly forced his open palm into the guard's throat. Before the human could drop to his knees and choke to death, Galanör wrapped his left arm around the man's head and flicked his hand away, taking the human's head with him. The speed and force of such an action were enough to break the fragile vertebrae between his head and shoulders.

With four dead men in the tavern, a great many of the patrons decided to leave with all haste. Chairs and tables were knocked over in the rush to flee the murderers.

"That was fun..." Adamar swigged an abandoned tankard of ale.

Galanör looked at Farney's dead body, slumped over the table. He was angry with himself for going down this route, for thinking it could be as simple as buying the women and children. Now, he had put his companions and the mission in peril. They would be hunted by the Trigorns and their element of surprise would be lost when they took the humans.

A pang of guilt gnawed at his conscience when he looked upon the dead bodies. Being trained to kill and actually killing were two different things. He soothed his guilt by reminding himself that these men were scoundrels and rogues.

"We need to leave, now." Galanör strode towards the exit, with Adamar following close behind.

Outside, the patrons ran in every direction to get away. As the crowd dispersed, Galanör caught sight of the elves, each with a body at their feet. With no guards to follow them, the elves climbed the walls of the tavern and fled across the rooftops.

"We should have done this *my* way!" Adamar stood in the centre of their apartment. "Eliön had already scouted the location. We knew their numbers, their weapons and, best of all, they didn't even know we existed. Now they'll think they're under attack and increase their security. Not to mention the mages at the Trigorn's disposal. They will use magic to hunt us now!"

Galanör leaned against the wall, looking out of the rain-soaked window for any sign of the Trigorn's men. He could feel all of their eyes on him, judging him for his tactical error. Damn this storm, he thought. It had ruined everything!

"We will reach Korkanath's shores and fulfil our duty, even if it sees the end of us!" Galanör turned on the group with fire in his eyes. "We will burn the Trigorn family to the ground if we must. Not a hundred men could stand against. You fear these humans, Adamar, but you forget, brother, we are not the elves that fled Illian and left the humans to our lands. We are as mighty as the elements. We are *elves*. We will take what we need and complete our task. When we return to Elandril, we will be heroes. Think about what we're bringing back! Our names will be carved into history when the future of our race hears how we saved all of Verda."

He only believed a handful of his own words, but that wasn't the point. Galanör had successfully manipulated Adamar by inciting his fear of the humans. The large elf offered no further challenge but instead appeared eager to see their duty through with as much violence as possible. The others looked convinced, with Lyra nodding her head in agreement.

"Eliön, take Ailas and scout the brothel again." Galanör met Lyra's eyes, a silent message informing her of his *need*. "Adamar, Naiveen, return to The Anvil and observe the investigation. I have a feeling the city guard will be taking orders from Mr Farney's replacement."

They all accepted their tasks and readied themselves to leave. Lyra walked ahead of Galanör into the bedroom, his signal received. The evening's violence coupled with his rousing speech had put him in the mood for a different kind of physical activity.

CHAPTER 10
A RANGER'S PRICE

"No, no, this will not do!" Lovani, the master of servants, looked Asher up and down with disgust. "You cannot be presented to his Grace like this." He tilted his head with more disgust at the sight of muddy footprints and rainwater that trailed the group of Graycoats and the ranger.

With the click of his fingers, another servant ran off to perform some unknown task, while the castle guard stood firmly behind the master of servants, barring the way.

"The king wishes to see this man!" Darius Devale was clearly eager to please the king.

"I see no man before me, Brother Devale, but a beast! No, the smell alone will permeate the king's library and curl the pages of the books." He clapped his hands impatiently and the same servant returned with another man holding a leather satchel. This new man had recently been woken up, given his dishevelled appearance. "Jevano here will give you a shave and clean you up. Your clothes will be cleaned and dried." This was obviously news to Jevano, whose expression was a mixture of shock and fear at the sight of Asher.

"He's not touching me with any blade." Asher turned a threatening expression on the barber.

"Ah, but when he is finished," the master of servants said, commanding the three buxom maids to push past Jevano, "you will be cleaned..."

Asher had a sudden change of mind. "Well, a little trim wouldn't hurt." Without looking at Devale, Asher walked off with Jevano and the maids, smiling as he did.

"Brother Devale, might I suggest you sit by the hearth and dry off?" The master of servants indicated the large fireplace in the castle foyer, much to Devale's chagrin.

A couple of hours later, Asher admired his reflection in the floor length mirror. His beard had been trimmed neatly and his hair washed with expensive perfumes. He tied the top of his hair into a small ponytail that rested over his crown; it was a nice change to be able to put his hand through his greying hair. He looked back at the mess made by his bath. Soap and water had poured over the side with the lining of its interior crusted in dirt from his naked body. The ranger was glad to see the back of the maids, however, who had scrubbed him violently with large brushes on long sticks, crushing his dream of enjoying the three of them in the soapy bath. He couldn't help but feel a little tricked by the master of servants.

Asher fixed his cloak to the latches on his leather shoulder pads, impressed with its shade of green. Every inch of his armour had been cleaned and dried, except for the strip of red cloth hanging from his belt; his orders had been quite specific.

The master of servants soon returned and led Asher and Brother Devale to an unassuming door. The corridor leading to the door was sparsely decorated and off the castle's well-adorned halls. Asher knew a secret entrance when he saw one.

"This is Galkarus Vod," Lovani announced at the sight of the tall man, standing in front of the secret door. "He is King Rengar's court mage."

The tall man wore a long red robe, lined in gold, with a staff in one hand, almost as tall as himself. Galkarus stroked his bushy white beard and took in the sight of the ranger. The belt around his waist was covered in pouches upon pouches and appeared far too heavy for a man of Galkarus's age to carry. The wizard reached around his back and retrieved a thin wand, covered in growths like the burrs on a tree.

Galkarus waved the wand over Asher, creating a distortion in the air. Asher was happy to stand there and allow the mage to search him with his revealing spell, knowing that the stone in his ring would protect him. Not that it mattered. He had been relieved of all his weapons and had his armour picked apart while the king's servants cleaned it. With no reaction to his spell, Galkarus stepped aside, eyeing Asher with a suspicious look.

The door opened into a small library with an ornate desk situated in the corner, layered in scrolls and leather-bound books. A single arching window stood between the bookshelves, reflecting the candlelight from within the room.

"King Rengar the Sixth, of the royal house Marek, Lord of Alborn..." The master of servants introduced the king, who was taking his last step off the small library ladder, to their right.

The king was not what Asher had been expecting. He was devoid of the usual gems and jewellery that accompanied a man of his standing, with clothes no more majestic than a man of moderate wealth, though his simple shirt and trousers were no doubt made of the finest materials. The ranger guessed Rengar to be of a similar age to himself, with perhaps a few more wrinkles around his eyes. His short dark hair was slicked back and greying along his receding hairline, where Asher could make out the faintest of scars on the king's forehead.

"Thank you Lovani, that will be all." Rengar's voice commanded subservience. Here was a man who had been giving orders and getting his way since birth.

Lovani stood aside, staring at Darius Devale with his arm outstretched towards the door. Devale hesitated, realising the master of servants was indicating for the Graycoat to leave with him. A single look from the king, however, confirmed that *he* was to leave with the master of servants. Darius bowed once, with a distrustful glance at Asher, and left promptly.

The secret door closed without a sound behind them, revealing the bookshelf that disguised its presence. The king slowly made his way to the embellished chair behind his desk, taking in the ranger's appearance with a measured gaze. Rengar clasped his hands and tilted his head, considering his words with care and much fore-thought, as was expected of a king. Asher knew to wait for Rengar to start the conversation; even old assassins knew how to talk to royalty.

"I like to come up here to think, to get away from it all," the king began. "I would offer you a seat but only one was made for this room. I don't have guests in this part of the castle. I hope this demonstrates the gravity with which you have been invited. I have an unlimited supply of underlings more than ready to take secret meetings like this on my behalf, but I wanted to see you myself." A flash of lightning drowned out the candlelight.

"What can I do for you, your Grace?"

"It's not what you can do for me, Ranger, but what you can do for Illian." Rengar's pale blue eyes bored into Asher. "What do you know about the elves?"

The question took Asher by surprise. He knew more about elves than anyone else in Illian but, then again, so did every assassin trained at Nightfall. The ranger couldn't help but look away for a moment, while he tried to bury his memories about the Arakesh's biggest secret.

"The same as everyone else," he lied. "After the dragons started the war with us, they left for Ayda. No one has seen or heard from them since." As far as he knew, that last part was actually true.

"Until now..." King Rengar placed his hand on the scroll laid out on his desk. "They are returning, Asher; the elves are coming home. The Lord of Elves has dispatched an envoy with his daughter, Princess Reyna Sevari."

Something about that name triggered a memory in Asher's mind, but instead of recalling an image he could smell ash and smoke.

"On behalf of the elves, the Princess will start a dialogue between our two nations, so that we might begin to reintegrate our societies. We can start with trade and what not, but think of the knowledge they hold, not just about the past, but about magic, immortality and the lands beyond Illian."

Asher could see the hunger for power that twinkled in the king's eyes. He was just like every other man, ruler or peasant; he just wanted more. An alliance with the elves would give Velia a serious advantage over the other countries in Illian, especially Grey Stone, home to King Orvish and personal rival of Rengar's.

"I fail to see how I fit into all this, your Grace."

"I have already sent messengers to the other rulers of Illian, including the highest mages at Korkanath. As we speak they are journeying from all over the land to be here for the elves' arrival. After all, this is to be a monumental piece of history..." Rengar looked eager to shove it in their faces that the elves had chosen Velia.

"Tomorrow, I will announce this to my people so that feasts and parades might be prepared to welcome our guests, both royal and elf." That explained the extra guards and the curfew around Velia. "However, this damn storm has delayed events. My court mages tell me it cannot be shifted... useless lot. The elves have had to travel north, for calmer waters. Instead of arriving in Direport in a few days, they are now expected to make shore in the mouth of The Unmar. I want you to meet them and bring them back to Velia safely."

Asher raised his eyebrows at the king's request. It was a lot of information to take in at once, especially for someone who had been leading the simpler life for fourteen years. The elves returning to Illian was unexpected, given how things were supposedly left between their two kinds a millennium ago.

"Surely you have a thousand men more suitable for this than me. The Graycoats would do this for free, but if you've heard of me, your Grace, then you know my services aren't cheap."

"I don't want an army to be the first thing the elves see, and I don't want to send an organisation that has no allegiance. And you're right, I have heard of you, Ranger... or should I say assassin?" The king's gaze was piercing.

"Your past is infamous. To this day, Queen Isabella recounts the day you saved her life and that of her son from an Arakesh plot. It's your past that makes you so valuable to this endeavour. My spies tell me that a contract has been drawn up between the Arakesh and an unknown party. It is believed their objective is to sabotage this new alliance and assassinate the elves before they reach Velia. I offer *you* this job because you know how they think. You'll see what others could not, a difference that could keep the elves alive, I think."

"I take it I don't have much of a choice?" Asher turned briefly to the secret door behind him.

"Oh, you have a choice. Take the job and get rich... or don't. I should point out that the latter will see you returned to the custody of the Graycoats. Beyond that I cannot see you making any choices ever again."

"Well, when you put it like that..."

"Name your price, Ranger."

Asher took a moment to think about that number. It wasn't every day such an offer was made by a king. Of course, there was the chance he would never get to spend a single coin of it. If Nightfall really had accepted a contract to assassinate the princess of elves, Asher would be hard pressed to stop them. Elves would prove a formidable foe for any one, or even two, Arakesh, forcing the Father to send a team to kill them.

It had been a long time since the ranger had fought with the warriors of his old order. He had defeated three in the palace at Lirian and one before that, but he had felt the cruel bite of time since then. Asher knew he was still faster than any man, but the Arakesh were bred to be more than that. It was the first time in his career as a ranger that he had questioned whether he could accomplish the job.

"This is no ordinary job, nor is it easy..." Asher began with his usual bartering techniques, though for the first time he actually believed his words.

"I am more than aware of what I ask, Ranger. Name your price."

"I want an account set up within Stowhold." Asher's first request gave the king pause. Stowhold was the central bank used throughout all of Illian, with the many treasures of every kingdom stored inside, and overseen by the Addathorn family. "This account will never run dry for as long as I live but, don't worry, I'm a man of simple needs. Finally, I want the deed to five square miles of land on the coast, somewhere near The Willows." He wasn't sure why he made that last request; a glimmer of hope for his old age, perhaps?

"Is that all?" Rengar appeared more amused than anything. "Thinking of settling down are we? I don't blame you. Time beats us all..." The king inspected the back of his hand, where the faintest of liver spots were beginning to show. "You might reconsider, should you succeed. This endeavour will see you rise from humble ranger to a hero of the people, ushering in a new golden Age for Illian."

"Do we have a deal, your Grace?" The fame would certainly help with future jobs, but Asher had little interest in being a hero.

"Bring the princess and the elves back to Velia, and you can start your new life." Rengar leaned forward in his chair. "I take it this buys me your loyalty, as well as your services. You are to be my representative in this endeavour, Ranger. The Lord Marshal of West Fellion has charged Darius Devale and a group of Graycoats with accompanying you, but you are—"

"Graycoats? I work alone—"

"Do not interrupt me again." King Rengar maintained his steely gaze. "You are to be my representative, not precious Devale out there. Your skills are legendary, but I suspect the Arakesh will provide you with quite the challenge and, as much as I hate to admit it, the Gray-coats are the best fighters at my disposal, so they will accompany you."

"I thought West Fellion wasn't supposed to do king's work..." Asher couldn't think of anything worse than having a team of Devale's lackeys getting in his way.

"They need more money. After this, I have no doubt Lord Marshal Horvarth will find himself at my door, requesting I pledge more coin to their order. If Velia pays more, so too will the other kingdoms, to ensure the Graycoats show no bias towards me. Besides, if I send you and them, I risk no Velian lives. Now answer my question."

Asher's loyalty couldn't be bought. He had been free now for fourteen years and had no intention of giving that over to any king. But for the opportunity of a retirement he thought would never come, the ranger was willing to bow the head and play along. Asher knew he could get lost in the world and forget this meeting had ever happened, should he need to. They couldn't find him if he didn't want them to.

"You have my loyalty. I will escort and protect the elves on your behalf. But I'm in charge, Devale follows my orders..." Asher hesitated, thinking about his next demand. "...And I want the two Gray-coats who brought me here." The ranger couldn't fathom why he made such a request.

"Excellent! Galkarus, my court mage, will see to your horses." Rengar stood up and made for the opulent door to his left. "Lovani will see you out. You leave immediately."

Nathaniel and Elaith sat in the only tavern still serving food past midnight. They had been forced to seek out shelter beyond the walls of Velia, in the small village sprawled across the fields. Nathaniel had shovelled the food into his mouth, paying no attention to its taste, as he imagined punching Darius Devale over and over. With the exception of a couple of professional alcoholics, slumped over the bar, the tavern was deserted.

Elaith looked despairingly at the plate of ribs before her. "I've seen more meat on old skeletons."

"Eat up. If your hunting skills are anything to go by, it'll be the last good meal you get before we reach West Fellion."

The young woman grumbled and continued to pick off what meat she could. He knew the fight with the bandits was still playing on her mind. It was bound to. It wasn't the first fight he would have picked for her, but at least the outlaw she killed was a complete bastard of a human being. The bandit's face would haunt her for many years to come but, hopefully, the death wouldn't weigh on her conscience.

"What will happen when we return to West Fellion?" Elaith asked.

"You've performed well." Nathaniel wasn't used to giving praise. "I will give my report and you'll graduate."

Elaith didn't look too happy about the prospect. Even though she had been training for eight years, the final test was over in the blink of an eye. Nathaniel knew the month wouldn't be over before Elaith received her first patrol duty. Four out of ten students never returned from their first year patrolling. He kept that statistic to himself.

The tavern door creaked open and slammed into the wall. The sound of the rain and thunder blew in with the wind, as a tall figure stood in the doorway. Nathaniel's fist closed at the sight of Darius Devale striding into the tavern, water flowing off his long coat and his hair matted against his face.

The senior Graycoat's eyes quickly scanned the bar, before resting on Nathaniel and Elaith. He stomped over with an expression to match the storm.

"Darius...?"

Devale stood before them and briefly looked back at the door with a face of contempt. "We have been charged with a mission of great importance to the realm..." He paused, contorting his mouth. "There is a far greater chance of success if you would accompany us."

In a flash of lightning, Nathaniel caught sight of Asher outside, astride his horse, smirking mischievously at Darius Devale's back.

PART TWO

CHAPTER 11
HEADING FOR DARKER SHORES

Reyna hung over the side of the ship, clinging to the sheets attached to the sails, and bathed in the warm rays, under the midday sun. With Faylen's Seabreath in her veins, Reyna could finally enjoy the delights of sailing and the joy of the ocean. Looking down, The Adean was rushing by, spraying her with cold water, while Ölli flew overhead, circling the ship. They had escaped the storm and entered calmer waters with their northern bearing, though the dark clouds could still be seen on the southern horizon.

Using exceptional agility, Reyna swung around the sheet and flipped onto the deck. Faylen stood at the stern, ignoring the wheel and using magic to fill the sails with wind. Mörygan was below deck, using the diviner to communicate with Galanör on Dragorn. She looked at the storm again and knew it had forced them all to alter their plans.

"Mörygan spoke with your father last night," Faylen called from the stern.

Reyna slowly walked up the steps to see her mentor. "What did he say?" She knew it wouldn't be anything good. All her life, her father had been nothing but the Lord of Elves, his commands to be followed, and nothing more. If it wasn't for her mother's love, Reyna would have been convinced her birth was intended solely for her father's grand plan. Choosing not to dwell on her mother's absence, the princess focused on Faylen's words.

"He feels we are being opposed. The elders, including your father, have been unable to dispel the storm that has affected our plans thus far."

"Who would even know to oppose us?" Reyna asked, concerned. The plan had been put together over many years by her father and was only known in full to a fraction of their kind. There were certainly no humans aware of the plan.

"That is what troubles us all. To control a storm of that size and power takes considerable magic, but to maintain it for so long and against the will of the elders and human mages, that would require almost unlimited energy. Your father doubts it is any one caster, but several, combining their magic to harness the storm." The crystals that decorated Faylen's bracelet began to shine as if the stars themselves were trapped inside.

"Does the Lord of Elves think we are being sabotaged?" Reyna asked.

Faylen gave her a knowing look she had expressed before. Reyna's mentor knew how she felt about her father and found it difficult that the princess always referred to him by title. Reyna knew that Faylen had always wanted the relationship between father and daughter to flourish, as it had with her mother, but respect was the only emotion Reyna knew how to give him. His age and wisdom demanded it.

"Your father fears that there are some in Illian still loyal to Valanis."

"But how could that be? When Valanis was defeated at Elethiah, the humans were still scattered on the edge of The Wild Moores. Even the Darkakin arrived too late to be influenced by his dark magic." Reyna had studied history under Faylen herself, but it helped that her parents had lived it.

"The war didn't end in Elethiah. There were still elves bound to his insidious will after the battle. We hunted them down before leaving, but your father thinks it might be possible that a following of humans was cultivated first. If this proves to be true, their cult will only have swelled over a thousand years."

"So it could be someone loyal to King Rengar, someone who knows we're coming?"

"Not necessarily. As well as the high mages of Korkanath, we instructed the king to invite the kings and queens from across the land. There is a much larger circle of suspects now." Faylen adjusted the sails to change tack.

"What could these people want?" Reyna thought about a group of humans coming between them and their plans. It made sense to try to stop the elves from succeeding if they worshipped Valanis, but what could they possibly hope to achieve in the long run? Valanis was trapped in Elethiah for all time.

"If they exist, their only goal would be to free Valanis. But without the dragons it is impossible to break the Amber Spell. The dark one is beyond man's grasp, Reyna."

"Not according to the prophecy..." Reyna was aware of how sensitive the topic was.

"Your father doesn't believe in the Echoes of Fate. And you know he has deemed its words unreliable." It was clear to see the conflict on Faylen's face.

Reyna's mother was a firm believer in Nalana's dying words, putting her at odds with her husband, who had lost his faith in the gods and their gift of prophecy. Faylen had joined Adilandra in her belief, but the queen had commanded Faylen to stay with Reyna when she left for the southern lands of Ayda, back in the east.

"If he doesn't believe the Echoes, why has he made plans according to Nalana's words?" Reyna wasn't sure what she believed in, but the fact that her father was so against the prophecy only pushed her towards believing in it.

"He doesn't believe in the prophecy." Mörygan emerged from below. "But he does believe in man's power to destroy. If there is a way to free Valanis, man is sure to find it. They will not realise what they unleash that day, but they will come to regret it with the rest of Illian. It is our responsibility to ensure that mankind never gets the chance."

Reyna could feel the need for confrontation rising in her. "And the eve of this plan just happens to coincide with the arrival of Paldora's Star?" The princess looked to the sky where, any day now, the comet known as Paldora's Star would cross the night's sky, as it did every five hundred years. Its presence was well documented in Nalana's prophecy, as well as the peril that would accompany it.

"As you say, coincidence. Besides, Paldora's Star will cross the night's sky as it always has. Like every time before Princess, it will not be seen in the daylight, as Nalana's words claim," Mörygan replied.

"What about Galanör's part in this? If he succeeds at Korkanath, the Lord of Elves will be fulfilling part of the very prophecy he doesn't believe in!" Reyna could feel Faylen's eyes on her. It wasn't befitting of a princess to raise her voice.

"Focus on your part in this." Mörygan strolled to the edge of the deck, his hands clasped behind his back. "Forget the garbled words of a dying elf and see clearly what lies before us. We must destroy Valanis once and for all, before the dim-witted humans accidentally free him, and while he is vulnerable in Elethiah."

Reyna left for her room, seeing that Faylen wasn't going to speak for her or her beliefs. Mörygan couldn't be reasoned with, having his head firmly planted inside the king's behind. Ölli glided down to meet her, eager for his lunch having stretched his wings.

~

"You shouldn't allow her head to be filled with such nonsense," Mörygan chastised Faylen after Reyna left. "If there are no gods, there can be no prophecies. She must believe in the natural abilities of our kind, not the useless words of a believer in false deities."

"We believed in those deities once..." Faylen relinquished her hold over the wind and allowed the ship to sail naturally.

"We were young and naive, primitive even. Gods would not grant Valanis the power he claimed. They wouldn't allow for such devastation to be wrought across our land, our people. Valanis found a natural source of powerful magic and it corrupted him, that's all."

"What is magic, if not a gift from Naius?" Faylen had not been alive during The Dark War, but she knew Valanis had claimed Naius, the god of magic, granted him the power.

"Magic is a part of this world, like fire and ice. It's woven into the fabric of our reality." Mörygan ran a critical eye over Faylen. "Perhaps the king was wrong to put the girl in your care all these years..."

Faylen bit back her retort, refusing to rise to him. Instead, she looked to the horizon, south of the ship.

"How fairs Galanör?"

"His mission isn't without its difficulties," Mörygan explained, "but he assures me they will reach Korkanath at the appointed time."

"At this rate, we will reach Illian in a few days. Do you think King Rengar will have an emissary waiting to meet us?"

"No doubt. He will want to show us off to the other rulers of Illian. I wouldn't be surprised if he sent an army to escort us..."

CHAPTER 12
A WOLF AMONG SHEEP

After nearly two days of hard riding, Galkarus's spell faded and the company's horses needed their first rest, along with everyone's behinds. Barely a word had passed between the group since they left Velia, a silence Asher was grateful for.

As well as Nathaniel, Elaith and Darius Devale, six Graycoats accompanied him on the king's errand. Every time the ranger caught Devale giving Nathaniel a dirty look, he couldn't help but laugh to himself. Sending him into the tavern to recruit Nathaniel had been his first order to the arrogant Graycoat. It wouldn't be his last.

The storm was behind them now, its borders hanging over Velia in the distance. They had kept to The Selk Road on their journey north, the well-beaten track the fastest and safest way to travel. The road connected all the kingdoms in Illian, passing through some of the bigger towns and cutting through The Evermoore. Asher rarely used the road, preferring the isolation of the wild and the opportunity to travel across the land unseen.

The horses trotted along the road with the last of their energy.

Asher led the group with Nathaniel coming up on his side, ignoring the glances of the other Graycoats.

"We should probably stop soon," Nathaniel commented. "Let the horses rest. We've made good time; we'll reach the mouth of The Unmar tomorrow."

"Soon, but they have a little more in them." Asher patted Hector on the neck, as he looked over the group behind them.

The horses were covered in white foamy sweat and the men were haggard from riding non-stop. Elaith was half asleep over the mane of her chestnut mare.

"It's still hard to get my head around..." Nathaniel kept his voice low enough so as not to be heard by the others.

Asher wasn't sure what to make of the strange friendship forming between them. "They won't stay," the ranger replied. "When the elves realise that humans are just as barbaric as they were a thousand years ago, they'll return to Ayda. The only question is how many survive the Arakesh."

"Isn't that why you're here?"

"I've spent over a decade avoiding them for a reason, Galfrey. The Father won't send old assassins to kill the elves, he'll send the best. I might be able to predict their moves but that doesn't mean I'll survive an encounter with them." Asher shifted his bum in the saddle, resigning himself to the fact that there was no comfortable position.

"The Father... that's the head of Nightfall?" Nathaniel's tone had changed, his curious nature returning.

Asher silently laughed to himself, giving Nathaniel a sideways glance. The Graycoat was always searching for answers, though whether it was to elevate his status within West Fellion or just his curiosity was unknown to the ranger. Asher felt his old instincts kick in when probed about Nightfall's secrets, however. He had been brought up and trained to live a life shrouded in deceit and lies, with a foundation built around loyalty to the Arakesh. Every assassin was to die with Nightfall's secrets.

"Why keep their secrets?" Nathaniel pressed. "You've said it yourself, you're not an Arakesh anymore. You owe them nothing."

"Why share them?" Asher countered. "Nothing good has ever come out of that place. What would you do with the information? Even if you took every Graycoat to Nightfall there would be nothing but death waiting for you."

"So if you share their secrets, people will die, and if you don't share their secrets, people will still die..." Nathaniel's horse slowed down, leaving the ranger to carry on and think on his words.

After a brief pause for lunch, Asher drove the group on until nightfall, when they made camp south of Palios, the most northerly town within Alborn's borders. Devale and his men rested against their horses' sleeping bulk, having feasted on the hunted deer Elaith had caught. Asher had taken her out and allowed her to use his bow while teaching the young woman to track. Against Devale's protests, Nathaniel had allowed them to hunt alone, though Asher didn't doubt there was still some caution on Nathaniel's side.

Elaith had taken to him in a way most never did. She apparently didn't see him as an assassin or a natural enemy of her order, but as an interesting person with a rich life, filled with intrigue.

Asher was content to sit by the fire and take first watch as he polished his rune sword. Under the moonlight, the blade sparkled as if the silvyr was inlaid with diamonds. Nathaniel sat beside him, entranced by the hypnotic flickers of the fire. The Graycoat had naturally gravitated towards the ranger after the group made camp - the others having made it clear that they didn't want to socialise with him. Elaith too had come to sit with him by the fire. Was this friendship, the ranger wondered?

He had only ever called one person a friend.

"The Father is always the leader." Asher spoke into the fire, catching Nathaniel's attention. "It can be a Mother as well. It's a violent hierarchy. You can only ascend by killing the previous Mother or Father, but leading the Arakesh comes with a price. Once you claim the position, the order claims your sight, literally." Nathaniel failed to hide his shock. "From the day you're inducted, the order's alchemist puts you on a regime of Nightseye elixir - one vial every day until you're twenty-five. After that, you're permanently affected. But the elixir was developed for elves. In humans, the potion only works if the user is in complete darkness."

"That's why the Arakesh use blindfolds..." Nathaniel looked at the red cloth hanging from Asher's belt.

"When completely blinded, you can see, hear, taste, smell and feel everything. Your reactions are heightened as your senses tune you into the world in a way you can't imagine. It becomes addictive though. It makes you crave the next opportunity to flex your skills and kill on Nightfall's behalf. If you take on the role of Mother or Father, you're expected to live this way until you die. If you're good enough to beat an Arakesh who lives permanently attuned to their environment, then you're good enough to rule."

Nathaniel looked over the group of snoring Graycoats. "How are we expected to repel a foe like that?"

"They can be over-sensitised." Asher retrieved a small pouch from his belt and dropped into Nathaniel's palm. "Talo spices from Karath, in The Arid Lands. Set the bag alight and throw: it creates an almighty bang that plays hell with sensitive hearing. It won't last long, but it could be the difference between life and death. Do you know any magic?"

"Some, but I don't carry any crystals for storage. West Fellion discourages us from using it."

Asher knew that a novice in magic, without any crystals, ran the risk of draining his energy. He had never experienced this himself but had witnessed it first hand in others. In a fight, however, lighting the bag of spices with magic was the quickest way.

"Do you know the word for fire?" Asher asked.

"Vala..." Nathaniel opened his empty palm and, without

Demetrium to help conduct the magic, only a pathetic flicker of fire came to float above it. He closed his eyes, no doubt feeling the drain. "Your control over magic, is that another Arakesh secret?"

Asher twisted his silver ring. "Not exactly..." The ranger stopped at the sound of trotting hooves in the distance. He estimated at least twenty horses travelling south, along The Selk Road.

They had walked away from the fire to allow their eyes to adjust in the darkness when Asher heard the distinct sound of carriage wheels. The other Graycoats stirred and came to meet them beyond the firelight. From around the trees came an entourage of knights on horseback, surrounding a majestic carriage adorned with golden lion heads, each reflected in the glow of the fire. Every knight wore shining armour with golden cloaks draped over the back of their horses. As a natural reflex, Asher scanned the faces of them all, assessing for any threats.

"The royal house of Tion." Darius Devale released the grip on his sword.

The royal knights kept their eyes on the group as they rode by. The sight of the Graycoats was obviously unthreatening to the warriors of Namdhor, who continued on. Asher caught sight of a fair-haired woman peeking between the velvet curtains inside the carriage. She looked at them for a moment, before a man's hand grasped the curtain and closed them in.

"Lord Merkaris..." Nathaniel observed the carriage drive by, curiously. "He must be travelling to Velia for the festival."

"It seems he travels with better company than us!" one of the Graycoats jested, rousing a laugh from the others.

"Are they going to a celebration or going to war?" Elaith commented, noting the large number of soldiers.

The ranger watched Gal Tion's descendant disappear into the night. Merkaris Tion ruled Orith, the northern region of Illian, from the kingdom of Namdhor, just as the first king had, centuries ago. Asher had visited the city several times in his youth, as an Arakesh, and was yet to find a reason to return as a ranger. The ancient city was built into the rocky slopes of Vengora, in the north-west.

"What rumours?" Elaith asked the Graycoats muttering to one another.

"Murder's what I heard," one of them replied.

"His father, mother and sister died at sea... on stormless waters." The Graycoat spat on the ground.

"I've heard Merkaris has a wicked side. Sadistic behind closed doors apparently," a third man added.

"The hearsay of milkmaids." Nathaniel returned to the fire.

"Well, why don't we ask the old man?" The first Graycoat, with a black beard wider than his face, turned to Asher. "Aren't the Arakesh supposed to know everyone's secrets?"

"Would you like to know your mother's secret?" Asher rested a hand on the buckle of his belt.

The bearded Graycoat strode forward with violent intent, but he was halted by Devale, who stepped into his shoulder and placed a firm hand on the man's chest. The two men locked eyes for a moment before the bearded warrior breathed out a sigh and walked away.

"Perhaps we should get some more rest?" Devale suggested.

Hidden within his cloak, Asher pushed the dagger back into its sheath at the base of his back. "We ride at dawn."

CHAPTER 13
A DARK PACT

The sound of a noisy and chaotic world came back before her sight did. Through bleary eyes, Adilandra took in the spiked cage in which she lay, as it dragged her through the streets of the largest Darkakin city the elf had ever seen.

All around her, humans shouted at one another across a giant market, bartering for the lives of animals and slaves. As her senses returned, the smell of wild animals and human sweat filled her nose in a nauseating concoction.

Turning in her cage, she searched for her companions through the dust and sand, kicked up by the horses pulling her along. Fallön lay unconscious in an identical cage on the track, behind Adilandra's. Ederön and Lörvana, however, were nowhere in sight.

"Fallön!" Her cries were drowned out by the crowds.

The cage ran over a rock in the road, jostling Adilandra inside. She recoiled at the pain from bumping into a row of spikes that pointed inwards. When she looked up from the cut on her arm, the elf was greeted with the faces of a dozen humans, clambering on her cage. They shouted and spat at her with lust and rage, their hands jutting between the bars to claw at her.

The explosive crack of a whip drove the baying mob away from the cages. One man fell to the floor with a bleeding gash across his back and head.

The large Darkakin from the jungle came up alongside her, astride a giant lizard, twice the size of any horse. His dark face was half covered by what looked to be a real skull, though his cheeks remained exposed, painted in white patterns that accentuated the small fangs fused into his cheeks, as if he were a beast. A deformed and lipless mouth revealed bloodied gums and sharp teeth. The wooden armour, that barely covered his muscled body, was covered in similar horns, with two large fangs protruding from the fur around his shoulders. The club on his back was coated in the dried blood of Adilandra's friends.

The crowds parted at the sight of the large Darkakin, going back to their market stalls and watching the paraded elves from afar. Unable to stand up in the cramped cage, Adilandra placed her palms against the roof and the floor to steady herself, but when the cage was dragged into an encompassing shadow, the elf adjusted her position to look between the spiked bars.

The giant pyramid blocked out the sun.

All of Adilandra's instincts screamed about the danger of entering such a place. The structure emanated dark magic and sacrificial rituals. Rotting corpses, old and fresh, were nailed to posts outside the temple's entrance. The row of posts continued in both directions around the pyramid, surrounding it in dead bodies.

The large Darkakin barked an order in their native language. Adilandra had no time to react as the warrior beside him placed a slender pipe to his lips and blew a dart at her. The dart sank into her neck with a sharp bite, poisoning the elf's body with a powerful toxin. She tried to ignore the pain and pull the dart out but failed to lift her arm. Again, the large Darkakin was the last thing she saw, before darkness took her.

∿

"Adilandra..." The hushed voice was as familiar as the fear intoned in it.

Adilandra opened her eyes to find herself on her knees and a painted hand grasping her shoulder. Beside her were all three companions, also on their knees, with a Darkakin standing behind them. Fallön received a smack to the head for speaking. Adilandra didn't understand the words spoken by the guard but knew a threat when she heard one.

Ederön was being held up on his knees at the end of the row, his clothes stained with blood where the arrow had struck him. His skin was paler than the rest, but not as marred by fresh bruises and cuts as Lörvana and Fallön.

Adilandra blinked hard to correct her blurry vision and examine their surroundings. She felt the cool breeze coming from the long balcony to her right and realised they must be high up to feel anything but the heat of the sun. The chamber where they knelt was covered in large cushions, low tables and dark strips of fabric hanging from the ceiling. Perfectly toned men and women lay sprawled across the cushions, drinking out of goblets and sharing meat and fruit. Adilandra was shocked at what little the humans wore. Painted guards stood in parallel rows in front of them, each facing one another before the elf caught sight of the throne.

"...I want the terms of our agreement bound in blood, Alidyr." Sitting on the throne of bones was a beautiful woman, for a human, with black hair braided down to her waist and red paint across her eyes. Her lips were painted black, contrasting with an olive-skinned body, which was covered in tattoos that ran down her arms until they met sharpened nails.

"My master's word is his bond, Goddess."

Alidyr Yalathanil...

Adilandra couldn't see his face, but she didn't need to. There wasn't an elf alive who didn't know the name of Valanis's most honoured general. With his back to the elves, she could only see the long dark hair that ran down his back, over a floor-length white robe. The short-swords hanging on each side of his hip were intriguing, with their curved white hilts and gleaming crystals. Those blades had claimed many elven lives during The Dark War.

The Goddess bared her sharp teeth. "Words are but piss in the wind! Bind our fate together old one, or return to your master a failure..."

The robed figure paused before answering. "So be it." He delved into his robe and presented the queen of the Darkakin with something Adilandra couldn't see. "This is a diviner; I will contact you through it with my master's wishes. Until then, prepare your people."

"You think I require instruction on the matter?" The Goddess moved like a viper coiled to attack. "We are war incarnate, old one. All of Verda will tremble under our feet." She sat back and turned to the bald servant on her left. "Hyvark will see to the blood oath." The bald servant walked towards the elves, with Alidyr in his wake.

Time seemed to slow as their eyes met. Alidyr's reaction was far better controlled, but his surprise was still there to see. His flawless complexion was cut with a small scar that curved down from the corner of his left eye, forming a crescent moon. Alidyr deserved a greater punishment while serving in the Hand of Valanis. Those dark, elven eyes reflected a life older than her own, with a gaze that chilled Adilandra's bones. He hesitated in front of the kneeling elves, glancing back at The Goddess.

Upon closer inspection, Adilandra could see the short-swords were etched in the gold script of the ancients. Alidyr didn't stop or protest their capture but instead continued to follow the servant, as if they meant nothing to him. What was the Hand of Valanis doing in the Darkakin lands?

After the elf's departure, Adilandra and her companions were hefted roughly to their feet and pushed before The Goddess. A swift kick to the back of the legs put them all on their knees again, at the foot of the throne.

"Welcome to Malaysai," The Goddess began. "We don't see your kind for millennia and then I see five of you in a single day. Though some of your companions made their way to my palace much earlier." A wicked smile crossed the queen's face. Without any shoes, The Goddess's bare feet padded over the stone floor, as she circled the group. "It turns out your kind have many talents..." She traced a seductive line across Fallön's jaw. "...Delicious."

With every measure of control, the elves remained steady, trying not to react to the queen's words. The Darkakin were cannibals and rapists. "What's the matter old ones? Do you not speak man's language?" With no response, The Goddess gave an order in the Darkakin tongue.

Ederön dropped like a stone after the large Darkakin slammed his meaty fist into the elf's jaw. Adilandra's keen ears weren't required to hear the sound of his jaw breaking before he hit the floor.

"No!" Lörvana screamed. Her guard tugged her hair back to keep her in line.

"So you do speak." The Goddess clamped Lörvana's mouth in one hand. "Even I despise speaking the language of such pathetic creatures, but since you don't speak Darkakin and I don't speak elf, we are left with little choice."

Adilandra's eyes filled with tears at the sight of Ederön's unconscious form. "You must let us go," she pleaded. "We are on an errand of grave importance."

The large Darkakin stormed over, ready to punish her for speaking out of turn, until The Goddess held up her hand, stopping his own from falling across Adilandra's face. The queen moved closer, inspecting the auburn-haired elf with vibrant green eyes.

"You speak for the group? You are the one who has forced them to run for their immortal lives across my land?" The Goddess wiped the blood from a cut on Adilandra's eyebrow and sucked her finger clean.

"You *must* let us go..."

"Why?" The Goddess's face was inches away. "So you can find the *dragons?*"

Adilandra didn't know what to say. She was too stunned at the queen's knowledge and her face reflected it. How could she have come by such information?

The Goddess laughed wickedly. "You should see your face, elfling. I believe his name was Tölvarn."

The name pulled at the elf's heart. Tölvarn was the second elf to be taken by the Darkakin and sold on from clan to clan, constantly beyond their searching reach. He had been the youngest of their group and Adilandra had promised his mother she would see him safely returned.

"I played with him for some time," The Goddess continued. "We have many aphrodisiacs and hypnotic elixirs potent enough to affect even an elf. You can imagine my delight at the opportunity to sample such legendary wares. It is rare my appetites are sated by a single man.

"Of course, when I was bored of his body I handed him over to my inquisitors." Adilandra felt sick. "He lasted considerably longer than any human would, but there's only so much flesh they can lose before they spill all their secrets." Ederön's blood flowed across the cold slabs, slithering towards The Goddess's bare toes. "Krenorak..." The large Darkakin stepped forward. "Let my people see an elf up close."

Adilandra and the others struggled against their captors when the large Darkakin dragged Ederön off by the ankle. The sudden movement woke the elf up, who could sense his impending fate by the distress of his friends.

"NO, PLEASE!" Lörvana begged.

Ederön could only moan through a broken jaw, as Krenorak picked him up with both hands and flipped him over the edge of the balcony. There was only silence after he disappeared from view, the distance too far for the sound of his impact to carry.

Adilandra felt the tears running freely down her cheeks. She had seen too many elves die since they left Elandril, and every death was on her. The throne room spun, while Adilandra's stomach lurched and she threw up at The Goddess's feet.

"My ancestors told stories of the great wyrms of the sky," The Goddess continued as if ordering Ederön's death was trivial. "They also told of how your kind drove the Darkakin from Illian. Apparently, my ancestors were weak."

Her words were lost on Adilandra, who only wanted to fall to the floor and pass out, but the sharp tug on her hair kept the elf on her knees. Lörvana hung limply in her captor's hands, her eyes fixed on the balcony, while Fallön fought against the Darkakin with a face of rage.

"I assure you, queen of elves," The Goddess said as she returned to her throne, "the Darkakin are not weak. Soon the world will see what we are capable of..." With a wicked eye, she looked over the captive elves. "Krenorak, you have proven yourself with the blood of so many elves. You have tracked them for many moons and are deserving of a great gift. You may have that one." The Goddess's eyes rested on Lörvana.

"No!" Fallön doubled his efforts, but Krenorak barked an order in Darkakin and the elf was struck across the head by his captor. "I'll kill all of you!"

"I like this one's rage." The Goddess fixed Fallön with a predatory gaze. "Have him prepared for tonight. He may need a more powerful elixir than the last." Fallön was dragged away with a new cut across his temple.

Adilandra was left alone, surrounded by her enemies once again. She saw the world through blurry eyes, barely aware of the blade at her throat. The Goddess was suddenly by her ear, running a sharp nail over the pointed tip. Adilandra didn't even have the energy to pull away from her hot breath.

"What to do with *you*, elfling? There isn't enough room in my kingdom for two queens. But you did come all this way for the dragons." The Goddess lifted Adilandra's chin with a long nail. "So perhaps I'll grant you your wish..."

CHAPTER 14
A SHADOW IN THE DARK

fter another day of non-stop riding, the company came to a steady trot as dusk approached. Nathaniel closed his eyes and let his head roll back under the warmth of the sun. The Graycoat was thankful to have seen blue skies and white clouds for a couple of days. The storm hanging over Velia was far from sight but he had the feeling it wasn't going anywhere for a while.

Their journey had remained uneventful for the most part, with only a handful of caravans and traders passing them on the road. The other Graycoats had grumbled, with little subtlety, regarding their opinion of Asher's leadership, though Darius Devale had kept them in check, unsure, no doubt, of the ranger's tolerance and eager to keep his men's limbs attached.

Nathaniel looked from Asher to the others. The ranger had certainly committed terrible crimes in his life, crimes the Graycoats were commissioned to prevent, but having heard only a small part of the ranger's history and Nightfall's horrific regimes, it wasn't hard to see how children could be so easily moulded into killers. At least Asher had made the conscious decision to leave the Arakesh and make amends, even if they did come with a bag of coins for his troubles.

Looking at his worn leather coat, Nathaniel knew his duty should be black and white. Asher was, and always would be, an Arakesh; the ranger's rigorous training would never let him forget that. His knowledge of Nightfall and its inner workings was invaluable to West Fellion. Nathaniel knew that this should be the only reason to allow Asher to breathe, with the Graycoat's deepest instinct being to drive his blade through the assassin.

Nathaniel looked at Asher and knew he didn't feel that way.

Unhappy about his torn emotions, Nathaniel did the only thing he knew and kept it to himself. A life as an outcast amongst his own people and a job that kept him on the road didn't offer much in the way of friends.

"You know." Asher came up beside him and unexpectedly started a conversation. "With your skills, you don't have to stay bound to that coat. You're already accustomed to life on the road and I know the pay is better on my side."

"I'm a Graycoat - it's all I know." That was all Nathaniel knew to say. He felt it was in his blood.

"That's how I thought for a while."

"What changed?" Nathaniel knew he was asking a very personal question.

"They ordered me to do something I didn't agree with..."

The reply piqued the Graycoat's curiosity, but he refrained from asking further questions. Instead, he dwelled on the ranger's words and saw a similar dilemma in his own future. Whatever bargain had been struck between Asher and King Rengar, the Lord Marshal would still order his arrest. Nathaniel glanced at Darius, who was watching them intensely, and wondered what choice he would make when Devale gave that order.

"The Lord Marshal ordered my father to do something he didn't agree with once. Had he obeyed, we wouldn't be having this conversation right now."

"Where did he meet your mother?" Asher was more insightful than Nathaniel gave him credit for.

"Not far north of here, in Longdale. He had been sent to root out a band of rogue dwarves preying on traders in The Iron Valley. I didn't see him much growing up. My mother died giving birth to me, so I was raised by her brother, Uncle Job." Nathaniel looked to the north, where The Vrost Mountains sat, their image fading in the light of dusk. Beyond them was Longdale, where he often wondered what his uncle was doing. "He's a good man, raised me as well as he could on a farmer's income. My father was ordered to never return to Longdale, but he disobeyed often. Even after my mother died, he would journey north to check on me, always promising that the next patrol would be his last, until of course, it was..."

"I was in Karath when I heard of his death," Asher replied. "It's said he fought off an entire war band of Outlanders attacking Snowfell. There is a statue of him in the town square if I recall."

"I've seen it." Nathaniel avoided Snowfell whenever possible. Seeing his father depicted in stone only ever served to remind him of the life that he had been robbed of.

The two rode in silence after that, Nathaniel making it clear that he had nothing else to share. It was more than he had shared with anyone else for some years though, and the thought of his uncle rekindled fond memories as a child.

"You hear that?" Elaith called back to the group. "Running water!"

The horses sped up to round the cluster of trees that concealed the mouth of The Unmar. The ocean was narrowed for fifty miles until it formed the beginning of the river, where the group spotted the wooden ship beached across the shore. Nathaniel had a bad feeling on sighting the ship. Its design was different enough from any human ship to make it notably elvish, but something about it didn't sit right with the Graycoat.

Upon their approach, Asher jumped off his horse early, while the rest of the Graycoats continued on to the ship. Nathaniel looked back to see the ranger crouched, examining something on the ground.

"Hello?" Darius Devale cried out from atop his horse.

After several more calls, it was clear there was going to be no reply. The head Graycoat turned to his men and instructed them to search the ship before they lost all the light.

"There's no need." Asher came up behind them, pulling Hector by the reins. "Three tracks in the ground, all heading away from the ship. Two women and a man I'd say."

"Are you sure?" Darius asked, disbelieving of his skills.

"The tracks stop halfway down the shore, before veering off into the trees." Asher nodded towards the small forest that lined the south of the river.

"Why would they head into the trees?" Gorf asked through his bushy black beard. "It's safer to stay in the ship and wait, surely?"

"Not if we aren't the first ones here..." Nathaniel felt his hand instinctively rest on his sword.

"I see no tracks but our own," Gorf replied.

"The Arakesh don't leave tracks." Asher jumped back on his horse and charged into the woods without delay.

Nathaniel quickly followed, along with Elaith, while the others looked to Darius for their orders. Nathaniel didn't wait to see what he instructed but instead spurred his horse on. The ranger led the way, only slowing to inspect the ground or a broken branch. It wasn't long before the sound of clashing steel could be heard in the distance.

The other Graycoats caught up with them as the trees gave way to a small clearing, dotted with the old ruins of a forgotten temple. Their horses leaped into the open space and the warriors freed their weapons. The horses separated in an effort to avoid galloping into an ancient archway or a decaying wall.

Nathaniel's breath was taken away at the sight of the melee. Two female elves moved with incredible speed in a defensive circle around a third, lying on the ground at their feet. Eight Arakesh danced around them, probing for a weak point with their short-swords.

The assassins were a mix of men and women, each blindfolded with red cloth. Their armour comprised of dark leather that covered every limb, with padded areas around the large muscle groups. They were built for speed, agility and no lack of ferocity.

An arrow flew from Nathaniel's bow, as it had a thousand times before, only this one was cut from the air a foot away from its mark. The Arakesh moved like lightning, knocking his next two arrows aside with ease. The distraction worked perfectly for the blonde elf, who lashed out with her curved blade and opened up the assassin's chest cavity. The dark-haired elf pulled the blonde one back protectively and parried the attack from two other Arakesh.

The Graycoats charged across the clearing, swinging their swords from atop their horses. Not a single blow landed against the assassins, who either parried or dodged the predictable attack. Elaith followed Nathaniel in leaping from her horse and drawing her sword. The Graycoat suddenly felt very vulnerable with his ward by his side. He had the overwhelming urge to protect Elaith, who he knew was no match for this foe.

"Stay close!" Nathaniel instructed her, moments before the first Arakesh turned on him with short-swords slashing. Panic set in as he was pushed away from Elaith by the assassin's pressing attack. His ward tried to help him, but received an immediate kick to the gut by another Arakesh, forcing her to the ground.

Nathaniel couldn't get to her.

The Graycoat dodged and ducked, doing his best to meet every blow with his sword and counter-attack. The assassin was ready for his every move, knocking aside his sword and lashing out with every part of his body. Glimpses of Elaith showed her to be in greater peril than himself, as her attacker bore down on her with both swords.

"Elaith!" There was nothing he could do.

A familiar green cloak cut between Nathaniel and Elaith and Asher rammed himself into the girl's attacker. The assassin was thrown to the ground by the surprise attack and dropped both of his swords in the process. The ranger never stopped, continuing his attack with an arcing swing of his sword that came down to decapitate the Arakesh, spraying blood across the stone wall.

Nathaniel's relief was short-lived when his own attacker flipped in the air and kicked him across the face, putting him on the floor at the assassin's mercy. The whistle of a sword was all Nathaniel heard before the clash of metal over his head.

An exquisite blade was held over him, keeping the assassin's swords at bay. Standing by his head was the most beautiful woman he had ever seen, with flowing blonde hair and bright green eyes.

The elf flicked her wrist, causing her sword to spin and send the assassin's weapons flying into the air. Nathaniel didn't hesitate to kick the Arakesh in the knee, forcing the man's leg to snap back and his whole body to collapse on top of the Graycoat. He clamped his hands around the assassin's jaw and head and snapped his neck.

The elf's eyes met his for an instant, but there was no time for thanks.

"Get up!" Asher shouted in his direction.

By the time Nathaniel picked himself up, Asher had back-handed another assassin with the spiked pommel of his sword. The blow whipped the Arakesh's head around and the spikes tore up her skin, caving her skull in.

Together, two of the Graycoats managed to kill an assassin, but their own deaths were inevitable against the other Arakesh. Looking around, Nathaniel could see three other Graycoats, Gorf amongst them, lying still on the ground with blood pooling around them.

Darius was holding his own but had sustained several cuts across his body and a deep gash across his left arm.

The dark-haired female elf cut down another assassin with her sword and expelled a fireball from her palm, taking down a second and slamming them into a tree. The beautiful blonde elf continued to dance around the prone elf on the ground, keeping the Arakesh's deadly blows from landing.

Nathaniel charged and jumped, sword first, into the nearest Arakesh. Before his second attack landed, Elaith came to join him with her own sword swinging. The three fought across the clearing, kicking up leaves and dirt.

The assassin ducked Nathaniel's sword and used a sweeping kick to knock Elaith off her feet. Infuriated, Nathaniel doubled his efforts and used every technique he had ever been taught to drive his sword home.

They were soon fighting by the burning body of the recently killed assassin when Nathaniel had an idea. He retrieved the small pouch from his belt and threw it onto the flaming body. The resounding crack was loud, even for his human hearing, but it had the desired effect on the Arakesh, who had dropped his swords to cover his ears.

The Graycoat spun on the spot, bringing his sword around in a devastating swipe that cut the assassin from shoulder to waist.

The last Arakesh had put Darius Devale on his back, but failed to kill him when Asher dived into the fray. The two fought as mirrored images of the other. They knew each other's fighting style and used every part of their body as a weapon to give them an advantage.

The elves stayed back, helping the newly conscious male elf to his feet.

It was quite the sight to see the ranger in a fight. He was every bit as furious as the assassin, though he had to move quicker in order to avoid both blades.

A rapid counter-attack by the Arakesh led to Asher receiving a back-handed slash across his right arm. Nathaniel caught his breath and ran across the clearing to help the ranger.

They clumsily battled the assassin together, their fighting styles not attuned to one another. The assassin used this to his advantage, often forcing one to almost kill the other with a stray swing of the sword.

Nathaniel pressed his attack, fighting through the pain of the assassin's kicks and elbows that continued to knock him back.

Asher was able to deflect several of the Arakesh's swords away from Nathaniel, but he could do nothing when the assassin planted his boot square in the Graycoat's chest. Nathaniel felt his chest compress, forcing the air from his lungs as he was thrown to the ground.

Down in the dirt, it took a moment to gain his senses back. He heard a sword hit the floor somewhere nearby and the melee suddenly stopped, with a pained grunt from the ranger. Nathaniel looked up to see the Arakesh falling to his knees, a large broadsword impaled through his gut.

"I'm getting slow..." Asher staggered back and dropped to one knee. He had a knife protruding from his left shoulder, buried to the hilt. In one swift motion, the ranger pulled the dagger free and threw it into the woods.

The moon had replaced the sun now, casting the clearing in a pale light. Asher placed his palm over the wound on his shoulder, his silver ring glistening with its curious black gem.

Nathaniel had noticed the ranger dwell on his ring when asked too many questions.

To his surprise, Nathaniel was helped up by Darius, who kept his eyes on the elves. Elaith joined his side, as the male elf rose to his feet. He was taller than the women and dressed in a long black robe, embroidered with silver along its edges that sparkled in the light. He removed a small dart from his neck and dropped it to the ground in disgust.

"If this is the reception we receive upon Illian's shores, I can only imagine what awaits us in Velia." The male elf looked over the humans with dissatisfaction.

Nathaniel struggled to tear his eyes away from the blonde elf, but he felt concern for Asher. Before he could turn to help the ranger, however, Asher appeared at his side as if no injury had been inflicted. The Graycoat couldn't keep the look of surprise off his face. There was blood on the ranger's armour but the blood loss had been staunched miraculously. The ranger refused to meet his eye and Nathaniel realised it was no miracle, but magic.

"Just a scratch." Asher shrugged off the Graycoat's curious looks.

"My lord and ladies." Darius bowed to the elves. "I am Darius Devale of West Fellion. King Rengar sent us to..." He looked around at his dead men and lost his words for a moment. "We have been sent to escort you to Velia and give our lives for you if we must." Darius spread his arm to encompass his fallen comrades.

"Who were these people?" the dark-haired female asked, looking at the Arakesh.

"Assassins sent to stop you from reaching Velia," Darius replied. "Enemies of King Rengar, no doubt, but I assure you a full investigation is being conducted."

The male elf stepped forward. "I should think—"

"Thank you." The blonde elf silenced them all. Nathaniel was enchanted by her voice just as much as her beauty. The elf's gaze lingered on him before looking to Asher with more concern. "You are wounded?"

Asher rolled his left shoulder, allowing his cloak to fall over the wound. "I fare better than most, my Lady." The ranger pulled his broadsword free of the assassin's gut.

"Who are you?" the blonde elf asked.

"My name is Asher. I am a ranger in these lands."

"I am not familiar with rangers," she replied.

"He is an Outlander," the male elf spoke up. "I have seen tattoos like the one on his face before. Why has the king sent an Outlander and the followers of Tyberius Gray to receive us?"

"When the king discovered that there was a plot to assassinate you, he didn't want to announce your arrival by sending soldiers bearing his sigil," Darius explained. "The Outlander has experience with their kind, that is all. This is Nathaniel Galfrey, a fellow Graycoat and his ward, Elaith Nevandar."

"I am Princess Reyna Sevari. This is my mentor and protector, Faylen Haladör and my advisor, Mörygan Mörgö."

Nathaniel couldn't take his eyes off her. She didn't look like a princess to him, with her trousers, tall boots and leather jacket that fell over the back of her knees. The sword at her side and bow slung over her back were enough to distinguish her from any human princess, besides the clothes.

"It's an honour to..." Nathaniel glimpsed something moving in the shadows, beyond the elves.

The snapping of twigs underfoot was all that preceded the magical force that slammed into both the elves and humans.

For the third time that day, Nathaniel was thrown off his feet and onto the ground. He groaned as Elaith landed on top of him, though he felt Darius fly by his shoulder and skid across the dirt and fallen leaves. Luckily they all missed being flung into any of the broken stone walls.

The sound of Reyna's cry sent a bolt of fear through the Graycoat, but he couldn't see the princess over Elaith.

All he could see was Asher.

The ranger had defiantly remained standing in the same spot, his cloak swept out behind him in the maelstrom. Asher went for his sword but paused, stunned by the figure that slunk from between the trees, as if he were an extension of the shadows.

Nathaniel rolled Elaith's moaning form off his legs and tried to stand against the pain that shot through his back.

The dark figure slowly approached Asher, until he was clear to see in the moonlight. Only his eyes could be seen within the shadowy hood and the black cloth that covered his mouth and nose. The cloak billowed in the breeze and blended into the darkness behind him as if he was permanently tethered to the abyss.

Dull armour protected his body and forearms, with golden script etched along its edges and across his chest. It was hard to miss the menacing sword that hung from his belt: a guardless, two-handed hilt, crowned with a diamond crystal the size of a thumb. Even in the shadow of his hood, it was clear to see that the man had the palest skin against deep blue eyes. Nathaniel was sure he could see the faintest sparkle of light behind those eyes.

The hooded figure stopped and tilted his head at the sight of the unmoving ranger. Nathaniel looked from one to the other, sharing the mysterious man's curiosity. Asher let go of the broadsword's hilt and retrieved the rune sword from his back. The blade came to life in the light, as the silvyr responded to the moon's touch.

"Who are you to stand against me?" The intruder's voice was an inhuman rasp.

Asher was a man of few words...

The ranger charged the gap between them and jumped at the last second with his sword held back and high.

The Hood was fast. He intercepted Asher's sword arm before the blade could touch him and spun the ranger around with his own momentum. Asher collided with a tree before crumpling to the ground, his sword still tight in his unyielding grip.

The ranger lashed out, leaping to his feet with the rune sword coming up under The Hood's jaw. Again he proved too fast and side-stepped the attack, whipping an arm out under Asher's sword arm and catching him in the jaw.

The ranger staggered back and spat blood, before spinning on his opponent and using his cloak to hide the angle of his sword. It made no difference to The Hood, who deflected the blade with the armour on his bracer. The shadowy figure followed his parry with five blows to Asher's body in rapid succession. Against the odds, Asher remained on his feet, if a little dazed. The Hood easily pushed the ranger's next attack aside and held onto his wrist.

What happened next was more confusing.

The Hood pushed his hand out, palm open, and appeared to exert some form of energy that forced Asher's cloak out behind him, as well as all the leaves and branches on the ground. The Hood's eyes widened in shock as Asher remained still, with a cocky grin on his face.

"Guess you're a slow learner..." Asher followed his comment up with a swift punch to The Hood's face and a kick to his gut, forcing the man back to the trees. The ranger shot out his arm with an open palm and produced a ball of molten fire that exploded forth from his hand. The Hood was instantly taken off his feet by the impact of the spell and launched into the woods.

Beyond all belief, the hooded man picked himself up and ran off into the darkness, until the flames that consumed his body could no longer be seen through the ruins and trees.

"What the hell was that?" Elaith hadn't even bothered to wipe the dirt off her clothes as she rose to her feet.

"Was that an Arakesh?" Darius gripped his shoulder and grimaced.

"No, that was something else..." Asher gave Nathaniel a look that suggested he really had no idea.

As one, they all turned to the elves who looked immaculate, despite having been thrown to the ground not moments ago.

Nathaniel caught Reyna looking at him, but she quickly looked away to observe Asher, who was slowly manipulating his wounded jaw.

Faylen stared into the darkened wood and turned to Mörygan with a questioning expression.

The tall elf ignored Faylen. "Clearly humans have delved too deep within the realm of magic. Though, you I find curious, Outlander." Mörygan moved past Faylen and the princess. "How is it you were able to withstand such power, and without the use of a wand no less?"

Asher ignored the elf's interest and began to rummage through the dead assassins for anything useful. "I'm being paid to get you from one place to another, unharmed preferably. So I suggest we gather whatever supplies we need and move on, immediately."

"These men deserve to be buried!" Darius exclaimed, gesturing to his Graycoats.

"Perhaps you didn't see the man on fire that ran off into the woods." Asher gave Darius a condescending look. "I don't know what we're dealing with here, but it doesn't die easily." Asher examined his sword as if there was something wrong with it. "If he doesn't return with reinforcements, *they* certainly will." The ranger pointed at the dead assassins. "They can never be seen to fail; they always close a contract, no matter how many of them die in the process. Today we fought eight and lost seven of ours. Tomorrow, it might be twenty and I promise you we won't survive that."

Darius looked away, unable to conjure an argument against the ranger's logic. "So what do you suggest, *Ranger?*"

Asher looked around, exhausted. "You can find the horses for a start."

CHAPTER 15
THE ELDER BOOK

"**I** said I'm sorry, Abbey." Gideon had lost count of his apologies. They walked down the stone corridors of Korkanath's east wing, having left Master Vorn's office.

Abigail was yet to look at him. "You couldn't help yourself, could you? Master Vorn told you days ago to leave the teaching to the teachers! Now we're both in trouble and I'm losing my afternoon. I was supposed to have the rest of the day off after my morning classes. We'll be lucky if we finish before midnight with all of Korkanath's security measures!"

"He's punishing you to punish me—"

"I am aware of that, Gideon. Sometimes being friends with you can be a real pain. You could have just carried on walking and enjoyed the brief break from the rain, but no, you had to stop and help the fourth years climb that stupid tree."

An old red oak tree stood in the centre of the grassy courtyard in the middle of Korkanath's grounds. The courtyard was often dominated by the students in their breaks, who craved the fresh air over the musty lecture rooms. Gideon had intended to cross the courtyard, while the rain had stopped, and take a shortcut back to his dorm until he came across the fourth years determined to reach the top of the red oak.

"They were only a few years away from learning the spell anyway. I was just—"

"Showing off is what you were doing." Abigail moved aside as a class of sixth years rounded the corner like a herd of animals. "What were you thinking teaching fourth years to shift the pull of gravity? We've finished nearly ten years at this school and we're still novices in that spell. How could you think they would master it in a few minutes?"

"They did pretty well; they walked halfway up the tree before—"

"Before apprentice Huckerby fell and broke his arm in two places!" Abigail finally looked at him with a gaze that could pierce dragons' hide.

Gideon had a plethora of counter-arguments, but he replied with the only one that would work. "Sorry..."

They descended the winding staircase, in the north-east tower of the campus, and knocked on the wide-set door. It creaked with age and opened slowly of its own accord, revealing a chamber devoid of any occupants. With no windows, the room was dimly lit by candles placed around the room, leaving the corners in shadow.

Gideon and Abigail cautiously entered the chamber, where they were pleasantly surprised by the aroma of vanilla. The room was lined with bookcases, lined with thick books and bound scrolls. To their right was a long table filled with alchemy equipment and colourful formulas in glass vials.

"So you're the unlucky pair that incurred the wrath of Master Vorn."

The surprising voice came from the other side of the room, where there was another door, secured in place by thick bolts. The man standing in front of it was tall with a bald head and finely-trimmed white hair around the back and sides. His blue robes denoted his rank as an archmage and a member of Korkanath's council.

He approached the pair with a limp, supported by a well-crafted staff, similar to Gideon's.

"Master Tibit..." Abigail expressed the same confusion as Gideon. "I thought the council had left for Velia, with the Magikar."

"Alas, my duties to this school keep me here." His voice was that of an educated man. "As you know, I am responsible for Korkanath's fortification and protection. Once a month these measures require testing to ensure they're up to the task. However, my condition makes for hard work when touring the length and breadth of such a large campus. Hence the reason for your being here, besides the incident with apprentice Huckerby."

Gideon brought his own staff to stand by his side and tried to subtly compare the two. Master Tibit's was a few inches taller and housed a ring of small crystals around the tip of the staff, which branched out like the roots of a tree.

"Isn't Malliath protection enough, Master?" Gideon asked.

A coy smile crept across Master Tibit's face. "Have you ever seen our great protector, Mr Thorn?" With a shake of the head from both apprentices, the master turned to the bolted door behind him. "Perhaps you should learn about our first line of defence before we look to internal matters."

Master Tibit hobbled to the bolted door and knocked his staff against the wood. The heavy iron bolts shot out of their locks and the door creaked open into another steep stairwell. At its base was a circular chamber with an arching ceiling. The room had a foul, musty smell that Gideon had never come across before.

The master showed them in and made his way around the edge of the room, being careful to avoid the large hole in the stone floor. Once inside, he put his finger to his lips and signalled them to remain silent and hold their questions. After a moment of silence, both Gideon and Abigail looked to one another in astonishment.

The deep heavy breathing of what had to be a giant creature could be heard resonating through the caves below their feet.

"Do you know how he came to be this island's protector?" Master Tibit asked.

"It was his punishment for starting the war against humans," Abigail replied.

"Indeed, Miss Rose," Master Tibit continued. "When the great Garganafan died at the end of the elven Dark War, Malliath took his place as the dragons' patriarch. His reason for starting the war with our kind is unknown since he never communicated with another soul after The Lifeless Isles were decimated. But, many speculated that Malliath blamed us for the departure of the elves.

"When they were beaten, it was King Tion's son who reigned over all of Illian. He decreed that the dragon's punishment should be to live, but only those with knowledge of magic could harness such a creature. So, Malliath's scales were branded in the ancient script and bound to our spells for as long as they mark him. He cannot travel beyond ten miles of the island and he is forbidden from killing humans... unless it interferes with his primary spell."

"What's his primary spell?" Abigail's expression of disgust hadn't changed since Master Tibit used the word *branded*.

"Anyone who sets foot on Korkanath, uninvited by one of its occupants, is deemed an intruder. Malliath's binding magic immediately alerts him to their presence. He is allowed to deal with them as he sees fit." Master Tibit ushered them out of the chamber and back up to his laboratory. "Now do you see why other measures are required besides Malliath the voiceless?"

"Not really."

Master Tibit rolled his eyes. "What if an intruder used a portal or managed to reach the heart of the dormitories or the old hall before Malliath found them. His spell would require him to tear the walls of this school apart until he killed them. I must ensure that intruders never get that far. I have enchantments to stop portals from opening as well as conjuring circles hidden throughout the grounds to bring forth all kinds of unnatural beasts."

"Portals?" Abigail stopped examining the spine of a book. "Isn't that a waste of time, Master? That form of magic has never been understood."

"Don't tell me Master Rollo has stopped teaching you about Samuel Higgins? I shall have to stop by his office later. Samuel Higgins was an apprentice of this school about three hundred years ago. He had been reading some of the older scrolls on how the elves had the power to open portals and traverse great distances in a single step.

"Before he reached twenty and became a fully fledged caster, as you soon will, he began experimenting with teleportation. He became the first recorded human to open and pass through a portal. Samuel had planned his final experiment to give him a grand entrance to his graduation. However, only a certain percentage of the young mage made it to the intended destination. The rest of him was never found..." Master Tibit didn't dwell on the terrible ending to Mr Higgins's experiment. "So you see, he proved that it is possible for humans to do so, even if his calculations were wrong."

"So where do we come into this, Master?" Gideon had the sudden urge to find everything ever written about teleportation.

"I'm going to teach you a simple spell, and the two of you are going to test each of the protective enchantments around Korkanath. I have a map here somewhere..."

Master Tibit rummaged through a small chest in the corner of the chamber, where Gideon noticed a short stand with a book resting on top, protected by a glass box.

"Ah, I see you've noticed the Elder Book." The master appeared to take extra care in keeping his fingers from touching the glass. "It belonged to the mages of King Tion's court. Within its pages are the spells used to bind Malliath... among other things."

"Forgive me, Master," Abigail began, "but why is something so, well... dangerous, kept in the corner of your study? Should it not be guarded?"

Master Tibit chuckled to himself. "I would like to see anyone try and get their *hands* on this book, let alone read its pages."

Gideon looked upon the simple book stand and its glass covering with new wonder. A sense of morbid curiosity overcame the young mage, as he considered the possible horrors that could be unleashed by the protective wards set over the book.

Master Tibit hesitated before he continued. "There was an assault on our vaults within Stowhold…"

Gideon and Abigail couldn't hide their shock. The vaults of Stowhold were the only places more secure than Korkanath.

"Do not be alarmed; the break-in was thwarted by Stowhold's security measures, as expected. However, the would-be-thieves succeeded in penetrating the vaults farther than anyone before. It was decided that a few of the school's more, delicate possessions, should be temporarily kept under our watchful eye, just until the investigation is completed, that is." The master continued to potter with things on his table as if to downplay his statement. "Come now. For that spell…"

The sun had set before Abigail finally forgave Gideon. They had checked almost all of the places on Master Tibit's map and tested the strength of the enchantments. A mispronunciation from Abigail almost summoned a Banshee from one of the conjuring circles, before Gideon quickly corrected the spell.

"My feet are *killing* me," Gideon complained. "I can see why Master Tibit always gets students to do this. It would take him days with that leg of his."

"I don't see why he doesn't just have it healed." Abigail dropped like a stone onto the nearest bench. "It's like he enjoys having a limp."

"When Master Graf took me to The Vrost Mountains a couple of years ago, he had a little too much wine one night and told me a few things he shouldn't. Apparently, Master Tibit was bitten by a Basilisk when he took a student out on their field trip. This was before you and I even came to Korkanath. There's no cure for Basilisk venom. He's lucky to have escaped with a bad leg. It's also why he never leaves the campus, so Master Graf says." The rain picked up again, forcing the two to seek shelter under the walkway.

"Come on, we shouldn't be gossiping." Abigail retrieved her wand, ready for the next stop on the map. "I would very much like to have some dinner and a good night's sleep before the next sun rises."

"Just think, Abbey." Gideon had his wistful voice on again. "In a few months we get to decide what we do and when we do it..."

"I think the realities of this world, beyond these walls, will provide quite the shock," Abigail replied with an air of superiority. "You realise everyone else in our year has already sent out their applications for positions in several courts across Illian. You wait until we need to pay for our first meal or a roof over our head..."

"Come on, Abbey!" Gideon wouldn't hear it. "With our fine skills in the art of magic, what could possibly stand in our way?"

"Oh, I don't know - fitting your head through the door on our way out?"

CHAPTER 16

A STEEP PRICE

Thunder rolled across the night sky as if the gods themselves ran over the clouds. Lightning reigned over Dragorn, striking the high towers and spires that decorated the cityscape.

Galanör could taste the water in the atmosphere and knew the rain was only minutes away. He crouched over the edge of the high building, overlooking the Trigorn brothel across the street. As always, he felt comfortable at such heights, surveying the land around him from a safe distance. His elven eyes and ears made such a lofty vantage an easy way to spy on the less evolved humans.

The elf leaned out, holding onto a rail, as he tried to get a better look down the alley, adjacent to the brothel. The wooden cart Ailas had prepared remained off to the side, undisturbed in the alley. Eliön had managed to sneak through the Trigorn's building the previous day, using magic to conceal himself. His report had detailed the structure within.

Underneath the brothel was an extensive bath house reserved for the clients with larger accounts in Stowhold. The rooms were lavishly decorated with whores of both sexes throughout, each with a guard positioned at the door.

"We're ready," Adamar said from behind him.

Galanör took one last look at the brothel. He was at the turning point. Humans had been killed to achieve their goals so far but, after tonight, the elf knew innocent blood would have been spilled on his command. There would be no going back after this. He would be a fool to believe the children would survive whatever horrors the Mer-folk had in store for them.

His conscience fought with itself for a second before he stood and faced the group, each of them with a sword at their hip and hooded cloaks flapping in the growing wind.

The part of him that desperately wanted to walk away from this told him that he could and everything would be ok, but the faces of his comrades, ready and eager for what lay ahead, reminded him otherwise. Galanör had made an oath to his king and a promise to his own father. There could be no failure.

"You all know what to do." The group gave a single nod. "I will meet you on the shore." All but Lyra dashed off the edge of the building to reach their entry points.

"Be safe..." Lyra's words were almost a whisper, as she leaped from the building.

Galanör turned back to the edge, looking down on the street filled with tavern stragglers and beggars. He didn't see any of his group, but he knew Adamar, Eliön and Ailas would already be moving through the sewers under the brothel, where they would come up within the bathhouse where the children were kept.

Naiveen and Lyra would be working their way around the block to come up behind the brothel where they would climb to the third floor. Eliön had reported that the best-looking women were kept there.

Now for his part.

Galanör moved to the side of the building and stepped off, skipping from one wall to the other, quickly making his way down without a sound.

The elf strode into the road, pushing a drunken man aside and confidently approaching the three guards stationed outside the brothel. They noticed him right away, taking note especially of the fine scimitar on his hip. All three men put a hand on their own swords and eyed Galanör cautiously when he came to stand in front of them. They were clearly trying to decide whether he was a client or a threat and couldn't make up their minds whether to be welcoming or threatening.

Galanör never gave them the chance to decide.

Before a single sword could be lifted between them, the elf removed his scimitar and swiped it across the humans. The fine blade cut through each of the men, opening their throats in one smooth motion. Galanör was already stepping over the threshold when the humans hit the ground.

Blood dripped off his sword, staining the braided rugs on his stroll into the first room. The elf was met with screams when the whores and their clients caught sight of him.

A guard rounded the corner and charged at him with an axe aimed high. Galanör side-stepped the slow human and eviscerated him, spraying blood over several women. This worked to increase the pitch of their screams and create chaos. He picked up the sound of heavy feet on the floor above him. A group of armed men on the Trigorn's payroll barged into the room through a set of double-doors to his right.

"The Fenrig family send their regards!" Galanör shouted at the men.

"Fenrig scum!" they naturally replied with anger.

Galanör ran from the brothel as planned, having heard more guards approaching from under his feet and even more from the floors above.

The elf sprinted into the street but maintained a human speed so the guards could follow him. He had memorised the path that would take him to the nearest Fenrig establishment, filled with their own militia. The whole city knew the Fenrigs were at odds with the Trigorns over territory, and that their alliance was the weakest of all four ruling families.

It wasn't long before he found himself running towards the temple of Oemis, the god of the sea. The stone steps that led to the main doors were split by the ten-foot statue of the ocean god. Like all human effigies of the gods, it was wearing little clothing, exposing the god's perfect body of well-defined muscles.

Galanör knew he had to run down the alley to the temple's left and then make another left onto Button Street. The group of angry guards was close on his heel and their threats never let up.

The elf emerged from the alley and was forced to deftly flip over a passer-by leaving the temple. He heard one of the guards collide with the woman and curse, before backhanding her. The chase caught the attention of several people milling around, including a pair of city guards who changed direction, as if they hadn't seen anything.

One more corner and the Fenrig's gambling house would be in sight. Galanör thought about the others and felt confident that they had already achieved their goals. His own part in all this had ensured they met as little resistance as possible.

The elf rounded the corner at such speed he was forced to push himself off the adjacent wall to keep to the path. Two Fenrig guards were positioned outside the doors, minding their own business, when Galanör leaped from the shadows and drove both men through the door with an almighty crash. He needed to make as much commotion as possible.

Galanör stood up, leaving the injured men winded at his feet and reeling in pain from the impact.

The gambling house was scattered with round tables across the ground floor and masked with smoke from a plethora of pipes. Galanör could smell the various herbs and weeds being smoked and tried his best to inhale as little as possible to keep his mind sharp.

Some of the clients moved away from the elf, while others remained in their seats, unwilling to part with their winnings.

"The Trigorns rule this city!" Galanör yelled at the guards rushing at him from the other end of the casino.

It all came together beautifully, as the Trigorns' men burst through the broken door at the same moment the Fenrig's men reached Galanör. The two winded guards were trampled when both groups slammed into each other with their swords and axes raised.

Galanör nimbly jumped from one table to another, cutting down a pair of guards in his way. He was quick to reach the back of the casino, where he had already scouted ahead the previous day, and knew there to be a back-door he could disappear through.

Looking back, the casino had erupted into bloodshed, the men ripping each other to shreds for slights neither had committed.

After entering the alley outside, Galanör climbed the nearest building, using the balconies and tight spaces to push himself up. He found his way to the roof before the rain started. In the flashes of lightning, he could make out the twin turrets that sat either side of the northern main-gate, half a mile away.

The elf wasted no time, leaping from roof to roof, as he had in the great forests around Elandril. The run was simply fun for Galanör, who enjoyed the freedom of using his body's natural skills. Having avoided the winding streets, the elf made it to the farmland in front of the gate in no time.

Dropping to street level once more, he pulled over his hood and walked past the city guard. The sights and smells of the horrid city would soon be a memory he would do his best to forget. He didn't even bother to look back.

After an hour of traversing the shoreline, Galanör came across the abandoned cart in the sand, the tarpaulin ripped off. Beyond the rocks, he could hear familiar voices amidst the rhythmic splashing of the waves.

The group of elves stood at the base of the cave that ran under Dragorn, each holding a different hostage. They were up to their thighs in water with the three children standing up to their shoulders in icy cold waves. Galanör tried to hide his discomfort at the sight, but Adamar appeared to take extra note of his expression.

"Stop to take in the sights?" the big elf asked.

Galanör felt his frustration rise to the surface. "Perhaps it would be a good idea if one of us remained behind, to cover our tracks." It brought him true joy to see Adamar squirm. He leaned in and whispered, "It's a long way to portal back to Ayda..."

Galanör wished he could witness such a feat. Adamar would come out somewhere in the middle of The Adean between Dragorn and Ayda, too weak to create another portal and die at the mercy of the sharks.

Eliön and Naiveen struggled to hold their female hostages, who cried out at the same time when their eyes fixed on the horror emerging beyond Galanör. The elf didn't need to turn around to know the Mer-folk had arrived. Even the elves looked on, perplexed by the wonder of the twelve sea creatures, whose torsos floated above the water. The cries of the children had no doubt summoned them so quickly.

"You have delivered what you promised, elfling." The lead Merman snaked through the water, drawing closer. As before, the waves settled in the Mer-folk's presence, leaving only the sound of the rain.

"I have," Galanör replied. "Are you prepared to uphold your end of the bargain?" He assumed it was the same Mer-man he had encountered previously but, in truth, the elf couldn't tell them apart.

"If you believe you can survive the journey, then we are prepared to take you to Korkanath."

The Mer-man flicked his head at the children and three of the Mer-folk dived for them, covering the distance with a speed even an elf would find hard to achieve. They snatched the children from the elven hands and coiled back into the dark water with barely a splash. The children's cries were instantly cut short, as they were dragged under the surface, propelled by powerful tails.

Galanör closed his eyes in hope of never recalling the sight.

Two other Mer-folk slithered forward until the water was too shallow for their tails. Galanör took a step back when the sea creatures began to spasm and wail in pain, while their skin and scales split down the middle. Their fingers shrank and the webbing disappeared, along with their pointed nails. The seaweed-like tendrils that flowed from their head changed structure and took on the appearance of long dark hair.

With a piercing scream from both, their scaled tails split open completely and two slimy, human legs fell out and dropped into the water. The giant tails flopped to the side, imitating a dead fish, while the Mer-men crouched in the water, surrounded by slime and broken scales.

Galanör's wonder turned to disgust when the new men vomited into the ocean and tried to stand on wobbly legs.

Their perfect forms could easily have doubled as models for statues of the gods. On shaky legs, the new humans approached the women, who struggled and cried, unsure of their fate. The new men stood in front of a woman each and stared deeply into their eyes.

Galanör watched with fascination, as the women immediately calmed down and stopped panicking. Eliön and Naiveen released them and moved away, allowing the naked Mer-men to take the women by the hand and silently lead them into the cave under Dragorn. After a few moments, their movement could no longer be heard in the water and they were hidden in shadow.

"Are you ready?" the snaking Mer-man asked.

The elf turned to his group, who were still trying to pierce the cave's abyss and witness the creation of a hybrid.

Galanör cleared his throat. "It's nothing you haven't seen before." With their attention back on him, he continued, "Swallow the Maktacha." They all removed a small ball of sticky green weeds that Lyra had been preparing and enchanting for several days.

They all shared the same sour expression before the ball dropped into their stomach and the magic began to work. Galanör felt a wave of nausea rise up into his throat, only for it to change into a burning sensation across his neck. The pain broke his concentration and with it the human image he had been wearing for over a week. His hair reverted back to its natural, straight, brown gloss and the stubble on his face disappeared, leaving behind a smooth angular jaw. Even his eyes reverted back to their vibrant shade of blue.

When the burning stopped, his skin felt tight and stiff around the joints. Breathing the sea air was a laboured exercise that made Galanör feel light-headed and dizzy. Lyra and the others came up behind him, so they were up to their waists in water. From the look of them, they too were struggling to breathe the air.

Galanör turned to his companions with his last breath. "Let's free a dragon..."

In the same way the children had been snatched, all six elves were yanked off their feet and plunged into the icy depths of The Adean.

CHAPTER 17
AN INTIMATION OF HOPE

Reyna felt uncomfortable riding a horse that hadn't been intended for her. The saddle wasn't right for her form and the horse wasn't used to her instructions. Every time she tried to take in the new landscape, the horse would come to an abrupt stop.

Thankfully, they had slowed down after a night and day of galloping and the rest of the group slowly trotted by, while Reyna did everything she could to encourage the horse. As an elf, she knew there was an eternal connection between her kind and every creature in Verda, but the human-bred horse was certainly putting that legend to the test.

"Argh! Come on." The horse bent down to nibble on the grass.

"He's used to a harder hand." The handsome Graycoat came up on her side.

Reyna's reply was halted by the chastising thoughts she rebuked herself with. She was the princess of all elven kind; it wasn't befitting to be attracted to a human, especially one so *filthy*. His square jaw was covered in light stubble, a new sight to Reyna, and smeared with dirt from their fight in the woods. His dark eyes were annoyingly pleasant to look at. They softened his rugged appearance, offering the knight the added touch of mystery.

At such a young age for an elf, Reyna had yet to master her exaggerated senses and urges that were commonplace for her kind. She had met several other suitors in her short life, but seeing someone so different was exciting. The feeling of anticipation intensified under his lingering gaze. Still... he was nothing more than a man.

"Come on." Nathaniel tugged hard on the horse's reins to get it moving. "Is there something on my head?" The Graycoat met Reyna's eyes and suddenly became self-conscious of his hair.

"Oh, no it's just..." Reyna was embarrassed. "I've never seen hair like that before. It's shaved so fine." The elf could feel herself going red in the face and wished she could make herself invisible, but Faylen would seriously frown on the needless use of magic. Reyna looked to her mentor who, as it happened, was already frowning at her.

Nathaniel laughed. "It's certainly different from yours." The Graycoat looked at Mörygan and Faylen. "What's it like to be back in Illian? I bet it's changed a lot in a thousand years."

"I've actually never left Ayda. I was born there." The thought made Reyna a little sad, but she didn't know why.

"Sorry. Immortality makes age hard to guess." His comment was met with an awkward silence.

Reyna had always felt uncomfortable with her young age. Living amongst a race of people with hundreds of years behind them made her feel naive and child-like, even as an adult.

"Reyna..." Faylen called from ahead.

Reyna knew when she was being summoned and not spoken to. The princess sped up, giving Nathaniel a genuine smile she often reserved for her time in The Amara when she enjoyed the freedom of running through the forest.

When she caught up with Faylen there was nothing to say - her mentor's expression was enough.

The group rode on for another hour before they came across a herd of deer, grazing beyond The Selk Road. Seeing the familiar wildlife put Reyna at ease in unknown lands, but it also made her stomach rumble.

"We should make camp soon," Asher announced, looking at the setting sun. "Give the horses a chance to rest overnight before the hard ride tomorrow."

"Perhaps we could eat...?" Elaith's eyes were fixed on the deer, her hand hovering around her bow.

"I'll come too," Reyna replied eagerly.

"No." Faylen was quick to stop her. "We are hunted in these lands, Reyna."

"I don't think the deer pose much of a threat." Reyna was already notching an arrow and struggling to manoeuvre her stubborn horse.

Faylen was about to further her protest when Asher rode up. "I'll go with them." The ranger turned to Darius Devale. "Start a fire and make a spit." The Graycoat was clearly unhappy about his instructions.

"And why should I trust her life to you, *Outlander*?" Faylen's tone was harsh.

Asher threw his cloak aside and removed a wooden object from behind his back. Reyna heard the distinct click before the object unravelled into the shape of a bow. The princess was impressed with its practicality, but it wasn't nearly as well crafted as her own.

"I'll go." Nathaniel stepped in, meeting Reyna's eyes.

The princess was quick to reply, "I need no assistance." With her horse turned to the open field, Reyna galloped away.

On her way past, Reyna shot Faylen a look that told her mentor she had chosen her words poorly with regard to the ranger. It was clear that Asher was made of stronger stuff and wouldn't be affected by Faylen's words, but she still disagreed with her harsh choice of words.

After years together, they were able to share a lot of messages and unheard words with nothing but their eyes. Faylen rolled her own and made no move to follow the princess across the field, giving Reyna the trust she desired.

The deer scattered as the three riders galloped through the field, bows ready. Elaith fired first, missing a deer by a foot and striking a tree instead. Nathaniel released his arrow next, leaning out from his horse, but found as much success as his ward.

Reyna felt like showing off.

The princess adjusted her weight atop the saddle, placing her balance on her right leg while her left foot rested on the flat of the saddle. It was an unorthodox position but easily achieved with Reyna's natural sense of balance.

She took a slow breath as she drew back on the bowstring, anchoring the arrow and settling on her target. Releasing the arrow was the most satisfying feeling she knew. The intended deer skidded to the ground with an arrow protruding from the back of its head.

"Damn it!" Elaith cursed, missing her next target. The young Graycoat notched another arrow but the herd had already retreated into the woods.

To Reyna's elven eyes, however, the deer could still be seen amidst the trees. The princess raised her bow again and brought down the final deer.

"That was an impossible shot!" Elaith looked off into the woods.

"Not for an elf." Reyna heard Faylen's voice in her mind again; *a princess should never be smug.* "I would be happy to show you some of our techniques while we're on the road."

"I'm not sure Nathaniel would be happy with that," Elaith replied quietly. "He considers himself quite the archer..."

Before Reyna could reply, Nathaniel emerged from the woods with Reyna's kill slung over his shoulder. "You're good with a bow, Princess Reyna."

"Please, just Reyna..." The Graycoat's gruff appearance continued to pull her in, calling to the baser instincts that ruled many of her kind.

Nathaniel simply nodded, clearly unsure as to how to respond to such a request from royalty. The three returned to the makeshift camp as dusk settled in, heralding the stars.

When the moon had almost crossed the vastness of the starry field above, Reyna peeked her head over Faylen's sleeping form and stole a glance at the camp's guardians. Asher and Nathaniel sat by the fire, talking to each other in hushed tones.

The princess watched the two in fascination, each so very human in their appearance and movement. The ranger was old by the look of his greying hair and white stubble, with the smallest of wrinkles spreading out from his eyes.

Nathaniel was still young, with his smooth skin and short dark hair, though his jaw was chiselled in the style of many elves. The Graycoat's dark eyes were a stark contrast to the crystal blue of the ranger's in the firelight.

"I just can't believe we're sitting amongst *actual* elves," Nathaniel whispered like an excited boy. "Isn't this a little surreal, even for you?"

"I've seen stranger things." Asher sounded as if he was telling the truth.

Reyna promised herself to ask the ranger about his extraordinary life when she next had the chance. She wanted to soak everything up while she was surrounded by the humans - to take in and remember as much as she could about them and their various cultures before... The thought that came next disturbed Reyna.

"I must admit, they're not exactly what I imagined," Nathaniel continued.

"Forget everything you were ever taught about the elves," Asher warned. "They're not the people you heard about as a child or read about in books. Long gone are the days of singing to the trees to make the forests grow, or devoting themselves to the arts and music. We made them *hard*.

"They're faster than us, stronger, more intelligent and they can wield magic in a way that makes us look like children. They appear to be beautiful and inviting, but they're at the apex of any food chain, even the dragons'. We're lucky they decided to leave Illian when they did."

"Why?" Asher had Nathaniel's full attention.

"Because if they decided to fight us, humanity would be just another footnote in the history books."

Nathaniel turned to look at her and the others with a different kind of curiosity in his expression. The princess ducked down and stayed very still, imitating sleep, while her ears remained highly attuned to the humans.

How could Asher know such things about the elves? For a race that she had been told was very simple, the ranger was proving to be quite the mystery.

"How can you know such things?" Nathaniel asked, disbelieving.

Reyna quite liked the way the Graycoat saw her kind.

"Nightfall has extensive libraries. The knowledge the Arakesh have built over the millennia would dwarf even the archives of Korkanath."

Nightfall... Reyna had heard about the mysterious guild of assassins during their preparations. What was Asher's connection?

The princess dared to steal another glimpse over Faylen's sleeping form. Something about the old ranger didn't sit right with her.

The sound of thunder rumbling overhead accompanied the change in pressure around the elf. The storm was growing.

"We'll need to leave before dawn if we're to carry on through this storm." Asher and Nathaniel began to move, but Reyna kept her head down and pretended to be asleep. "We should wake the others and make our way."

"How do you wake a princess?" Nathaniel asked.

"I wouldn't worry about it," Asher replied coolly. "She's been awake for a while."

Even in the dead-cold of night, Reyna's face still managed to blush.

CHAPTER 18
THE HAND OF VALANIS

Deep within the thick rock, hidden in the canyons of The Arid Lands' endless deserts, reality was ripped apart for a fraction of a second, ushering in one of the oldest creatures in all of Illian.

Thallan Tassariön stumbled into the dimly lit room, carved out of the rust-red rock that made up the entire valley. His dark armour and cloak had stopped smouldering, but his pale flesh was still healing from the fire, cast by the mysterious ranger. In order to traverse five hundred miles with a single portal, Thallan had been forced to sacrifice more magic instead of healing his burns.

The elf was thankful for the depth of the cave and the cool air that blew through the open wooden door. The corridor beyond was lined with torches, illuminating its incredible length. The secret room in which he found himself was empty, with the exception of the fire-pit in the centre which cast shadows amongst the arches lining the chamber. The smoke drifted high, disappearing through small holes, bored into the rock.

Thallan thumbed the diamond crystal fixed into the hilt of his sword. He called on the magic reserves stored within to return him to full health but even the great sword had been depleted with the massive jump and would require meditation to fill it up.

For now, he would have to heal slowly and endure the pain. It was no matter; Thallan's master had taught him what real pain was centuries ago, in the depths of Vengora. With the help of the gods, Valanis had conquered pain and passed on the lessons to his chief disciples. The elf could draw on the pain and use it to fuel his passion and complete the master's work.

With one hand, Thallan removed the mask that covered his mouth and nose and pulled back his hood. Using delicate fingers, the elf stroked his bald head, feeling the severity of the burns that disrupted the flow of ancient glyphs, tattooed across his scalp. When the skin healed, the tattoos would be replaced as perfectly as his pale skin.

It had been a long time since Thallan had been on the wrong end of a fight. How could a simple ranger not only stand against his power but actually repel him? The elf relived the encounter in his mind and saw the ageing human produce the fireball without uttering a word. Who was he?

"You're late." The deep voice came from the shadows, filling the room with a power that Thallan was all too aware could rival his own.

"How can I be late, Alidyr, if the meeting doesn't start until I arrive?" Thallan met Alidyr's defiant expression with a stony gaze of his own.

Alidyr stepped out of the shadows, sweeping his long white robes behind him, to reveal the magnificent twin short-swords that hung on his waist. The tall elf circled the fire-pit with his hands behind his back, the light reflecting in his deep blue eyes. It was the only feature they shared, Thallan thought. The power bestowed on them by Valanis had altered their appearance, enriching their eyes with an unattainable blue. Unlike the rest of the Hand of Valanis, Alidyr kept his hair long to hide the ancient script.

Three flashes of light momentarily blinded the two elves and the smell of sulphur filled their noses. After a hard blink, Thallan looked over the three shadowy figures of his oldest companions, though rivals would be a better word. All three wore the same black armour and hooded cloak, with a mask covering their mouth and nose. Each was in possession of the gifted weapon, granted to them by Valanis.

"Brothers, sister..." Thallan greeted them with a nod, turning his head to hide his burns in the shadows.

Alidyr simply came to a stop in front of the wooden door, clasping his hands inside the sleeves of his robes.

"You are injured..." Samandriel Zathya stepped towards Thallan, her own deep, blue eyes scanning his burnt attire.

"He failed." Alidyr's flat tone ignited a fire inside Thallan.

"Perhaps you should train your assassins to a better *standard.*" Thallan met the eyes of all four, daring any to challenge him as openly as Alidyr had.

"What happened?" Nakir Galvörd gripped the deadly whip coiled at his waist, each of its tendrils capable of cracking stone.

Thallan thought of the best way to convey his failure without making himself sound weak. "The Arakesh couldn't even defeat the Graycoats." The injured elf scowled at Alidyr. "The princess still lives, and is now being escorted to Velia by the survivors and..." He hesitated, unsure how to describe the other human.

"What is it?" Adellum Bövö's rough voice cut through the crackling of the fire. His mask and cloak concealed the scar that marred his throat, a souvenir from the siege of Elethiah, a thousand years ago.

"There was another," Thallan continued. "A human ranger stood unaffected by my power." The elf detected the slightest hint of curious movement from Alidyr. "He commanded magic as if he were an elf, without a wand or staff."

"Impossible," Adellum asserted.

Samandriel shifted her double-ended spear to one side. "My sources in Velia tell me King Rengar has hired an Outlander to travel with the Graycoats. There is only one Outlander I know of who lives as a ranger."

The new information caused all eyes to fall on Alidyr. If this ranger really was the traitorous Arakesh, then it would only serve to highlight more of Alidyr's failings.

"You're awfully quiet, Alidyr." Thallan moved closer to the fire-pit. "Wasn't there an assassin under your tutelage who also happened to be an Outlander? The very same Outlander who fled the order, I believe."

Even under the scrutiny, Alidyr's expression remained passive. "Asher never showed any talent for magic. He preferred to be up close when he took a life."

"A deception, perhaps?" Nakir offered. "To hide his real skill."

"As a human, he shouldn't even have that skill," Adellum countered, his eyes still on Alidyr. "No human has ever commanded magic as we have. They're too primitive."

"He was Nasta Nal-Aket's pet-project, as I recall," Alidyr added, casually.

Thallan could see through the elf. Alidyr was trying to make it appear as if the ranger was of no concern, and certainly with no ties to him. He was trying to make Thallan look weak, but it wouldn't work. Alidyr had lost his place as head of the Hand and it would never revert.

"Then it seems, Alidyr, that you are in the perfect position to unravel the mystery of this... Asher. You are to use your role within Nightfall to investigate this man, and discover how he is able to resist the power of Valanis." Thallan looked in the direction of the corridor behind Alidyr. The secret room in which they resided had been constructed centuries ago as an annexe to the rest of Nightfall.

"As you wish..." Alidyr bowed, in what Thallan felt was mock-respect.

"The ranger is a side-note." Samandriel cut through the tension. "What of the Darkakin?"

"Arrangements have been made," Alidyr replied. "The Goddess is amassing her people from across the south. They are preparing for war."

Nakir laughed. "Only a human would have the arrogance to grant themselves such a title."

"The Darkakin will not be enough if Ayda comes to the aid of Illian," Adellum pointed out. "Our cousins must be taken out of the picture. Thallan, allow me to hunt the princess. My bow never misses."

"Our strike must be surgical." Thallan rested a hand on Adellum's shoulder. "I fear your methods would reveal our existence; the master would not want that yet. The Lord of Elves has no desire to help the world of man, and a war between the two lands will weaken them *both*. His daughter is already here to begin their own invasion."

"Then why is it essential that the princess be killed?" Nakir asked. "We are wasting resources."

Thallan responded with authority. "Killing her will anger the Lord of Elves and disrupt their long-term plans. We will force their hand and make them focus their efforts on immediate retaliation."

"What of the elves' infiltration of Korkanath?" Adellum looked to Thallan.

It appeared the entire Hand needed reassuring of his execution of the master's plans. Would they question Alidyr so much?

Thallan remained calm to show his confidence and control. "Our allies in Ayda have embedded an acolyte within the team; they have informed me that their attack on Korkanath is imminent. Their machinations on that island will only prove to serve our purpose and that of Valanis. Malliath will provide us with the natural magic required to set our master free."

"We are foolish to believe they can simply take a dragon, especially one so deeply enthralled," Samandriel added, confirming for Thallan that the group had no faith in his abilities.

"They will succeed, Samandriel." Thallan was finding it harder to contain his temper. "When Valanis is freed of his confinement, he will deliver death from the skies astride the voiceless one." Thallan couldn't help but notice the expression of doubt on Alidyr's face. "Do you have something to add?"

"You speak of returning our master to power." Alidyr remained in the doorway. "A dragon will not see to this. We should focus on our primary goal. Valanis will not be returned to full power without Paldora's Gem. He is vulnerable without it."

Thallan didn't hesitate to respond. "You led us in that quest for a millennium, earning your demotion, Alidyr. Perhaps you have a new insight as to where we should be looking?"

Alidyr took a breath, leaving the bait. "Paldora's Star will be crossing the heavens soon. For a few precious days we will be able to sense its presence."

"The master's vision will be seen to fruition by us!" Thallan spat. "This is not the time to abandon years of planning. Your business in the south is complete. Now discover the depth of this ranger's involvement and send more of your assassins to kill the princess. I don't care how many it takes." Alidyr bowed again in a way that made Thallan want to bury his sword in the miserable cur's heart. "The rest of you, return to Kaliban."

Nakir, Adellum and Samandriel disappeared as quickly as they arrived, leaving Thallan and Alidyr alone. Thallan felt his grip naturally fall onto the hilt of his sword, always anticipating Alidyr's attempts to take back control of the Hand.

"You might have Nightfall at your back, brother," Thallan began, "but you are not the *Father*. They are not your army and they will not follow you without question. Do not forget why you started the order of the Arakesh in the first place. All live to serve Valanis."

"How could I, under such wisdom and guidance?" With that, Alidyr turned and strode away, down the corridor. Thallan resisted the urge to throw a knife into his back.

CHAPTER 19

NIGHTFALL

The wall slid back into place, behind Alidyr, sealing the entrance to the Hand's meeting room. The segment of wall was adorned with a floor-to-ceiling tapestry of Kaliban, the formidable-looking fortress built into The Vengoran Mountains, in The Ice Vales. Most of its magnificent architecture was now buried under tons of rock after a thousand years without upkeep.

It was in that place of solitude that Valanis had taught Alidyr and the others the real commandments of the gods. From within its dark embrace, they had each learned to use the magic of Naius under the master's watchful eye.

With a tender hand, Alidyr caressed the canvas, as if he could will the fortress to return to its original majesty. His failure to Valanis weighed heavy on his heart. For a thousand years he had searched for Paldora's Gem, even creating the Arakesh to help him find it and generate wealth to increase his resources, but the stone was lost to all. For four decades Alidyr had paid the price and suffered under the new reign of Thallan, as head of the Hand. Thallan was determined to steer events across all of Verda to meet the master's original vision, foregoing the search for the gem. Alidyr was the only one who truly believed in Nalana's prophecy and the gem's significance.

He had to find it.

Thallan's details about his encounter with Asher had piqued Alidyr's interest. He stated that the ranger stood unaffected by the power bestowed upon them by Valanis. Alidyr had seen countless humans and elves fall under the power of that magic; there were no counterspells or wards that could keep the raw magic of Naius at bay. As a god, Naius was infallible and therefore unchallenged by anything that roamed Verda's lands.

Except...

Alidyr paced the floor of his luxurious chamber, working through his thoughts to find a logical explanation. The only thing capable of challenging the power of a god was *another* god. The powerful magic given to Valanis had been a gift from Naius, but the gem was a gift from Paldora, the goddess of the stars. The master had told them that the goddess created the gem to help Valanis control the untameable magic of Naius. Without the gem, the magic would consume Valanis and end the work of the gods.

Could Asher be in possession of Paldora's Gem? If he not only stood against Thallan but repelled him, it stood to reason that the traitor must be wielding something of great magical significance, if not the gem. Perhaps the gem had been handed down through his family's generations?

He would have answers.

Alidyr's feet echoed through the cold corridors of Nightfall. Being the most respected and feared master in the order, he took no care to hide his passage through the maze of hallways.

Travelling deeper into the hive, the sound of clashing swords from the training arena became ever more distant. Day or night, the Arakesh fought against one another to harden themselves, seeking out their own weaknesses and eradicating them, whether that be a characteristic or an individual.

The pitch-black would inspire terror and primordial fear in any other being to walk Nightfall's corridors. There wasn't a single torch or lantern outside of the individual rooms. Most feared what lurked in the dark, the monsters that took shape in the shadows of a fearful imagination.

The Arakesh thrived in the dark - they needed it to live. With the power of Valanis flowing through his veins, Alidyr had no trouble seeing in the dark and finding his way to The Cradle.

Taking greater care with his footfalls, Alidyr slipped into the darkness of the great hall via one of the balconies that lined The Cradle's top tier. Without a sound, the elf balanced himself on the balcony rail with the ease of a cat. Like so many of the Fathers and Mothers before him, Nast Nal-Aket sat cross-legged, praying at the altar of Ibilis, the god of shadows. There were no guards keeping watch over the Father since he was to appear strong at all times and require no such protection.

Alidyr had mentored and personally taught every Mother and Father who had ruled Nightfall. The elf had always taken the necessary steps to ensure he found the next replacement puppet, guiding and manipulating them in the best way to eliminate the current ruler or any competitors for the throne.

Nasta Nal-Aket had been the first to slip through Alidyr's plans and kill the elf's chosen successor, after assassinating the Mother at the time. Nasta had never shown great promise, much like his pet, Asher, who had never shown a talent for magic. For twenty years the human's rule had put Alidyr on edge, forcing the elf to make certain he still held the upper hand.

As he always did, Alidyr dropped into the chamber without a sound. He approached the Father with every element of stealth he knew, as well as some added magic to conceal him against the Father's heightened senses. In moments, he found himself within striking distance of Nasta, reaffirming the knowledge that, if he needed to, Alidyr could take the human out of the picture.

The elf genuflected. "Father..."

"Every time you sneak up on me, Alidyr, it makes me wonder why I bothered to have my eyes removed."

The Father's white, curly hair and beard, matched with the wrinkles that lined his tanned skin, gave him the appearance of an old man, fragile and weak. But Alidyr knew better; for a man in his early seventies, Nasta Nal-Aket was in peak physical condition, thanks to his daily fighting rituals with the other assassins.

With no notion of effort or pain, the old Father came to his feet in one swift motion. Shadowy craters stared back at Alidyr in the dark. The only sound from Nasta's robes falling into place.

"To what do I owe the visit, old mentor?" The Father slowly walked over to his throne at the head of The Cradle. "Do you require more ingredients for the Nightseye elixir?"

"No, Father." Alidyr came into step beside him. "I have come to regretfully report the failure of an assassination."

Nasta continued to walk at the same pace, his expression giving nothing away of the surprise he must have felt. Alidyr had hoped to keep the attempt on the princess a secret, but the death of so many Arakesh wouldn't escape the Father's attention. Feeding him a half-truth would help to keep the status quo and maintain order through the ranks.

"I wasn't aware of any active assignments." The Father's tone made it hard for Alidyr to ascertain the truth in that statement.

"I responded to a contact of my own, in Darkwell, in the north," Alidyr lied. "The request was put through the appropriate channels and I responded in the interest of the order. The infamous Graycoat, Darius Devale, was finally causing enough trouble to warrant a desire for our services. My information was that he travelled with a group of Graycoats... and a *ranger*."

Alidyr watched the Father's expression closely, as he took his seat on the angular stone throne. Word of the ranger made no difference to Nasta's passive look, and he didn't appear to detect the lies hidden within the partial truth, either.

"Continue," the Father ordered.

"From what I can gather, Devale survived by the skin of his teeth, while the other Graycoats succumbed to our forces. It was the ranger who dispatched each and every one of our assassins and lives to tell of it, besmirching our reputation." The Father remained irritatingly quiet. "The ranger had a name: Asher, an Outlander by his markings. I believe it to be the same man who abandoned our ranks over a decade ago."

Nasta's bottomless eye sockets bored into Alidyr. "Curious. If this ranger dispatched all of the Arakesh, how is it you came by such accurate information?"

The ancient elf had mastered the beating of his heart centuries ago, allowing him to fool the lie-detecting ears of the Father.

"I have spent a lifetime amassing spies across Illian, Father. For the sake of our order, I maintain a constant vigilance over the land. One of these spies watched the fight between the Graycoats and our assassins. He reported the most interesting of encounters upon sighting the ranger. Apparently, he used magic without any spells or the use of a wand..."

"Is there a question in there, Alidyr?"

"I believe Asher was something of a prodigy of yours, was he not?" Alidyr casually walked over to the small table in the corner of the hall and poured himself a cup of wine in the darkness.

The Father sighed and bowed his head on the throne. "To this day I wonder what happened to him that night." Alidyr had never seen Nasta display so much emotion - a potential weakness. "I'm sure you recall better than I that he slew one of his brothers the night he ran from his duties. I was sure for a long time that he would replace me someday."

No, he wouldn't, thought Alidyr. The elf had always, and still was, planning to replace Nasta with Ro Dosarn, a peer of Asher's.

"What I *recall*, Father, are the bodies of our brethren that began to show up after he disappeared." Alidyr inhaled the wine's aroma before sipping it, making certain it hadn't been poisoned by an over-confident assassin. "I personally saw to the retrieval of them."

"His betrayal stung me, personally. It was I who brought Asher to Nightfall as a boy and initiated his training. When he fled I sent many to hunt him down and return him to these walls."

"On the occasions that I taught Asher, there was never any indication that he knew his way around magic. He presented as a very average student in that regard..." Alidyr tailed off in hopes of Nasta offering some explanation, but the Father sat in silence. "Where, may I ask, did you find the boy?"

"In the swamps of Elethiah, just beyond the border of The Wild Moores."

Alidyr hid the surprise he felt at the sound of the elves' old capital city. That was where everything changed, not just for the elves, but also for humanity and all of Verda. His master had been defeated there by the combined magic of the dragons and the elves, ushering in the end of The Dark War and the disappearance of Paldora's Gem.

"What was he doing there, Father?" Alidyr pressed, hungry for information.

"It was *forty* years ago, Alidyr, and I am no elf. Besides, I don't see what this has to do with locating him now. I stopped actively sending the Arakesh after him years ago. Now, they are to bring him back should they come across him."

The elf returned his empty cup to the table before replying, downplaying his interest in the ranger. "He appears to be a more capable killer now than when he was an Arakesh. I suppose I'm just curious as to how he acquired such new skills, in magic no less."

Nasta placed his bejewelled hands on the armrests of the throne. "He was always a capable killer, Alidyr. His real talent was hiding that capability."

A lesson he learned from you apparently, Alidyr thought.

"Perhaps," the Father continued, "his newfound strength in magic is a skill he has been forced to learn hiding from us."

"You are right, of course, Father." Alidyr bowed, detecting restraint on Nasta's behalf.

There was more to Asher than he was willing to divulge. Such secrecy only served to fuel his interest in the ranger. "I will right this wrong and see to it that Darius Devale is eliminated, immediately. If he is to be found in the company of Asher, what instructions should I give?"

"The order stands. He is to be brought in alive, Alidyr."

"As the Father wills it..."

In the twilight before dawn, Alidyr sat cross-legged in the middle of his personal chamber, meditating. The knock at his door had been anticipated seconds earlier when the elf's keen ears had picked up the sound of soft boots.

"Enter," he replied.

There was a moment of hesitation upon entering the candle-lit room as Ro Dosarn's eyes quickly adjusted to the light and his heightened senses faded away.

The man was covered in head-to-toe black leather armour, with two short-swords strapped to his back. His short grey hair and neatly trimmed goatee were as uniform as his appearance. The only individual aspect to the assassin was the twin-braid of hair that hung from his chin. Ro's skin spoke of a hard life, with a web of lines around his eyes and a permanently furrowed brow. The scar across the bridge of his nose was the most prominent of the old wounds his face bore witness to.

Alidyr didn't know where Ro had originally hailed from and the elf didn't much care, either. The man had been chiselled into a being of war, his only purpose in life to kill and serve. Alidyr had secured his allegiance years ago, with promises of him one day killing Nasta Nal-Aket and ruling the Arakesh.

"You called for me, Master..." Ro bowed on one knee in front of Alidyr.

"The order requires blood. Will you serve?" Alidyr rose to his full height and began to circle the assassin.

"As the Father wills it," Ro responded in the only way he had been taught.

"But the Father does not will it... *I* do. I have a mission for you that will trigger a chain of events that will put you on the throne." Ro looked up, eager to hear more. "You are to travel to Velia as soon as we are finished here. There, you will track down and kill the traitor, Asher. This will unhinge the Father and give you the edge and the opportunity to strike him down. The traitor's body must be returned, however, and to me alone. I would inspect his person before you present him to the Father."

"Inspect, Master?"

"Should you be unable to bring the body back, you are to search Asher for any jewellery, specifically a black crystal. Above all else, you *must* return this item to me, even if you fail in killing him." Alidyr rested a hand on the assassin's shoulder to emphasise the point.

"I will not fail, Master. If the traitor is in possession of the jewel you seek, you will prise it from his cold dead corpse yourself."

"I would expect no less." Alidyr continued to circle the man. "I suspect you will find your target in King Rengar's palace. He will be in the company of Graycoats and three elves, but do not despair, you will have allies waiting for you in Velia."

"Elves?"

Normally, Alidyr would punish an Arakesh for asking so many questions, but confiding in Ro would only serve to convince the assassin into thinking he was valued.

"Great events are unfolding, events that will change Verda's landscape for ever. You have been chosen, Ro Dosarn, to play a pivotal role on behalf of the gods. I will tell you more before the sun rises, but first, to ensure you are up to the task of defeating these elves, I have prepared a special elixir for you..."

CHAPTER 20
FIRST IMPRESSIONS

Under the cover of the rain and strong winds, blowing between the buildings, the company of elves and humans secretly entered Velia. King Rengar's men had already cleared a passage through the streets to keep the group away from the prying eyes of the city's early risers.

The elves wore large, heavy hoods to conceal their pointed ears and keep the weather from disturbing their immaculate features.

Nathaniel had remained close to Reyna, convincing himself that he was only being diligent in his duty. In appearance, the princess looked to be a young woman of a delicate nature with an inviting smile and attractive body, but the Graycoat had seen her in battle and knew better than to judge her based on appearances.

The group was offered a glance of Direport, packed with ships and boats of every size. The port was so big it could have been a town unto itself. Nathaniel's gaze was drawn to the largest ship in the bay, with its flag waving high upon the mast in the wind. The dragon that adorned the flag was impossible to miss. Dragorn's elite had already arrived in Velia, it seemed. The Graycoat looked up at the king's palace and realised he was about to meet all the royalty in the land.

Then again, he was walking behind an elf, so meeting a few kings and queens was rather dull by comparison.

As usual, Elaith stuck to Asher like a baby cub. The ranger didn't appear to mind, however, often taking the time to impart some of his own lessons from the road on the young Graycoat.

Darius Devale shot him a look from under his hood, a silent order in his eyes: *be ready*.

Nathaniel scanned the area, checking the alleyways and windows for any sign of his fellow Graycoats. As soon as the elves were safely inside the palace, he knew they would pounce on the ranger and take him to West Fellion. He couldn't allow that. Could he?

The streets remained empty with only the occasional door opening, whereupon the city guards would quickly force the occupants back inside. Nathaniel kept his grip tight on the bow slung over his shoulder. He wiggled and scrunched his right fingers to warm them up and keep them flexible in case an arrow required notching in a hurry.

What was he doing? Would he really fire upon his brothers-in-arms to defend the ranger, a man who had killed Graycoats in the past? Nathaniel looked back at Asher again, catching his eye under the billowing green hood. There was honesty in the ranger's face, an honesty Nathaniel was unaccustomed to seeing.

The Graycoat hated that there was a longing in his heart to travel with the ranger and have an honest, uncomplicated life on the road. But the order was all he had ever known. Oaths had been taken to protect the realm, and protect it he would. *No, not the realm*, he thought, *the people...*

The streets soon opened up into a grand square, guarded at every entry point by soldiers in red. Servants of the king were hurrying about in the rain with decorations and bunting, climbing the buildings and hanging more flags of the wolf-head. By the end of the day, the entire city would be ready for celebrations, when King Rengar introduced the elves to the people.

The servants looked up at the group, curious about the king's new guests, eager to see what all the fuss was about.

Two soldiers opened the large double doors that led into the palace foyer, where an extravagant red carpet had been laid out with gold trimming. Standing at the bottom of the marble staircase was Lovani, the master of servants. When the doors closed behind them, the lanky man bowed in front of the elves, who had now removed their hoods and revealed their elegant features.

"Princess, esteemed guests, may I present King Rengar the Sixth, of the royal house Marek, Lord of Alborn..."

King Rengar descended the staircase from the left, while his wife, Queen Helena, came down from the right until they both met in the middle. Behind the queen were the royal couple's three teenage daughters and several maids, one of whom was holding the baby prince. The king was backed by his advisors and the court mage, Galkarus Vod. Dressed in their finest clothes and capes, the royal family glistened with jewellery and crowns adorning each of their heads.

Lovani raised an eyebrow at the collective grubbiness of the group, giving special attention to the ruined carpet under their muddy feet. Nathaniel stifled his laugh but did nothing to hide his smirk at the servant's dismay.

The elves bowed out of respect to the royals, their beauty evident despite the muddy clothes that clung to them. Even stood next to the immaculate family, the elves appeared more regal and majestic.

King Rengar waved his hands as if welcoming old friends. "After so long, it is truly a pleasure to welcome you in my home."

The king went on to introduce his wife and children, while Nathaniel let his gaze wander to count all the guards he could see. There wasn't a chance that the king would allow the ranger to be taken during such a historic occasion, but the Graycoat couldn't ignore his training and took stock of his surroundings.

"It is we who are honoured to be invited into your home, King Rengar." Reyna gave what Nathaniel suspected was a rehearsed line and smile to match. "This is my guardian and mentor, Faylen Haldör and my advisor, Mörygan Mörgö."

The king laughed with glee. "Come, I have gathered the rulers of Illian as you requested. They're positively shaking with excitement at the prospect of meeting you all."

The princess made no move to follow the king. "Perhaps, your Grace, we might rest for a short while, before meeting such a venerable group?"

"But of course!" The king seemed to take in the elves' attire for the first time. "I shall have my servants see to your clothes immediately."

"That won't be necessary," Faylen interjected, adjusting the sack-cloth bag that hung on her back.

"As you wish." King Rengar bowed and snapped his fingers at the master of servants. "Lovani will show you to your rooms at once."

The elves were ushered away until Reyna turned back to Nathaniel, who had remained behind, awaiting instruction.

"Are my *protectors* not to follow?" Reyna asked with an equal mix of sarcasm and expectation in her tone.

"Ah, what a fine job the Graycoats have done in escorting you to Velia." King Rengar bowed his head in thanks. "But the palace guard will see to your safety from now on, Princess Reyna."

"We were attacked upon landing on your shores, King Rengar. Had it not been for the bravery and skill of the Graycoats, we would not be standing here." Nathaniel suspected that last part to be an exaggeration. "I see no reason why they cannot continue to watch over us..."

The king hesitated before replying, "Of course. As you wish, Princess. But rest assured, I have my best investigators looking into the people who attacked you. They *will* be brought to justice."

Reyna flashed Nathaniel a glance, before turning to follow Lovani. Did she want him to stay? His own desires for the elf had caused his imagination to run wild. There was no way the princess of the elven nation could have any interest in him. Could she?

Nathaniel had never had so many questions in his life. Meeting Asher and the elves had complicated life somewhat. Or was it simply more interesting? The Graycoat shook his head to rid himself of such internal toil.

Elaith and Darius were frantically whispering to one another behind him, keeping their distress away from the departing royal family.

"What's the matter?" Nathaniel could already see the problem.

Asher was gone.

"Where the bloody hell has he gone?" Darius drew close to Nathaniel, gripping his arm as they continued to follow the elves.

"How should I know?" Nathaniel wondered if the ranger had even passed through the palace doors.

"If I discover that you had a hand in helping that vagabond flee, I will personally see to your exile from the order, if not your execution." Darius shoved Nathaniel's arm aside and strode on.

Nathaniel paid little attention to Devale's threat, instead, taking the time to survey the foyer before it disappeared from sight. There was no sign of Asher between the columns or the balcony above. The ranger must have slipped away before they entered the palace. Even *his* tradecraft couldn't see him vanish in the middle of the palace.

Elaith came up on his side. "Where *did* he go?"

"I have no idea. But something tells me we haven't seen the last of him."

Asher ducked into the shadows of the nearest alley and scaled the building in seconds. The rainwater dripped off every inch of his body, forcing him to take extra care with his grip.

From the safety of the building top, the ranger looked down on the three Graycoats as they rounded the corner. They stopped short until one of them ran on ahead to check the next street at the end of the alley. The knights proceeded to check behind abandoned crates and clear out the darkened doorways. Asher stalked them from above, a predator hunting its prey. The assassin inside him was hungry to finish his efforts and pounce on the Graycoats, killing them effortlessly.

The ranger pulled away from the ledge and closed his eyes, allowing the urge to pass. Killing them would only attract attention he didn't need. The city was crawling with extra patrols, and no doubt every Graycoat would be looking for him now. Retrieving Hector from the stables would be problematic, but he'd deal with that later.

They were coming.

The Arakesh had failed to fulfil their contract to whoever hired them. The Father would send more to make things right, and he would send someone deadlier.

Asher was too close to the intended target to see everything around him. He needed to step back to see the bigger picture. Whatever assassin was sent to finish the job would have to sneak into the city and infiltrate the palace, and Asher knew every way they would try.

The old ranger pulled his cloak tight against the lashing rain, and sat with his back to the chimney, his thoughts clouded by the mysterious assassin that accompanied the Arakesh. Had he travelled with them? Or had he lain in wait to see if the Arakesh succeeded in their kill before revealing himself? The way he had moved was familiar, especially the speed with which he danced around him. The ranger had only ever seen one other individual fight in such a manner.

"Alidyr Yalathanil..." He whispered the name inside his hood.

The elven master was Nightfall's biggest secret, the creator of the Nightseye elixir and the longest serving instructor in all forms of combat. The elf's twin-blades were legendary. Asher had personally seen Alidyr cut steel to pieces with his diamond-edged swords. The ranger had spent a long time in Nightfall ensuring the elf overlooked him; a lesson his oldest friend and father-figure had taught him.

Nasta Nal-Aket...

It had been a long time since he had allowed himself to even think that name. Was this new assassin connected to Nightfall, to the Father? He moved like an elf and wielded magic like an elf, but Asher would have recognised Alidyr's voice if it had been him. Besides, everyone knew the elf never left Nightfall.

Asher glanced at the black gem, poking out of his fingerless glove. He was thankful for the protection it had granted him during the encounter with the inexplicable elf. Something told him he was going to have to rely on its protection again before this was all over.

When the Graycoats had moved on in their search, Asher jumped onto the adjacent, taller building and climbed onto the roof. The ranger surveyed the city and the palace, looking for the entry points he knew any assassin would take. When they came, he would be ready.

CHAPTER 21
DUTY-BOUND

Reyna explored her new chamber, while Faylen and Mörygan examined their own, each connected by a door at the back of the room. Gold and silver antiques lined the drawers and mantel shelf. A large hearth dominated the far wall, the flames reflecting in the long mirrors, which hung in almost every corner.

A giant four-poster bed dominated the centre of the room with luxurious fabrics for bed-linen. A bowl of fruits and sweets had been placed on the circular table at the foot of the bed. The cold stone floor was almost entirely covered by the fur and head of a brown bear. The animal's expression of anger and pain must have been its final moments.

The elven culture she had grown up with was hardened, with lessons devoted to hunting and fighting and using magic for combat and protection. It was the only way Reyna had ever seen her people, though secretly, when she sneaked out at night and ran through The Amara, the princess had felt a connection to the wildlife that had never been explained to her. The trees called to the elf and the creatures that lived in the great forest trusted her.

Was that how her people had once lived? she wondered. Were those the elves Nathaniel spoke of from the human history books?

That sense of belonging was greatly missed right now, in man's halls of stone.

Faylen had always told Reyna that her inquisitive nature was born of her young age. Her mentor believed that the princess would eventually come around to their new ways, despite having never lived through the wars.

Reyna did not agree with that theory. Surely her nature was simply how elves were created to be and that all other elves, by comparison, were unnatural in their chosen evolution to become predators. Her people were supposed to be noble and regal, with pure intentions. They were certainly capable and warriors even... but not killers. The thought of her father's plan opened a hole in her stomach.

Could she really go through with this?

Faylen entered her chamber unannounced, via the connecting door, putting a swift end to Reyna's musings. Mörygan was close at her heel, his black robes flowing behind his stride.

"These chambers will suffice." Mörygan stopped by the glass doors to Reyna's balcony. "Now, Princess, remember your instructions. When you meet with the mages of Korkanath you must..." A knock at the door silenced Reyna's advisor.

"Enter." Reyna knew she should have dismissed whoever was at the door, but she just couldn't go over the plan *again*.

To her delight, Nathaniel entered the room with his ward, Elaith. The princess noted that Darius Devale was not with them, but could only see that as a good thing. As an elf, Reyna felt she was an excellent judge of character, and Darius Devale had a devious feel about him.

"Any luck finding Asher?" the princess asked, all too aware of the stir it had caused between the Graycoats. In truth, Reyna still wasn't sure what significance the ranger was to the knights' plans, but they appeared to be distressed at his sudden disappearance.

"Yes, I would very much like to speak with him," Mörygan added. The older elf was more interested in Asher's magical abilities than anything else.

"I'm afraid not." Nathaniel motioned for Elaith to close the door behind them. "Darius has left to organise the remaining Graycoats to search for him."

"Do we think something untoward has befallen the ranger?" Faylen asked, no doubt fearing that the assassins had returned.

"Asher fulfilled his agreement with the king in escorting you safely to Velia," Nathaniel explained. "I believe this form of exit is quite normal for a ranger."

"A shame," Mörygan remarked. "He was perhaps the most interesting human I've met."

Reyna rolled her eyes, hearing the passive insult her advisor threw at Nathaniel. The princess was just happy to see his dark eyes and unusual hair again. His rough exterior was wonderfully new to the elf.

Nathaniel became very interested in Faylen's handling of the sack-cloth bag she placed on the floor. Reyna knew what was coming and smiled, knowing that the Graycoat was about to be astonished.

The elven mentor opened the bag and reached inside until her entire arm appeared to have gone through the stone floor. Faylen pulled up and began to work the cloth bag around the edges of an emerging wooden chest.

The Graycoats' mouths fell open in speechless wonder, as the impossible unfolded in front of their eyes.

"There was a chest inside that... bag." Elaith nudged Nathaniel's arm as if to ensure that he had seen the same thing.

"Do they not teach you magic at West Fellion?" Reyna asked, bemused.

"Not really," Nathaniel replied, his eyes fixed on the chest. "Nothing like *that*."

"This magic is nothing." Faylen opened the chest to reveal fresh clothes. "Even your mages possess this knowledge."

"Now we require privacy, young knight." Mörygan dismissed the Graycoats with a look at the door.

Nathaniel met Reyna's eyes once more before he bowed his head and ushered Elaith out.

The Adean waves battered Galanör and his team as they reached the rocky shores of Korkanath. The elves were exhausted, having been abandoned by the Mer-folk well over a mile away from the island. The sea creatures feared Malliath's piercing gaze, his dragon's eyes capable of spotting their glimmering scales beneath the surface.

The group floated on their backs in the rain, metres away from the black, rocky beach. The magic allowing them to breathe underwater and survive the pressure of the Mer-folk's speed had dissipated.

"If I don't see another Mer-man for the rest of my immortal life, I will be a very happy elf." Adamar's strong arms recovered faster than the others, bringing him closer to the shore.

"Wait, Adamar!" Through laboured breaths, Eliön called for caution, when Adamar found the rocky surface beneath the water. "We don't know if the princess has—"

"I'm not freezing in the water, waiting for a signal we'll never see." Adamar waded through the ocean up to his waist. The diviner would be useless on the island, leaving them to more traditional methods of communication with Mörygan. "This storm will cover any sign from Velia."

"Adamar..." Galanör intoned his authority, hoping to stop the big elf in his tracks.

Thunder erupted overhead, drawing their gaze to the high walls of Korkanath. The stone walls which grew out of the natural rock gave the school its shape.

Adamar strode onwards until his first foot left the water and settled firmly on Korkanath's dry land. The next thunder-clap to tear apart the sky did little to mask the angry undertone that roared across the world. All five elves, still in the water, looked at each other in concern, before slowly turning to Adamar on the beach.

Galanör didn't have time to be angry with him. "Everyone out of the water. NOW!"

Adamar unsheathed his sword, while the others scrambled from the water. Ailas was the first to reach the shore, tearing the protective cover from his quiver and notching an arrow in the blink of an eye. The two elves searched the stormy skies in every direction, waiting for the group to break the water's edge.

"Put your weapons away!" Lyra ordered. "They will do no good against Malliath. We need to find the binding spell first."

Galanör shoved Adamar aside as he strode onto the island, not bothering to hide his despair at the elf. "*First* we need to find cover, or we'll never even breach the walls."

The group ran over the uneven terrain, skipping over the sharp rocks with long strides. Galanör led them around the curving wall, desperate to find a cave under the school. He soon picked up the distinct sound, however, of giant wings over the wind and rain. The others stopped with him to look at the sky - the warrior in him wanted to see death when it came for him. A black shadow seemed to glide through the thick grey clouds above, but only for a second before it disappeared. They were being hunted by the oldest predator in Verda.

They had made a terrible mistake.

The banquet hall was lined with servants, eager to attend to the various needs of the royals. Tables, covered with every kind of food, lined the walls between the servants, with smaller tables dotted around for discarded drinks and plates.

Reyna was greeted at the door by King Rengar, who took the utmost pleasure in introducing the elves to the great audience. The elf felt everyone's eyes on her at all times, as the king of Velia escorted her around the hall to meet the individual rulers of Illian.

The princess could feel Mörygan behind her, desperate to take over from the king and steer them towards the mages of Korkanath. The group of wizards were easy to spot amidst the well-dressed royal parties. Against the backdrop of the pale grey sky, beyond the wall-length, open balcony, the mages congregated in their billowing robes and hoods, each sporting a substantial beard.

"May I introduce Queen Isabella of house Harg, and ruler of Felgarn..." King Rengar extended his hand out to a woman in a sweeping green dress and silver crown, reminiscent of a stag's horns.

Reyna wasn't used to judging human ages yet, but the queen's face appeared slightly older than that of any elf. The princess guessed her to be around forty years old, but she dared not ask; Faylen would have her head.

The queen bowed her head. "An honour to meet you, Princess Reyna. You should visit my home in Lirian soon; I think you would find the forest quite reminiscent of your home in Ayda."

"Thank you, Queen Isabella." Reyna bowed in return. "My parents lived in The Evermoore as children and speak fondly of that time," she lied. Though her parents had lived in The Evermoore for a time, they had never spoken highly of it - or at least her father hadn't - always dwelling on the humans' emergence and how they ruined everything.

The queen became very excited. "Well, your *parents* are always welcome in the heart of Illian, Princess. I should love to host you all, of course." A young freckled boy, yet to see ten winters, appeared by her side. "This is my son, Timothy. He was very keen to meet the fabled elves he read about growing up."

There's nothing in your books about what we are, Reyna thought.

The young child was ushered forward until he bowed and became red in the face, preferring the folds of his mother's dress.

King Rengar gestured to the tall man, slowly approaching from behind Queen Isabella. "Ah, Lord Tion..."

As the king was getting ready to introduce the next rulers of the land, Reyna caught sight of Mörygan's sideways glance, indicating their need to meet with the mages. The princess nodded subtly, before settling on Nathaniel on the far side of the room. The Gray-coat's chiselled appearance looked irritated at whatever Darius Devale was talking to him about.

"Princess Reyna..." King Rengar's introduction was cut short, when the tall human waved off the king of Velia and reached for the elf's hand, kissing it lightly.

"I am Lord Merkaris of house Tion, ruler of all the north."

The gold crown over his shoulder-length blond hair came to a point, with the head of a lion. Merkaris's elegant clothes did nothing to hide his strong physique - he was no lazy king.

"The north..." Reyna made chit-chat, unsure of why she felt uncomfortable in his presence. "You speak of Orith, the northern region under Vengora. You share a border with Dhenaheim, no?"

"Yes, my Lady." Merkaris maintained his intense gaze. "Though, we have more trouble with the Gobbers that reside within Vengora, than we do with the dwarves. Not to say that our lands aren't *safe*. Our people have grown strong making the land our own. The elves are always welcome in my home, Namdhor, to see for themselves." He smiled with his perfect teeth and square jaw.

"I would enjoy a tour of the north," Reyna lied again. The princess had a feeling she would be lying a lot from now on. "The house of Tion? Your ancestor was Gal Tion, the first human king of Illian?"

Merkaris smiled as if he had a fish on a hook. "Indeed he was, Princess. My lineage is the oldest in the land. From our home in Namdhor, the king ruled from Vengora to the The Undying Mountains."

A man cleared his throat from somewhere behind the gathered group. Merkaris raised an eyebrow, unimpressed with the inter-ruption.

When they finally stepped aside, the princess was surprised to be greeted by the sight of a small boy, with olive skin and a completely bald head, covered in tattoos of thick black patterns the elf didn't recognise. The child wore very little by human standards, adorned with more jewellery than fabric. His nose, eyebrows, ears and lips were all pierced and connected by golden chains. Big brown eyes looked up at the princess with passive interest.

"Princess Reyna..." King Rengar stepped in front of Lord Merkaris. "For the first time in our history, the ruler of Karath has graced Velia with his presence, all to meet you. May I present Emperor Faros the First, of the bloodline Kalvanari and lord of The Arid Lands."

Reyna blinked in an attempt to hide her confusion. A child ruled everything south of The Moonlit Plains? How could anyone bow to the wisdom of a boy? There was a moment of silence that carried on for too long, while Reyna stared at the child-emperor.

The man standing next to Emperor Faros cleared his throat again. "I am Sivilis, high court mage to Karath and vizier to the emperor." Styled much in the same way as his master, Sivilis's bald head was covered with a tall hat that stood above his magical staff. A long black cylinder of beard jutted out from the vizier's chin at an odd angle, adding to his strange appearance. "On behalf of the emperor, I invite you to spend time exploring the wonders of our extraordinary land to the south. The city of Karath is home to some of the greatest pleasures imaginable..."

King Rengar sucked in a tight breath. "Yes, lovely I'm sure." He took Reyna by the shoulder and gently guided her away from the curious emperor and his strange vizier. "Some refreshments for our guests, perhaps?"

The mages drew closer.

～

The large rocks of Korkanath had given way to a stony beach that stretched beyond their vision. The elves kicked up the tiny pebbles in their frantic search for shelter.

They had all heard the dragon's roar between the thunderclaps and even seen a shadow flit across the beach once or twice. Korkanath's protector knew that uninvited guests had entered its territory. Now, Galanör knew what it meant to be hunted from above.

"Over there!" Eliön fought against the wind and pointed at an archway built into the rock.

With a dragon on his heels, Galanör felt the instinctive urge to pray to the gods, despite his lack of faith.

The group ran faster than any human could manage, closing the gap between them and salvation. Galanör reached the entrance first and ushered his companions through the archway, his elven eyes scanning the skies for the beast that hunted them.

The archway gave way to a long corridor that cut through the island rock and stopped somewhere underneath the school. Beyond the stony beach, lay the sunken decking of the small port that harboured the ships that kept Korkanath stocked with supplies.

"This must lead to the stockrooms under the school!" Naiveen shouted back, as they approached the wooden door at the other end of the corridor.

"I don't care where it leads as long as it's inside!" Even Adamar's bravado failed when faced with a dragon.

"Stop!" Galanör barked the order before they could barge through the door.

The group came to a sudden stop in the dark tunnel, inches from the door, Ailas's hand poised over the thick metal knob. They turned to regard Galanör as if he were mad, unaware of the dragon that hunted them.

Thud!

Somewhere beyond the archway, behind them, Malliath had dropped onto the beach, his massive wings collapsing and blowing a gust of wind through the tunnel. Even with the sound of the heavy rain and the raging gales outside, the elves heard the sharp breath that escaped Malliath's nostrils. As one, they looked from the open archway to Galanör with the same silent question.

"Think where we are," he instructed. "Assume everything is hexed and magically barred. There will be traps everywhere designed to stop invaders in their tracks."

Lyra quickly faced the wooden door again and waved her hand over the surface, commanding the magical wards to reveal themselves.

"It's been warded with a spell designed to collapse the tunnel. I can see the magic that protects it but..." Lyra looked back at them with defeat in her eyes, before looking further down the tunnel, where defeat changed to fear. "We don't have time for the counterspell."

The tunnel was cast in complete darkness when Malliath stepped in front of the archway. The narrow corridor was filled with the foul stench of rotting meat and sulphur, as the dragon's mouth encompassed the archway. The elves felt the air around them being sucked back down the tunnel, away from them.

Galanör had never seen or heard a dragon in battle before, but he knew that when they drew in a sharp breath, it was never a good thing that followed.

Reyna could practically feel Mörygan's eyes rolling in his head when King Rengar steered them away from the mages of Korkanath.

The princess maintained her smile and made certain to meet the eyes of everyone that watched her, exhibiting confidence and control. Rengar's family and advisors followed them like sheep around the hall, letting the other rulers know where the strongest alliance with the elven nation would lie.

King Rengar leaned into Reyna, as if they were old friends, and spoke quietly. "I know you wish to meet all the rulers of Illian,

Princess Reyna, but I must apologise in advance for the barbarian you are about to meet."

Reyna smiled politely, hiding her displeasure of the king's voice in her ear. With less animation, King Rengar stepped to the side to facilitate the meeting between Reyna and a dishevelled looking man.

"Princess Reyna, this is King Gregorn of house Orvish, ruler of The Ice Vales."

"Princess..." King Gregorn made no advances to take her hand or embrace, as Reyna assumed he would, instead settling for a curt nod of his silver-crowned head.

Gregorn's lack of enthusiasm for meeting her only helped to endear the king of The Ice Vales to Reyna.

His long scraggy, grey hair and beard were very unkempt for a royal, especially when standing next to the immaculate King Rengar. All of Gregorn's fingers were adorned with rings of every mineral, which did nothing to distract from the king's dirty nails. A floor-length cape of dark brown fur flowed out from the high collar that surrounded his neck, ending with the head of a bear on his shoulder.

Reyna knew from her studies on the voyage to Illian that the bear was the animal that decorated the flag of The Ice Vales, much like the wolf for Velia or the horse for The Arid Lands.

"I have wished my entire life to speak with one of your race." King Gregorn's voice was as rough as his appearance, though his expression was that of a desperate man. "There are ancient tomes known to only a few, that state The Ice Vales were once as lush and habitable as Felgarn, my neighbouring land..."

"Not this again, Gregorn." King Rengar tried to silence him with a hand. "Perhaps this is a conversation for later?"

"I agree." Mörygan nodded his agreement and looked at the mages by the balcony.

King Gregorn persisted. "Is it true that the land was cursed during The Dark War, Princess? Orith is north of my kingdom and suffers no winter like my people. Perhaps there is a counterspell known to your kin?"

Reyna's mouth opened, but she couldn't find the right response. It was a well-known fact that Valanis had cursed the land around his fortress, Kaliban. The Western Vales, as they had been known to the elves, had frozen over after the Amber Spell had trapped the evil elf in Elethiah. It was this curse that caused the avalanches and earthquakes in the mountainous region of Vengora, sealing off Kaliban and the dark secrets Valanis kept there.

"Ah, Magikar Pondaal..." King Rengar turned his back on Gregorn and directed the group towards the balcony.

Mörygan was only too happy to walk away from the king of The Ice Vales, his eyes fixed on the mages.

Reyna promised herself that she would find time later to explain all she knew about the curse over his land. She only regretted that there was no counterspell to free the people of their never-ending winter.

Not that it matters, she thought...

As they approached the mages, Reyna dwelled on the fact that they were moments away from performing their part in the great plan. Her next conversation would have ramifications that would go on to affect all of Verda. When her part was done, Galanör would no doubt go on to complete his and, in so doing, start the beginning of a new era that would remove humanity from the map. Reyna looked at Nathaniel once more and felt a cold dread fill her bones.

"Princess Reyna, may I introduce Magikar Pondaal, head of Korkanath, Illian's premier school of magic." King Rengar placed his hand on the Magikar's shoulder, another display of the king's influence and power in front of his peers.

Continuing her attempts to guess human ages, Reyna judged the Magikar to be in his sixties, maybe seventies. Standing a little taller than herself, Pondaal was dressed in a long purple and gold robe with a chunky golden chain around his neck, adorned with a large ruby. Reyna could sense the magic contained within, stored there by the Magikar.

He had a kind face with startling blue eyes and long white hair and matching beard. It was slightly amusing to the princess that this revered human, with less than a century of life, was the master of Illian's magical school. The younger looking Mörygan and Faylen beside her both had more knowledge and experience of magic than Pondaal could imagine.

"It is a great honour to meet you, Princess." Magikar Pondaal bowed. "To be in the presence of those who first instructed our kind to use magic is truly a dream come true."

"The honour is all ours, Magikar Pondaal." Reyna knew her lines well. "My companions and I are curious as to how far humans have progressed with your exploration of magic."

Pondaal lapped up the attention. "Oh, we have made great strides in your absence, Princess, though that's not to say that we don't have so much more to learn. Perhaps with the new alliance between our two lands, we can work together to bridge the gap?"

Here it comes, Reyna thought. "I know of many elves who would be interested in your work at Korkanath, Magikar. My father feels there is a lot we can accomplish together."

The Magikar couldn't wait to get his words out. "Well, that's wonderful, Princess! All of elven kind is welcome in Korkanath..."

There it was, the legendary invitation to Korkanath. Reyna missed Pondaal's next speech, instead looking from Mörygan's smug expression to the lashing rain and gathering mist beyond the open balcony. Somewhere out there, Galanör and his team would be reaching Korkanath's shore, preparing to take the first act of aggression against the human race.

What had she done?

The elves could do nothing but brace themselves for the inevitable.

Galanör could feel the magic building between them, each ready to project a barrier that would hold back the dragon's breath. But even their combined power would never hold out against the might of Malliath. They would be engulfed by fire and their mission would be brought to an abrupt end - all their efforts for naught.

In his last moments, Galanör thought of the children he had served up to the Mer-folk and was surprised to find his deep sadness at sacrificing the younglings. The elf had tried to live his long life without regrets but found himself wishing he had confronted his father and stood up for himself. He didn't want to marry Princess Reyna and he wasn't even that interested in starting a war with the humans, despite his disdain for them.

Galanör had been duty-bound for so long and now, at the end of his life, he wished he could have been free, even for a short time.

He looked down at Lyra in the dark, crouched beside him. Galanör wasn't surprised to find he felt nothing at the thought of her dying; she had been nothing but a lover to pass the time on Dragorn.

The air being sucked out of the tunnel stopped when Malliath had taken his breath - that final moment an eternity in the blink of an eye.

Galanör didn't want to die here, like this.

The moment went on; the only sound their ragged breaths in the darkness. Where was the fire? Galanör could feel his heart pounding in his chest. Was Malliath deliberately prolonging their fate, drawing out their final moments to torment them?

The meagre light that pierced the storm clouds flooded the tunnel once more, confusing the elves. Malliath's bulk shifted across the beach, his mighty claws digging up the dirt underneath the pebbles. Galanör held his breath, wondering if the dragon had simply decided to attack them a different way. The sound of giant wings flapping in the wind could be heard, moments before an explosive splash resounded further out to sea.

"They did it..." Eliön gasped in disbelief.

Galanör had come to the same conclusion. Reyna and the others must have finally met with the mages of Korkanath and had their invitation extended to their entire race.

The elves looked at one another in relief, sagging against the walls, while they took a minute to appreciate how lucky they were. That particular part got under Galanör's skin. There was no place for luck on a mission like this. They had to use their skill and magical abilities to achieve success. It had only proved that their current situation stood upon a knife's edge.

The elf tried not to dwell on his thoughts during what he had assumed were his last moments on Verda. He would be slave to his duty forever.

"There's no time to rest." He looked to Lyra. "We need that door opened."

～

Gideon Thorn skittishly entered Korkanath's grand library, aware that his current attire would be frowned upon by the librarian.

In the hope of tempting Abigail from her studies, Gideon had dressed in his sparring gear - the same clothes Master Vorn had forbidden him from wearing - and placed his shrunken staff in the sheath on his back. His dark red leather jacket had a collar that dug into his neck, with tarnished golden buttons that fastened up on the right side of his chest. The creaking leather combined with the rustle of his sandy trousers and tall brown boots made a racket in the silent library.

Gideon mouthed the word 'sorry' to the disgruntled students, who looked up from their books to the sound of his heels on the wooden floor.

Gideon turned the corner of one of the towering bookshelves and saw a dozen floating books rushing into the spaces between the shelves. The mage quickly spun on his heel and strode out of the corridor in the knowledge that the floating books preceded the grumpy librarian.

Mistress Gurtru rounded the corner, missing the sight of Gideon slinking away, and continued to wave her wand left and right at the parallel bookshelves, *tutting* as she was forced to rearrange the misplaced books put back by lazy students.

With a sigh of relief, Gideon passed further into the never-ending library. It had been enchanted centuries ago to ensure that it had no end, thereby making certain that the mages would never run out of space for their books and research.

There were plenty of school legends that students had become lost and died in the labyrinth, their ghosts now haunting the deepest recesses of the library.

Never one for taking the chosen path, Gideon climbed the ladders fixed to the bookshelf on his left and used the top shelf to place his boot and push himself over the balcony above. As always, Abigail was sitting in her usual booth, with her head buried in a thick leather-bound book.

Without looking up, she said, "The stairs won't bite you, you know."

Gideon sat on the other side of the table and placed his hands over the pages, stopping her from reading. "Come spar with me. I think I've found a way of using the hexes Master Tibit had us use on the grounds. If we set them up around the training hall we can work together to fend off whatever *nasties* come our way. It'll be fun!"

Abigail gave him her usual look of derision. Gideon knew it was a more dangerous way to train than usual, but he felt like a challenge today. He pouted and emphasised his pleading look to convince her that sparring with him would be better than reading. To his joy, Abigail's mockery slowly turned into a coy smile and she pulled aside her robe to reveal that she too was wearing her sparring clothes.

"You're so predictable, do you know that?" Abigail closed the book and touched the cover with her wand, instructing it in the ancient language to return to its rightful place.

"Yes!" Gideon's glee was dampened by nearby students shushing him. "Sorry..."

Being extra careful to avoid Mistress Gurtru, they left the library and made for the training hall. They hadn't reached half way when the commotion from the wall caught their attention. Deciding to investigate, despite the rain, Gideon and Abigail rushed up the spiral staircase and out onto the top of the wall. An entire class of sixth years, journeying between classes, had huddled together at the wall's edge, each of them cramming to see over the side.

"What's going on?" Gideon asked.

Before anyone could answer, a savage roar rippled over the wall, filling the students with dread and excitement.

Gideon knew that roar could belong to only one creature. Both Abigail and he dived for the side, craning their torsos over the edge to see the majestic animal. Every jaw dropped at the whipping black tail that plunged into the ocean after its owner. Gideon could barely contain his excitement at seeing even a part of Malliath. The tail had been incredibly long, leading Gideon to rethink his original estimate of how big the dragon was.

"Did you see his tail?" he asked Abigail.

"We saw more than that!" one of the students next to Gideon exclaimed. "He was trying to fit his head inside there. He's massive!" The gangly young boy pointed to the outcropping of a stone archway on the beach. Gideon recognised it immediately as the entrance to the stockrooms for supply ships.

A clap of thunder elicited a cry of panic from the entire class. Everyone crouched or hid behind their friend while scanning the stormy sky. Gideon and Abigail kept their eyes on the water.

"I can't believe we missed him!" Gideon remained fixed to the wall.

"Why do you think he was on the beach in the first place?" Abigail pointed her wand in the air and the rain immediately curved around both of them, keeping them dry.

"Hunting maybe?" Gideon suggested.

"What could he possibly be hunting on the beach?" Abigail didn't sound convinced.

Gideon shrugged, disappointed. "I don't know, but I wouldn't want to be it..."

PART THREE

CHAPTER 22
THE POINT OF NO RETURN

It had taken several minutes longer than Galanör expected it would, but Lyra finally managed to open the door without setting off the hex. It was a testament to the humans' ingenuity and comprehension of magic. They were not to be underestimated, it seemed.

Without instruction, the group split up like a highly trained team of invaders, each heading in a different direction to check the stuffy stockroom. Lit with only torches, the large room was lined with twenty-foot high shelves stacked with foodstuffs. The outer walls were hidden behind rows of barrels filled with wines, ales and water.

The elves couldn't hide their sour expressions, forced to inhale the foul combination of the potent human food.

"What is their fascination with cheese?" Adamar was the last to return to the huddled group.

They said nothing of their close encounter with the dragon. Galanör was impressed with the team's ability to carry on, without dwelling on the fact they had almost died only minutes ago.

"Who has the map?" Galanör asked.

Ailas pulled a rolled up piece of parchment from within his cloak and laid it out on the floor. The group crouched around it and placed weights on the corners to keep it flat. The state of the paper suggested it was very old, with yellow and brown stains across the surface.

Galanör waved his hand over the blank parchment, magically commanding it to reveal its secrets. Dark lines immediately appeared, outlining Korkanath's walls and rooms throughout the vast grounds. Using mental commands, Galanör poured more magic into the map, changing the dark ink into fluorescent blue lines that lifted from the parchment, building a more complex and detailed image of Korkanath in three dimensions.

"We're here." Naiveen pointed at the lowest room on the floating map.

Eliön tied his dark hair into a knot. "We have no hope of freeing Malliath without the spell-book that holds his enchantments. Finding it must be our first goal."

"I hate to bring this up again," Ailas said, "but what happens if we free Malliath and he decides he doesn't *want* to return to Elandril with us."

"Trust in Galanör, Ailas," Lyra replied softly. "The king himself instructed him on how to speak with Malliath. Once the dragon hears of our proposal, he will surely fly us all home at great speed." Ailas nodded, apologetically.

Galanör kept his own reservations to himself. He feared that they were overestimating the mentality of a dragon, branded, enthralled and imprisoned for nearly a thousand years. There was a very good chance that Malliath would simply fly away, never to be seen again. Or he'd kill them all. Or both.

"So how do we find the book?" Galanör kept his team focused.

"Simple." Adamar had a menacing grin. "We find one of the teachers and *ask* them."

Galanör knew exactly what the big elf meant. There would be more blood spilled before this mission was over, he thought. They had killed thugs and even innocents to get them this far, but they had never resorted to torture.

He looked back at the glowing map that floated between them all; there were too many rooms to check. The book was no doubt guarded as well, making their task that much harder, and if every locked room was as heavily enchanted as this one, they would be undone in no time.

"Very well." Galanör was sure to hide his disdain for the plan.

They spent the next few minutes plotting their route through the underground network of tunnels. The stockroom had been built well away from the greedy hands of the school's students. Two levels up, they spotted what looked like a classroom or laboratory. They decided to start their hunt for a teacher there.

"Until we are discovered, we must remain as shadows. We can't leave a trail of bodies." Galanör was looking at Adamar. "If the mages rally against us we will perish. Do not underestimate them."

In complete silence, the elves moved swiftly through the torch-lit corridors. Their swords were drawn, with Ailas and Eliön each notching an arrow as they ran around the curving walls. While ascending a wide set of stairs, the wooden double doors at the top burst open, stopping the team in their tracks.

Following Galanör's lead, the group hugged the sides of the stairs and used concealing magic to hide. The portly mage continued on down the stairs, oblivious to the six immortals either side of him. To the human's eyes, they simply weren't there since the magic they each employed bent the rays of light around their bodies.

Before the door could close behind him, Eliön held it open to allow the others to pass through unheard. Once the corridor was safe, the elves reappeared, as if from nowhere - they had to be cautious with their use of magic when up against fellow magic-users.

Galanör knew that they each wore a crystal with magic stored within, as well as other smaller crystals hidden on their person, but drawing on that power had to be reserved in case of an all-out confrontation.

Using hand signals alone, Galanör led the group through the empty corridors until they reached another set of stairs and arrived on the floor they had chosen to start their search.

They were forced to hug the wall again before stepping onto the floor when a class of human children thundered down the corridor. Shouts of joy about the hot lunch coming their way and hushed whispers about another group sighting Malliath, was all Galanör could hear. As the students bypassed them, the group of elves remained in the shadows of the spiralling staircase, until the rabble disappeared.

"Well, we know *that* teacher's alone..." Adamar was desperate to draw blood.

"We should wait to make certain no other class takes their place," Galanör cautioned.

Aside from Adamar, the team was content to wait a few minutes before leaving the shadows and entering the classroom. Inside, they found several rows of wooden tables and benches, the room flooded with light from the bank of windows fitted high at the head of the class.

Standing with his back to them, a man Galanör guessed to be in his forties, was using his wand to erase information from the chalkboard. It appeared the mage was a history teacher, judging by the dates scrawled across the board.

Adamar cleared his throat to get the teacher's attention. Galanör rolled his eyes at the elf's dramatics, always wanting to make an entrance. He shot the big elf a warning glare that instructed Adamar to do only as he was ordered.

A small gasp escaped the mage's lips when he looked upon the unnerving vision of six strangers with swords and bows at the ready, each wearing dark cloaks to match their menacing expressions. Oddly, Galanör thought of the water, still occasionally dripping from their clothes, and leaving a trail. They would have to see to that after acquiring the information about the book.

"Who are you? What do you want?" The mage held his wand defensively in front of him, the tip pointed at Galanör's face. Everything about the history teacher screamed of a weak and pathetic individual who couldn't hold his own against another human, let alone six elves. "How did you even get in here?"

"Naiveen...?" Galanör didn't take his eyes off the mage.

"No one can hear us," Naiveen coolly replied.

Galanör had hand-picked this particular team because he could rely on them to predict his commands. They could be trusted to think for themselves and perform whatever was required for the mission. Adamar was a different matter, however, having been forced upon him by advisors who had the king's ear - a fact that Galanör could not easily forget.

As she had in their apartment, in Dragorn, Naiveen had already set up a magical barrier around the classroom to keep the inevitable screams from being heard outside.

Galanör hated the thought of what was about to happen, but he didn't dare show it. "Excellent. Ailas..."

Galanör stepped an inch to the side before the arrow exploded from Ailas's bow, sinking into the mage's wand-hand, up to his wrist. The teacher shrieked in agony and he dropped the wand to the floor, before falling back into the blackboard. Lyra casually kicked the wand away, as the group closed in on the mage from all sides.

Adamar was stopped by Galanör's outstretched arm. "Eliön will retrieve the information we seek." The mage looked up, whimpering and terrified, cradling his wounded hand.

"You doubt my abilities?" Adamar was ready for a fight with anyone.

"I doubt the mage would be able to say anything at all if I let *you* question him." Galanör dismissed Adamar with a flick of his hand, asserting his dominance while motioning for Eliön to get to work.

Eliön crouched down to the mage's level, where the human was able to observe his elven ears. For just a moment his fear and pain were replaced with curiosity and awe.

For just a moment.

Eliön gripped the arrow protruding from the mage's hand and tugged it harshly, eliciting another scream.

With a calming tone, Eliön looked intently into the human's watery eyes. "To stop the pain, you will say anything to appease me. Know that when you lie, I will know, and the pain will increase tenfold." The elf ripped the arrow out of the mage's hand and towered over him. "Let us begin..."

CHAPTER 23
A DAY IN THE SUN

Adilandra concentrated on her breathing and took slow and steady breaths to keep back the tears. Two Darkakin had snatched her from The Goddess's chamber, where the elf had been chained up, and dragged her roughly by the arms through a series of tunnels under the pyramid.

Her first night as a captive had been unbearable; she couldn't even bring herself to think what Lörvana had been through. Krenorak had claimed her as his prize and taken her back to whatever hell he came from. The thought of the big Darkakin brought back the images of Ederön being thrown from the balcony.

You have to survive...

It was the only thought that kept back the tears and reminded her how important their mission was. Adilandra looked down at her manacled feet, being dragged over the sandy ground, as the two Darkakin pulled her along. The elf had lost track of how far they had come or where they were in relation to the pyramid. She remembered being dragged up a great number of stairs, where she barely noticed the jeers and insults that were hurled her way by stray Darkakin.

Eventually, the guards dropped her in a new room with a single tunnel leading off it. Daylight poured through the tunnel and into the room, exposing an array of weapons and shields on the walls. Almost every weapon was coated with several layers of dried blood, accounting for the room's hideous smell.

In the distance, beyond the lighted tunnel, the sound of a thousand voices chanting in unison rang out.

The Darkakin flipped Adilandra over without warning and laid her flat on her back, where they hurriedly went to work on the chains around her wrists and feet. When they were done, the two guards left the room via the same door and barred it from the other side, leaving Adilandra with only one way to go.

The queen of elves stood up and tentatively massaged her wrists, where the chains had cut into her skin. Why had they left her in a room of weapons? Where was she? The chanting continued, only now Adilandra could hear it above her, from where powdered rock began to rain down into the room. The elf started to put it together in her mind; the weapons, the chanting...

She would have to fight if she wanted to live.

Removing a sword, shaped like a hook, Adilandra readied herself for what was about to happen next. If they wanted to see an elf fight they were going to sorely regret it. She thought of the atrocities they had suffered under the Darkakin for years and felt her grip on the sword tighten. With what little strength she had left, Adilandra would go out taking as many of them as she could.

You have to survive...

There it was again; the reminder that death wasn't an option. Valanis would be freed soon, she knew it, and when the dark elf rose back to power, he would bring with him a time of darkness for all the people of Verda, a scourge to dwarf the evil of the Darkakin.

Adilandra blinked away the final tears and strode down the tunnel, into the light. The hot sun beat down on her face and the dry air attempted to steal the breath from her lungs. She wiped the sweat from her brow and the back of her neck, sweeping aside her auburn hair, while she adjusted to the intense light.

The sight of her was greeted with a thunderous uproar of chanting from all around. The elf was standing at the edge of a gladiatorial arena, shaped like a massive amphitheatre, with hundreds of rows of blood-thirsty Darkakin. The walls stood unusually high and curving spikes and blades adorned the very top.

Adilandra looked down at her feet, checking the grip of her boots in the sand, heavily stained with old blood. Thinking back to all the stairs she had been dragged up, Adilandra felt confident that the arena had been built high above the ground.

The baying mob was silenced when The Goddess's cruel voice shouted down at Adilandra from behind. "I promised you that I would grant your wish, fulfilling your futile journey into my lands." The Goddess stood at the top of the high wall, amidst a dozen guards, with her throne situated behind her. The Goddess was given the best view of the carnage. "But first, my people need entertaining!" The entire arena erupted into cheers. "Should you survive today, I will show you the dragons tomorrow." The Goddess wore a headdress made of black bones, shaped around her head to give her the appearance of a cobra.

Adilandra's attention was instantly drawn to Krenorak. The hulking Darkakin was standing to the side of The Goddess's throne, with Lörvana chained up on her knees. Krenorak rested his meaty hand on the elf's shoulder, keeping her down and stating his claim over her. It broke Adilandra's heart to see the state Lörvana was in. Both of her eyes looked swollen and bruised, surrounded by smaller cuts that split her lips and marred her cheeks and nose. The elf's keen eyes could see the tears constantly running down her face. Fallön was notably, but disturbingly, absent.

For the first time in her long life, the queen of elves was feeling wrathful.

One of the Darkakin guards handed The Goddess a sheathed sword, Adilandra's sword. The wicked ruler pulled the blade free and held it up to the light, inspecting the ancient glyphs engraved into the steel.

"Let us see how your elven steel holds up against Darkakin brutality. And no magic! It's so very boring..." The Goddess threw the sword end-over-end until it dug into the ground at Adilandra's feet.

The elf didn't hesitate to drop the rusted heavy blade and pick up her sword - a manoeuvre that saved her life. The spear whistled past her ear and carried on into the wall, below The Goddess's podium. The arena erupted in more cheers as the first wave of gladiators charged the elf.

You will survive today...

Adilandra focused her mind and sharpened her senses, using the few precious seconds to assess her opponents before they were on her. The four Darkakin rippled with muscles and rage, sprinting across the sandy arena. They wore little armour, making Adilandra's job that much easier. Between them, she caught sight of two swords, an axe and shield and the lead runner with a net and a spear.

As the queen of elves, Adilandra had enjoyed lessons at the hands of her people's most skilled warriors. Her husband had made certain that his wife could defend herself when the war was upon them. Until right now, she had never felt the need to kill, as so many of her kind often did. The Darkakin had forced this hidden nature from within her, and now they would pay for it.

Predictably, the first gladiator threw his net at Adilandra. The hooked edges spun round and round, designed to either impale its victim or secure them to the ground. The elf deftly rolled under the flying net, feeling one of the hooks brush her hair. The gladiator leaped into the air, with his spear angled down at Adilandra, when she came out of her roll. The man couldn't compete with the agility of an elf, however.

Tilting her head to the right, by only an inch, Adilandra avoided the tip of the spear and made a slicing motion with her sword. The gladiator's momentum pushed him through the elf's sword, almost separating him from his legs.

Adilandra didn't look back; confident the warrior was dead or soon would be. The first death created an eruption of cheers from around the arena. The Darkakin didn't really care who died - as long as there was blood and gore to be had, they were entertained.

The two swordsmen attacked her as one, having witnessed the folly of the net-thrower. Parrying both slashes of their swords, Adilandra whipped her leg around, catching the gladiator on the right in the face. She felt the man's jaw dislocate before he spun away, tumbling to the ground.

The gladiator wielding the axe and shield quickly took his place, swinging the curved blade at the elf's head. Adilandra arched her back to avoid the axe, while simultaneously flicking the remaining swordsman's blade aside, ensuring the axe embedded itself into his chest. The axe bit through the gladiator's breastplate until it severed major arteries inside. His shock at being mortally wounded by his fellow gladiator was short-lived. Adilandra twirled on the spot and brought her scimitar to bear across the swordsman's neck, removing his head with a single swipe.

The axe-man snarled when the headless body dropped to the floor and took the axe with him, leaving the remaining gladiator without a weapon.

With only his shield, the warrior blocked the elf's attacks. Adilandra drove him back with every swipe of her powerful sword, its edge scoring the metal shield from top to bottom. When she realised she was using too much energy to kill an inferior opponent, Adilandra changed tack and ducked low, swiping at the gladiator's legs. Everything below the man's knees was cut away in a flash of steel and an agonised scream. He could do nothing but fall backward, with his shield covering him.

The shrieks and whimpers that escaped his lips only drove Adilandra's bloodlust on. The elf dropped to one knee and brought all her strength down on her sword, plunging it through the shield and into the gladiator's chest. His death was horribly satisfying.

A mangled war-cry was all the warning she had before the

swordsman with the dislocated jaw charged her from behind. Adilandra's scimitar was lodged in the shield and refused to come out in the time she had to avoid the swing of his blade. Instead, the elf opted to roll over the dead axe-man and take on the last gladiator with her bare hands.

The swordsman's jaw wobbled independently, while he jumped over his dead friend, muttering profanities even a Darkakin would struggle to understand.

Adilandra deftly came up inside the man's swing and shoved the edge of her open palm into his throat. The counter-attack halted the gladiator instantly, causing him to drop his sword. The elf forced him to the ground with a hand around his throat. Thankful for her flexible body, Adilandra stepped on the man's sword arm, pinning him with her hand around his neck. She squeezed. The elf didn't stop until his eyes bulged and turned red, at which point she wrenched his head sideways.

Snap!

The gladiator stopped squirming. The mob remained silent, watching with fascination and glee at such ferocity.

Adilandra slowly stood up, catching her breath and looking around at the hungry eyes of thousands of Darkakin. The arena was holding its breath. Her eyes finally rested on The Goddess, seated regally on her throne, like a snake coiled to attack.

"More!" The Goddess shouted to the cheers of the crowd.

Iron gates fitted into the wall around the arena were rising on their pulley system. Adilandra counted twelve more gladiators entering the arena. The queen of the elves casually walked over to the dead axe-man and retrieved her sword. Just for today, she would be everything her husband wanted her to be.

You will survive this...

CHAPTER 24
THE NATURE OF ELVES

The Velian guards remained at the end of the corridor, while Nathaniel and Elaith followed the elves back to their rooms.

"You can get some sleep." Nathaniel motioned for Elaith to return to the servants' quarters they had been allocated. "You can relieve me at dawn." The Graycoat knew he was being too good giving her that much time, but the reception in the hall had been awfully boring for the young knight, and the elves were far safer this deep into the palace.

Elaith's eyes lit up at the prospect of having a whole night's sleep on a bed. Without another word she turned around and disappeared down the corridor.

Nathaniel chuckled to himself and looked at the wooden chair that was to be his post for the night. He suddenly felt very sorry for the sore behind he was about to get.

The thought of a sore arse naturally made him think of Darius Devale. During the reception, Darius had told him that Asher was nowhere to be found and that he had been forced to send a messenger bird to West Fellion, informing the Lord Marshall that he had failed to bring in the elusive ranger. It was followed by more threats that he would see to it that Nathaniel was thoroughly punished. It was less amusing, however, to hear that King Rengar had sent men to fetch the bodies of the fallen Graycoats for proper burial, though he was thankful for it.

Nathaniel sincerely hoped that the ranger was miles away from Velia by now. He had come to enjoy the company of the man, despite his past misdeeds. A part of him hoped that they might meet again on the road, though whether he would still be a Graycoat remained to be seen.

The knight spent the next hour or so going over the events of the last few days. The fact that he had survived a confrontation with so many Arakesh was a miracle. No, he thought, a testament to his skill. Nathaniel didn't completely believe that and remembered Asher and Reyna coming to his aid at the right moment.

Who was the mysterious assassin who fought Asher? Had it not been for the ranger's affinity for magic, Nathaniel may well have fallen to the assassin's blade in defence of the elves.

It troubled him more to think of who hired the assassins in the first place. The men and women they had just met in the reception hall were the only people in Illian who knew in advance that the elves were coming. It stood to reason that one of them had made contact with the Arakesh. But why? What did any of them have to gain from the assassination of the princess?

Nathaniel lost track of time while he chewed over his thoughts. The door in front of him creaked and pulled him from his reverie.

"It occurred to me that you didn't get to eat at the reception." Reyna stood in the doorway, a vision of beauty. Her clothes had been replaced by a long nightdress that clung to her body. Nathaniel's reply came in the form of a blank expression. Reyna laughed softly. "Come inside."

The Graycoat checked to see if the guards were watching before he followed the elf inside.

A gentle breeze drifted through the open balcony, lifting Reyna's nightdress to reveal her bare feet. She indicated the food laid out on her central table, but Nathaniel ignored it and followed her out onto the balcony. He couldn't take his eyes off her golden hair, blowing in the breeze. Everything about the elf was enchanting to him as if from the moment they met a spell had been cast over him.

Nathaniel came up on her side and did his very best not to look down her dress. Remember, you're a knight, he thought.

"So what do you make of the world of man?" Nathaniel had to say something before he gave into the urge to kiss her.

"The world of *man*? You might want to change the name." Reyna's eyes were piercing.

Nathaniel smiled apologetically and looked out to sea, afraid that he would be drawn in by her exquisite green eyes. Direport lay below, a sprawling network of masts and decking that curved round into the ocean.

"It seems you arrived on our shores with a lot more knowledge about us than we have of you." Nathaniel kept his tone light.

Reyna smiled. "You didn't think the Lord of Elves would send his only daughter without learning about current affairs?"

"Should I even ask how you came by so much information?" Nathaniel met her smile and they both shared a laugh at the unspoken.

Nathaniel had no doubt the elves had taken precautions to learn more about humanity, possibly even sending other elves ahead in secret, but he also didn't much care. It was hard to care about anything around Reyna.

"What would you like to know about elves?" The princess turned to look at Nathaniel while leaning against the rail.

The Graycoat thought about what Asher had said over the fire. "Everything..."

Reyna laughed again and Nathaniel found it intoxicating. He glanced over her shoulder at the adjacent balconies that belonged to Faylen and Mörygan, hoping they wouldn't hear them and order him to leave.

The princess looked away as if considering her words. "We're everything you are, only *more*. All our emotions and urges are the same; we just feel everything more... intensely. And we're immortal."

"You're right, we're *practically* the same." They laughed again before Reyna became serious.

"We're not like the elves that lived in Illian before our departure to Ayda. At least that's what I hear; I haven't yet seen thirty winters myself. I'm still considered a child by elven standards..."

Nathaniel could see some resentment in her eyes. There was a lot more to Reyna than he could see on the surface, and he was instantly filled with the need to discover it all.

"Well, you don't *look* like a child." Nathaniel couldn't help taking in Reyna from head-to-toe. He paused, fascinated at the sight of her pointed ears, protruding from her hair.

"You're very sweet." Reyna met his eyes with an intense gaze. "I'm unaccustomed to your own appearance, but I can't say I don't enjoy it."

Nathaniel was stunned by the statement. He was as ordinary as any human, at least in appearance.

"I think you had too much wine at the reception, Princess."

"Reyna..." she corrected, gently. "And I don't drink alcohol; it affects our ability to use magic."

"Very wise," Nathaniel added with a wry smile.

"Well I am an elf, you know?" The princess laughed in her melodic way again, drawing him closer.

"You don't seem *that* different from a human," the Graycoat commented in jest, knowing just how different the immortal was.

"Is that right?" Reyna held Nathaniel in a predatory gaze. "Because we're faster." The princess took two impossibly quick steps, putting her face under his, their bodies touching. "We're stronger." Reyna grasped both of Nathaniel's arms and pinned him against the wall. "And..."

There was no time for words. Reyna pushed her soft lips into his and any thoughts of his oath to the Graycoat order was forgotten.

The elf released her strong grip and slid her hands up, behind his head, while Nathaniel tugged on her waist, pulling her even closer.

Unyielding in their embrace, the couple stumbled back into the bedroom, knocking every piece of furniture on their way to the bed. The Graycoat was more than happy when the princess's owl fled the room and out onto the balcony.

Nathaniel became very aware of how much gear he was wearing and the awkwardness of having to stop and remove it all. Apparently, Reyna had thought of the same dilemma and decided to take care of the problem. With a strength that didn't belong to a person of her size, the elf ripped his leather coat open without pulling all the gold buttons off. In a second she had stripped him of his coat and was already removing his shirt. The Graycoat had a moment of self-conscious thought when Reyna looked upon the scars that covered his torso, each a story in themselves.

Relieving him of such doubt, the princess kissed him again while massaging her hands into his chest and abdomen, taking every inch of him in, until her hands found the buckle to his belt and trousers.

"You're very forward, for an elf," Nathaniel managed between kisses.

"I'm *really* not..." After dropping his belt and sword, Reyna pushed him backward, onto the bed. With delicate fingers, the elf hooked her fingers into her nightdress, around her shoulders, and pulled the gown off, allowing the silky dress to fall at her feet.

Nathaniel was speechless before the perfect body that crawled onto the bed, between his legs. It had only been seconds since their lips were parted, but the addiction was undeniable now.

He needed her.

CHAPTER 25
SECURITY MEASURES

Galanör took a precautionary step back after Eliön announced that he was finished with the history mage. The man had been levitated upside down and suspended in the air beside his desk, immobile and defenceless against the elf's techniques in torture. Eliön's disinterest in the mage was the only indication that he had released the magic holding him there.

The body fell to the floor, narrowly missing Galanör's foot. Blood had pooled on the floor, running into the cracks between the flagstones and spreading across the classroom.

"I'm fairly confident he was telling the truth from the beginning," Eliön explained, wiping the blood from his hands, "but I had to be certain..."

That certainty had cost the mage several fingers and most of his facial features. Looking down, Galanör no longer recognised the man who had aimed his wand at him earlier. The elf hid his discomfort at such a gruesome sight.

Ailas rolled out the map on a nearby table - the mage's desk was unusable - and waved his hand over the parchment to bring it to life. Doing his best to ignore the dead body, Galanör examined the map, searching for the room described to them over and over again by the mage. The room was easy to spot, though on the other side of the school, due to the annexe built beneath it. A set of spiral stairs led down into a circular room with a hole in the middle. There were no grounds beneath it on the map.

"The book is in this room." Adamar pointed at the chambers next to the spiral staircase.

"Well done Adamar," Ailas replied sarcastically, evoking a laugh from the others. Adamar grinned at the elf with a smile that said, *I'll get you later.*

"So..." Galanör brought the group back. "We move with caution and take every measure to reach the room undetected. When we find the book we destroy it, ending Malliath's enthrallment. Now, to make certain he doesn't just fly off, I will head to the highest point in Korkanath before you destroy the book. The king has shown me a spell that can attract a dragon for miles. I will pass the king's message on and..."

Galanör didn't really know what would happen next. This particular part of the mission relied heavily on hope. No, he thought; trust in the king. The Lord of Elves had more knowledge about dragons than any other of their kind.

Doubt ate away at him.

They had come so far from home and accomplished so much. There was nothing for them but to move on with the plan and give everything they had to see it through.

The door creaked open and Galanör chastised himself for not hearing the footsteps beforehand. The elves instinctively wrapped themselves in magic and concealed their bodies. Except for Adamar.

"Master Rollo?" The voice of an older man preceded his entrance. "'tis' only me, Master Tibit."

Galanör could do nothing as the man hobbled into the room with his tall staff and looked upon Adamar, standing defiantly between the rows of tables. The new mage looked in horror from Adamar to Master Rollo, dead and mutilated on the floor. Galanör wanted to lash out and punish Adamar, but he was beaten to it by Master Tibit.

Adamar took one step towards the mage with a malicious smile, which Galanör wanted to strike from his face, until Master Tibit waved his staff to the side with more speed than was expected of his age.

Adamar was swept aside by an invisible force that flung the elf with enough power to put him through the wall and into the next classroom. The explosion was ear-shatteringly loud, taking chairs and half a table into the adjacent room behind the elf. If Adamar wasn't dead, he deserved to be, Galanör thought. The stupid elf had forced their hand.

Naiveen revealed herself first, throwing a small knife at Master Tibit's throat. The mage's look of surprise was to be expected when he gripped the knife protruding from his neck and looked on as the elves came into being in front of him. Naiveen's attack, however, had not been a killing blow.

"Yala..." Master Tibit's spell came out as more of a gurgle, but his willpower continued to fuel the magic.

Naiveen had not expected any retaliation and, as such, hadn't seen fit to erect a barrier that would deflect, or absorb, the ball of fire that erupted from the mage's staff. The elf was hit square in the chest and launched backwards into the wall, her body leaving the floor completely. Galanör winced at the sound of her head slamming into the stone. Naiveen wouldn't be getting up anytime soon.

Master Tibit dropped to his knees, still holding onto the hilt of Naiveen's knife in his throat. The pressure he exerted on the blade wasn't enough to stop the blood from trickling down his robes. His eyes darted wildly between the four remaining elves. Seeing their ears, the mage's suffering turned to curiosity, unable to comprehend his final moments or the reason for his death.

A deep groan and falling rubble came from the hole in the wall. Adamar stumbled through the jagged gap with his head resting in one hand, blood streaking down his cheek. The big elf settled on Master Tibit with a look of rage.

Galanör was annoyed that two of his team had been injured by the mage, but Adamar's revenge would be more severe than the man deserved for defending himself.

With a tug of telekinetic magic, Galanör pulled the blade free from the human's neck. Blood poured out in deadly amounts, spilling onto the floor and adding to the massacre. In a final breath, Master Tibit's eyes glazed over and he slumped to the floor.

Adamar growled at the dead body and advanced to kick the mage for good measure until Galanör stopped him with a firm hand.

"Gather your wits. We need to move." Galanör motioned for Lyra to wake up Naiveen.

Putting Adamar through the wall had shattered the boundaries of Naiveen's spell. It wouldn't be long before others arrived to investigate the commotion.

Naiveen awoke with a start before she patted her chest down to put out the tiny flames that licked at her clothes. Lyra helped her up and inspected the damage done to the elf's skin. Galanör could smell the burnt flesh and urged Naiveen to use some of her stored magic to heal it. They would need to be at full health if they were going to make it across the school.

Gideon and Abigail scrambled out of the sparring hall, drenched in sweat, and used their bodies to slam both doors shut behind them. Not a second after the doors closed did the bombardment start from within the hall. The mages' weight was all that kept the horrors trapped on the other side from breaking free.

"*It'll be fun*, he says..." Abigail sarcastically reiterated Gideon's comment between laboured breaths. "I thought you said you had found a way to use the hex-traps as a sparring tool?" Another heavy knock from the other side threatened to send the mages flying down the corridor.

"I'll admit it got a little out of hand." Gideon frantically waved off two fourth years walking by.

"A *little*? Gideon, there's a fully grown Hydra on the other side of this door!" Abigail was forced away from the door after one of the Hydra's heads thundered into the panel where her back was.

Gideon held out his staff and used it to bar the door until she recovered. "Well, it wouldn't have been such a problem if you hadn't removed so many of its heads on our way out!" With every decapitation, the Hydra had grown two more heads in its place. Gideon searched both ends of the corridor, hoping all the masters were detained elsewhere.

"You're right." Abigail's pitch was steadily rising. "I should have just let it devour us instead! You said the biggest thing we'd face would be a Banshee, maybe a Gorgon!" The doors began to crack around the hinges as multiple high-pitched and very hungry roars threatened to break their resolve.

"So how do we fix this?" Gideon tried to ignore the pain in his back and head every time the door slammed into him.

"You're asking *me*? You're the one who botched the hex-trap! How could you forget to place it under a boundary spell?"

Gideon rolled his eyes. The boundary spell would have limited the size and number of monsters that could cross from the shadow world into theirs, keeping the portal inside the hex-trap a moderate size. The Hydra that had crawled out was large enough to eat the Gobbers whole, and it did...

The gnashing jaws only served to increase Gideon's resourcefulness. His mind raced through all the texts he had ever studied about Hydra, specifically their weaknesses.

"We have to pierce its heart!" Gideon exclaimed. "That means no more decapitations, Abigail!"

"Oh, well I think I left my spear in my other robes!" she replied dryly, shouting over the banging doors.

Gideon's mind raced through every possible idea. The Hydra's scales were thick, requiring some force to pierce its hide. *Think Gideon!*

He made a series of ape-like noises before he could find the words. "I've got it! The statue of the old knight, the one outside the alchemy lab!" A statue of a knight from The Dragon War had been guarding that corridor for centuries.

"What about it?" Abigail asked.

"The spear he's holding was inserted afterward. They're two separate pieces!"

"That would mean us outrunning this thing until we reach the alchemy lab..."

Gideon could see the flaw in his plan now; the alchemy lab wasn't even in this wing of the school. But it was close to Master Tibit's room. If they failed to defeat the Hydra, the old mage would surely know what to do. Of course, it would come with some severe punishment for Gideon and Abigail but, at this point, punishment from the masters was better than being digested by a Hydra.

"We'll throw everything we have at it to slow it down!" He made a list of spells in his head, ready.

"We're never graduating..." Abigail was looking as tired as Gideon felt.

"I'll take surviving over graduating any day! Are you ready?" She nodded between fighting the door. "Run!"

The two mages sprinted down the corridor to their right, just clearing the doorway before the Hydra burst through it in an explosion of splintered wood. Its momentum propelled the beast straight into the opposing wall, where the Hydra's bulk crumpled the stone and shattered the bay window. The torches lining the wall fell across the monster's writhing body, aggravating the creature even more.

Gideon regretted looking back upon the nightmarish vision. A dozen heads, that could torment the minds of lesser men, battled one another into lead position to find their prey. Four thick legs, with sharpened claws, lifted its girth and dug into the hard floor, crunching the stone to dust. A long reptilian tail followed the Hydra out of the sparring hall, as it launched itself down the corridor, after the mages.

"Just keep running!" Gideon shouted. "And don't look back!"

Abigail looked back...

"What was that?" Lyra's expression was more curiosity than fear.

"It sounded like a Basilisk..." Ailas replied, notching an arrow.

Galanör had heard that particular screech before. As a younger elf, he had taken many expeditions on his journey to become a warrior worthy of his family name. The Shalarian Woods, the northern crown of Ayda, was home to many unnatural creatures and had served as his father's personal training ground for Galanör.

"That was a Hydra." His statement drew the attention of all.

"Why is there a *Hydra* in the grounds?" Eliön asked, puzzled.

"There could be a hundred reasons in this place," Adamar replied, a little louder than Galanör appreciated. The knock to his head was potentially more severe than the gash he had healed.

"We need to keep moving, *quietly*." Galanör pressed on, sticking to the walls and taking cover behind pillars and hiding in archways.

As the sun had set, a pre-cast spell swept through Korkanath, lighting all the torches and hearths. The flickering shadows served them all, allowing them to avoid the rush of masters and students that flocked to the history classroom. There had been no point in concealing the presence of the bodies when they couldn't hide the giant hole in the wall or the smell of sulphur from the fireball.

The elves sharpened their hearing as they passed through an indoor courtyard, filled with the sound of splashing water from the central fountain. A nod from Galanör was all the communication needed for the team to conceal themselves from sight. Concealment magic was among the most taxing, even for an elf, and the team was slowly absorbing the power that ebbed from their various hidden crystals.

By the time Galanör felt the stinging sensation spreading across his skin, it was too late. Their concealment spell was broken by the wards placed on the room, exposing them to three separate hex-traps. The elves rallied together, back to back, when the first demonic arms, claws and tentacles emerged from the circular portals on the floor. The ancient glyphs lining the traps glowed with brilliant purple light, powering the portals to the shadow world.

"I didn't feel any wards," Lyra said, holding her scimitar in both hands.

"They must have activated Korkanath's defensive measures when they found the dead teachers," Eliön replied, aiming his bow, along with Ailas, at the Ghoul being birthed on the other side of the fountain.

Galanör braced himself, twirling his one-handed sword and feeling the weight of it.

The plan was falling apart.

The odds of the elves reaching the Elder Book were becoming slimmer. The noise about to be created closing the hex-traps would attract every mage in the grounds. How far would they go to achieve their goal? There was a good chance that the students would rise to defend their masters and protect the school.

More children to the slaughter. Galanör's resolve faltered at the thought.

A ten foot Gorgon slithered from the nearest portal, with dozens of snapping snakes whipping out from its semi-human face. The horrific combination of snake and woman was enough to focus all the elves. Preternatural speed launched the Gorgon across the gap in the blink of an eye, two outstretched arms with clawed fingers ready to rip his head off.

Ailas unleashed his arrow into the Gorgon's breast, halting it just enough for Galanör to slice its neck, removing its horrific head from its body. He was careful not to look the monster in the eyes, while it tumbled to the floor, for fear of being turned to stone.

There was no time to catch their breath when the Gorgon was replaced by a charging Minotaur and several hungry Gobbers.

The elves responded with centuries of training. They each moved their own way, allowing the Minotaur to pass through the huddle and be dismembered by a slash of their swords. The separate limbs flew off into a pile, carried by the monster's momentum.

Adamar, never one to pause, picked one of the Gobbers up with his free hand and threw it into one of the portals, causing a backlog of creatures to fall into the hex-trap.

"We need to close the portals!" Galanör looked from Lyra to the hex-trap beside the fountain.

Naiveen followed Lyra, helping to cut a swathe through the advancing horde of monsters. Their swords slashed in every direction, parting limbs from bodies and turning the fountain's water red.

Eliön and Ailas fired their bows with deadly accuracy, never requiring more than one arrow to put a beast down. Whenever a Gobber or Sandstalker was inside their aim, the elves resorted to using the limbs of their bows to beat the enemy away. Then Adamar would wade in with his blade. They were a force to be reckoned with.

Galanör cut open the bellies of two Ghouls in one slice when a familiar voice screamed from beyond the fountain. Naiveen had been slashed across the back by the razor sharp claws of a Gorgon as she tried to defend Lyra from the very portal they were closing.

Galanör reacted with reflexes honed over centuries of fighting and threw his sword across the room, sending it spinning end-over-end to pin the Gorgon's head to the wall. It gave Naiveen the precious seconds she needed to get up and fend off a flying Imp.

Now, without a weapon, Galanör ran to their aid, relying on magic to cut his way through. A flick of the wrist sent a sharpened icicle, formed from thin-air, between the tiers of the fountain and into the heart of a Gobber. With his other hand, Galanör unleashed a fireball into a Werewolf, setting its fur alight.

Calling on the magic of the earth, the elf manipulated the stone on which they stood, creating an eruption of rock that scattered a group of Gobbers and killed a small Troll in the explosion.

When Galanör reached Naiveen and Lyra, he looked back to ensure the survival of the others. Adamar looked happier than ever, while Ailas and Eliön moved with intrepid speed, firing arrows in every direction. Lyra rose to her full height, exhausted, after deactivating the hex-trap.

"Are you hurt?" Galanör asked, as he yanked his sword free of the Gorgon's head.

"These hex-traps are powered by great magic," Lyra replied. "I feel we have been misinformed about the humans' capabilities."

"We need—" Galanör's order was cut short by the blast of telekinetic energy that blew half the fountain to rubble and threw Ailas across the room.

A group of mages had entered the foyer with their wands and staffs held high. They were a mix of teachers and older students by the look of their different robes. Unfortunately, the hordes of monsters flooding the room paid no attention to the mages.

The elves were out of their depth. The school was designed around protecting its students and secrets, and their knowledge of magic had been underestimated. Or had it? Had the elves simply been too arrogant in their assumption that they were superior in every way?

Galanör was forced to roll across the wet floor to avoid a volley of fireballs, icicles and lightning that tore through the horde of monsters. The mages' spells could barely be heard over the howls, screeches and roars bellowing from every creature.

Ailas and Eliön didn't hesitate to drop four of the mages in quick succession with a hail of arrows. The oldest of the mages held up his staff, stopping the final arrow mid-flight with an invisible shield, saving his life.

Galanör could only react with self-preservation in mind. The elf jumped up from his roll and stepped on the remains of a dead Imp to launch himself into a group of Gobbers advancing on Adamar. A swift twirl of his sword killed three in one swipe, while Adamar turned at the pivotal moment and cut the final Gobber in half.

Galanör's momentum never ceased, as the elf continued to run around the fountain, dodging spells and cutting a bloody path through the exotic gathering of beasts.

He charged at the three remaining mages. He conjured a fireball in his open palm and released it in their direction, knowing full well that the mages would easily deflect the spell. The older mage held up his staff, creating a translucent shield that exploded in sparks and flames when the spells collided.

The blinding burst of light was the effect Galanör had intended. The elf skidded on his knees, coming up under the mage's defences, and whipped his sword up with enough force to separate the man from waist to shoulder. Another flick of his sword chopped the second mage's hand off, causing him to drop his staff. But, before the man could scream in shock, Galanör let loose with a barrage of green lightning that launched the mage back down the corridor. He was dead before his body hit the floor.

The last mage was a young girl with short dark hair and glassy blue eyes. She was terrified of Galanör. Of all the monsters in the room, the elf was the only one that scared the girl.

The young mage set free a pathetic ball of fire that Galanör didn't even need magic to avoid. The elf dodged the spell with a quick turn of his shoulders and retaliated by whipping his sword across the girl's hand. He deliberately held back, making certain to cut her fingers rather than remove her whole hand.

The mage's wand fell to the floor, as the girl pulled her hand into her chest, clutching the lacerated fingers. Galanör decided he would hit her with a wave of telekinetic energy and leave her unconscious, but alive. The others would never know of his mercy.

As the magic coalesced in his palm, Lyra appeared from behind the bulk of a dying Gorgon, her speed impossible to stop. Galanör could see what was about to happen but knew he would never be able to come between the mage and the elf in time.

Lyra's sword sliced across the young mage's neck in a blur of motion.

Galanör's lover took no notice of his shock, moving on to kill another Ghoul before tackling another hex-trap.

Her wounded hand forgotten, the mage gripped her gaping throat in futility. Galanör wanted nothing more than to take her in his arms and ease her passing with a friendly face and a kind smile. But he could feel Adamar's eyes on him from across the room. Anything but deadly precision would be taken as weakness and exploited by the large elf.

Before the tears could reach her bloody throat, Galanör strode forward and plunged his blade into her heart, ending her suffering in an instant. The elf pulled his blade out of her body and the young mage collapsed to the floor, dead.

A rage was building inside Galanör. A rage he very much wanted to take out on Adamar, or his father, or even the Lord of Elves! He had pretended for too long to be something he wasn't. How many people had been taken from the world because of his façade? Were the lives of so many worth his noble sense of duty?

The elf's momentary lapse in concentration cost him. By the time he noticed the two new mages, dashing into the hall, Galanör was already under the shadow of a fully grown Hydra.

The overriding fear of being eaten by the maws of a hungry Hydra drove Gideon and Abigail into the violent chaos of the central foyer without a care.

It was only when they reached the broken fountain that Gideon turned back, realising that he had jumped over several dead mages in his frantic dash to escape death. Then there were the cloaked strangers battling the many monsters that poured out of two hex-traps.

Gideon's distress at the dead mages was mirrored in Abigail's expression of horror. Who were these strangers? How had they infiltrated Korkanath? They moved so fast, cutting the beasts to ribbons with ease.

There wasn't time for anything else. The Hydra had caught up with them.

A dozen thick, reptilian heads exploded into the foyer, using brute force to push through the doorway and litter the room with more debris and broken stone. The monster towered over the strangers, who were crouched around one of the hex-traps, and screeched at the top of its mighty lungs.

The feral sound was just bearable for Gideon and Abigail, though it appeared to cause some distress among the strangers, who all covered their ears in pain.

A wet *crunch* smothered the noise of the female stranger's scream. She had been defending the other woman on her knees, apparently trying to close the portal.

"Naiveen!" The name was shouted in anger by one of the archers.

The woman's legs were all that could be seen, poking out from one of the Hydra's jaws. They kicked furiously, for only a moment, but inevitably went limp in the creature's mouth. Two more heads coiled round and ripped off a leg each, swallowing them whole.

An Imp squawked over Gideon's head, fleeing the ravenous Hydra, and paying the two mages no attention. In fact, all the monsters were ignoring them. If it hadn't been for the surrounding mayhem and dead bodies, Gideon would have stopped and admired Master Tibit's spells. Instead of doing that, however, he raised his staff and used a deflective spell to stop an arrow from piercing his chest.

Abigail gripped his arm. "We need to get out of here!"

She was right, of course. They had intended to kill the Hydra, but now that the beast was helping the other monsters in attacking

Korkanath's intruders, it made sense to leave the creature to it and escape before they were caught in the cross-fire.

One of the strangers shouted over the din in a language Gideon had heard many times but never spoken so fluently. The words were unmistakably elvish, with the exception of two words; *Elder Book*. The question of why these people were communicating in elvish was lost to the fear of what they wanted with the Elder Book.

"They're after the Elder Book! We have to get to Master Tibit!" Gideon immediately noticed the attention of the stranger who had spoken in elvish fall on him. The mage instantly regretted his actions. "Run!" They ran for the only door that hadn't been reduced to splinters.

The elvish speaking stranger barked another order between the slashing of his sword. Gideon looked back to see one of the archers break away from the fighting and make for the same door they had escaped through.

Gideon aimed his staff over his shoulder and thought of the ancient word for earth, filling the spell with the urge to explode. The stone floor burst open as if a volcano had erupted from beneath, firing chunks of stone towards the approaching intruder.

With incredible speed, the man ducked back into the room of monsters, narrowly avoiding the explosion. Gideon dared to look beyond, if only in curiosity at how the strangers combatted the beast.

The Hydra was making a mess of things.

The largest of the group, with two long braids on the side of his bald head, had somehow managed to actually climb onto the Hydra and use the creature's thick necks to navigate between the snapping heads.

As impressive as the man's agility was, his chosen method of attack was doomed. The stranger's scimitar lopped off heads left, right and centre. He either didn't notice the multiple heads growing back or he didn't care.

The remaining archer had the smarter idea of trying to pierce its hide with his arrows. Gideon almost stopped to watch, as his uncanny accuracy put every bolt between the Hydra's tough scales and into its soft flesh.

A flash of purple light, at the base of the monster's bulk, told Gideon that the kneeling woman had succeeded in closing the hex-trap.

The cloaked intruder, who had avoided Gideon's spell, dashed back into the corridor after them, notching an arrow as he did. The corridor leading to the west wing was long with no doors to their left and only a wall of glass to their right. There was nowhere to escape the inevitable arrow being aimed at them.

Abigail flicked her wand over her shoulder, creating a momentary shield behind them. The arrow whistled through the air, only to collide with the shield in a flash of light and snap into pieces.

More arrows hurtled down the corridor with more speed and accuracy than Gideon thought possible from a running man. Between them, they managed to deflect every arrow, until they reached the door at the end.

"It's locked!" Abigail pulled and pushed on the door with some force.

"It's Korkanath's defensive wards! Each wing is in lockdown!" Gideon turned to face the archer, only twenty metres away, with his bow held high.

The stranger came to a halt with a menacing smile that chilled Gideon's blood. This man was going to kill them and he was going to enjoy it. As if to savour the moment, the stranger took a long slow breath.

"Get the door open," Gideon instructed Abigail. He brought his staff to bear in a defensive manoeuvre he had learned years ago.

Abigail wouldn't die, and neither would he.

Gideon would fend off his attacker with every spell he knew. He had to. The young mage didn't know if he had it in him to take a life, though he had always wondered how far he would go to save himself. With Abigail behind him, there was no question.

The archer appeared to take Gideon's stance as a challenge and replaced his bow with the sword from his hip. As sharp as the blade looked, Gideon knew it couldn't even chip his staff, which had been enchanted with spells designed to make it as tough as diamond. At least six spells sat ready in his mind, each one harmful and capable of striking a mortal blow.

The rain lashed against the tall arching windows, covering the sound of the melee at the other end. It was just Gideon and the intruder. Abigail was protected behind him, while she used her wand to reveal the spells that covered the door.

The stranger charged at Gideon. The mage braced himself, ready to let loose a telekinetic wave strong enough to shatter bone.

Everything happened at once.

Gideon heard the massive intake of a sharp breath, so loud it could be heard beyond the dark windows, which were being pelted with rain.

The stranger turned to the window mid-charge; his malicious smile turned to one of fear.

Gideon shouted at the top of his lungs for Abigail to take cover, but he never heard the words over the almighty explosion that filled the corridor.

The windows blew in and the stone arches were reduced to flying shrapnel.

A jet of fire engulfed the stranger and continued to spread throughout the corridor.

Gideon dropped to one knee and braced the base of his staff against the floor. He shouted the spell, but his voice was drowned out by the wave of fire flowing over the translucent shield, protecting both Abigail and himself. The magical shield kept the fire at bay, but the spell wasn't strong enough to keep out all the heat.

When, at last, the fire stopped pouring into the corridor, Gideon released the spell and rose unsteadily to his feet. The stone walls had melted and glowed bright orange with steaming droplets falling from the ceiling.

There was nothing left of the stranger that could identify him as even being a man.

Gideon turned to Abigail, who shared his look of complete shock. They were both covered in sweat, their hair matted and ash smeared over their faces.

Malliath's hovering bulk sheltered the corridor from the relentless rain, his giant wings drowning out the winds and turbulent storm.

Gideon took a cautious step forward, tilting his head to catch a glimpse of the dragon, but the sound of his wings faded and the rain returned. The incoming water created more steam, as it cooled the molten stone.

Both mages were stunned into silence. They had spent years at Korkanath having never so much as glimpsed Malliath and, in a single day, they had seen his tail descend into The Adean and actually survive his deadly breath.

How the intruders had set foot on the island without Malliath killing them was a mystery, but now that they were openly attacking mages, the intruders had obviously activated another of Malliath's enthralled spells.

The locking mechanism in the door *clicked* and the door swung open. They still couldn't find the words to describe what had just transpired. A silent agreement was made that they would press on for now and talk later.

They had to reach the Elder Book.

CHAPTER 26

A KING BY ANY OTHER NAME

Merkaris marvelled at his own physique, barely aware of the woman sharing his bed. He considered himself the pinnacle of what any man could hope to achieve with their body, his abdomen and chest dripping with sweat while his muscles worked into the nameless woman.

His mind wandered in the rhythm and the heat. Before the night's proclivities had begun, he had received word via the diviner that he kept on his person at all times.

Alidyr Yalathanil's voice had cut through the ether like a knife, commanding all of Merkaris's attention. "Your lord would have use of you..." the elf had said, his image a distorted reflection across the void.

"I live only to serve Valanis," Merkaris had replied, knowing that an order from one of the Hand was to be taken as if Valanis had commanded it himself.

"Indeed you do. Your assault upon Stowhold was impressive, even I didn't expect you to get as far as you did."

"My spies tell me they moved the Elder Book to Korkanath the very next day," Merkaris explained, smugly.

249

"I am aware," Alidyr replied flatly. "I am sending an Arakesh to Velia, to see our master's needs are accomplished. You are to help this assassin." Alidyr's tone left no room for debate.

"What can I do to serve the great Valanis?" Merkaris had asked.

"Princess Reyna travels with two elven companions. They will make my assassin's job near impossible to complete. You were shown many wonders during your time in Kaliban, Merkaris. Your grasp on the magical world surely surpasses that of any human, even the Magikar."

Merkaris had felt a swell of pride overwhelm him at the memories of his time in Kaliban. His knowledge of magic was beyond the comprehension of the pathetic mages inside Korkanath. The king had been made into the perfect secret weapon for his master and, at the same time, granted more power than any other in the realm. He owed everything to the majesty of Valanis.

"You are to kill the elf known as Mörygan Mörgö," Alidyr had continued. Perhaps Merkaris's acknowledgment had been too arrogant, but the elf felt the need to explain the gravity of his command. "Mörygan is well accomplished in the art of magic and will offer a challenge you have never faced. But know that in completing your task, you will please the Hand of Valanis, and therefore Valanis himself."

"It will be done, my Lord."

Merkaris returned to the present and manoeuvred himself so that he might discard the exhausted woman across the bed. It didn't take long for her to fall into a much-needed sleep, while he sharpened his mind and thought of the task ahead.

The king spent another hour in meditation, dwelling on the lessons imparted to him all those years ago. By the pools of Naius - the only human to ever do so - he had absorbed every detail of the magical world and all it had to offer.

The power given to him... no, the power he *earned*, was what granted him the courage and the skill to usurp his parents, plotting the scheme that saw to their demise and that of his sister. It was only fair in Merkaris's mind. His parents had been weak, unfit to rule, with designs on sending their magically talented son to Korkanath, where his potential would be wasted.

Now, he ruled all the north with a purpose that his parents could never have imagined.

Merkaris opened his eyes, satisfied with the soft glow that emanated from the three crystals that sat on the stone floor before him. The magic stored within them would aid him in the battle to come.

The king collected the crystals and began to dress himself in the dark robes, hidden within one of his chests. Before he could conceal his face with the black cloth, the woman began to stir in the bed. She gasped at the sight of his shadowy image, a pair of long daggers sheathed on each hip.

"Shh..." Merkaris held a finger to his lips, which had stretched into a malevolent smile.

Without another word, the king strode over to the bed and picked the woman up by her throat in one hand. It was a strength that men could only dream of. She squirmed and gurgled in his grip, desperate for precious air. Merkaris carried her out to the balcony and surveyed the mass of ships that made up Direport, below.

"Know that in the swift death I am granting you, you will avoid the suffering that is coming to this land..." The woman's terror-stricken expression told only of her fear that death was imminent, and that there was nothing she could do to stop it.

Merkaris pushed the woman over the lip of the rail and turned back to his room, her death unworthy of his time. Instead, he finished fitting a pair of bracers to his wrists, each inscribed with the ancient language, giving his hands supernatural speed.

Inside the same chest, he opened a secret compartment that held a slender box, the size of his forearm. Merkaris took the box out as if its contents were sacred and delicate. The king couldn't help but smile at the sight of his wand, crafted himself in the heart of Kaliban.

The black shaft was perfectly straight with an elegant strand of rare silvyr coiled from end-to-end. The handle was made from the bone of a centaur, personally hunted and killed by Merkaris for the very purpose of crafting the wand. In his hand it was more deadly than any sword could ever be.

A light knock at the door indicated the arrival of his men. Merkaris called on the magic that filled every fibre of his being and flicked his wand towards the locked door. The mechanism *clicked* and the door swung open, allowing the group of equally shadowy figures to enter the room.

Despite only being able to see their eyes, Merkaris trusted them all. They were killers - *his* killers. They had each proven themselves to him over the years, taking lives on his order without question.

They moved through the halls of Velia's palace like reapers, sending anyone unlucky enough to get in their way to the afterlife.

The wing housing the elves was easy to find, with the extra guards placed along the corridor. Merkaris used magic to douse all the torches and candles in the corridor, casting the killers in darkness. As instructed, the men moved swiftly, eliminating the guards with as little noise as possible, using their bare hands to crack necks or throw small knives.

Merkaris could feel the magical aura on the other side of the door, his skin almost humming in its presence. After years of training in Kaliban, he was always aware of magical beings. Mörygan was clearly a master of the arts, as Alidyr had stated, but it only served to fuel the king's need to challenge himself.

Trusting his men to organise their own attack, Merkaris touched his wand to the door handle, unlocking and opening Mörygan's door. He cast a concealing spell to cut off the sound of the creaking hinges.

The ancient language filled his practised mind, allowing him to wield magic at the speed of thought and without hesitation. It made him feel powerful, like an elf.

Using magic in such a way had taken most of his adult life to master and, as far as he could tell, the teachings of Valanis were the only lessons that could impart such wisdom. The mages of Korkanath had grown lazy over the centuries, wasting time learning new ways to use magic, instead of taking the time to understand it.

The king entered the room boldly, but quietly, while his eyes scanned the room trying to discern the various shadows. It was dark and the balcony doors were closed, keeping out the howling wind and constant rain. It made Merkaris's breathing sound like that of a giant in the quiet room.

The door closed behind him at the same moment all the candles and torches came to life in the room. Standing before him, where only a second ago there couldn't have been, was Mörygan Mörgö.

"You weren't so arrogant as to think you could sneak up on an elf, were you?" Mörygan stood defiantly in his long grey robes with perfectly straight, black hair draped over his shoulders.

Merkaris could only smile, though it was hidden behind the dark veil that concealed his face. This was going to be the fight that finally proved he was worthy of Valanis.

"Do not fear, master elf, I want to look you in the eye when I make history..."

Mörygan looked confused. "History?"

"I am to be the first man to kill an elf in a thousand years!"

"We shall see..." Mörygan held out an open palm and conjured a ball of fire.

CHAPTER 27
RO DOSARN

Resting her head on Nathaniel's bare chest, Reyna rose and fell with his heavy breathing.

The elf was impressed with the Graycoat's stamina. She had been led to believe that humans made terrible bed-mates, due to their inferior bodies. There was nothing inferior about Nathaniel's body. He was strong, yet soft and attentive. Their bodies had come together as if the gods themselves had made them for each other.

Glistening with sweat, the princess rolled over to cool off, unable to remove the smile from her face. Turning back to Nathaniel, she found him looking at her with content. His beautiful dark eyes were easy to fall into and be transported away from the reality of her reason for being there.

While the two were so engrossed in each other, Reyna caught the glimpse of a green flash outside the balcony, when Mörygan released a magical flare. The princess doubted that the flare would be seen amidst the storm and gathering mists between here and Korkanath.

With a delicate finger, Reyna traced the outline of Nathaniel's muscled stomach, up to his chest and over the scars, until she rested her hand against his cheek. His rough hand caressed her thigh and gently spread out across her hip, which he used to pull her closer and kiss her with an intense passion that left the elf craving more.

Using her greater strength, Reyna rolled over Nathaniel and pulled him over again so that she was underneath him. They giggled like children and kissed again, enjoying the warmth and touch of each other's bodies.

The moment was spoiled when Reyna's elven ears picked up a sound outside the room - a sound her instincts told her was danger. She pushed Nathaniel back to inspect the door and he followed her gaze with surprise.

"What's wrong?" The Graycoat was oblivious to the sounds beyond the door.

Reyna could hear someone taking great care to muffle the sound of a dying moan. Another carefully placed one of the armoured guards on the floor rather than letting them fall.

The princess threw Nathaniel onto the other side of the bed and slipped out of the covers to put her nightdress on - all before the Graycoat could even look up.

Two swift strides put Reyna in front of the door, pausing only for a second to retrieve her sword on the way. There was a person on the other side of the door now, she was certain.

The elf angled her sword, ready to plunge it through the wood and into the skulking shadow outside when commotion from Faylen's room distracted her. In her hesitation, the would-be-attacker made their move.

The wood splintered around the lock and the door violently swung open on its hinges. Reyna's reflexes saved her from the concussive blow, allowing her to spin out of the way and twirl her sword around in a defensive manoeuvre.

A man, disguised in dark clothing, sprang into the room, followed by two more similarly dressed, each with a black hood and mask covering their mouth and nose. All three lashed out at the elf with a sword in one hand and a dagger in the other.

The blades came at the princess from three different directions, each angled to remove her head or a limb. It was immediately clear that, despite their skill, they were no Arakesh. Reyna easily deflected two of the swords and dodged another, whipping her leg back to send one of the men flying across the central table, where it collapsed under his weight and sent food tumbling to the floor.

Nathaniel came bounding over the bed, naked, and jumped onto the fallen warrior as he was getting up. The Graycoat's momentum sent the two of them spinning into the nearby wardrobe, splintering more wood. Reyna moved to help him, until Nathaniel exploded from the broken wardrobe and tackled the masked warrior around the waist, picking him clean off the floor and charging him into one of the bed-posts. The knight could handle himself, it seemed.

The princess deflected another barrage of slashing blades and used her elven speed to slip between the two warriors and strike both, one across the thigh and the other across his arm. A dagger dropped to the floor, covered in its owner's blood, while the other limped back to put some distance between himself and Reyna.

The two killers took a breath, reassessing their attack. She was clearly faster and stronger than they had anticipated. It was almost insulting that only a few had been sent to dispatch her.

The painting of a summer landscape fell to the floor beside Reyna, at the same moment as the chest of drawers was knocked from its position beneath it. The princess could hear Faylen fighting on the other side of the wall, and strongly suspected that one of her attackers had been thrown into the stone with a little magical assistance. For the would-be-killers' sake, Reyna could only hope that they had been smart enough to send more than three men to kill her mentor. Faylen could wield a sword just as well as she could muster a lightning bolt.

Behind her own attackers, Reyna could see Nathaniel's naked body ducking and weaving between the warrior's sword, slicing through the air. The Graycoat caught the man's sword arm by the wrist and bent it downwards until the bone snapped and the blade fell to the floor with a clatter. The black-clad warrior was quick, however, indifferent to his pain, as he brought his dagger around to cut Nathaniel's shoulder. The Graycoat fell back, gripping his new wound, but never taking his eyes off the warrior.

His attacker had only one good hand now, leaving Reyna confident in his ability to fend off the man. The elf shook such worries from her mind. Nathaniel Galfrey was a knight and an accomplished fighter, easily capable of besting one assassin... even if he was naked.

The elf's attackers came at her again with renewed fury, seeking revenge for their injuries. Their aggressive attack was sloppy, giving into their pain, with wild slashes that Reyna easily parried and evaded. An upward thrust of her scimitar cut the man with the injured leg up the centre of his body, slicing everything open from groin to head.

A high parry kept the second attacker from removing her head, their intense gaze meeting in the soft glow of the candlelight. The man's eyes were full of hate and determination, desperate to end her life out of duty and personal need.

With her free hand, Reyna called on her innate magic and cooled the air around her palm at an incredible speed. She produced a foot-long icicle that was launched from her hand and into the attacker's chest, killing him instantly. He fell backward and landed on the cold floor with a loud *thump*, the bloody icicle shattering into pieces.

Looking up from his body, Reyna's eyes were drawn to the wet footprints leading from the open balcony, shimmering in the candle-light. The prints were too fresh to belong to Nathaniel or herself and... Her attention was prised away by the fitful gurgling of the last attacker's final moments. Nathaniel held him tight around the neck in a headlock. A swift turn of his powerful arms snapped the man's neck, ending the struggle.

Both were left panting in the dim light, both splattered in the blood of others.

Nathaniel groaned as he stood up, making no effort to staunch the blood running down his injured arm. Reyna's skin tingled - as it did in the presence of magic - before she saw it, the air rippling behind Nathaniel and the dark figure emerging from the shadows.

With a single step forward, the Arakesh plunged his short-sword through Nathaniel's back until it pierced his abdomen. The Graycoat gasped, frozen in place with shock, while the blindfolded assassin rested his hand on Nathaniel's shoulder, keeping him upright.

The princess stopped, too afraid to attack in case the Arakesh adjusted his sword and killed him.

Blood dripped off the end of the sword, dulling its shine. The Arakesh held a stony expression beneath his blindfold. This was a professional killer, not an amateur as the others had been.

The assassin spoke in a gruff voice, with a hint of intelligence not dissimilar from Asher's. "Where's the ranger?" He twisted the sword just enough to elicit pain from Nathaniel.

"Stop!" For the first time, Reyna didn't know what to do while holding a sword. Wielding a blade was one of the few times the princess felt in control of her life, but now she could only hesitate.

"Where's the ranger?" the Arakesh asked again in the same controlled tone.

The short-sword moved again, doing more damage and causing more blood to flow down Nathaniel's stomach.

Reyna didn't know what to say, she didn't even know where the Outlander was. Beyond her room, she could still hear Faylen fighting her own intruders and knew that there was no one coming to help her.

∽

You're getting too old for this...

Asher pulled himself up the palace's outer wall, ascending the slippery stone and fighting against the relentless rain. The ranger had been climbing the high wall for nearly an hour after catching sight of the familiar shadow tackling the same wall.

It bothered Asher that he had only seen one Arakesh. Nasta Nal-Aket would surely have sent more than one assassin to complete the task.

A misplaced foot almost sent Asher to his death. His muscles reacted with pure reflex and his arms reached out for the nearest handholds. Looking down, there was no question of whether he would die or not. Death, however, had accompanied the old ranger as far back as his memory could go. Nightfall had banished the concept of fear long ago, honing the warrior into a beast, fit only for killing.

The sound of clashing steel floated down on the wind, strengthening Asher's resolve to finish the climb. The Arakesh had already scaled the palace and disappeared over the lip of the balcony he assumed was the princess's.

It troubled Asher to think of the speed with which the assassin had scaled the palace. They were taught magic at Nightfall, but most preferred to rely on their combat skills rather than sorcery. It was possible, however, that in the fourteen years since he had gone into exile, the practices of the secret order had changed. Either way, this Arakesh was certainly using magic now, leaving Asher with only one option if he wanted to keep up.

He hated this part.

Using magic felt horribly unnatural to the ranger, as if he wasn't completely part of reality when he used it. He thought of the ancient word for air - not that he needed to, it just helped him to focus - and willed himself to float upwards, towards the balcony.

Asher didn't look down, as his hands and feet left the wall, afraid that it would break his concentration and end the spell. He flew ever upwards and the balcony came up fast through the rain. Timing was everything when it came to ending the spell. Asher released his hold on the magic when the bottom ledge of the balcony was in reach.

The ranger hung there for a moment, holding up his body weight with his hands alone. Climbing canyons, in the south of The Arid Lands, had more than prepared Asher for traversing every kind of terrain. His hands were rough from a youth spent competing with other students of Nightfall to scale the high walls that encompassed the caves they called home.

On top of the balcony rail, Asher perched there while he assessed everything he could see and hear. Two balconies along, the glass doors blew out in a purple flash, in what could only have been a magical explosion. The clashing steel he had heard earlier was coming from the adjacent room, between the three balconies. The room in front of him, however, was quiet and concealed by the flapping curtains in the wind.

Moving undetected was as easy as breathing for the old ranger. He moved to the edge of the door and allowed the curtain to hide him, while he took in the room's contents.

It was a mess.

Broken furniture and food littered the floor between three dead bodies and several pools of blood. Asher saw Reyna first; facing him with terror etched across her face and splattered with blood over her nightdress.

The elven scimitar she wielded was coated in blood but held down in what the ranger recognised as a defensive stance. Following her gaze, Asher found what was causing the princess's look of panic. A naked Nathaniel was being kept upright by an Arakesh, who had driven his sword through the Graycoat's back.

Once again, Asher's stomach flipped as it had when Nathaniel and Elaith had nearly been killed, south of The Unmar. Besides Hector, the ranger had never really cared who was hurt in the big bad world, but the thought of his friends being harmed...

Friends?

Asher couldn't believe the foreign word that ran through his head. A Graycoat of all people; ironic, he thought. Nathaniel gasped in pain, ending his reverie. Friends were distracting, apparently.

"Where's the ranger?"

The unforgettable voice of Ro Dosarn gave Asher pause. Ro had been his equal many times at Nightfall and offered a greater challenge than any of the assassins sent previously.

Like Asher's, his hair had lost most of its colour, but his physique was still that of a younger man. The red blindfold did little to hide the new scars Ro had earned across his face.

Why was he looking for Asher? Had he not been sent to kill the elves like the others? It was possible, however, that the diligent assassin was making certain that he knew where any and all threats might come from.

The amount of blood leaving Nathaniel's body was becoming alarming. It wouldn't be long before the man's knees buckled and the colour would leave his skin.

Asher began to think through every scenario that would allow him to save Nathaniel before Ro could deliver a killing blow. As it turned out, the ranger wasn't giving the Graycoat enough credit, who, in a burst of action, stepped forward and elbowed the Arakesh in the face at the same time.

Both actions sent the two men in opposite directions, releasing Nathaniel from the bite of Ro's sword. Free of the blade, the knight fell to his knees and more blood poured from the wound in his abdomen.

Asher didn't hesitate to leap into the room. He drew his broadsword and set upon Ro Dosarn. The Arakesh reacted as if he had always known the ranger was there, moving naturally into a defensive stance and parrying the first slash of his sword.

Jumping back, Ro dived over the bed until he landed on the other side, where he retrieved his second short-sword from his back.

The two previous students of Nightfall looked at each other across the bed. Despite the blindfold, Asher knew that Ro was looking at him with magical eyes that took in the ranger and everything else besides. The blindfold would give the Arakesh an advantage in this battle, but Asher refused to wear his own, wanting to believe in his natural abilities.

The usual confidence he had, when facing an opponent without his Nightseye vision, was lacking. It wouldn't help either that Asher was sure he was using some other form of magic that helped him climb the palace so quickly. Extra precautions had clearly been taken to ensure the assassin's success.

Behind the ranger, Reyna came to Nathaniel's aid, pressing her hands onto the open wounds on his stomach and back. The blood found every gap and continued to pour out, taking the knight's life with it. Asher stepped out from the side of the bed and met Ro in the middle of the room, each sizing the other up.

"You're looking old, *Ranger*."

Asher had nothing to say to the assassin. They had been rivals like so many others in Nightfall, but the ranger had never taken it personally. Nasta Nal-Aket had taught him early on to put such feelings aside and focus on what was in front of him.

Launching himself at Ro, Asher brought his broadsword down in an arcing motion that would cut any man clean in half. Faster than should have been possible, Ro side-stepped the attack, leaving Asher's sword to collide with the stone floor.

The assassin's counterattack was too fast to dodge and both short-swords cut into the ranger's shoulder and ribs, slicing through the tough leather. The pain could be ignored, but the force of the blow could not, exposing Asher's torso for a swift kick. The impact took the ranger off his feet and threw him into the wall.

Ro smirked at the fallen warrior. "You've become slow, too..." The assassin raised both short-swords, ready to deliver a mortal blow.

As it had in the past, the black gem inside Asher's ring called to him in moments of peril. The instinct to raise his hand and unleash the magic stored inside, instead of raising his sword, was overwhelming. He needed the assassin to move slower and give him time to recover, and so the ring responded with his desire.

Asher raised his hand and felt the invisible force ripple across his open palm, expanding outwards until it captured Ro within its spell.

The Arakesh almost stopped completely, as if he was moving through tar, his expression frozen with aggression.

Asher didn't know how long the spell would last and rolled out of the way, retrieving his fallen broadsword as he did.

Rising to his knees, the assassin's blades came down where Asher had just been lying, his speed returned. Ro couldn't hide his look of surprise at the empty space. With the Nightseye elixir coursing through his veins, the assassin didn't need to physically look at Asher, but he whipped his head around anyway as if to check that his senses were still working.

The ranger took advantage and came up, twirling his broadsword either side of the Arakesh to push him back, away from Reyna and Nathaniel. Ro parried and evaded every swing as he stepped back towards the door, their swords clashing together with enough force to remove a limb.

Asher saw the opening and didn't hesitate to give the assassin a considerable fist to the jaw, knocking him back and out of the room.

Ro slammed into the wall of the darkened corridor, tearing up the hanging portrait of a relative of King Rengar. Blood trickled from his mouth and stained the assassin's grey goatee.

Asher pressed his attack, trained to never give an inch in combat, and brought his broadsword down in heavy sweeps that would remove the head from a Minotaur. Ro was faster than he should have been and ducked and rolled away from the incoming blade.

The two fought through the corridor with furious abandon, each parrying the other's attack as they stepped over the dead bodies of the Velian guards.

The narrow corridor forced them to tailor their strikes and stay close to each other. Asher kept pushing the fight down the corridor, away from Reyna's room, and into the light of the foyer beyond.

Ro had the advantage in the darkened hallway, with the Nightseye elixir keeping him constantly aware of his surroundings.

The ranger could see his error in not wearing his blindfold. For the last fourteen years, it had hung at his belt and reminded him to trust in his own skills. It tempted him always with the power it gave him in battle, but he felt stronger every time he claimed victory without it.

The corridor opened up into a small foyer with a central table, decorated with lavish flowers and fruit. The Arakesh wasted no time utilising the extra space to fall on his acrobatics, flipping and contorting his body into every unorthodox position to gain the upper hand.

It had been a long time since Asher had need of such skills, and his joints had only become worse with his years on the road. The ranger took hit after hit, as Ro kicked and punched Asher from head-to-toe. The blunt force only made the ranger slower, giving the Arakesh more opportunity to slash him with his short-swords.

Asher lunged at the assassin and roared, trying to make as much noise as possible. The ranger knew his only hope of winning this fight now, was if the palace guards heard the commotion and came to investigate.

Fatigue was well past setting in and Asher could feel the weight of his broadsword for the first time. He no longer had the energy to perform the exotic twists and turns of the large blade, putting him into a purely defensive stance.

Ro's swords whipped around the ranger, cutting his arms and legs, always searching for the mortal strike that would end the fight. The heavy footsteps of armoured guards echoed through the hallways, coming up the stairwell behind the assassin.

Asher had one trick left up his sleeve. The ranger dropped his broadsword and fell to one knee before Ro Dosarn, feigning pain from the injury in his cut leg. He looked up at the assassin with very real exhaustion. The blindfold hid the look of victory in the Arakesh's eyes, but Asher knew it was there. That overconfidence was everything the ranger was relying on to give him the perfect opening.

Ro lifted both of his short-swords over his head, preparing to bring them both down on Asher.

The ranger threw himself at the assassin, his momentum taking them down the stairwell. The two men tumbled and rolled over each other, down the spiralling steps, slipping punches in between their tangled bodies.

Ro landed on top of Asher and surprised the ranger by abandoning his swords in favour of using his hands. The assassin held Asher's right arm down and grasped for his fingers, desperately clawing at his index finger where the black gem resided in its silver ring.

"Stay down..." Ro growled, struggling to get a hold on the ring with his knee on Asher's chest.

Asher fought all the harder when he realised the Arakesh was trying to steal the ring.

How did he know about the gem? Had he been sent to retrieve it, or kill him, or both? The ranger was suddenly filled with a lot of questions, but decided to think about them after he had escaped from under Ro Dosarn.

Retrieving a slim blade from the sheath on his hip, the ranger jabbed it into the assassin's thigh. Ro howled in pain and stopped grasping for the ring. His face was consumed with anger, manifesting in the backhand he gave Asher.

"Halt!" A dozen guards in red and blue capes rushed towards them, swords drawn.

Asher could see Ro gathering his strength at the sight of more men to kill. The Nightseye elixir combined with whatever else he had clearly taken was fuelling the assassin to keep going and kill anyone that got in his way.

The ranger could feel the tug of the black gem again, begging him to be unleashed. Magic had never been his way, but he couldn't deny the advantage it gave him when all else failed. In the past, keeping a sliver of the crystal in his ring had made sense if only to protect him from the magic of others.

Ro was too busy - calculating the different ways he was going to kill the guards - to notice Asher pointing his open hand at the assassin's chest. A concussive wave erupted from the ranger's palm and caught Ro, hurling the assassin high into the air until his back and head collided with the ceiling. A small impact crater was left in the ceiling, with a web of cracks where Ro's head had slammed into it. His fall to the floor looked just as painful as his collision with the ceiling.

Asher groaned in pain and exhaustion as he rolled onto his knees, keeping one eye on the assassin at all times. Ro remained where he fell, blood matting his spiky grey hair and dripping onto the white floor.

The ranger hadn't even straightened his back before the guards surrounded him. They looked from him to Ro with confusion and no small amount of fear. The guards recognised the blindfolded Arakesh and knew of Asher from his first meeting with King Rengar. Neither were men they wanted to get into a fight with.

"This assassin tried to kill the guests of your king..." Asher arched his back and sighed in dismay at the many *cracks* and *pops*. "There are more upstairs." The ranger looked up the spiral staircase, but none of the guards followed his gaze.

Four guards broke off and tentatively investigated Ro's prone form. "He's still breathing," one declared.

"Take him to the dungeon!" the only guard with no helmet ordered.

Asher watched them drag his body down the corridor and collect his short-swords. "He's going to need chaining up, preferably suspended from the ceiling with another set of chains keeping his feet secured and off the ground. Strip him naked and burn everything you find on him. Oh, and make sure he's never in the dark..." Asher stopped offering advice when he looked at their faces and realised they weren't listening to him.

The sound of a man in gut-wrenching pain reminded Asher of what was happening upstairs.

Nathaniel was dying!

The ranger made for the stairs, only to be blocked by the sidestep of two guards. Their swords had the slightest wobble to them, betraying their fears.

Asher gave them a hard stare while clenching his fists, cracking the knuckles. Certain that he had made the desired impression, the ranger stepped forward and carried on up the stairs. The guards didn't get in his way.

CHAPTER 28
KEEP YOUR ENEMIES CLOSER

The Hydra lay dead in the middle of the hall, its bulk completely burying the fountain and several dead fiends. Adamar had hacked his way into the creature's heart and plunged his sword through to the hilt.

Lyra placed a hand on the monster's scaly hide, taking a moment of silence for Naiveen, her body somewhere inside the Hydra's belly.

Galanör felt nothing for the death of Naiveen. The loss would only make their mission that much harder to achieve, nothing more.

Galanör dragged his eyes from the lifeless corpse of the girl, killed by Lyra. The terror frozen on her dead face would haunt him with the faces of the children, snatched away by the Mer-folk.

"Ailas?" Adamar walked over one of the dead Hydra heads to stand beside Ailas at the door.

The archer stood as still as a statue with his bow in hand, his gaze fixed on the corridor where they had all heard a great explosion.

Adamar sighed, drawing Galanör and Lyra to their sides. The corridor was a ruin of glass and rubble, the walls and floor consumed by fire. In the middle of the destruction were the charred remains of a body and a broken, half-melted bow. Eliön was dead.

Galanör put a hand on Ailas's shoulder and gave the elf a reassuring squeeze. The two archers had been friends for nearly three centuries and had trained together for this mission for years.

"What magic is this?" Adamar looked on in awe.

Galanör noted the melted stonework. "This is no magic. It's Malliath..."

The other elves turned to each other, questioningly. "Why is Malliath attacking?" Lyra asked. "He didn't kill us on the beach, which can only mean that Princess Reyna received the invitation."

"It must be an addition to the enthralling spells," Galanör mused. "The mages must have enacted a silent magical alarm when they found the teachers' bodies. That's why the hex-traps have awoken in our presence and why Malliath is seeking us out. We have openly attacked the mages and now the entire school is against us."

"You have led us to ruin..." Adamar was quick to blame Galanör.

If they hadn't already lost two of their companions, Galanör would have seriously entertained the idea of separating Adamar's head from his body. He didn't trust the big elf, but his particular skill set would most likely be required between here and the Elder Book.

"We push on," Galanör ordered, striding into the heat of the corridor. A small spell kept the molten droplets from burning his flesh and the fires at bay.

The elf paused to take in the sight of what remained of Eliön, a vision of what was to come in the war they were starting. The efforts of Korkanath's mages were already a testament to the casualties that would be suffered on both sides.

~

"Come on!" Gideon stood guard over Abigail while she studied Master Tibit's door. He held his staff up, training it down the hallway from which they had come.

"This isn't as easy as pointing my wand and commanding the door to open!" Abigail replied, sharply.

They were both stressed. Seeing the bodies of their fellow mages didn't help, but being inside the maelstrom of Malliath's fiery breath was hard to forget. They had both nearly died several times in the last hour, putting their nerves on edge and making them overly sensitive to every noise and shadow.

Gideon glanced over his shoulder to see Abigail carefully scanning her wand over every inch of the door. The sound of lightning being discharged, somewhere beyond the hallway, yanked Gideon's attention back to guard duties. The whip and crack of the lightning were followed by screams and steel clashing against wooden staffs.

The mage pointed his staff to the floor and commanded the elements to coat the stone in a layer of slippery ice. If the intruders came at him, they would have a hard job moving as fast as the archer had.

The unmistakable sound of fireballs scorching the walls and rebounding off magical shields resounded down the hallway. They were drawing closer.

"Who do you suppose they are?" Abigail asked, feeling for the vibrations in her wand.

"I don't know," Gideon said, hefting the staff in his hands and adjusting his grip. "But they're well trained in the magical arts, or they wouldn't have made it this far."

"The Black Hand, perhaps?" Abigail's tone was that of great concentration.

Gideon considered the suggestion for a moment. It was entirely possible the rogue group of mages had finally had enough of being hunted by Korkanath's mages and decided to strike back. The mysterious group of dark wizards had formed centuries ago. Very little was taught on the subject, but plenty of myths and legends had been built around them and the constant battling in the shadows that had taken place between the two groups.

"I don't think so." Gideon winced at the sound of a distant explosion. "They seem to prefer weapons to magic, and I didn't see any wands or staffs."

"I've got it," Abigail announced triumphantly. A silent revealing spell exposed the door's secrets. The dark oak was suddenly overlaid with blue and green light that twirled and spiralled until words began to form.

"What is it?" Gideon asked, wondering what the delay was.

"The door can only be opened with the correct phrase," Abigail answered with dismay.

"What do you mean?" Gideon asked more frantically.

"I've commanded the locking mechanism to reveal the clue built into the magical ward that protects the room. Listen to this." Abigail cleared her throat before reading the words projected on the door. "I am the king of my kind, the greatest of all. My fangs are legendary, delivering everlasting pain, but to look upon me brings only death. Should you survive our meeting I will stay with you always, but know that my presence is what makes you stronger...?"

Gideon's mind went blank. He thought through every page of Palantine's Bestiary, trying to connect the riddle to the monster. The sound of arrows being loosed and swords slicing through flesh grew ever closer, distracting him from the riddle. An agonised yelp escaped the lips of another fallen master, who skidded across the floor at the end of the hallway, his robes smouldering around his chest.

"Oh, of course, *the king of my kind*!" Abigail repeated with excitement. She stood back from the door and boldly spoke, "Basilisk." The blue and green writing disappeared as the metallic lock unbolted and the door opened by itself. "Yes!"

"Get inside!" Gideon wasted no time in bundling her into Master Tibit's room and slamming the door shut behind them. With his staff pointed at the lock, Gideon resealed the magical ward that barred the door shut.

Both mages turned to meet each other's gaze and immediately embraced with a comforting hug. They had been each other's rock throughout all their years of tutelage at Korkanath, often relying on the strength of the other to keep them going through hard times.

Surviving Malliath's fiery breath topped the list of things they had endured together.

"The book!" Abigail seized Gideon's arms, catching sight of it in the corner of the room. "How do we protect it?"

"If Master Tibit's warning is anything to go by, we shouldn't touch it." Gideon looked around the room for inspiration. The master was clearly in the middle of several experiments, though Gideon could only fathom half of it all.

Abigail gasped and covered her mouth. They could both hear several voices talking on the other side of the door. The ice had done little to slow the intruders' progress, apparently.

"What do we do?" Abigail whispered harshly.

Gideon continued his frantic search around the room, only now he was looking for somewhere they could hide. In his desperation, Gideon always found he became more resourceful and, there it was, staring him in the face. He grabbed Abigail's arm and dragged her over to the large wardrobe, opposite the Elder Book. The young mage opened the doors with haste, ripped all of Master Tibit's ceremonial robes off their hooks and flattened them to the wardrobe's base.

"Get in!" He had no idea how long it would take the invaders to breach the warded door.

Abigail complied and stepped into the wardrobe, keeping her wand out of her leather holster.

Gideon aimed his staff at the Elder Book. "Ebori..." he spoke the word aloud to give it stronger meaning, aware of the magic it would consume. The book and stand faded from sight, becoming completely invisible to the eyes of any being.

Satisfied with his spell, Gideon mentally commanded his staff to shrink so that he could fit it inside the wardrobe. Abigail pushed her toes into one of the doors so they could still see into the room.

They didn't have to wait long.

The door to Master Tibit's room exploded into the room, splintering into chunks and crashing into the many experiments. Glass was shattered and tables were broken under the impact of the door, sending exotic liquids and potions in every direction.

The two mages braced themselves against the *shudder* that overtook the wardrobe. Gideon couldn't believe the power of the intruders. Clearly, that explosion was intended to go the other way if the door was ever breached, but somehow they had repelled the entire warding spell.

Gideon tilted his head to get a better look through the crack between the doors. Four people strode into the room with the confidence only gained from killing so many. They all wore dark cloaks, with their hoods down, exposing their elegant features and prominent cheekbones.

With the exception of the bald one with braids, the other three had long beautiful hair that appeared softer than silk. The only thing that lessened their visage was the spatters of blood that stained their clothing and skin. The dark haired woman scanned the room and continued to speak in perfect elvish.

"We should converse in man's tongue for now," the one with long brown hair said. "We shouldn't give away our identity yet. Now find the book. The human said it was in here."

Everything he said gave Gideon pause and alarm, forcing him to inspect the invaders again with a careful eye. The young mage felt his mouth drop at the sight of the bald one's pointed ears.

Elves!

Judging from her vice-like grip, Abigail had come to the same conclusion.

The elves spread out and began to investigate everything in Master Tibit's possession. Gideon could feel exhaustion setting in as his concealment spell started to take its toll. He called upon the magic stored in the small crystals, interlaced around the centre of his staff. Sweat gathered around his temples and dripped down his cheeks, as the magic called for more energy to keep the spell alive. The knuckles on his hand turned white under his intensifying grip.

He had to hold on.

Galanör kicked the wooden debris, left by the door, making certain the Elder Book hadn't been buried underneath.

At first glance, it appeared the book wasn't stored in the room at all, but Galanör knew it was more human trickery. The mage had told them nothing but the truth and the elf didn't doubt it.

Another door inside the master's chambers caught Galanör's eye. The magic woven into the wood was impossible to ignore. From what he recalled of the map, however, the room beyond was a spiral staircase that led to a lone room beneath this one and nothing else. In fact, the three-dimensional map showed there to be a hole inside it.

Galanör moved to investigate the door when he felt the over-bearing presence of another. Adamar was close behind him, appearing to look busy inspecting the contents of a small cupboard.

A sixth sense, honed after centuries of training, told Galanör that something was very wrong. The small hairs on the back of his neck stood on end when he considered the way in which Adamar had been forced upon his group.

The big elf had shown nothing but contempt for Galanör since they left Ayda's shores, and had done nothing but try to undermine him every step of the way. The advisors to the king, responsible for thrusting Adamar upon them, were all elves who sought a loftier position within their hierarchy.

Was it possible that another family had designs on removing the rising Reveeri family from the picture by killing Galanör?

Moving away from the door for a moment, Galanör ensured his back was never to Adamar, who would surely make his move the instant they located the Elder Book.

"It's here!" Ailas exclaimed.

Galanör kept Adamar in his peripheral vision, while he walked across the room to Ailas's side. The archer had his hands out, gesturing in the direction of an empty space in the corner of the room.

"I can feel the power of the spells inside," Ailas continued. He used a revealing spell to break the concealment.

As if emerging from an invisible fog, the Elder Book took form in front of them, nestled within a glass covering. The book itself was bound in thick leather, its colour faded over a thousand years, and the pages a tint of yellow.

All thought of Adamar's ill intent was forgotten at the sight of the book and the prospect of finally returning home, victorious. Though, for Galanör, he felt he would simply be happy to forget his time on man's shores and do everything he could to erase the images of the innocents he had killed.

"What are we waiting for?" Ailas's grief made him impatient and careless.

Galanör didn't move quickly enough to stop the elf from reaching out and lifting the glass covering. "No!" His plea was too late for Ailas.

The spell protecting the book was merciless, its singular purpose created to bring instant death to whoever removed the covering.

Ailas gasped in frozen terror as the glass box turned to ice in his hands before it slowly moved up his fingertips and continued along his arms. From his skin to the marrow in his bones, everything was turned to solid ice, including the clothes and weapons he wore.

"Help... help me..." The words barely left his lips, which were losing their colour.

The other elves stood back, afraid to touch Ailas in case the curse could be passed on. The archer dropped to his knees with the frozen glass box stuck in his shiny, ice-covered hands. His legs were soon covered by the encroaching ice, cementing him to the floor.

"Help..." Ailas's last plea was just audible before the ice froze his vocal cords and his entire head glazed over.

The moment of silence was only broken when the archer's body shattered into a thousand pieces, spreading him across the floor and between the feet of his companions.

Another one dead.

Galanör crouched low, hesitantly picking up a piece of ice that resembled the side of Ailas's face. Like the other killers who had died under his command, Galanör felt nothing at his passing, except that he wished a swifter death had met the archer.

That curse had been designed not only to kill but to deter anyone else from trying to take the Elder Book. To steal the book wasn't just to die, but to die slowly and painfully.

"Will we all perish under your leadership, Galanör?" Adamar was behind him again, his large shadow looming over the elf.

His sixth sense screamed at Galanör now, urging him to take immediate action or face certain death. Under the cover of his cloak, Galanör rested his hand on the hilt of his sheathed sword. He could have it out and brought to bear before Adamar knew what was coming.

The distinct sound of a sword passing through a person's body came from behind Adamar. Galanör turned on the large elf, confused but battle-ready. Standing before him, Adamar gurgled and dribbled blood.

Galanör followed the large elf's gaze to the elegant scimitar protruding from his chest cavity, coated in warm red blood. Adamar's eyes betrayed his anger and confusion, all too aware that his death was imminent, but also unjustified.

The blade slid out of his back and the elf dropped to his knees, falling flat on his face in the icy remains of Ailas.

Standing in the place of Adamar was Lyra, her sword wet with the blood of her kin. She had seen the coming calamity and acted to save Galanör at the price of killing one of her own. He sighed heavily at what had transpired but managed to give Lyra a warm smile of appreciation.

Lyra's reflecting smile vanished like a candle blown in the wind. Galanör didn't have time to see the deception until it was too late.

She flicked her hand over his face, unleashing a wave of magic that lifted the elf off his feet and launched him across the room.

～

After the book had been found, Gideon was barely able to regain his strength enough to remain standing, but events outside the wardrobe kept his attention fixed.

The protective spell that killed the archer had been hard to watch, and he felt Abigail's head fall on his shoulder more than once, seeking comfort. Everything after that had only created more confusion for Gideon. The female elf killed the larger elf and hurled the apparent leader across the room.

All the while, the young mage kept his eyes on the exposed Elder Book.

Abigail and he looked at each other, the same thought passing through their minds. Now there were only two of them, and from the look of it there would soon be only one; a massive improvement to their odds.

A strange question Gideon had never had to entertain crept into his mind after following that train of thought. He had already decided that he was prepared to take a life to protect Abigail and himself, but did he have the same gumption to protect a book?

To lose the Elder Book would surely mean the possible death of many more than just the two of them. The power to control Malliath the voiceless could be devastating, though why any elf would seek that end, Gideon did not know.

"Lyra..." The one known as Galanör rose unsteadily to his feet. Gideon could just make out the thin line of blood that ran down the elf's face. "Why? I don't understand."

"I should hope not." Lyra stalked round the dead body of the large elf, her tone laced with superiority. "We have spent a long time planning this, longer still than your precious king has planned to re-take Illian from the humans. Keeping all of you in the dark was a crucial part of the plan," the elf purred patronisingly.

"*We?*" Galanör leaned into the archway that divided the room.

"*We* are everywhere," Lyra continued. "We advise your king. We fill your ranks. We know your secrets." The elf laughed with a glee that made Gideon's blood chill. "*Paldora's celestial star graces daylight sky, and in its beauty ordains calamity...*"

Gideon had never heard that phrase before, but judging by Galanör's expression, the elf knew of it well.

"Why do you speak of this?" Galanör asked.

"Come now, lover." Lyra adopted a seductive tone. "You know of the Echoes of Fate as well as I. A few days from now, Paldora's Star will reveal itself for the first time in daylight sky, and Valanis will rise again... so it is foretold."

Galanör's expression turned from confusion to horror. "You serve the dark one?"

"It is folly to serve any other," Lyra replied quickly.

"Paldora's Star has streaked across the *night's* sky nine times since that prophecy. What makes you so sure this time will be any different?" Gideon could see that Galanör's horror had quickly turned to anger.

"That's the problem with our kind; no faith anymore." Lyra didn't wait for a reply but, instead, burst into action and threw a small, previously concealed knife at Galanör.

Caught off guard, the elf was struck in the shoulder by the blade, forcing him back towards the sealed door.

Gideon didn't know what to make of any of it. The two mages could only watch in fascination as the two elves collided with their swords in a flurry of twists and turns so fast that human eyes struggled to keep up with them. The name *Valanis* rang a bell in Gideon's mind but he couldn't place it. He mouthed the name to Abigail who replied in hushed tones.

"The Dark War. The civil war between the elves."

Gideon nodded his understanding. Valanis had been the key

instigator in starting the war, though the mage could hardly remember why. An elven war a thousand years past wasn't at the top of his to-know-list.

The two elves fought with speed and grace, reminding Gideon of a dance rather than a fight to the death. It was hard to make out who was winning though; when it came to sword fights, the mage was no expert.

Again, he found his eyes drawn to the exposed book. They had to protect it from both elves, for it didn't matter which one survived. Apparently one wanted it to help the elves overthrow Illian, and the other wanted to use the book to serve Valanis, a being wholly associated with evil.

Gideon was about to suggest a plan when current circumstances forced the mage's hand. Both Abigail and he jumped from the wardrobe in a desperate attempt to avoid the stray fireball. The wardrobe exploded into pieces, raining splinters down amid a thousand chunks of the frozen dead elf.

Gideon looked up through bleary eyes to see that Galanör and Lyra had paused their fight to look upon the fallen mages.

"We need to get the book!" Abigail scrambled to her feet before Gideon could stop her. Her wand levitated the book from its stand, but her genius was for naught.

Gideon could only watch with dread when Lyra levelled her hand at Abigail and loosed an icicle, sharper than any sword. The elf moved so fast that, it seemed, the icicle could be heard plunging into Abigail's chest before it was seen leaving Lyra's palm.

Her pained gasp stole the breath from Gideon's lungs, leaving him to relinquish his staff in place of catching her falling body. The Elder Book landed on the floor at the same moment he caught her. He didn't know what to say. He only knew that she would certainly die from this wound and that there was nothing he could do. That helplessness stung deeper than any wound Gideon had ever suffered.

The world and its troubles disappeared in that moment.

Abigail's copper ringlets fell over his crouched knee and her bright blue eyes looked longingly into his. He couldn't bear to look at the icicle protruding from her chest. Her wonderfully pale skin was turning a deadly shade paler every second.

With a soft hand, Abigail stroked Gideon's cheek, as if the mage knew she would never get the chance again. Gideon held it tight in his own, shocked by the speed at which she was losing her warmth. Tears flowed freely from his eyes at the thought of never being greeted by her warm smile again. He was barely aware of the clashing steel behind him.

Without a word, Abigail's hand went limp and the life faded from her eyes. She was gone, forever.

Shock set in. Gideon held her body, his senses taking everything in but his mind unable to process it. The two elves continued their dance, wreaking havoc across the room. The young mage brought Abigail close to his chest and embraced her with all his strength as if he might bring her back with his love alone.

"It doesn't matter what you accomplish today!" Lyra's voice sounded a hundred miles away. Gideon's vision took in the sight of the elf, on her knees and at the mercy of Galanör's blade. "Valanis will rise and usher in a world fit for the gods—" Her words were literally cut short by the sweeping motion of Galanör's sword.

Gideon placed a gentle kiss on Abigail's forehead, oblivious to Lyra's rolling head. The silence that followed woke the mage from his grief, revealing him to be the only living thing in master Tibit's chamber. Galanör was gone, and so too was the Elder Book.

The mage felt his grief turn into a burning anger that demanded his attention. Lyra was dead, but Abigail's death could still be laid at Galanör's feet. Gideon quickly unstrapped Abigail's wand holster and applied it to his own leg. He then sheathed her wand and retrieved his staff.

Now, the elf would pay.

～

Galanör burst through the door and into the lashing rain, atop Korkanath's high walls. The relentless wind and ice-cold droplets did nothing to numb the betrayal of Lyra or the killing of yet another innocent girl.

Somewhere between sadness and rage, the elf screamed into the night. He knew that the king's machinations were ultimately to remove Valanis from being a potential threat, but Galanör had no idea that Valanis had people fighting back, and so close!

There was a war brewing; only he had a feeling it wasn't going to be between elves and men. How long had the dark one been manipulating them? Had his entire quest so far been at the design of Valanis's followers?

The faces of the dead haunted him once more, along with the despair of the young mage who held his dying friend in his arms. Was his duty worth the suffering of so many?

The sound of great wings flapped overhead, drawing the elf's keen eyes to the night sky. The pouring rain made it almost impossible to spot the black dragon. Galanör looked to the Elder Book, floating by his side and protected from the rain by a spell of his own. The elf levitated it before him and commanded the pages to turn without touching it, fearful of any curses. He would have to act fast now, before Malliath descended on him.

The spell was easy to find, thanks to his education in the ancient language. There was no counterspell or incantation to recite. He need only burn the pages, expressing his intent to Malliath before offering the invitation from his king.

Galanör hesitated. Now, in the final moment of his mission, the elf didn't know if he was doing the right thing. The sound of gliding wings rippled through the sky, making his decision for him. It didn't matter what Galanör did after he freed Malliath, the important thing was that he freed Malliath. It might just be the only good thing he had done since leaving Ayda.

A blast of superheated energy, akin to lightning, caught Galanör on the back of his shoulder and knocked him to the floor. With his concentration broken, the Elder Book collapsed with him, its pages sprawled open.

"ELF!" The rage-filled scream exploded across the night.

Galanör lifted himself from the floor, flexing the same shoulder joint that had now been stabbed and burnt by magic. The young mage from the master's chamber stood opposing him in the rain, his staff aimed high. Galanör had never seen so much fire in a human's eyes before. This man, if he was old enough to be called one, intended to fight a superior foe with no concern for his own life.

"GO BACK!" Galanör shouted over the pelting rain.

The mage took no notice and came at the elf, wielding his staff as if it were a spear. A high jump brought the young man down on Galanör with the tip of his staff angled to strike the elf's head. To Galanör's superior senses, his every action was easily anticipated. He didn't have it in him to counter the mage, however, and continued to dodge and evade his every swing and thrust. More than once, the mage let loose with another blast of energy or a fireball, both repelled by Galanör as an afterthought.

Before the next lunge, both elf and man stumbled under the buckling wall. Galanör had seen the look on the mage's face before, on the faces of others who looked upon something awe-inspiring, yet terrifying at the same time.

Malliath was behind him.

Galanör turned quickly to see the great head of the dragon, his purple, reptilian eyes fixed on the elf. Four curving horns sat above his eyes and extended into the air, as a crown on the head of a king.

Malliath's head coiled in the manner of a snake, ready to strike, as his magnificent wings spread out beside him, each glistening with a tough, purple membrane. The dragon sat upon four thick legs, plated in black armour, natural to his kind, ending in claws sharp enough to score the stone wall he rested on. In the darkness behind him, a giant black tail that ended in the shape of an arrowhead, swished through the air, hypnotically.

The elf moved back, slowly, the mage long forgotten in the face of such a creature. Malliath's maw opened to allow a forked tongue to slip out between razor-sharp teeth. Galanör could sense it coming as if the dragon was waiting for the mage to move aside so he could reduce the elf to ashes. He only had one move left to make, though whether it would save his life or not, he didn't know.

Galanör unleashed a fireball at the open pages of the Elder Book, setting the enthralling spells alight.

The wall shuddered again, knocking the two bipeds over when Malliath the voiceless roared for the first time in a thousand years. The elf guessed the dragon's roar to be somewhere between pain and a cry of freedom.

Malliath thrashed about, dealing more damage to the crumbling wall, while ancient glyphs shone a brilliant violet along his body. Until now, the imprinted glyphs had remained hidden, blending into the dragon's dark scales and plated armour. As Galanör watched in wonder, the ancient glyphs slowly vanished from Malliath's body, causing the dragon more distress.

Somehow, through it all, the mage found the balance and courage to renew his attack upon Galanör. This time, he came at the elf firing from both a staff and a wand, forcing Galanör to deflect both attacks while watching his footing on the crumbling wall.

More than once, the two combatants were made to duck under a wing or jump over flying debris. Still, the mage came at him, all fury and abandon. Whether the young man could see it or not, the wall was coming down and Malliath intended to fly away.

Galanör knew in that moment that his only hope of survival was to latch onto Malliath and let the dragon take him far from here. How far, he didn't really care anymore.

"Run!" was his final warning to the mage, as he turned for the dragon.

With elven agility, Galanör nimbly scaled Malliath's muscled leg and wrapped his arms around one of the many horns that ran along the creature's spine. To the elf's great surprise, the human mage didn't hesitate to follow him. Only his speed could not compare to that of an elf. Malliath launched into the air, off his hind legs, with enough force to bring down the entire wall.

Galanör wanted to turn away, sure that he was about to witness the death of another, too young to die. The mage surprised the elf again with his determination and no small amount of luck. At the last possible second, the young man leaped across the opening chasm and grasped one of the spikes on Malliath's tail.

Korkanath quickly dropped away and both were taken high into the heavens, astride the beating wings of a dragon.

CHAPTER 29
MAKING HISTORY

Mörygan crawled across the floor in a way that Merkaris felt was beneath an elf. He should have known when he was beaten and met his maker with some dignity, while his honour was still intact. The arrogant elf had assumed his power was levels of magnitude above Merkaris's, and now he would die because of that miscalculation.

The king of the north limped behind the elf, using every technique he knew to ignore the pain in his leg... and his back, shoulder, chest and head. Mörygan had wounded Merkaris from head-to-toe, but the human was still standing and that was what mattered.

Merkaris patted down his left arm - which was still on fire - as if it was no bother. The limp in his leg would take more of a seeing to since it wouldn't look good for the king to be limping after doing nothing but sleeping.

The elf's chambers had been obliterated in the fight. The balcony doors were missing, having sprayed glass everywhere, some of which was still lodged in Merkaris's body. The bed linen was on fire with several scorch holes burned into the mattress. Not one piece of furniture had escaped the devastation, littering the room with splintered wood and broken chandeliers.

One corner of the room was completely frozen over with a thick layer of ice. That particular spell had delivered a rather nasty frost-bite to the elf's hand, turning it black. Worming between it all was a thick trail of elven blood, slowly being smeared over the stone floor by a crawling Mörygan.

Merkaris pointed his wand at the elf's back and with a flicking motion, the king flung Mörygan across the room, slamming him hard into the wall. The sound of bone cracking was just audible over the cry of pain that escaped Mörygan's lips. Merkaris bit down on his own pain when he realised at least two of his fingers were broken in his wand hand.

"Impossible..." The word came out of Mörygan's mouth as a whisper, looking upon the foreboding shadow that advanced on him.

Merkaris laughed. "Nothing is impossible through Valanis. He has the knowledge of the gods. The same gods your people have forsaken..."

"Were you sent to talk me to death, then?"

Merkaris lashed out immediately, silencing the whelp with a spell he had learned from Nakir Galvörd, one of Valanis's Hand. The spell acted as a whip, producing a red-hot line of energy from the tip of the wand. It cut through the air as easily as it did Mörygan's face. The elf moaned in agony, covering his cheek, but failed to keep the blood from gushing between his fingers.

Commotion in the adjacent rooms demanded Merkaris's attention. It seemed the fight was over and someone was still alive, but in pain. His men would be dead, of that he had no doubt, but nor did he care, since they were all replaceable.

The fate of the Arakesh was unknown, but he was sure all would be revealed in time. For now, though, he had to finish his work and get back to his chambers unnoticed. It wouldn't be long before someone came to check on Mörygan Mörgö.

Without a word, Merkaris aimed his wand at the elf and unleashed a barrage of lightning that consumed every inch of his victim's body. The king of the north smiled to himself. The elf's body would be smoking long after he was dead.

By the time Asher returned to Reyna's room, his new wounds were demanding attention as they spread aches and pains throughout his body. The sight of Nathaniel's prone and pale body helped him put aside such troubles.

The elven princess knelt over his torso, her hands covering the wound in his abdomen. Blue light emanated from between her fingers and Asher noticed the deep look of concentration on Reyna's face.

The ranger paused on his way over, stopping to check the faces of the dead assassins on the floor. Two of them were hard to place but looked familiar, but the third, closer to Nathaniel and with a broken neck, was easy to place. He had seen the man's face when King Merkaris's convoy passed them by on The Selk Road. Asher scrutinised the would-be-killer's features one last time, making certain it was the same man. Chances were high that the other familiar faces belonged to men he had seen in the convoy. Though doubtful, it was entirely possible that Merkaris had no idea that some of his men were rogues.

Asher couldn't see how the king of the north fitted into the attack, however, as it had clearly been orchestrated by the Arakesh.

The ranger looked up to see a white owl staring at him from its perch atop a splintered wardrobe. He couldn't recall the name of the bird, but he found its intense stare to be unsettling.

"Is he alright?" Elaith asked, her expression full of concern for her mentor.

"He will be," Faylen replied, standing over Reyna with her scimitar in hand.

The princess was wearing a long nightdress, stained red with blood. Not her blood, Asher noted.

Nathaniel gasped and his brown eyes opened wide for a moment. Sweating, Reyna visibly relaxed and removed her hands to inspect the new flesh, though it was still coated in dried blood. Asher couldn't help but smile at the look of surprise on the Graycoat's face.

Elaith's grin outshone them all. "Why are you naked?"

Asher chuckled heartily, while Reyna turned a shade of pink and Faylen rolled her eyes. Nathaniel just let his head fall back and rest on the floor, relieved and surprised to be alive.

"Thank you..." The Graycoat took Reyna's hand in his own.

"You should thank Asher." Reyna glanced at the ranger, a warmth in her eyes that Asher wasn't accustomed to. "Had he not arrived when he did, I wouldn't have been able to heal you."

Asher simply nodded at Nathaniel's grateful smile, still enjoying the look of adoration he had received from the princess. The ranger enjoyed the new feelings his friends evoked in him and yet, at the same time, his instincts told him it was futile. People died around him. They always had and they always would, he thought. Not only that, but allowing himself to feel anything for anyone put him at risk as well.

Nightfall had bred that into his bones.

"Where is the assassin now?" Faylen asked, doing her best to ignore the naked Graycoat on the floor.

"Rengar's guards have taken him into custody."

"He *lives*?" Faylen's words intoned her disappointment.

"Barely..." Asher blinked hard to stop the room from spinning. "The guards took him away before I could finish him."

"At least he failed." Reyna looked at Asher again with a knowing look. It seemed the princess knew Ro Dosarn hadn't come for her.

"Indeed..." Faylen looked back to her room, distracted. "Where is Mörygan?"

"Probably interrogating anyone he left alive." Reyna didn't appear bothered by the elf's absence, clearly trusting in his abilities.

Faylen disappeared into her room, while Reyna and Elaith helped Nathaniel to his feet. The Graycoat was still a sickly shade of grey, and he nearly lost his footing concentrating on maintaining the blanket now wrapped around his waist.

"Where the hell have you been, anyway?" Nathaniel asked Asher through glazed eyes.

The ranger took Nathaniel's weight from the elves and half-carried him to the edge of the bed, where the Graycoat appeared happy to sit, no doubt feeling the effects of blood loss.

"Doing what I was paid to do," Asher replied casually.

Nathaniel smirked, as if intoxicated. "I think you've gone above and beyond what the king paid you to do..."

Before Asher could find a witty reply, Faylen called for help in the distance. "Wait here," the ranger ordered. Without his assistance, Nathaniel flopped onto the bed.

Elaith stayed with him so Asher could accompany Reyna into Faylen's room and then into Mörygan's. Asher scanned the debris. It was more of a mess than the princess's chamber, with evidence of a significant magical battle all around.

The ranger couldn't leave his wounds much longer and placed his hand over the cut on his thigh. Magic flowed out of the black crystal and into the wound, healing it by the time he caught sight of the dead body, lying at Faylen's feet. The smoke rising from the body was evidence to the charred scent Asher had stuck up his nose.

"He's dead." Faylen rolled Mörygan over so they could see his burnt and lacerated face.

Asher didn't detect any heartache on Faylen's part, or Reyna's for that matter, but rather a sense of distress that Mörygan could be killed at all. The ranger couldn't judge them; from the brief time he had spent with the elven advisor, he had come to the conclusion that Mörygan Mörgö was an arrogant ass.

"Who could do this?" Reyna asked.

"The elf from the woods, perhaps?" Asher suggested with a coy look cast over Faylen. Her recognition of the masked attacker hadn't been lost on the ranger.

"Elf?" Faylen was quick to respond. "What elf?"

"*Come on*, we both know an elf when we see one." Asher walked away to inspect the rest of the room.

"We will talk about this later..." Faylen added at the sound of heavy boots marching down the corridor.

"Worrying about *that* shadow is the least of our problems." Nathaniel walked into the room, with his arm slung over Elaith's shoulder, now partially dressed and ignoring their looks of concern. "The men who attacked us; I recognised them. They're part of King Tion's escort; they work for Merkaris."

"It isn't safe to stay here," Asher added, making no comment that he had made the same observations. It seemed that even in his debilitated state, the Graycoat wasn't to be underestimated.

"That much is obvious, Outlander." Faylen was already gathering any belongings she could find of Mörygan's.

Asher met Reyna's apologetic look but made no acknowledgement. Faylen's disdain for the ranger was clear to see, though he didn't know why and he didn't really care.

The entire realm had similar feelings for Outlanders and often with good cause. The black-fang tattoo below his eye, however, was there to stay. Asher only wished he knew how it came to mark his skin.

The door burst open as two Velian guards entered the room and parted, making way for King Rengar in his flowing robes. His face portrayed a dramatic performance, though the ranger couldn't tell if it was rehearsed or not. Had it not been for the gain the king stood to receive from the elven alliance, Asher may have suspected he had a hand in the assassination.

King Merkaris was involved in some way, but it would be foolish to assume he was working alone. Either way, they had worked in concert with the Arakesh. All roads led to Nightfall.

"This is unacceptable!" Rengar roared. The king gasped at the sight of Mörygan's body and covered his mouth in shock. "I assure you, Princess Reyna, the people responsible for this will be hung, drawn and quartered! My men tell me we already have an assassin locked away in the dungeon, an Arakesh no less. He will..." The king stopped talking when he caught sight of Asher. "Ranger, what are *you* doing here? How did you get in?" Before Asher could give him an answer, Rengar continued his tirade. "Never mind. Arrest this man!"

Everyone, including Faylen, moved at the same time to block the guards. Princess Reyna came between them first, halting the guards with a mere look. Nathaniel and Elaith had their hands resting on the hilts of their swords behind Asher - a statement in itself.

"Princess, this man has ties to the assassins that—"

"Asher arrived in our moment of need, King Rengar, a moment in which *your* men did not." Reyna spoke calmly but authoritatively. "To that end, my mentor and I no longer feel safe in your kingdom."

The shock displayed across Rengar's face was genuine this time. Asher could see the fear in his eyes, with the new Velia he had imagined crumbling around him. The ranger tried to hide his grin but wasn't sure how well he succeeded.

"Princess, please!" King Rengar pleaded. "The guard has already been tripled. Why don't you sleep on it and we—"

"Sleep where, your Grace?" Reyna replied sharply. "In the same rooms where my advisor lies dead?"

Rengar winced at the sight of the smoking remains. "New rooms are already being prepared..." The king could tell it wasn't going to be enough.

"Your people will prepare a pyre. Mörygan will be given back to Verda under the sun's first light. Until then we will make use of these new rooms you offer. But, we *will* be leaving, King Rengar." Reyna turned away to signify her disinterest in continuing the conversation.

"Where might you go, if I may ask, that you feel is safer than Velia?"

Asher could see that Reyna hadn't thought her plan all the way through. The elves would be welcome in every kingdom across Illian, but none would be any safer than Velia. The Arakesh could get to them anywhere. They needed a fortress with high walls and guards up to the challenge of repelling an assassin of the highest order. A place that wasn't densely populated, making it harder to blend in or slip by unnoticed. The answer hit the ranger like a club to the head.

He wasn't going to like this.

"West Fellion..." Everyone turned to Asher. "We'll go to West Fellion."

"Asher..." Nathaniel started, before the ranger held up a hand to quiet his protest.

"They are sworn by plenty of oaths to do the right thing." Asher waved his hand dismissively. "The point is, they're neutral with nothing to gain by an elven presence in these lands, and they despise the Arakesh who are apparently hell-bent on killing you." He looked at the princess. "And besides all that; they live in a fortress..."

Rengar appeared deflated with their choice to leave his kingdom. There were no protests from the elves, but Nathaniel and Elaith continued to look on with grave expressions.

"They will welcome you and protect you... Princess." Nathaniel added her title as an afterthought, though he spoke with a heavy heart. The Graycoat knew, as Asher did, that when they finally arrived at West Fellion, the ranger would be taken into custody. If he was lucky.

"There you have it, King Rengar. We will need horses as well. When we are situated and feel safe again, I will contact you with regards to my father's wishes about our... future *alliance*." Reyna walked out of the room without even looking back at Mörygan's body.

There was something about the way the princess had spoken of their future alliance that gave Asher pause.

The ranger kept that thought to himself.

∿

Merkaris slipped back into his room, having used a concealing spell to move through the palace's corridors unseen. When the door closed behind him, he slumped back and slid to the floor, exhausted after his battle with the elf.

His body ached from head-to-toe, with several cuts and lacerations making themselves known. Blood trickled down his right arm from a particularly nasty cut and pooled around his supporting hand. Merkaris groaned when the burn across his back stuck to the door, pulling at his raw nerves.

The king of the north let his head loll back, while he laughed at his good fortune: no, not fortune, but *skill*. He had killed an elf and a powerful elf at that! As promised, Merkaris would sit at the right hand of Valanis in the new world and rule over the humans. If he could defeat an elf such as Mörygan then there was nothing that could stop that future from happening.

Craving the softness of his bed, Merkaris attempted to stand but found his left leg could no longer support him. He decided to sit a while longer and rest. As long as he appeared respectable come morning, all would be well. The king of the north drifted off to sleep with a smile on his face. Soon, he would be the king of more than just the north.

CHAPTER 30
PRISONERS

Exhausted, bleeding and starved, Adilandra was thrown into her cell with little care. The Darkakin guards sneered and spat at her before walking back into the darkness, beyond the torchlight.

The queen of elves hated the dark but knew better than to use magic to illuminate her surroundings. The Goddess had made it very clear what would happen to Fallön and Lörvana if she called on her innate abilities.

Without hesitation, the elf dived for the scraps of meat, left on the dusty floor, and consumed them in a few mouthfuls. There was only enough water in the mug for a few sips, leaving her thirsty and craving more.

Her cell was situated somewhere inside the giant arena, hidden from everything else in the dark. Adilandra refused to cry, but rogue tears trickled down her cheeks. All was lost and she knew it. Her friends were dead and those left alive were suffering a fate worse than death.

The Goddess had promised to show her the dragons tomorrow, but the elf knew this to be more lies. Adilandra was being kept in the arena, rather than the palace, because they planned to have her fight again. Already today, she had killed twenty-two Darkakin gladiators under the sweltering sun, and she remembered every face.

Remembering all the blood made her feel sick and, for a moment, she feared the only food she had consumed in many days was about to come back up. The bloodlust and rage the elf had experienced during the battle had soon left her when it was all over.

"Great Atilan, give me the strength to see this through..." Adilandra offered a prayer to the king of the gods.

It had been a long time since she had prayed to any of the gods and often practiced it in secret, away from the prying eyes in Elandril, the elven capital in Ayda.

The gods had long been forgotten and ridiculed by the elves after their departure from Illian, seeing them as nothing more than fables created by their ancestors.

Adilandra knew better.

She knew that the elven nation had forsaken the gods out of spite and anger. The Dark War, between the elves, and The Dragon War, between mankind and the dragons, had been too much for her people and their thinking was overly simple: If the gods were real, how could they let so many die?

Adilandra's mother and father had never lost faith, however, teaching their daughter about the heavens and raising her to love the gods. It was this faith that reassured her that Nalana's prophecy was true; the Echoes of Fate had been sent by the gods themselves - a warning of what was to come.

Crouching in the filth and the dark, her faith was waning. Adilandra thought on the prophecy she had memorised many centuries ago and, as she had many times before, the elf recited the last verse to herself in the fading light of the torches.

"Children of fire and flame offer great promise, but only one perceives the time we will fall. As the gods recast their fortune and power, one will suffer the burden of destiny for all..."

Adilandra had been convinced since she was a young elf that she was the one who would perceive the time they would fall, that she alone could sense the impending doom and the return of Valanis. But now, sitting where she was, Adilandra was convinced that she too might be the one destined to suffer for all.

The elf thought to cheer herself up by peering across the void and seeing her daughter through the eyes of Ölli. Using such magic was undetectable to the human eye and would, therefore, go unpunished. Adilandra groaned in frustration when her sight failed to pierce the ether. She was too weak to control the spell, leaving her alone to her torment.

In her mental state, holding back the despair was simply too hard. The queen of elves curled into a ball in the centre of her cell, afraid to sleep near the edges in case a Darkakin reached for her through the bars. Sleep would not come easily that night.

The inky abyss surrounding Alidyr quickly gave way to the dim light of Velia's dungeons. The dry desert air of The Arid Lands was left far behind, now replaced by a cool chill that penetrated his long white robes. The portal had transported him farther than he would have managed, had he not drawn on the crystal he held in his hand. Looking at it now, what had glowed so magnificently only a second ago was just a hollowed out husk, as dark as a common rock.

The meditation required to store such magic was taxing and time-consuming, but Alidyr made certain that he always carried two on him at any time.

The elf's sharp eyes and ears picked up the rats scurrying in the shadows, sticking to the walls as they searched for scraps. The walls and ceilings were damp, with drips falling from the archways between the cells.

Alidyr wasted no time in striding through the dank corridors, passing the curious onlookers, from within their cages, with little interest. He knew that Ro Dosarn would not be kept in an ordinary cell.

Without a sound, the master assassin moved through the dungeon with ease, its layout memorised from the maps archived in Nightfall's library.

Alidyr looked in a few rooms from which the strong aroma of blood clung to the air. As with so many dungeons in the human realm, the elf felt their torture devices and techniques were lacking, unrefined and uninspiring. Valanis had shown him the ways of inflicting real pain, of inducing enough fear to kill a man or elf without so much as a touch. Soon, he thought, soon the old ways would return and the human race would quake before Valanis's power.

And his own...

It wasn't long before the sound of jovial chit-chat filled the halls. Alidyr could tell by smell and sound alone that there were eight Velian guards around the corner, huddled around a table and playing cards.

The twin, hourglass short-swords on his hips called to him, desperate to be unleashed and to taste blood. His time as a master at Nightfall had kept his swords sheathed longer than they would have liked.

In the forty years since Thallan took command of the Hand, the blades had urged him many times to strike the usurper down. Alidyr was confident, however, that he was finally close to tracking down Paldora's Gem. Seeing Thallan's expression after such a success was worth allowing him to keep it attached to his face.

The elf rounded the corner without caution, his white robes flowing about him in his haste. The guards before him were of the brutish variety, a stupid breed, which saw no threat in an opponent if he wasn't wearing garish armour and brandishing an oversized weapon. Not one stood up from their stool to challenge him. Not that it would have made a difference.

"Who the hell are you supposed to be then?" the farthest guard asked with his playing cards still in hand.

"I'm afraid the answer awaits you in the next world..." Their grasp of Alidyr's answer was slower than the swing of his majestic blades.

Blood sprayed off the steel and across the faces of every guard before the first head hit the floor. Alidyr could feel the glee of the sentient swords, gifted to him by Valanis, as they sent another soul into the afterlife.

The remaining guards reacted as one, reaching for the swords scattered around the table, but none could stop the master-assassin from taking another life. The elf dashed and sliced, rolled and plunged, flipped and removed another's head from their shoulders. Parrying their sluggish attacks was child's play to Alidyr, who had fought against the greatest warriors in the elven nation.

A strong side-kick sent one guard into the wall of the small annexe, cracking his ribs before his back broke on impact. The short-swords moved as an extension of his arms, delivering a swift death to any who strayed too close. It had been only seconds since the first guard had questioned his appearance, and now that same man was backed against Ro Dosarn's cell door. His fear-stricken face was smeared with the blood of his friends.

"Stay back!" The guard waved his sword wildly. "What *demon* are you?"

Alidyr remained defiantly in his stance. His white robes were perfectly clean, without a single drop of blood in sight.

"Demon?" Alidyr slowly twisted the hilt of his blade, feeling the exquisite balance. "I am something far worse..."

A flick of the wrist sent the blade spinning end-over-end until it impaled the guard where he stood, throwing him back. The elf held out his free hand and the skewered sword flew from the man's chest and back to its master, as they always did.

Alidyr replaced the swords, still dissatisfied with taking so few lives. He waved his hand over the dead guard, using magic to fling him back into the room and out of the way.

The door to Ro's cell was locked. The elf stood aside and, with another wave of his hand, the door exploded off its hinges, breaking the lock, and colliding into the table where the guards had sat.

The cell was irritatingly bright, with extra torches mounted on the walls and candles lit across the floor. The room was occupied by a single wooden post, to which Ro Dosarn was shackled in chains. The assassin's arms were bound high above his head and his feet were tied to the bottom of the post. His armour had been stripped away and his weapons no doubt taken far from the dungeons.

Alidyr looked on in bitter disappointment at the warrior's wounded body. Ro had suffered many cuts and bore a plethora of bruises. It crossed the elf's mind then to abandon the failed assassin and leave him to his fate, as punishment, but he was still an able hand with a blade and would serve Alidyr now with fervour to impress him. He didn't believe for a second that Ro had been beaten by any guard or even a Graycoat. The assassin could only have been defeated by the ranger.

A slow-moving trickle of blood flowed down Ro's neck, from the back of his head - clearly the source of why the highly-trained killer hadn't awoken yet. Alidyr removed a small vial from within his robes and popped the cork. Wafting the bottle under the assassin's nose awoke him in a daze, startled as he was to see his master standing before him.

"What a disappointment you are," Alidyr remarked.

"Master—"

"My spies tell me that not only did you fail to do as I instructed, but you couldn't even kill a simple Graycoat."

"He has the black gem!" Ro exclaimed. "The one you're looking for! He wears it on his finger, in a silver ring!"

Alidyr kept his expression guarded, hiding the elation that swelled within him. Paldora's Gem had been found! After a thousand years it had finally resurfaced, and with an Outlander of all people.

The elf was greatly interested to know how the ranger came by such a powerful artefact.

"Wait..." Alidyr recalled Ro's words again. "He wears it in a ring?" the elf asked.

"Upon his right index finger. I would have had it but..."

"But what?" Alidyr drew closer, hungry for information.

"Asher defeated me with magic, powerful magic. And I swear he had no wand to hand!"

Alidyr turned away, considering his options. He knew that the crystal was larger than that which Ro had described. It could never have been placed into a ring. Did the ranger only hold a piece of the crystal? If so, did he still have the rest or had he lost it? Perhaps he never even had it?

The elf considered his options, knowing full well that a discovery of this magnitude should be discussed with the Hand. Asher was no doubt still inside Velia, possibly this very palace, but he was in possession of the gem, and that made him more powerful than even the ranger probably knew. The elf had to be smart about his next move.

Being so close to the magical gem was exciting, and he wanted to storm the palace immediately until he found Asher and took it from him. But that would be folly. The ranger would be surrounded by Graycoats, Velian guards and the two surviving female elves.

There was a chance that he would expose himself and fail to recover the ring, jeopardising everything. Alidyr had waited a thousand years to get his hands on the gem; he could wait a little longer. What he had in mind was extremely drastic, however, but worth it for his master's prize.

"Release me, Master, and I will not fail you again. The gem will be yours." Ro pushed against his manacles, desperate to be unleashed once more.

"There isn't time for that now. Word has reached me that Asher is to accompany the elves to West Fellion at dawn. There, they will be heavily protected against a fool such as yourself." Alidyr goaded the assassin. "No, we will come at them with a force that is *guaranteed* to retrieve the gem. You will return with me to Nightfall, Ro Dosarn, and prove your worth. I have but a final task for you."

Alidyr used magic to break the assassin's bonds, setting him free. The elf picked out the remaining crystal, feeling its energy emanating into his hand, offering its magical aid.

The air *crackled* and distorted in protest, as the fabric of reality was torn apart to make way for the assassins. One step into the void and they were transported back into the warm embrace of Nightfall.

CHAPTER 31
TAKING FLIGHT

The sound of rushing wind filled Gideon's ears, drowning out the rhythmic flapping of Malliath's great wings. They had been flying now for several hours and dawn was beginning to break on the horizon.

The young mage clung to the dragon's bony spike with both hands, while his feet remained lodged on top of another, further down the tail.

It hadn't been long into the flight when Gideon had decided to use Abigail's wand to freeze the muscles in his left hand, ensuring his grip never faltered.

Abigail...

The thought of his best friend made him angry again. Gideon searched for the source of that anger, farther up the length of Malliath's hide where Galanör, the elf, appeared to be sitting comfortably between two larger spikes.

The elf's strength and agility made the dragon's scaly body a lot easier to traverse, though whether he found it any easier to breathe remained to be seen. Luckily, Malliath chose to fly below the clouds, allowing the mage just enough air to breathe, providing he kept his head to the side, away from the oncoming wind.

There was little to stop the biting cold, however, from chilling him to his bones. He was sure the only reason he hadn't frozen to death yet was because of the constant warmth that ebbed from the dragon's scales.

Every now and then, he dared to shift his body and look down at the gliding landscape below. Malliath was travelling fast, covering a vast distance with every motion of his wings. Gideon found it hard to believe that he had gone from wondering what Malliath looked like to being permanently attached to his tail. Hundreds would kill for the opportunity to ride a dragon, though Gideon felt that might be an exaggeration of what was taking place.

It had been several hours since Korkanath had disappeared and the many lights of Dragorn had come and gone, along with the rest of The Lifeless Isles, south of it. Malliath had clearly flown off in a southerly direction, but since then there had been nothing but black ocean below them, making it harder to determine their location.

Gideon popped his head up and searched the skies for the source of the rays of light that pierced the clouds. The sun was coming up on his left, meaning the dragon was still flying south, but where were they going? How long could a dragon fly for? Having been enthralled to Korkanath, this must have been the farthest Malliath had flown in millennia.

It dawned on Gideon that Malliath could simply be looking for somewhere nice to settle down and eat them...

Nathaniel watched from afar as the pyre burned away Mörygan's body, reducing the elf to floating ash. Reyna had told him the ashes would be carried on the winds across Verda. The princess had also said that it was an elven affair and that Faylen wouldn't want him or any others to be present.

As far as the Graycoat could tell, there was no love lost in the passing of Mörygan, but there was a deeper sadness that an elf had been killed. Nathaniel could sympathise; the death of an ageless being was a great loss when he considered how much knowledge and how many experiences the elf had collected over the centuries.

The elves stood on the shore of The Shining Coast so that the pyre was facing Ayda, to the east. Velian guards stood farther still, ensuring the funeral was kept private and the beach off limits.

Asher and Elaith were not far from Nathaniel, both in quiet conversation while they prepared the horses on a grassy knoll. It had been the first reprieve Velia had enjoyed without any rain, but stormy clouds gathered overhead, threatening to unleash all the water in the heavens.

The first light of the new dawn pushed through the gaps in the darkness, revealing a choppy Adean. Fog in the distance kept Korkanath hidden, but Nathaniel cared little for such sights. Everything paled next to Reyna.

The Graycoat pressed his hand into the area on his abdomen where the Arakesh's sword had wounded him. That wound should have killed him, slowly and painfully too, if not for Reyna and Asher. The magic of the elves was not to be underestimated, along with the resolve of the ranger.

Nathaniel had always known that Asher was close by, refusing to believe that the ranger had simply vanished back into the wilds. Something kept the older man close, but whether it was the current mystery they were all embroiled in or some notion of friendship, he couldn't tell.

All of his Graycoat instincts appeared to be fraying at the edges. Befriending Asher should have felt like a betrayal to his order, but sleeping with Reyna was a direct disregard of the oaths he had taken.

Sex had always been considered a grey area among many of the Graycoats, despite the hard line the order supposedly had. As a hardy group of men and women, who spent a long time on the road and were often revered by locals, it was a very hard line to stick to. But, it was still a mandate that they never lay with another person for fear of starting a family.

Nathaniel knew better than anyone that having a family and being a Graycoat was unacceptable.

But, Reyna was different.

The elf had disarmed Nathaniel in every way, making him forget the troubles of the world and his poor standing within the order. The princess had an honesty to her, much like Asher, that endeared the Graycoat to her. Reyna had been his first, though he hadn't the courage to tell her at the time, and it didn't really come up after being stabbed in the back by an assassin.

Doubt began to creep into his mind. What if Reyna didn't feel the same way? What if he had simply been her entertainment for the evening? It seemed very un-elf-like, but then he had been told by Asher and Reyna that everything he knew about elves was wrong.

Should he even care? he thought. Even if the princess did feel the same way, it wouldn't matter. The princess of the elves couldn't be with a lowly knight of a human order. She would be destined to marry some noble elf far above Nathaniel's station and they would live forever, together.

That was something the Graycoat would never do. In fact, during his training, he had been told that he would be lucky to see his fortieth birthday, let alone live forever.

The sound of galloping horses coming to a canter could be heard from the direction of the guards. Nathaniel replaced his worries with new ones at the sight of Darius Devale and three Graycoats, riding up to meet him. He turned to Asher and Elaith, raising a hand to keep them where they were. He could handle Darius Devale.

"The king has informed me of your plan," Darius began before he jumped off his horse. "You're either very stupid or very smart." The Graycoat looked over Asher in the distance. "Since I don't credit you with enough intelligence to be setting a trap, I'm going with stupid.

If you think your ranger friend over there will be allowed to walk freely inside West Fellion..."

"It was his idea," Nathaniel stated bluntly.

Darius's frown formed into one of suspicion. "And did it never cross your mind that *he* might be setting a trap?"

"To what? Trap every Graycoat inside their own fortress with little-old-him?" Nathaniel had always felt like fighting in the presence of Devale.

"Lord Marshal Horvarth may see it differently," Darius added quickly.

"He's already recalling every Graycoat in the realm." Nathaniel took a moment to relish Darius's dumbfounded expression. "Haven't you received the message yet? I asked Galkarus to send one of his owls last night. The Lord Marshal replied immediately."

Darius gritted his teeth, reserving his ire. "Then we shall accompany you, as the Lord Marshal commands."

"Oh great..." Nathaniel replied, sarcastically. He walked away, leaving a seething Darius Devale.

"What did he want?" Elaith had as much love for Devale as Nathaniel. It pleased him.

"They're returning with us to West Fellion." Nathaniel met Asher's cold, blue eyes. "You should reconsider coming with us." The Graycoat was happy to travel with Asher, but he didn't want to see any harm come to the ranger by his own people.

"There's more going on here than a simple assassination contract." Asher observed the elves in the distance. "I mean to find out what."

Nathaniel wanted to ask the ranger why. He knew Asher had been paid and had seen him take away some papers given to him by the king himself, though the knight had no idea what Asher's final prize might be. So why was he sticking around? By the very definition of his title, the ranger should have hit the road once more, seeking out the next job or adventure. Nathaniel decided against asking him, not wanting to put the ranger in an awkward position.

More galloping horses caught the attention of the group. A captain of the Velian guard was riding up to meet Darius Devale. A heated discussion, followed by a dramatic obscenity from Darius, drew the three companions across the beach to investigate.

"What's going on?" Nathaniel inquired.

"The Arakesh has escaped..."

Everyone turned to look at the elves, still standing with their backs to the shore. There was no time to lose, Nathaniel thought. They had to make it to West Fellion, and quickly, before Ro Dosarn struck again.

"Take me to his cell." Asher's request surprised them all. "And have King Rengar's court mage meet us there." The ranger directed his request at the captain, who looked to Darius and Nathaniel for permission.

"You heard him," Nathaniel ordered.

Reyna stood and watched as the embers of Mörygan's pyre were whisked high into the air and carried out to sea. The elf's body was barely visible between the consuming flames that cremated him.

The princess was filled with a strange mix of emotions. It was the first funeral she had ever seen since no elf had ever died in Ayda, and yet her feelings towards Mörygan confused the way Reyna knew she was supposed to feel. It was a tragedy that a being of such an age had been taken from the world, as it would be if any elf died, but her advisor had not been a pleasant one.

On more than one occasion, Reyna had overheard the cruel things Mörygan had said about her mother. His family lineage had been linked to Valanis at one point, though the princess tried not to let that cloud her opinion. Mörygan had a way of making people dislike him all by himself.

The truth of the situation was far more profound. Now that he was dead, Reyna felt as if she wasn't bound to her father's plans for

Illian. It had been Mörygan who had constantly reinforced her father's will on Faylen and herself. In her heart, Reyna knew that Faylen didn't agree with the invasion and that she had secretly wished to accompany her mother on her pilgrimage to the south.

It dawned on Reyna that it wouldn't matter what she did or who she warned. The world of man would be shattered by the elves. But, perhaps she could save a few? The elf glanced behind her to look at Nathaniel, who was talking to Asher and Elaith. The humans she had met thus far had been a mixed bag of personalities, but Reyna wasn't filled with the urge to kill them all as her father was.

Reyna looked past the burning pyre and out across The Adean. Somewhere out there, Galanör and his team would be laying siege to Korkanath and freeing Malliath the voiceless. Her father's plan was coming together, whether she wanted it to or not. The next stage in their plan, however, would take many years, giving Reyna more time to prepare.

Prepare for what? she thought. What was she going to do exactly? Ruining her father's plans would have dire consequences that she couldn't truly fathom. Yet the alternative was hard to think about as well.

"He was a vile elf..." Faylen announced over the fire's crackle.

Reyna turned in surprise at her mentor's irreverent comment. It was very uncharacteristic of Faylen to speak her mind so freely, especially to say something so derisive.

"He didn't make the best impression." Reyna compensated for her mentor's words and kept her own opinion somewhat more guarded.

Faylen glanced at the princess, apologetically, as if realising for the first time that she had said anything out loud. Reyna kept her smile hidden, enjoying the carefree attitude of her mentor.

"I recovered his diviner," Faylen said. "When we have privacy I will inform the king of his death, though I can't see it changing anything greatly."

Reyna faced her mentor with glassy eyes. "Are we really doing this, Faylen?"

"Do not let your emotions cloud what must be done. I disapprove of your choice to bed the knight, but you are old enough to make your own decisions, so I won't stop you. But it will change nothing, Reyna. There is nothing we can do to stop what is coming." Faylen didn't take her eyes off the pyre.

"Does that mean we shouldn't try?" Reyna continued. "I know you disagree with my father's plan, just as my mother did. You are older and far wiser than I; surely you can see how far we have fallen?"

"Fallen?" Now Faylen turned to meet Reyna. "We have grown strong under your father's rule. It is my age and wisdom that allows me to see the danger we face. The humans will inevitably release Valanis. They are too inquisitive and curious for their own good, always striving to cross the next line and achieve more."

"Are they not to be respected for that? I know you don't truly believe your own words, mentor."

"They are dangerous, Reyna."

The princess could see that, despite everything else, Faylen truly believed her own words.

Faylen continued, "When this business with the Arakesh is over, we will return to our duties and see our part in the plan completed."

Reyna turned back to Mörygan's burning body, feeling more trapped than ever. She glanced over her shoulder again and saw a captain of the guard conveying what looked to be grave news to Nathaniel and the others.

"I think something bad has happened..." Reyna said.

"Thank goodness." Faylen's words surprised the princess yet again. "If we stand here any longer, we'll never get the smell of smoke out of our clothes."

~

309

Nathaniel looked at what was becoming an all too familiar sight since he had taken up new company. The hacked and broken bodies of eight Velian guards lay strewn across the small room in front of Ro's cell. Asher stood at the forefront of the group, taking in the scene with experienced eyes.

"What do you see, Ranger?" the king asked.

"He didn't escape." Asher surprised them all. "He was broken out."

"How can you tell?" Reyna looked around but, like Nathaniel, she couldn't see what the ranger did.

"The position of the bodies," Asher explained. "Look at how they fell, the positions of the wounds. They're each holding their sword, or it's close by. Yet they were all killed by blades, fine ones if their broken armour is anything to go by."

Nathaniel looked at all those things but still couldn't see what Asher did. The room was a bloody mess, with a solid door lying in the middle of the room atop a broken table. It seemed perfectly plausible that Ro had escaped his cell and killed them all.

"Galkarus..." Asher faced the court mage. "In my travels, I once came across another ranger who favoured magic. I saw him use Kayt dust to look into the past and see what monster had attacked a merchant convoy. From then on I have always kept a pouch of Kayt dust ne me but, I confess, the spell eludes my memory. Do you know of it?"

Nathaniel thought about Asher's natural grasp on the magic world and doubted the man couldn't use the spell without knowledge of the ancient language. Was the ranger asking Galkarus to help simply to hide his own talents?

"I do," Galkarus replied coolly, not meeting his king's questioning look.

"Then why haven't you already used it?" King Rengar snapped. He was clearly displeased with his entire staff after last night's events.

Galkarus bowed awkwardly and moved to take the pouch of Kayt dust from Asher. With his powerful staff in hand, the wizard threw the pouch high into the air so that the blue coloured dust rained over the room. His staff boomed as he slammed the bottom into the floor and an unintelligible spell could be heard under his breath.

Nathaniel looked on in wonder. As the dust fell and sparkled in the torchlight, figures became visible, made from the blue dust.

"Incredible..." Elaith looked on with the same wonder as Nathaniel.

Galkarus moved aside as a tall figure in long robes took his place in the dust. The guards were all sitting around the table that was still visible through the dust. After a moment's pause, where Nathaniel assumed some verbal altercation had taken place, the robed man burst into action with two short-swords, hacking and slashing at the men. They fought back, but to no avail, all dispatched by the robed figure. The dust was incredible, but it wasn't accurate enough to discern the features of the man's face.

When the last guard had been slaughtered, the shadowy figure used what must have been magic to remove the door with such force, and without touching it. Nathaniel noted the absence of a wand or staff and wondered if the others had seen the same thing. There were only two people the Graycoat knew of that could manipulate magic without Demetrium; one was Asher and the other was an elf. Since it couldn't have been Asher, Reyna or Faylen, it could only mean there was another elf out there. A bad one.

Galkarus used his staff to drive the Kayt dust into the cell, where the group continued to watch as the robed figure made his way inside. There was a long moment while they spoke in silence until more magic was used to break the assassin's bonds and then...

Nathaniel squinted and narrowed his eyes as if that would clear up the unusual sight. The two men stepped into a swirling coalescence of blue dust, before vanishing completely.

"What was that?" Elaith asked.

Thankfully, Nathaniel wasn't the only one with surprise on his face, though he noticed the look that Reyna and Faylen shared. The elves knew something, but the Graycoat knew better than to ask in front of the group.

"Could it be...?" Galkarus asked himself more than anyone.

"What is it?" King Rengar urged.

"They used a portal," Asher stated flatly.

Galkarus nodded his agreement and the elves kept quiet.

"I thought such magic was unknown." King Rengar looked to his court mage, suspiciously.

"It is!" Galkarus was quick to reply. "Or... it should be. Korkanath has never unlocked the secrets to teleportation. The elves, perhaps?" The wizard looked to Reyna and Faylen in hopes of unravelling the mystery.

"No." Faylen didn't hesitate. "We would not have sailed across The Adean if there was another way."

Nathaniel didn't know Faylen well enough to determine whether she was lying, but he could see that she wasn't telling the whole truth either.

"It must be The Black Hand!" Galkarus exclaimed. "They must have discovered the ancient magic. We must inform the Magikar at once."

"No!" Rengar raised his hand. "No one except those present is to know of this." The king was worried about losing face, no doubt.

"It was Nightfall," Asher announced, crouched by the body of a dead guard. His fingers traced the edges of the chainmail that had been sliced apart by the attacker. "They were just clearing up their mess, leaving no trace."

"You call this clearing up a mess?" Darius opened his arms wide to the room full of bodies.

"Silence!" Rengar held up another hand. "Explain, Ranger."

"I have seen those blades before." Asher waved his hand at the floating blue dust. "This was just another assassin sent to make sure

312

that no one retrieved any secrets from Ro Dosarn. He'll be punished for his failure."

"But they will come again..." Faylen wasn't asking.

"Then why are we still here?" Nathaniel turned to make room for the elves, as the unlikely companions made to leave. "We ride for West Fellion."

CHAPTER 32
ANCIENT HISTORY

The ten-foot wooden doors groaned and protested as Alidyr pushed his way into Nightfall's archives, with Ro Dosarn close on his heel.

Just as every other room was steeped in darkness, so too were the archives. High-back chairs were tucked neatly underneath the long tables that lined the centre of the room. The walls matched that of a grand library, its shelves filled with scrolls and parchments dating back to Nightfall's earliest days.

Alidyr's sharp nose wrinkled from all the dust that clouded the room, though his exquisite hearing and extra magical senses informed him of their privacy. The information stored in this room was but the first part of putting together the puzzle that surrounded Asher.

Ro followed him perfectly through the darkness, thanks to the Nightseye elixir flowing through his veins. Alidyr could sense the man's trepidation in his presence - the assassin was still expecting to be punished for his failure. Alidyr was certainly tempted, but he had a better use for the human.

"You now know of the one I serve." The elf continued to search through the scrolls in the pitch black. He had informed Ro of the part he played in the larger game, and that Valanis was the true master that they all served, even if the Arakesh didn't know it.

"Valanis will rise again," he continued, "and the Arakesh will be his fist. In serving him, you will be rewarded more richly than you could ever be as the Father of Nightfall." Alidyr stopped and faced the assassin, each able to see the other with perfect clarity. "Your failure in Velia has forced my hand. Paldora's Gem must be retrieved at all costs, but I see no reason why we can't take out two birds with one stone. The elves and the ranger seek shelter at West Fellion, a long-standing thorn in our side and a potential threat to Valanis's grand plan for Illian." Alidyr was building up to his deception, a well crafted and rehearsed speech.

Humans were so easily manipulated.

"You, Ro Dosarn, are to seek out any and all allies of Nasta Nal-Aket." Alidyr ignored the assassin's curious expression. "If their allegiance to the Father is confirmed, you are to quietly remove them."

"Master?"

"Make no mistake - what we do next will shake Nightfall to its core, but it is necessary to make it stronger. When you have taken care of his allies, I will replace Nasta Nal-Aket as Father and lead the Arakesh into a new era." Alidyr could see the betrayal Ro felt in his expression. "Have no fear, you *will* be Father. When the gem is in my hands I will gladly hand Nightfall over to you, as my services to Valanis will take me away from my duties here." There it was, the perfectly crafted lie. The elf could tell Ro had lapped up his every word and taken it as truth.

Fool.

"As the master wills it." Ro bowed his head.

"No. As *Valanis* wills it..." Alidyr corrected, before dismissing the assassin.

When the doors closed behind Ro, Alidyr went back to his search. The elf knew that Asher had joined their ranks a few decades ago, but he couldn't remember the exact year. He started at three decades past and worked his way down from there, fingering every scroll to check the name. At last, when he reached as far back as four decades to the year, Alidyr pulled free the bound parchment that belonged to Asher.

The master assassin pulled the knot and laid the scroll out across the table, weighing it down with decorative candles that had never been lit. The elf took in every detail of information on the page. This piece of parchment was the only thing in all of Illian that had anything about Asher before his initiation.

Just as he had remembered, the scroll confirmed that Nasta Nal-Aket was the one who brought Asher to Nightfall. As a boy, he had claimed to be nine years old when he arrived at the order's door. Knowing that the ranger was forty-nine in age, however, did nothing to inform Alidyr of why he had a piece of Paldora's Gem.

The elf skimmed through the details of the boy's height and weight, pausing over the detail pertaining to the black-fang tattoo, below his left eye. Why did that give him pause? The elf had seen that Outlander tattoo himself when the man had been an assassin. So why did he read it over and over again?

Frustrated, Alidyr read on. Nasta claimed that the boy was an orphan without a clan or tribe, or whatever the Outlanders liked to have. The assassin had found the boy outside...

Elethiah!

Asher, an Outlander without a clan, had been found wandering outside Elethiah. There was no mention of the boy wearing a gem or a crystal, or anything that matched Paldora's Gem. It was too much of a coincidence that the boy had been found in the last place the gem had been seen. And yet, Elethiah was impenetrable thanks to the Amber Spell and the protective spells, placed over it by the elves after The Dark War. A small boy couldn't have found a way inside, and that's if the gem was still inside the old capital.

That thought set off a chain of older thoughts, long forgotten inside Alidyr's mind. Now he knew why the tattoo felt relevant.

The elf scrunched up the scroll in his hand and marched from the archives with haste. His thoughts raced around inside his mind, as the puzzle began to unfold, however unlikely it might be.

Once returned to his chambers, Alidyr locked the door and clicked his fingers, setting every candle and torch alight. In a place where the dark gave the predators power, it was always sensible to rest in the light.

To complete his investigations and prove his theory correct, Alidyr had to check a very different archive. He kicked the small rug aside, at the foot of his bed, and knelt down to where a circle of ancient glyphs was engraved into the stone. With his hand flat in the middle of the ring, Alidyr sent a mental command that activated the magical ward placed over the stone. The elf stood back and the circle separated into large chunks which, one-by-one, descended below the floor until a spiral staircase was created.

Alidyr made his way down into the secret room, aware that he hadn't been down here for many years. Another click of his fingers illuminated the room with candles and a single torch at the end of a small table.

Like the archives, this room was walled with shelves lined with leather-bound books and scrolls lodged between the gaps. No searching was required in his personal library, however. Alidyr knew exactly what he was looking for amongst the many diaries and journals of hundreds of elves, each chronicling the history of the land and their immortal race.

A light brown book, larger than most, was taken from the shelf and placed delicately on the table. He released the scrunched up piece of parchment and opened the great book with care, riffling gracefully through the pages. This particular volume had been one of the first accountings of the events after the attack on Elethiah. It was among the oldest of tomes owned by the elf.

After finding the entry he desired, Alidyr sat down and slowly read through every line. It spoke of the brief hunt for Paldora's Gem after the Amber Spell was enacted. Nalana, a Dragorn and princess in the court of the king, told of how she gave the gem to a human, an

Outlander, shortly after Valanis stormed the city. She had hoped, it seemed, that the boy could smuggle the gem out of the city unseen and that she knew the boy well.

The hunt had been brief of course, when the boy, a native of The Wild Moores, could not be found. The elves had scoured the vast forest and questioned many of the tribes, but the boy with the black-fang tattoo was gone. Deciding that the gem might be better lost; the hunt had come to an end and with it the power to either free or destroy Valanis.

This was the same Nalana who heard the gods and first spoke the Echoes of Fate. Could this small boy from a thousand years ago be the ranger that had yet to reach fifty? It seemed that destiny was weaving quite the web.

Alidyr looked up from the book, dismissing the entire notion. Asher had been a boy when he arrived at Nightfall; he certainly wasn't a thousand years old! An ancestor, perhaps? It was possible that the gem had been passed down through the generations, though why Asher only possessed a piece of the gem, he did not know.

The explanation struck him like a lightning bolt!

How could he have been so short-sighted? He was truly undeserving of ruling the Hand to have missed what had been under his nose for so many years.

Asher had arrived forty years ago, to the year, after being found outside Elethiah with no tribe to speak of. There had only been one event of significance that had taken place, exactly forty years ago...

CHAPTER 33
INTO THE WILD

Galanör blinked hard to keep sleep at bay. He had been awake for almost two days now and was thankful for the icy wind that kept him alert. Should he fall asleep, the elf was sure that he would fall from Malliath's back and die upon impacting The Adean.

Sitting back, against the largest spike on the dragon's hide, he looked over the horizon, noting the sun had passed noon and done nothing to warm his chilled skin.

Malliath had altered his course in the late morning and moved in a south-easterly direction. Galanör couldn't fathom where they were going or what might be motivating the dragon. It was astonishing alone that Malliath had tolerated their presence at all, rather than barrelling through the air and dropping them to their doom.

Thinking of his human companion, the elf adjusted his precarious position and turned back to spot the young mage, clinging to one of the spikes for dear life.

The elf was impressed. It was a testament to his stamina and strength to be holding on for so long. Or it could be a testament to the young mage's rage and desire to kill Galanör, that he would abandon his home and jump onto a dragon. It was, unfortunately, more likely to be a combination of the two. Galanör had witnessed the heartbreak on the young man's face when the girl had been killed by Lyra.

There was another face that would torment him, but not like the faces of the others did. Lyra had betrayed him but, more than that, she had betrayed every elf in Ayda. The conspiracy of which she spoke was greatly disturbing to Galanör.

The elf sat back, now accustomed to the level of oxygen, and reflected on every conversation between Lyra and him. Had he missed something glaringly obvious? He thought back to the moment he had chosen her to be on his team and realised there had been no trickery. Lyra had truly been the best among her peers, though it now appeared as if she had been trained by someone else in secret.

Planting Adamar into the group had been the ploy to keep his attention off Lyra. All the times he had laid with her and conversed in private, baring his fears and desires... How could she have aligned with Valanis? The dark elf had been defeated and trapped inside Elethiah since before Lyra was born. It was troubling to think of sympathisers and disciples of Valanis living in secret among his people in Elandril.

Turning his head to the left, Galanör looked north, to where Elandril sat in the heart of The Amara. With every beat of Malliath's wings, he was taken farther from his home, putting everyone in danger. He had to warn them, urgently. Lyra had said it herself; whatever plans the elves had, Valanis had been planning long before. No, not Valanis, he thought. The dark elf was incapable of having a single thought, let alone plotting against his cousins in Ayda.

Galanör wished he had taken more time with Lyra, and pressured more answers from her. There was someone at the top of this conspiracy, someone keeping Valanis's plans alive. Galanör swore then that he would find this person and personally see to their end.

There was that duty-bound voice again.

To protect his people he would take more lives. Did he have any boundaries? Was there a line that he wouldn't cross in service to his people? Killing all those in service to Valanis felt more like a service to the world than just the elves. If that tyrant was ever set free, he would bring war to all of Verda, the humans included.

As the clouds whipped above his head, Galanör had thought himself free for the first time. Now he knew that to be folly. In one form or another, he was duty-bound to do what was right, to protect not just the elves, but the creatures that walked all of Verda's lands.

As long as the shadow of Valanis fell over the realm, Galanör would be forced to fight. A voice inside told him that it wouldn't matter if he defeated the greatest evil ever known, it still wouldn't atone for the innocents he had already killed.

But he had to try.

Without warning, Malliath banked to the left, dipping his huge shoulder as he did. Galanör braced his legs and reached out for the spike in front of him, holding onto it with all his considerable strength. A loud yelp from behind told of the mage's distress. Galanör wanted to look back and make sure the man was still there, but the elf dared not move.

As suddenly as he banked, Malliath levelled out and continued to fly straight, only now they were heading for land. Galanör's keen eyes could make out the forests in the distance, beyond the shoreline of what the elf knew to be The Opal Coast of Ayda.

Illian had been left far behind now, having crossed the breadth of The Adean. They were far south of Ayda's eastern shores, heading into lands unknown.

Where was Malliath going?

The sun was setting on the horizon, casting the Alborn countryside in an orange hue. Riding out from Velia, the group had made good time crossing The Selk Road, heading into the wild grasslands.

Alborn was a fairly civilised part of Illian, a region of flat, lush fields and small archipelagos of woodland, home to a variety of animals. It had been a pleasant day's riding in all, with very little drama.

Reyna smiled, happy to feel the warmth of the fading sun on her face. It had been the first time since their arrival in Illian that the storm hadn't overshadowed them, though it was certainly following them in the distance.

The group came alongside a small wood, skirting around its edges to continue heading west. Another smile broke across Reyna's face when Ölli dived down between the trees, hunting for his dinner. The white owl disappeared into the woods, but Reyna knew well that the bird would find her with ease. He always did.

Wiping the smile from her face, Darius Devale and his Graycoats came riding up alongside the companions from the rear. They slowed upon reaching Asher at the head of the convoy, and Reyna's elven ears heard everything they spoke of.

"We should rest here and make camp before we lose the light," Darius suggested. "Let my men check the perimeter before it's too dark."

Reyna could see that Asher was tempted to ride on. The ranger had no fear of the dark, and he wanted the elves within the safety of West Fellion's walls.

The Princess had grown to like the older man. It hadn't escaped her notice that Asher was now assisting them without the promise of payment which, Reyna had recently learned from Nathaniel, was an essential part of procuring a ranger's skills. The mere fact that the man simply wanted to see them safe endeared the ranger to her. She felt, however, that expressing such affections or gratitude would be unappreciated by Asher.

"Very well." Asher brought his rather intelligent horse, Hector, about and addressed the group. "We'll stop here for the night and set off again at first light. West Fellion is still three days away."

Darius instructed his men to comb the area and check the woods for any wolves. Elaith and Faylen set about making the camp with some tents, given to them by King Rengar. Asher headed into the woods to search for firewood but turned to Reyna and Nathaniel before disappearing.

"You two are the best archers," he stated flatly. "Go and find us something to cook."

Reyna detected the hint of a smirk on the ranger's face and appreciated what he was really trying to do.

"I will accompany you." Faylen made to join them before Reyna stopped her.

"There's no need. I can protect the knight all by myself." The princess beamed. "Don't worry Mr. Galfrey, I won't let anything harm you." Reyna walked away, unable to hide her smile. It wasn't very often, if ever, that she used her royalty to command Faylen.

Leaving their horses and a displeased mentor behind, the two walked off into the plains in search of deer. It pleased Reyna to see that the Graycoat was back to health and fully recovered. They walked in silence for a time, simply enjoying each other's quiet company in the sun.

"I'm very sorry about what happened to Mörygan," Nathaniel offered his condolences.

"You'd be the only one..." Reyna replied under her breath.

"What was that?"

"Oh, nothing. It is a great loss to my people and a shame that it has disrupted our alliance. But those of us that remain must strive to make things right."

Reyna thought that Faylen would be proud of her diplomatic response, even if the princess just felt sick about what they were really doing. The urge to come clean and tell Nathaniel and Asher everything was overwhelming.

"I am sure you will do a fine job. And do not fear, we will bring an end to these assassins that hunt you."

They shared a warm smile and walked closer together until their hands brushed against one another. It wasn't long before they came across some tracks and followed them across the plains and into the tall grass.

The herd grazed in the distance, unaware of the predators that stalked them. Ducking into the tall grass, they crouched with their bows ready and arrows notched, relishing the hunt together.

"Where did you learn to hunt?" Reyna asked. She was momentarily embarrassed to think that she didn't know much about the Graycoat. Her elven urges hadn't given her much pause while in King Rengar's palace.

"No one leaves West Fellion without the skill to hunt... except for maybe Elaith." They both stifled their laughter. "Where did you learn? It seems a strange skill for a princess."

Nathaniel's question was only more proof that the elven culture was a secret to man. They had no idea that the life of a warrior was the only way to exist anymore.

"Elandril, my home, is situated in the heart of The Amara, a forest greater than any you can imagine. My mother and Faylen would take me on long expeditions through those woods, hunting for days to stay alive. I miss the trees..." Reyna thought of the Redgrove trees that grew higher than any tower built by man or elf.

"And your mother?" Nathaniel had stopped watching the deer.

"You would like her." Reyna smiled more to herself. "Her name is Adilandra. She is strong and brave... untamable"

"Like you," Nathaniel added with his own smile.

They were only inches away from each other now. Reyna's emotions were heightened, exaggerated all the more by her elven youth. She couldn't help herself. The princess dived into his lips and knocked them both over into the grass.

Nathaniel dropped his bow and cupped her face in his hands. For just a moment, Reyna forgot all her worries, succumbing to the passion that overwhelmed her. The tall grass flattened around them as they rolled over one another, unrelenting in their grip.

They kissed for a while longer, enjoying the touch and embrace of the other, forgetting the world and its troubles. As the sun faded, the night's cool air brought them from their reverie. They had spent at least an hour just lying in the grass, telling stories of a childhood spent in The Amara and Nathaniel's time in Longdale before growing up in West Fellion.

The princess was beginning to see that there was more than just a knight and handsome features to the man. His experiences as a child and growing up were in their own way similar to her own. But he was still human...

Reyna popped her head slightly above the tall grass to see if the herd of deer still grazed nearby. Amazingly, the animals had moved closer to the pair while they had remained hidden beneath the grass. Before they lost all the light, elf and man shot up from the grass and fired an arrow each into the closest deer, killing it instantly.

"We will have to find a suitable excuse for our time away," Nathaniel commented with a mischievous smile.

"Using you for my own ends *is* a suitable excuse. I am a princess, remember?"

The Graycoat laughed. "You are refreshing..."

Reyna frowned. "The women in your land are stifled beneath the boot of man. I will see this imbalance corrected when our alliance is formed."

Nathaniel returned with a genuine smile. "Now that would be worth seeing." He slung the animal over his shoulder. "I thought elves were all vegetarians..."

Reyna thought of the warrior-race they had become. "My ancestors used to be, but not anymore. You see; your knowledge of elves grows every day."

They returned to camp, smiling and laughing as they did.

CHAPTER 34
ASPIRING HEIGHTS

Alidyr considered himself to be above all things; men, elves, the Arakesh and even the Hand. He was second only to Valanis, and rightly so. His master had been chosen by the gods, and so he was worthy of leading.

It had stung the elf greatly when Thallan had wrested control of the Hand, claiming Alidyr had failed Valanis *and* them. Thallan was a fool, however, for thinking that any progress could be made without Paldora's Gem. It was the key to everything and the task of finding it had been entrusted to Alidyr.

And now it was within his grasp.

The elf waited patiently, in the secret room behind the Kaliban tapestry, with his white robes wrapped around his arms. Since the revelations of his investigation into Asher, Alidyr had been putting the larger picture together.

The elves' invasion of Illian was ultimately a way of ensuring that Valanis would never be set free by the humans, though Alidyr believed there to be some greed on the part of the Lord of Elves. Now that a piece of the gem had been allied with the princess and her mentor, there was a greater possibility that they would try to breach Elethiah's wards and destroy Valanis once and for all.

Like chess pieces on a board, Alidyr could manipulate both sides. His tongue could be just as wicked as his legendary short-swords. A push here, a siege there, and everything would fall into place, and the gem would be his, elevating his status once more.

A portal opened on the other side of the fire-pit and Adellum entered the secret room. As always, the elf was shadowed in his black cape and hood, with his nose and mouth concealed behind a mask.

In the presence of Alidyr, he removed both mask and hood to reveal his bald head, tattooed in ancient glyphs. The golden patterns laced around his powerful black bow glistened in the fire-light. Alidyr had seen the devastation that weapon had wrought in the past and knew well that it would serve him in his new plan.

"Why have I been summoned?" Adellum's tone was harsh.

Forty years ago, the elf wouldn't even have spoken until Alidyr addressed him. That would change soon.

"Because of all my brothers and dear sister, you are the wisest." Alidyr knew how to wield words better than he did swords.

"You want something." Adellum folded his arms.

"No brother, our *master* wants something..." Alidyr walked slowly around the fire-pit, his gaze locked with Adellum's.

The ancient general scrutinised Alidyr, searching beyond his mysterious answer. "It cannot be..."

"But it is." Alidyr smiled. "Paldora's Gem has been found."

"But how? When?" Adellum unfolded his arms and stepped closer to the fire-pit.

"The ranger who defeated Thallan." Alidyr was sure to recall that little fact.

"We must tell the others!" Adellum turned to leave until Alidyr stopped him with a firm grip.

"I summoned only *you*, brother. Thallan does not believe in the power of the gem, nor its importance. He still heals by the pools of

Naius in Kaliban. He is weak. The gem is being taken to West Fellion as we speak, where it will be guarded well. Let you and I return Valanis to power and bring down a great foe at the same time."

He could tell that his words had struck a chord in Adellum. The opportunity to rise above the others and prove himself to Valanis was too good to pass up. It helped that he knew Adellum always craved a good fight and often spoke fondly of the battles they fought in The Dark War.

"What do you suggest?" There was some respect in Adellum's tone now.

"I will command the Arakesh to follow you into battle, brother. They will be eager to finally bring down the walls of West Fellion."

"You're talking about marching hundreds of assassins across Illian, into an outright war. Do you even have that power? I thought the Father commanded here..."

Alidyr hadn't expected such caution from Adellum. "If I order the Arakesh to attack West Fellion, then that is what they will do," he replied with authority. "Will you lead them and retrieve the gem?"

"I could want for nothing more." Adellum bowed his head. "But where shall you be, brother?"

"I am not one for grand battles; I would leave that glory to you." Alidyr knew exactly where he would be, but Adellum didn't need to know that.

"You always were one for the shadows."

"Indeed..." Alidyr made for his room once more. "When your army is ready, I will call on you again." Adellum bowed deeply and vanished into the dark.

Yes, Alidyr thought, the gem would be his very soon.

Galanör nimbly shifted his weight, while holding onto the giant spikes on Malliath's back, balancing himself on the balls of his feet.

The elf was still concerned that too much activity would disturb the dragon and spell his doom. He couldn't help but feel that there was mental instability where Malliath was concerned, though it was to be expected after a millennium of servitude to the mages of Korkanath.

Peering around and above the spikes, Galanör searched Malliath's scaly hide for any sign of the young mage. His keen ears hadn't picked up any sound from the human since the dragon banked hard to the left, hours previously.

With his long brown hair whipping about him, Galanör caught sight of the young mage who, miraculously, was still clinging to Malliath's spikes and small bony protrusions. Galanör suspected that magic was being used to keep him in place.

As if aware that he was being watched, the mage looked up and returned a hard gaze at the elf. Their prolonged flight across the world had done little to temper the fire that still raged in the human's heart. Galanör wasn't looking forward to dealing with him when they finally touched down. That was providing Malliath didn't eat them both first.

Shifting his weight once more, Galanör craned his neck to see the land below and was shocked at what he saw. The treetops of Ayda's forests had disappeared and had been replaced with sparse desert.

How far south had they gone?

Great canyons and valleys spanned the horizon, with little or no vegetation in between. It occurred to Galanör that he had never seen a desert before with his own eyes. The paintings and descriptions he had seen didn't do the barren landscape justice, failing to depict the sheer scale and vastness of the waterless ocean.

There wasn't a cloud in the sky either, exposing them wholly to the sun on Malliath's black scales.

Galanör quickly lost interest in following the arc of the sun and keeping up with time. It seemed that Malliath had plans to fly forever. There was a moment when the elf thought the dragon would land in a valley, between two mountains, but Malliath's gliding wings simply flapped once and they soared back into the sky.

Later in the day, Galanör's attention was gripped by more than the changing landscape, which beyond the mountains quickly became jungle-like. His elven eyes became fixed on thousands of humans moving across the land.

From their lofty height, the humans appeared as ants, but Galanör's eyes were able to pick out details. Swords, axes and spears glistened in the sun, amidst the amble of the marching men and women. He knew it had to be an army, but they certainly didn't travel like one, with no discernible ranks or formation.

Far in the distance, Galanör could see a dust cloud, much like the one that enveloped the humans below, rising over the jungle canopy. Was there another army heading in the same direction? Who were these humans?

Galanör had been sure that since Malliath had banked left and flown inland, they had entered the continent of Ayda, and yet there were humans below him...

"Impossible," the elf said to himself, the truth dawning on him.

He looked down at the marching army once more with new curiosity and no lack of alarm. Not only were there humans in Ayda's south lands, but there were Darkakin!

Galanör knew well of the skirmish between his ancestors and the war-like Darkakin that had emerged alongside the more peaceful humans, from within The Wild Moores. They had been driven south of Illian, exiled to fight amongst themselves since that was all they craved.

They embodied every aspect of the humans that the elves had come to despise. How had they settled in Ayda? Galanör cursed his own people's insular nature and their lack of desire to seek out new lands and explore, as the humans did.

The Darkakin had obviously explored the lands south of Illian and discovered a way of crossing into Ayda. The elf took heart that the armies weren't heading north, to Elandril, but moving farther south, towards...

Galanör sat up, peering over the four sloping horns of Malliath's head, to see the city in the heart of the jungle. Standing above it all was the unmistakable shape of a pyramid.

CHAPTER 35
BETWEEN A DRAGON AND A HARD PLACE

Adilandra lashed out in three different directions, her elven scimitar parrying two swords before splitting another man in half from groin to shoulder. Seeing their fellow gladiator's blood spill over the ground only fuelled the remaining two men to attack wildly.

The queen of elves had been taught to detach herself when fighting, in order to keep her mind sharp and disciplined. An emotional fighter made many mistakes. That philosophy worked well when fighting elves, but was not entirely required when faced with weaker, slow-moving humans.

Adilandra unleashed her rage, enjoying the ease with which she tormented and wounded the gladiators. Slipping easily between their attacks, the elf cut and slashed both men across their thighs and arms, severing major arteries.

There was no fight to be had after that.

The arena erupted in cheers from all around when the baying mob was finally appeased with the daily offering of blood and gore. Adilandra slowly turned to regard them all, her chest heaving visibly from the exertion of fighting all day on such little sustenance.

The lust for more death was expressed on every Darkakin face. They always needed more.

The sun was past midday and hidden behind the arena's high walls, but it did nothing to cool Adilandra in the tropical heat, who dripped from head-to-toe in sweat.

The Goddess stood up from her throne, silencing the jeering crowds immediately. Protected on her podium, the olive-skinned queen walked to the edge and looked down on Adilandra. Her cobra head-piece cast her features in dark shadows, giving the woman a menacing appearance.

"You have proven entertaining elf-queen," The Goddess began. "I find you almost as entertaining as my pet..." The Darkakin flashed Adilandra a wicked smile, knowing the reference to Fallön would sting. "Nevertheless, you have fought, and fought well! You are deserving of the reward you seek." The Goddess's sly tone suggested that Adilandra wasn't going to like what came next.

At the far end of the arena, metal gates were being opened on their pulley system. The elf slowly turned with a lingering look, straying from The Goddess to Lörvana, shackled on her knees.

The ground shook as if the earth itself had its own beating heart. The contrast between the shadows, beyond the gate, and the light of the arena made it impossible to see what was emerging from the darkness. Adilandra squeezed the grip on her sword, mentally preparing for a very different kind of fight.

"You have traversed a continent in search of the ancient wyrms, old one!" The Goddess was playing to the crowd now. "I give you... DRAGONS!" The arena exploded into deafening cheers when not one, but two dragons thundered out of the hidden depths.

Adilandra lost her breath at the magnificent, yet disheartening, sight. The two dragons were clearly adolescents; otherwise, they wouldn't have both fitted through the gateway. Between their heavy footsteps, the giant chains, shackled to their ankles, *clattered* and *rattled* as they were dragged across the sand.

The dragon on the left was a beautiful, deep green with flecks of gold across its scales. The other dragon slammed its light blue head into the green one, shoving it aside, while unleashing an almighty roar.

The green wyrm flexed its jaw of razor-sharp teeth and reared up on its hind legs, showing off its impressive wing-span. They were both angry if the empathetic waves that emanated from the creatures were anything to go by.

Adilandra knew it was unusual for dragons to communicate so openly and on such a wide scale, but these were young and sadly inexperienced. The elf tried her best not to let the dragons' mood affect her own, but she could feel the rage building inside of her, the hunger and desperate need to rip and tear muddying her own emotions.

The dragons' emotions spilled out and infected the surrounding mob, turning their elated cheers into angry howls and bellows.

Adilandra fought the urge to run at the dragons and slay them. She knew it would mean certain death if she tried, but the dragons' extraordinary form of communication was impossible to ignore.

The elf combatted the effects by focusing on their details, such as the blunt and chipped horns on their heads, or the broken spears that protruded between the scales on their legs and bodies. They were leaner than a dragon should be at their age, implying the horrific conditions they were being forced to live in.

How had the Darkakin even captured two dragons in the first place?

Her question would have to wait. Both dragons bounded across the arena with their reptilian eyes fixed on Adilandra. Though she had seen them as a young elf and studied them thoroughly, there was no training in all of Verda that could prepare a person to fight a dragon. Even an adolescent dragon was a giant compared to an elf, with scales that could deflect any sword.

Adilandra braced herself, unsure how she was going to survive the next few seconds. Magic would be the only advantage, but besides The Goddess killing Fallön and Lörvana for it, dragons were notorious for being immune to most spells, as they were magical beings themselves.

The thick chains were dragged across the sandy field and their clawed feet tore up the arena. This was it, the moment she either survived or died on her quest. The irony wasn't lost on Adilandra, in her potentially final moments, that fulfilling her quest to find the last of the dragons would be the very creatures that killed her.

No, she thought. This was not fulfilling her quest and it certainly wasn't fulfilling Nalana's prophecy. Finding the dragons was only half the quest. Convincing them to return to Illian and finally destroying Valanis and stopping a war between her people and the humans was the rest.

The queen of elves couldn't die here, she *wouldn't*. Adilandra believed, truly, that she was a part of that prophecy and that she alone would be the one to see it fulfilled.

The light of the sun was overcast when the dragons were finally upon her. Adilandra looked up, realising that the giant shadow could not belong to either of the young wyrms.

The dragons came to a sudden halt, skidding over the sandy ground, and looked up, as Adilandra did. Once more, the elf's breath was taken from her, as a full-size dragon with black scales and a wing-span that stretched from one side of the arena to the other, dropped onto the ground with a resounding *boom*.

The empathetic waves of anger ceased immediately, replaced by a strong feeling of hope and anticipation. The dragons' form of communication didn't reach as far as the crowd, whose cheering instantly turned to screams of terror as they ran for the nearest exit, creating chaos.

The black dragon inhaled a sharp breath before engulfing the closest stand in flames. The fire spread around the arena's curving sides, setting every man and woman alight.

Though stunned, Adilandra still caught sight of the two people that fell off the huge dragon's back and tail, tumbling to the ground, while simultaneously trying to avoid the dragon's stomping feet and swishing tail.

"Kill the beast!" The Goddess screamed from her podium. Her personal guard ushered the queen from the makeshift throne, taking a weak Lörvana with them.

Darkakin guards posted around the arena were slow to react at first, struggling with the urge to run away. Spears and arrows were soon being launched at the black dragon, however, though neither were successful in penetrating its thick scales.

The two younger dragons threw themselves up the high walls, clawing at the rock to reach the Darkakin above. Their attack was cut short, as the chains around their ankles were being pulled back into the depths of the arena. They must have been on a pulley system since there was no amount of humans that could drag a pair of dragons across the ground.

The black dragon's head swivelled around, stopping the flow of fire, and roared in protest. The larger dragon's roar was harder on the ears and dwarfed that of the younger ones.

The black dragon turned to face the helpless younglings and a tail as thick as a tree tore through the stands of the arena, killing scores of Darkakin. Its mighty front legs pounced onto the chains and gripped them between hardened claws. Then its powerful jaws clamped down.

It wrestled and whipped its head about in an effort to break the chains. All the while, the two men who had fallen from its back jumped and rolled in every direction to avoid the thrashing.

Gideon leaped to one side, narrowly avoiding Malliath's thundering back legs. The mage hit the ground and rolled, aware that the tail always followed the back legs.

Sand and dust were kicked up in a storm around the three dragons, making it hard to see and breathe. It was certainly a lot warmer than it had been on Malliath's back for the last couple of days.

The mage could hear the screams of thousands between the roaring dragons, but he was currently too occupied to take in the new surroundings. Before landing, he had seen what looked to be an arena, standing on three rocky pillars in the middle of a sprawling city with a pyramid at its heart.

Through it all, Gideon heard Galanör coughing in the sandstorm. The mage turned to see him ducking under the outstretched leg of a blue dragon, its claws inches away from impaling him.

Seeing the elf brought the mage's thirst for vengeance rushing back. Gideon removed the staff from its sheath on his back and commanded it to grow, as he made his way towards Abigail's killer. He made no distinction between Galanör and the other elves who had taken so many lives at Korkanath.

Malliath gripped the thick chain in his maw and thrashed wildly, giving Gideon an opening to charge at Galanör. The mage broke into a sprint with his staff held tight in one hand, a spell ready in his mind.

Using the fighting form Ali-maktah, Gideon jumped into the air, his staff high and pointed down like a spear. He had practised the technique a hundred times in the sparring hall and knew how to time it perfectly. At the apex of his leap, the mage fired a single bolt of energy at Galanör and, as predicted, the elf twisted his shoulders and dodged the spell.

Gideon touched down at the same moment and spun on the spot, bringing his staff around to bear. The magically hardened wood slammed into the elf's chest with all of Gideon's strength, putting him on the ground.

As satisfying as the blow was, it wasn't enough for Gideon. The mage came at the elf again, bringing his staff down in hammering arcs. Galanör rolled and evaded every attack, already recovering from the Ali-maktah.

In his frustration and anger, Gideon realised he was relying on physical attacks instead of his true strength. His staff came up with a sweeping motion and exploded with a telekinetic wave that collided with the elf, throwing him into Malliath's front leg.

The great dragon's body puffed up, as Malliath inhaled a sharp breath. Gideon and Galanör locked eyes for a second, both aware of what came next.

"Run!" Galanör's warning shocked Gideon, making him pause for a near-fatal moment.

The elf burst into motion and threw himself into the mage before Malliath's fiery breath super-heated the air. The fire swirled around them, just as it had around Gideon and Abigail in Korkanath's halls.

With his eyes shut tight, Gideon could only feel Galanör's body pressed against his, sheltering him from what the elf thought was certain death. Why would Galanör try and save him?

The fire dissipated as suddenly as it had started and Gideon opened his eyes to see another elf standing over both of them, her hand outstretched to her sides, having kept the fire at bay. Despite her dishevelled appearance, her beauty was undeniable. Her auburn hair was swept behind her in the wake of Malliath's outburst, exposing her pointed ears.

"Galanör?" The female elf looked down at them in confusion.

"Adilandra..." Galanör went on to speak to Adilandra in elvish, losing Gideon completely.

Before she could answer, Malliath roared again, now in triumph as the chains were melted and the smaller dragons set free. All three dragons shifted their considerable weight, giving the elves and Gideon cause to dash and avoid the curling tails and stomping feet.

From flat on his belly, the young mage looked up to see the dragons launch off their back legs and take flight. The elves had managed to stay together, holding each other by the arms, while they watched the dragons disappear.

Gideon finally had a good look at his environment and instinctively reached out for his staff. It wasn't there. He got to his knees, searching frantically for his most treasured possession. It was next to the elves, beyond his reach.

Galanör turned to look at him, and the instinct to survive reminded him of Abigail's wand on his thigh. The elves ran over to him, picking up his staff on the way, and avoided the occasional arrow or spear hurled their way. Gideon whipped out the wand and pointed it threateningly at them, his mind racing through the various spells he could use.

Instead of attacking him, they simply stood before him, offering his staff back. There was an urgency on their faces that he didn't understand, but it felt like a trap to take his staff back.

"Take it," Galanör spat, looking anxiously around the chaotic arena.

"Get away from me!"

An arrow impaled the ground beside Gideon and Adilandra reacted immediately by holding her hand out once more. She created a mirage-like shield that deflected another two arrows, mid-air. Gideon followed their flight back to a group of men and women with bows and spears; each was dressed in animal skins and painted in tribal tattoos.

"They're Darkakin!" Galanör yelled. "You know what they are, don't you? You can either come with *us*, or you can stay with *them*."

Gideon looked from the Darkakin, a savage people he had never wanted to meet, to the staff in Galanör's hand, the hand of the elf responsible for Abigail's death. More arrows whistled through the air, only to be halted by Adilandra.

The choice was simple, but hard.

PART FOUR

CHAPTER 36
A HALF TRUTH

On the second night, the group made camp on the eastern banks of The Unmar, only a day's ride away from West Fellion. They had decided to camp a mile north of the bridge and avoid any travellers crossing the river.

The ranger had taken precautions to keep the companions off the roads and beaten tracks, choosing, instead, to take them over the wilder lands in between. They were far enough to the south that the woodsmen of The Evermoore wouldn't come across them on their hunts, and north enough to avoid The Moonlit Plains, where the sea of fields was roamed by teams of Centaurs and other intelligent creatures who disliked humans.

To Asher's surprise, he had been left to take the group in any direction he pleased, having no resistance from Darius Devale and his knights. Darius had seen firsthand what the Arakesh were capable of and the other knights had seen the massacre in the dungeons. They were clearly of one mind that the ranger should guide them home, to where they thought they would be safe.

How wrong they were...

Asher looked over the horizon, to the south, where he knew

343

Nightfall lay in secret. What was the Father planning next? His first two attempts had failed, though the second attack in the palace had been very different. Ro Dosarn had tried to take his ring as well as his life. The Arakesh had been sent after Asher specifically, despite the elves having been the first targets.

For a moment, it crossed the ranger's mind that he had made a great mistake in getting involved. He had gained the attention of the Arakesh once more, after fourteen years of getting lost in the world and avoiding them.

The sight of Nathaniel and Reyna soothed his doubts, though he knew not why. It felt good to be doing good; that was the sum of it.

He had slain many monsters and foul beasts since carving out this new life, but he had always charged for it. Asher reasoned it to be his way of surviving without breaking the law, but it had never felt as if he was doing a good deed, always a service. And yet, now, the ranger had fulfilled his obligations with regards to the elves' safety and delivering them to King Rengar. It simply felt good to be helping them. It would never atone, he thought, but then nothing ever would.

Perched on a small log, Asher cupped his cheeks in contemplation and realised his stubble had quickly become a short beard. His clean clothes and armour were dirty again, along with his green cloak, which was covered in mud up to his calves. Life outdoors took its toll on those who dared. The elves appeared to be the exception, for both appeared as immaculate as the day they left Velia.

The Graycoats watched Faylen in wonder as she removed the large heavy chest from her sack and unpacked the necessary parts for their tents. The Graycoats were not as accustomed to magic as Asher and had never seen the use of pocket dimensions.

In Nightfall, the ranger had seen his elven teacher, Alidyr, use pocket dimensions to store potions and other belongings in his training halls.

Personally, Asher's eyes were more drawn to Faylen, easily the most beautiful woman he had ever seen, if a little cold towards him.

It was clear that the elf didn't like Outlanders and had already judged the ranger accordingly. Asher couldn't blame her. He had no memories of living in The Wild Moores, but he had met his fair share of its inhabitants. Outlanders were no Darkakin, but they were still savages and barbarians by comparison to Illian's human population.

Faylen was watching him staring at her. Asher blinked hard and looked back to the horizon and the fading sun, somewhat embarrassed. His interaction with women had been limited. As an assassin he had bedded many women, enjoying the luxuries of the order's wealth and rewards. As a ranger he had kept to himself, enjoying the touch of a woman only when suitably intoxicated. Like him, those women had never been looking for anything but self-gratification.

Despite knowing there was no world in which Faylen and he could be anything of note, he still had no idea how to talk to her. The elf was undoubtedly intelligent, wise and a lot older than he, with more experiences now than he would have in his entire life.

Asher pushed the thought aside, focusing on the here and now. The black gem poked out of his fingerless glove, reminding him that their troubles were far from over. It seemed that he had become a target once more, along with the elves.

How safe was West Fellion really?

If an Arakesh wanted to breach its walls they would, and after two failed attempts there was no telling what measures they would employ next.

Elaith appeared at his side. "Nathaniel says I have to go through my routines again..." The young girl looked down at him, her finger tapping the hilt of her sword.

Asher turned to regard the other Graycoats, all three of them watching the ranger. There was a chance that sparring with Elaith would end the peace between the knights and himself. Still, Elaith looked down at him with big brown eyes, pleading to learn from someone she apparently respected more than those in her order.

The young woman's interest in him was possibly more curious

than the friendship he had struck with Nathaniel. Another new connection in his life.

"Try not to die this time." Asher rose from the log and removed his cloak and sword belt. He propped the broadsword against the log and stood to face the young woman, much to her surprise. "The Arakesh fight with short-swords." The ranger slid the silvyr blade from his back and spun it a few times in his hand. "You have the advantage of distance and leverage, but you lack their agility and speed. An Arakesh will move to get inside your reach."

Asher came at Elaith with a long stride, flicking her sword away and coming to a halt with his hourglass blade at her throat. He turned his back on her, knowing that the Graycoat would attack.

Her technique was predictable, as she brought her sword down in an arc. Using reflexes honed over years of fighting, Asher side-stepped, deflecting her sword with little effort and jumped to her side, pointing the tip of his blade into her ribs.

"With a short-sword, the wielder is less likely to parry. They favour evasion." Asher put some space between them again, making every effort not to laugh at Elaith's frustrated expression.

The Graycoats had stopped preparing their tents and moved closer. Asher looked to Nathaniel, who surveyed the entire scene, ready to intervene if his fellow knights made a point of getting involved. Reyna also watched with fascination, but Faylen ignored them and continued to prepare the camp, indifferent to it all.

Elaith came at him again and Asher decided to let her get some of that frustration out. The ranger parried most of her attacks, evading and twirling out of the way of others, yet still, she pressed the offensive.

Every now and then he came back with his own attacks, forcing Elaith to think about her footwork and the different ways a short-sword could be used against her. He was impressed with the speed with which she adapted to his fighting style and quickly used it against him, wielding her sword with a different technique to keep the long blade closer to her body.

The ranger had no right to be proud of her, having had no role in her life up until recently, but he couldn't help how he felt.

Asher decided to teach the young knight one last lesson. He ducked and rolled under the swipe of her sword and grabbed a handful of mud at the same time. When Elaith turned to challenge him again, the ranger flung the mud at her face and momentarily blinded her, putting her off balance. With the flat of the silvyr blade, Asher wrapped her knuckles, making her drop the sword to the ground.

Elaith howled in pain and wiped the mud from her eyes. "That's not fair! You cheated!"

"Fighting isn't about being fair, it's about surviving. The Arakesh are trained to survive..."

"They're trained to kill," the Graycoat, who Asher knew to be called Orvin, remarked with some disdain.

Nathaniel stood up but Asher subtly waved his hand to calm the knight. This confrontation had been building since they departed Velia; even Darius did nothing to stop the inevitable. Asher had a feeling the senior Graycoat was eager to watch him fight some more, in the hope of studying his techniques. Such knowledge, however, would do nothing to sway the fight in the Graycoat's direction.

"Is that not what you are trained to do?" Asher countered, walking away from Elaith.

"We are trained to protect!" the other Graycoat, known as Tick, exclaimed, resting a hand on his hilt.

"At the point of a sword..." the ranger added, glancing at their blades.

"Perhaps you would like to see the point of my sword a little closer, ranger?" Orvin unsheathed his blade and Tick followed suit.

Asher looked at Nathaniel again, seeing the concern on his face. The ranger knew well enough that it wasn't a concern for his life, but that of the Graycoats' and any future peace. Reyna came to stand with Nathaniel, her hand firmly gripping the hilt of her magnificent scimitar. Faylen continued to potter around the small camp as if nothing was happening.

Asher walked towards the two knights, happy to pass them by, if they allowed it, but also ready to fight. Either way, it was up to them.

Orvin attacked first, his broad arms lifting his sword to cut Asher down the middle. To ensure he didn't kill them, the ranger threw his silvyr sword into the ground, sending it end-over-end, until it stopped at Orvin's feet. The throw gave the Graycoat just enough pause to allow Asher the time to move inside the knight's swing. A single open-palmed thrust into Orvin's throat halted the bigger man's attack immediately, causing him to stagger back and drop his sword in order to grip his neck.

Before Orvin had dropped to his knees, Tick came at Asher from his left. The old assassin dodged three consecutive attacks with minimal movement, avoiding the blade by mere inches.

Tick was a more cautious fighter than Orvin. The lean knight stopped attacking and circled the ranger with his sword out in front of him. Asher casually followed the Graycoat's circling motion, only half watching him. In truth, the ranger was a little worried that he might have killed Orvin, who was now going a shade of blue.

Nathaniel was on the periphery, itching to get in the middle of it, but clearly unsure how he would stop them.

Tick launched at him again with a jabbing strike that would pierce Asher's head. The ranger did everything he could to fight the muscle memory that demanded he take action and kill the knight.

"Darius!" Nathaniel called for his senior to stop this, but Devale simply shrugged in reply.

The lean knight twirled and flipped his sword in ways Asher could only imagine were ceremonial, since his blade was neither distracting nor effective at landing a blow. This kind of sword-mastery might be effective against Outlanders and thugs or even good for confusing monsters, but it was pointless in the face of an assassin trained at Nightfall.

At the apex of a particularly delicate twirl of the sword, Asher closed the gap in two rapid steps and ensnared Tick's wrist in a vice-like grip, bending it just enough to cause the tendons in the knight's hand to release his hold on the sword. Before the blade hit the ground, Asher landed a square punch across Tick's nose, splattering his cheeks with blood and putting the man on his back.

In the commotion, the ranger had failed to detect Orvin's recovery and the sword that was now cutting through the air in a decapitating motion. The only reason Asher had the time to dwell on his error was because an elven scimitar blocked the path of the sword, inches from his neck. It was, perhaps, even more surprising when he realised that Faylen was on the other end of that exquisite blade.

The elf was lightning fast in following up her parry with a strong hand that caught Orvin in the shoulder and drove him to the ground.

With the two Graycoats groaning and rolling around in pain, Faylen sheathed her sword and shot Darius a glare that cut deeper than any sword.

"Humans..." Faylen shook her head and returned to her chest. "Some firewood, perhaps..." The elf looked directly at Asher.

The ranger looked at Nathaniel, unsure what to do next. He wasn't a man who was used to thanking people and he mentally chastised himself for his inaction. Orvin shouldn't have been able to surprise him like that; more proof that he should be getting out of the game before he got any older.

"Firewood." Asher repeated Faylen's instructions, replaced his green cloak and sword belt, and headed into the nearby trees. He was sure to sheath the silvyr blade on his back, easily the most treasured item he owned, beside his ring.

"I'll accompany you." Nathaniel made to follow until Faylen stood in his way.

"No, you will prepare the food." The elf was not to be argued with.

∾

Many hours later, when the moon was at its highest, Asher took up watch by himself on a collection of large rocks, away from the coursing Unmar. The sound of the river was loud, and the ranger didn't like how the rushing water would mask the approach of any would-be-attacker.

The group had eaten in silence, while Tick nursed his crooked nose and Orvin flexed his sore shoulder and bruised throat. Both Graycoats made a point of not meeting Asher's eyes, each intensely fixed on the fire between them. There was certainly some wounded pride to go along with their injuries.

Faylen had silenced most grumbles with a single expression. Asher chuckled to himself; the elf had a look that could make a Mountain Troll quiver.

"You don't make friends easily, Outlander." Faylen appeared at his side, as if from nowhere.

Again, Asher chastised himself. He was getting old indeed, though he reminded himself that it had been an elf that crept up on him this time, not a lumbering oaf like Orvin.

"I could say the same thing about you," Asher replied without looking at her. He kept his eyes on the dark landscape.

"I didn't come here to make friends."

"In that case, you're doing a great job," the ranger replied dryly.

"I came here to protect Reyna, nothing more." The elf sat beside him on the rock. Her perfume was sweet and distracting.

"I've seen the girl in a fight. I don't think she *needs* you." A sly smirk crept over Asher's face.

"I came to protect her from *everything*." Faylen shifted her shoulders to regard Nathaniel's sleeping form.

Asher laughed quietly. "Good luck with *that*. It doesn't matter if you're a human, an elf or a dwarf; there are some things you can't deny. It's nature."

"You're very philosophical for a hired killer." Faylen raised an eyebrow at the ranger.

"I thought I was an *Outlander*?" Asher glanced back, before returning his gaze to the dark.

An almost undetectable smile flickered across the elf's perfect features. "You have the unfortunate luck of being both."

The two sat in silence for a while, as the light of the moon illuminated the fields and woodland beyond. Thick clouds continued to roll over the sky from the east, threatening to hide the stars. Like the Arakesh, the storm would inevitably find them.

"How is it you recognise an elf so easily?" Faylen asked softly.

Asher considered his answer. Nathaniel's words rang clear in his mind, weighing on him; *so if you share their secrets, people will die and if you don't share their secrets, people will still die...*

There was no running away from the past now - the Arakesh were coming for the elves *and* him. It made less and less sense to keep their secrets, even if he was doing it to keep others safe.

"I was trained by an elf." Asher couldn't miss the look of surprise on Faylen's face. "There are many teachers at Nightfall, but the best of them all is Alidyr Yalathanil."

The elf looked away for a moment, her expression instantly changing from one of surprise to grave concern.

"What is it?"

"What do you know of The Dark War, Ranger?" Faylen's tone matched her concern.

"A little. There were history lessons in Nightfall, but it was more for strategy than anything else."

"You have been taught by none other than the head of the Hand, Valanis's greatest general." Faylen stood up from the massive boulder and began to pace along the edge.

"Valanis?" Asher recognised the name from Alidyr's history lessons, though it struck a deeper chord he couldn't quite grasp.

"The mad elf who started the civil war. He's..." The elf looked up at Asher, who had risen with her, and stopped herself from saying any more.

The ranger could tell Faylen was hiding something, or not telling him the whole truth. Their mission had been to start communications between Illian and Ayda, yet they had left Velia all too easily. Now, it turned out, he had been under the tutelage of one of the most famous elves who ever lived. There was more coming together here than just the Arakesh fulfilling a contract.

"Well, it wasn't Alidyr who attacked us in the ruins," Asher said. "He fights with—"

"Twin short-swords," Faylen finished his sentence. "They were given to him by Valanis, along with his enhanced magic. The Hand consists of five generals; each gifted a weapon of choice, capable of mass destruction on the battlefield. Is that why the Arakesh fight with two short-swords?" she asked as an afterthought.

"Possibly. It was always rumoured that Alidyr started the order centuries ago, but the oldest records are lost. Who attacked us in the ruins, south of The Unmar?"

"He wielded a single sword..." Faylen cupped her jaw. "It must have been Thallan Tassariön, another member of the Hand. I studied them all in Ayda." The elf clenched her fists but contained her anger to a silent expression. "I can't believe they survived the purge."

Asher raised an eyebrow questioningly, lost among the new names and events.

"Before my people left these shores, they swept the land, ridding Illian of any stragglers or sympathisers of Valanis. There were pockets of followers, but they were all dealt with. It is an injustice that the worst of them all survived."

"So that's why the Arakesh are coming for you." Asher was putting it together now. "They're not seeing out a contract, they're working for Alidyr."

"For Valanis," Faylen corrected. "Alidyr must still be seeing out his master's last wishes. He must know we're..." The elf looked away again, the weight of the world apparently on her shoulders.

"Know you're what?" Asher pressed.

Faylen turned to regard the ranger, looking him up and down.

Asher could see the turmoil behind her eyes, as the elf struggled to keep her secrets.

"What does Alidyr know?" Asher asked again.

"We should tell them." Reyna came up behind them on the rocks, Nathaniel by her side. "We *need* to tell them."

"Reyna!" Faylen kept her voice just low enough to be drowned out by the flow of The Unmar.

"We will only get through this if we work together," Reyna protested.

Faylen sighed and turned away, her silence the only form of agreement she would give.

Nathaniel stepped to the side, looking from Reyna to Asher with curiosity. "What's all this about?"

"The reason we're here," the princess began, "the real reason, is to..."

"Destroy Valanis once and for all," Faylen interrupted.

Asher had become a master of lies during his time as an assassin and knew the elf's words to be true, just not the whole truth. If nothing else, Reyna's reaction was proof of his suspicions. The princess's shock quickly changed from surprise to shame, though the ranger couldn't figure out why.

"In the final days of The Dark War," Faylen continued, "Valanis marched his army on Elethiah, our capital city. Word had reached him that Paldora's Gem had been recovered by Lady Syla, a great hero of that time, and that the gem was under the guard of the royal family."

"Wait." Nathaniel waved his hand. "What's Paldora's Gem?"

"A celestial stone that broke off from Paldora's Star," Reyna explained. "It was believed by Valanis that Paldora, the goddess of the stars, had sent the gem to help him control his powers."

Nathaniel's expression told of his understanding perfectly, or rather his lack of understanding.

Reyna continued, "Valanis started The Dark War after he discovered the pools of Naius, the god of magic. Nobody knows where they are, but after he entered them he possessed more magic than any elf could rightly wield. It made him unstable and his powers hard to control.

He believed that the gods were trying to find a way to walk on Verda, and that Naius and Paldora had charged him with preparing the way. Paldora's Gem is said to allow its wielder perfect control over magic."

"However," Faylen continued, "Lady Syla recovered the gem first. And so the dragons offered their assistance to end his tyranny once and for all. The greatest and oldest of their kind, Garganafan, enacted the Amber Spell with the help of our elders. Garganafan sacrificed his life-force to trap Valanis and all of Elethiah in time. After that, wards and spells were set over the city to keep everyone out."

"Valanis is *still* in there?" Nathaniel clarified. "So you've returned to, what, kill a frozen elf?"

Asher was momentarily distracted by the tug of a memory he couldn't hold on to. The smell of sulphur filled his nose and the roar of a great beast echoed through his mind. The ranger was sure he had heard some of Faylen's words before, but where? From Alidyr perhaps?

"It was felt that steps should be taken to eradicate the threat, permanently." Faylen looked at Reyna, a silent conversation passing between them. "Humans have made great strides in the world of magic. Our king fears that Elethiah will inevitably be breached and Valanis freed."

"That's why you were happy to be escorted to West Fellion." Asher's attention had returned in full. "It's halfway between Velia and Elethiah."

"We have studied your maps carefully," Faylen stated with a sly smile.

"The Graycoats will help you." Nathaniel squared his shoulders.

Reyna squeezed the knight's arm with an affection that didn't match her smile. "It's too dangerous, Nathaniel. The wards that protect Elethiah are powerful; it will take elven magic to find a way in."

"That's if there even is a way in," Asher added.

"Leave that to us, Ranger." Faylen made for the camp, wishing to end the conversation.

"Aren't we getting ahead of ourselves?" Nathaniel said. "You're talking about going to Elethiah, but the Arakesh are still coming for you. I don't think West Fellion will deter them for long."

Faylen stopped and the companions looked at one another in silence, the gravity of that statement setting in.

"Wake the others," Asher instructed. "We're not waiting for dawn."

CHAPTER 37
THE PIT

The time had come. After a thousand years of nurturing and guiding the Arakesh, the time had finally arrived when Alidyr could use them to serve Valanis. No more controlling from the shadows and manipulating others to do his bidding, but the outright command of the most skilled warriors in all of Illian.

They could never be compared to the elven soldiers under his command during The Dark War, but the Arakesh surpassed every other fighting force in the world of man.

The ancient elf lurked in the corner of the surrounding balcony, always in darkness, as the men and women in their final year of graduation, bowed before the Father. The centre of the rectangular room was dominated by a circular hole that ran deep into the earth, known to all Arakesh as the pit.

It was, in fact, a test devised by Alidyr just over seven centuries ago. In their final year, the would-be-assassins were required to enter the maze of tunnels beneath Nightfall and find their way out, back to the surface of The Arid Lands.

Only the survivors could call themselves Arakesh, and survivors they would be if they could fight their way through the nightmarish creatures and fiends that called those dark tunnels home.

"You have trained tirelessly for many years." The Father was giving his usual speech below. "Pass this final test and you will be true masters of the dark."

Alidyr surveyed the group of twenty. He recognised them all, having taught them at various stages of their life in Nightfall. Some of them would meet their end in the pit; it was a statistic that had never changed.

The elf found himself committing some of their faces to memory for future manipulation and potential replacements for the Father or Mother. He almost laughed out loud when he realised it would no longer be necessary.

Ro Dosarn, a master assassin among his peers, was unable to sneak up on Alidyr Yalathanil. The elf turned to regard the man before he joined him by the railing.

Thanks to potions provided by the elf, Ro's wounds had almost completely disappeared, though there was no potion to heal the assassin's pride.

In the pitch-black, every assassin's senses were heightened, including the students below. None, however, were sharper than Nasta Nal-Aket's. The Father was no doubt aware that Alidyr and Ro were watching from the balcony since the elf had taken no magical precautions to hide their presence. Both elf and man were trained to keep their heart rates at a steady beat, so as not to give away their intent.

Ro used his hands to communicate in the silent language, known only to the Arakesh. *The Father's allies have been taken care of.*

In the perfect darkness, Alidyr could see every flexion of the man's fingers and hands, understanding him perfectly. **Were there many?** the elf signed.

More than I would have thought, but now he is alone.

Then it is time.

Ro understood and made another hand gesture that signalled for the other assassins, hiding beyond the balcony's entrances.

More than a hundred Arakesh filled the balcony, with just as many pouring into the rectangular room below. They made no move against the Father, who looked impressively passive towards the unusual gathering. The students appeared surprised and moved away from the pit.

"What is the meaning of this?" the Father asked, his eyeless lids looking directly at the elf.

Alidyr strolled to the centre of the balcony, his hand sliding over the rail, while he enjoyed the moment. For so long he had bowed to whatever pathetic human ruled over Nightfall, and now he was finally going to be rid of the last Father.

"I challenge Nasta Nal-Aket for the right to rule!" Alidyr announced to the masses that crowded into the room.

Curiously, the Father didn't flinch or make any outward appearance that the challenge bothered him. It put Alidyr on edge. Had Nasta perceived this threat and made plans? The old elf used his extra senses in the dark to sweep the room, searching for anything out of place, any heartbeat that betrayed a hidden ally of the old man.

"You have enjoyed your position within these walls for a millennium, Alidyr." Nasta walked around the pit, his hands concealed within his sleeves. "Why now do you choose to challenge the Father?"

"It's time the Arakesh realised their full potential," the elf replied. "I am going to take this order into a new dawn. I'm afraid that the future of which I speak does not require Nasta Nal-Aket."

Alidyr deftly flicked his legs over the rail and dropped silently to the floor below. He slipped his long white and gold robe from his shoulders, revealing the twin short-swords on his hips.

Nasta looked around for a moment, scanning the faces of the assassins surrounding them. It amused Alidyr that the Father was no doubt searching for his allies, whom he had prepared for this moment. Allies that Ro Dosarn had already seen to.

"You reap what you sow, Alidyr Yalathanil." Nasta swept his robes aside and slid the curving sabre, known as Reaver, from its sheath.

The sword of the Father or Mother was an impressive blade, forged by Alidyr himself at the appointment of Nightfall's first leader, long ago. Its edges were lined in the ancient script, designed to inflict extra pain that lasted long after the wound had been tended to.

In a flash, Alidyr's magical swords were in his hands, hungry for death. The stored energy within the crystals gave the elf a surge of adrenaline, pushing his heightened senses to their apex. Nasta made no attempt to advance and make the first move, but Alidyr's blades didn't care, they needed the elf to lash out and draw blood.

"Fall on your sword and die with honour, Nasta." Alidyr fought through the urge to strike out, the sight of Reaver giving him pause.

The Father laughed in the dark, surrounded by enemies. "If you fear the bite of my blade, elf, why not send another to fight for you?"

Alidyr leaped the distance between them in two powerful strides and jumped high into the air at the last second. Nasta's reflexes were proportionate to his stature, as the Father side-stepped the attack and whipped his sabre across Alidyr's midriff. The slightest of shifts in balance allowed the elf to avoid the blade, though he felt its razor edge slice through the robes across his ribs.

After his feet hit the ground, the fight began in earnest, the two skilled warriors colliding with deadly force. Alidyr's twin blades whirled around Nasta as if the elf were naught but a wraith. Nasta danced around him, twirling and spinning, his sabre parrying every blow from the short-swords.

Reaver was an extension of the Father's body, with the blade rolling, twisting, and whipping around his body in defensive and attacking stances. More than once, Alidyr was forced to duck or step back when the human found an opening or pushed one of his magical blades aside. Nasta Nal-Aket was certainly one of the most skilled swordsmen to have held the position of Father.

The pitch black was illuminated by the sparks that exploded from the clashing steel. Each warrior struck the other with more force than any ordinary being was capable of.

The surrounding Arakesh moved aside, avoiding the fight which quickly spread across the room, with each combatant leaping and flipping through the air, their swords slashing in every direction.

Alidyr ducked under the sweeping arc of Nasta's blade before it sliced through one of the pillars like butter. The elf came back up with a combination that set the Father back, towards the pit.

Alidyr used his superior strength and kicked Nasta in the sternum, sending the old man flying backward. The Father's tumble quickly turned into a controlled roll that brought him back to his feet, ready to parry the elf's next attack, an attack Alidyr was more than willing to provide.

He spun on the ball of his foot one way, then the other, striking from different angles every time. Alidyr felt his blades rejoice as they cut Nasta's ribs and then his thigh. The Father stumbled back and fell to one knee, using the tip of his sabre to support him.

The Nightseye elixir allowed for every assassin to smell and taste the blood that trickled from his wounds, their keen ears picking up the sound of the thick liquid dripping on the floor.

"You see, Nasta, I was always meant to lead them. The Arakesh follow the strong, and you are weak..." Alidyr slowly circled his prey, enjoying the superiority that befitted his race.

With Nasta's head bowed low, the elf could feel the blade in his right hand urging him to decapitate the Father. It would be so easy. Let us be done with it then, he thought.

Nasta Nal-Aket was impossibly fast. Using his bent knee, he spun on the spot and came to a stop beside Alidyr, before the elf's blade impacted the floor. Reaver's deadly edge whipped around with the Father and cut deep into the back of Alidyr's leg, just above the knee.

The elf cried out in pain, a physical experience he hadn't felt in many years, and dropped to his knee. The wound blazed like a fire in his leg, as the magic ate away at his nerves. Nasta came up behind him now, landing a heavy blow to the elf's back, using the end of his hilt. Alidyr sprawled across the floor, face down, barely aware of the pain in his back, the wound in his leg burning hot as an iron.

Nasta had no words but instead came down on the elf with Reaver. Alidyr had enough of his senses to roll aside, ensuring the curved blade buried into the floor and not his head. The Father came down again and again, each time narrowly missing Alidyr, who flipped around on his back to bring his powerful legs to bear in a spinning motion. Both feet collided with Nasta's face and launched him into the air, bringing him to the floor in a tumble of limbs.

Through the inky darkness, Alidyr could see the pit perfectly beyond the Father's fallen body. His leg screamed out in agony when he tried to walk normally, forcing him to limp over to Nasta. The human had survived the fight longer than Alidyr had expected, but the elf could feel the man's end was near.

As Nasta rose unsteadily to his feet, Alidyr's elven ears heard the various bones crackle and pop throughout the old man's body. His jaw appeared to be broken or perhaps dislocated, while his chest heaved in a struggle to breathe through what was certainly a broken sternum. Blood had soaked through his robes around his ribs and leg, filling the air with the smell of iron.

It impressed Alidyr more when the Father launched himself once more, ready to fight. Reaver cut the air either side of his head and limbs, never actually touching him, as he used his exceptional speed to dodge every attack. The elf went very quickly from being impressed to angered, when Nasta changed his tactics and thrust his head into Alidyr's nose, shattering it for sure.

Momentarily dazed, the elf could do nothing to stop Reaver from slashing his shoulder and drawing more precious blood, blood which coursed with elven magic that had been enhanced by the great Valanis and blessed by the gods. It filled Alidyr with rage at the thought of it being spilled by this old wretch.

Fighting through the new shooting pains in his shoulder, Alidyr thrust his hand out and hit Nasta with a wave of magic that threw the man into the air. Reaver was flung from his hand, where it skidded across the floor and disappeared down into the pit. The drop was so far that even Alidyr's incredible hearing didn't hear it land. Nasta came to a stop on the very lip of the circular pit.

Infuriatingly, the Father began to laugh to himself as he rose unsteadily to his feet. "You think yourself so smart, Alidyr. *I* am the Father of Nightfall; I know everything that transpires inside these walls. You think I don't know who you answer to, who you truly serve? You have used my Arakesh for your own purposes, breaking the very laws you helped to create."

Alidyr's eyes narrowed. "You're the one?" The elf couldn't believe the pieces of the puzzle that now fitted together. "*You* told King Rengar's spies that the Arakesh had taken out a contract on the elves."

Nasta smiled wickedly. "I have always known your true goals, Alidyr. I will not allow you to use my order to bring about your master's vision."

Alidyr did his best to hide the true surprise at the revelation. "What do *you* know of that vision?"

"I know that it will be a world where both our kinds cannot exist." Nasta swept his robe aside, assuming an aggressive stance.

"It will be a world for the *strong*." Alidyr fought through the pain and opened his arms out to encompass the surrounding assassins. As one, the Arakesh erupted with a sharp cheer, endorsing Alidyr's takeover.

The elf did his best to stride over towards Nasta without giving in to the pain in his leg. He easily batted away the Father's attempts to punch and kick him, his twin blades cutting the old man in several places, until he was reduced to his knees once more.

Nasta looked up at him with sunken pits where his eyes had been burned away. "You will never get the gem." He spat blood at the elf's feet, his words surprising Alidyr even more. "Asher will beat you..."

Alidyr sneered before kicking the last human Father of Nightfall into the pit. Nasta Nal-Aket disappeared into the darkness that even the Nightseye elixir couldn't penetrate.

The heightened senses of over a hundred Arakesh were on Alidyr now. The students appeared more confused than the assassins, giving the elf an idea.

"A new dawn rises on our order. A dawn that will bring about the first age in which the Arakesh rightfully rule." Alidyr could see his words were hitting the right chords. "Are you not the greatest warriors Illian has ever seen?" Again they erupted with a single cheer. "Should the strong not rule over the weak? We will show the kingdoms of this land that the Arakesh are to be bowed before!

"The armies of Illian *and* Ayda will tremble at the sound of our name!" They cheered with every statement, lapping up his words. "My first act as Father is to unleash you upon our sworn enemies, the Graycoats of West Fellion. There will be little resistance from the other kingdoms when they see the heads of their precious knights adorning pikes at their front gates. Prepare yourselves - the first army of Nightfall leaves without delay." Alidyr walked over to the confused students. "There will be no test of the pit. Instead, you will be tested on the battlefield. Gather your brothers and sisters. Today, we are all Arakesh!"

Together, the assassins and students ran from the pit to spread the word to all who had not been present. The Nightseye elixir would be fuelling their aggressive behaviour, filling them all with the need to fight and kill.

This is what they were bred for, Alidyr thought. He nodded to Ro Dosarn who knew to take charge and keep any who doubted Alidyr's vision in check. The elf flinched under the pain in his leg and shoulder, but kept his back straight and limped to the edge of the pit.

It was troubling to think of Nasta Nal-Aket's knowledge regarding his activities. How long had the human known of his allegiance to Valanis? Did Asher know as well? Were the two still working together, against him?

Alidyr would have liked to have kept the old man alive a little longer to extract such information, but his death was also required to take control.

Reaver's bite stung all the more, giving Alidyr cause to smile at the thought that Nasta's body would be ripped to shreds in the pit before the sun rose. All that was left now was for the elf to call on Adellum and his powerful bow. West Fellion would fall and the ranger with it.

The gem was so close he could almost feel it in his hand.

CHAPTER 38
ALLIANCE OF TWO SHORES

The first light of the morning sun shone over the densely populated shanty homes which made up the Darkakin's capital city. With no discernible architectural style, the houses and tiny apartments were built atop one another at every angle and in various states of disrepair.

A dozen different animals made their morning calls and the open air markets came to life, as the owners set up their stalls and displayed their wares.

The assorted smells and sounds assaulted Galanör's exceptional senses from his vantage point, between two third-storey apartments. The three unusual companions had taken refuge on a decrepit balcony, amidst the hanging pig carcasses and hide canvases before the stars had disappeared from the sky.

"*What do you see, Galanör?*" Adilandra asked in a hushed tone from the corner. Her legs were tucked up and her arms wrapped around her knees. Her scimitar was never beyond her reach.

It truly pained Galanör to see his queen so diminished and wounded. He wanted to personally kill every Darkakin who had even looked at her.

During the days when Galanör's father had secured his marriage to Reyna, Adilandra's disapproval had been clear to see, though not because she didn't approve of him, but because she could see that it wasn't what they wanted.

There had always been an understanding in her eyes that warmed Adilandra's subjects to her, Galanör included.

They hadn't long found refuge on the balcony, so the queen's recent history wasn't well known to him, but judging from the way they found her, Adilandra had been pushed to the edge of survival. It made Galanör's blood boil.

The mage notably cleared his throat at the sound of her elven words. He had insisted during their escape that they speak in man's language so that he might understand, though he was yet to tell them his name.

Nevertheless, Galanör was impressed with the young mage, who had climbed every wall and building as they had during their chaotic escape from the arena. The human had no right to be as agile or fast as the elves, yet he had continued to keep up, while simultaneously firing spells at their savage pursuers.

Despite being in better condition than Adilandra, the young man still appeared haggard and in need of a bath. He had barely spoken since they found refuge and kept his staff in his hands at all times.

"They're still looking for us," Galanör explained in man's tongue. "But the arrival of the other clans has slowed them down."

He referred to the thousands of Darkakin warriors as clans, but in his head, Galanör knew they were an army. From astride Malliath, he had seen other armies heading towards them from different directions, kicking plumes of sand high into the air in their wake.

Even now the markets were being flooded with hundreds of the tattooed warriors, who came out of every doorway in the neighbourhood. Many had simply camped out in the streets and Galanör had been thankful for the timing in which they found the abandoned balcony. The hunting parties had been easy to see before the sun rose, but now the gathering crowds and animals littered the streets.

"Where are we exactly?" the mage asked. If his eyes were daggers, then Galanör would certainly be dead by now.

In truth, Galanör had no clue where Malliath had abandoned them. They were definitely in the southern lands of Ayda but, beyond that, the elf was utterly lost. He looked back from peeking over the lip of the balcony and looked to Adilandra for any answer.

"This is the Darkakin capital city. They call it Malaysai." The queen's voice was hoarse, dry in the desert heat. "It's ruled by The Goddess, but she's as human as the rest. Can you see the pyramid?"

Galanör returned to the edge and cautiously peered down the street where the massive structure stood.

"She lives inside it, at the very top." Adilandra dropped her head, covering her face with her long auburn hair. When she faced them again her fresh tears were visible. "She had Ederön thrown from her balcony so the masses could feast on his..." The queen closed in on herself again.

Galanör didn't know the name, but it stirred the same feelings. He gripped his sword, filled with the urge to leap from the balcony and slaughter as many of the savages as possible. The thought of putting Adilandra and the mage at risk, however, stayed his hand.

The thought of keeping the mage alive struck him as odd. Was it Galanör's responsibility to keep the human alive? Aside from the fact that the mage could defend himself, he wasn't an elf and he certainly wasn't royalty. And yet, Galanör felt responsible for his being here, as well as his part in the death of the girl and all the others that haunted his dreams. Helping the young man wouldn't atone for his actions, but it couldn't hurt.

"What is your name, mage?" Galanör asked softly.

"Abigail Rose," he replied flatly. "That's the only name you need to know, elf."

Galanör felt his heart quicken as the shame cut into him deeper than any blade. Abigail Rose was the name of the girl Lyra had killed. His shame began to set in when he realised he didn't know the name of the girl Lyra cut down in front of the Hydra, or any of the names of the children and women he had offered up to the Mer-folk.

"I'm sorry..." Galanör almost choked on his words. Any apology felt foreign to the elf, having been bred to be the ultimate warrior and leader. His time on Dragorn had made him harder, having to deal with Adamar and commanding the others.

"When we're out of this hellhole, I'll show you how much your apology means." The mage's knuckles turned white around his staff.

Galanör couldn't meet his eyes and just nodded, trying to think of anything else but the faces of his victims.

"There is no escape," Adilandra replied from within the cover of her hair. "They're natural hunters, like animals. Once they have your scent they'll track you indefinitely. Time and distance mean nothing to them, only the hunt."

The mage was trying to keep up a wall of confidence, but it was clear to see that Adilandra's words had created a crack.

"What happened to you?" Galanör asked. "When you left Elandril four years ago, the king said nothing of where you were going, only that you had gone on a pilgrimage to study the dragon wall at Mount Garganafan."

Adilandra looked up with years of pain reflected in her eyes. "Eleven of us departed Elandril, seeking the dragons that left Mount Garganafan... Now, only three of us remain." The queen paused and Galanör waited, happy to give Adilandra the time she needed. "We encountered the first tribe of Darkakin towards the end of our first year, travelling south. They didn't care who we were or where we came from; we were just prey. Something they could hunt that would entertain and feed them.

Word travelled fast between the tribes and before the end of the second year, we had four hunting parties on our heels. They knew the terrain, the wildlife and the heat never seemed to slow them down. They could ambush us in the light of day and we would never know it until it was too late. By the end of the third year, they had killed five and captured two. After meeting The Goddess there were only three of us left."

"Where are the others?" Surprisingly, it was the mage who asked.

"The Goddess keeps Fallön locked up in her personal chambers." Adilandra blinked hard, forcing tears out of her eyes. "Lörvana was given to Krenorak, a savage among savages, as a gift for capturing us. They're both inside the pyramid."

"Why did you come looking for the dragons?" Galanör asked. "They left Mount Garganafan centuries ago. They don't want to help us, that's why the king sent us to retrieve Malliath." He noted the mage's interest instantly shift towards him.

"Why?" Adilandra countered fiercely. "So Malliath can open the dragon wall and my husband can personally raise an army of dragons?" The queen met his eyes between the parting in her matted hair. "*Children of fire and flame offer great promise, but only one perceives the time we will fall.*"

Galanör recognised the phrase from Nalana's prophecy, though he had never paid much attention to it growing up. Like the king, his father had never given it any credence.

Adilandra continued, "It will take decades to raise and train those unborn dragons, and that's *if* Malliath opens the dragon wall. Judging by the way he dropped you two and flew away, I don't think that plan is going to work anymore." She wiped a tear from her cheek and her tone took on a new resolve. "Valanis will rise soon, I can feel it. We need old dragons, experienced dragons that can harness the magic required to defeat Valanis once and for all..."

Galanör heard the Darkakin before he saw him. The door to the apartment on their left swung open and a barrel-shaped Darkakin, covered in tattoos and wielding a jagged knife, stormed onto the balcony, grumbling in his native tongue.

Galanör reached for his blade, having already decided he was going to plunge his sword into the Darkakin's exposed throat, killing him quickly and silencing any call for help.

It was Adilandra, however, who exploded into action first. With unparalleled speed, her foot snapped out and ploughed into the Darkakin's leg with enough force to invert his kneecap. The big man's cry was stifled by the open-palm thrust that the queen jammed into his throat, collapsing his windpipe as well as shoving him back into the apartment.

Galanör could only look on in shock at Adilandra's ferocity. Her time in the savage lands had left her a bag of raw nerves, constantly exposed.

The Darkakin gargled and suffocated, while Adilandra sat with her knee firmly on his chest, pinning him down until he died. Her shoulders heaved from the exertion of her laboured breaths.

Galanör could see the queen watching the Darkakin intensely, as his life faded away. It wasn't that she enjoyed it, but rather that she needed to see it, to see the savage die and feel something, anything.

Watching her friends die and be taken away had made Adilandra numb. Galanör could relate to such numbness, only his had been created by all the lives he had taken. Perhaps killing the Darkakin gave Adilandra some semblance of who she was or some justice that was owed to her. It was the opposite for Galanör now; who felt he had to save lives to regain something of his soul.

Adilandra fell back and scrambled onto the balcony without looking at either Galanör or the mage. Galanör held his breath for a moment, waiting to see if anyone responded to the queen's outburst. The noise from the street below only increased with the swelling army that had arrived.

Galanör crawled across the balcony and closed the apartment door since the smell inside was worse than the smell drifting up from the street and the hanging carcasses above them. The elf had thought that nowhere in all of Verda could smell as bad as Dragorn, yet the home of a single Darkakin made the island-city seem almost refreshing.

"You're not like the elves I read about at Korkanath." The mage stared at the doorway concealing the dead Darkakin.

Galanör didn't know what to say. He could imagine well enough what might be written in those books; ancient scripts about a race of vegetarians that spent all day writing poetry and songs while mastering the art of magic with ever-lasting lives. How wrong they were. That was why the elves would beat the world of man when it came to war.

"We need to start thinking of a way to leave these lands." Galanör changed the subject. "Elandril is well north of here, so we'll need to steal supplies for—"

"I'm not returning to Elandril." Adilandra looked up, meeting Galanör's eyes with defiance.

"My Lady..."

"I am not your queen, Galanör, not out here. I will not order you to leave me and I will not order you to follow me. But, I am going to find the dragons and stop Valanis from returning. In so doing I might just be able to prevent another war from ravaging Illian."

"What war?" the mage asked, his interest suddenly piqued.

Galanör looked at the young mage but found his mouth had clamped itself shut. Even now his duty kept him from divulging secrets about a war he didn't want to a man who could do nothing about it anyway. Instead, he turned back to Adilandra with concern in his eyes.

"My queen... Adilandra." Galanör didn't know what to say to convince her. "Before we arrived here I saw several armies of Darkakin crossing the land, all of them coming here. Very soon we won't be able to move through the city unseen, let alone cross the jungle and reach the desert. We have to leave *now*."

"What war are you talking about?" the mage asked again.

"I have no intention of staying in Malaysai," Adilandra replied, ignoring the man. "The dragons flew east from here, away from the Darkakin. As soon as I free Lörvana and Fallön, we will flee this city with all haste."

Galanör felt his expression go blank as he considered Adilandra's plan. If she thought that rescuing the elves from the pyramid and fleeing Malaysai was something that could be done with haste, then the queen had lost her... He couldn't finish the thought. Seeing the determination on her face now, Galanör knew there would be no changing her mind. With that thought, he also knew there was no way he could let her go alone. She was his queen after all.

His blank expression turned to one of sad contemplation when he realised that his days of killing were not as far behind him as he had hoped. A new beginning would have to wait, providing he survived.

"What *war*?" the mage asked with more urgency.

Adilandra didn't have the same reservations as Galanör. "The war we avoided by leaving Illian a thousand years ago," she explained. "A war between your race and ours. Though I dare to call it a war, slaughter would be a better description."

The mage couldn't decide whether to be confused or horrified. "Why would we fight each other?"

"The elves will fight to destroy Valanis and end the threat of his return once and for all. *Your* people will be forced to fight simply to survive. That is the nature of war." Adilandra looked through the mage as if seeing into the past.

Galanör respected her for that alone. Her age dwarfed his own, lending to her experience and wisdom beyond his comprehension.

"When is this happening?" The mage looked at Galanör now.

"It has already begun," Adilandra replied instead. "The world of man just doesn't know it yet."

In the constant noise that surrounded the companions, silence sat between the three. Galanör felt every precious second slip by, aware that their window of opportunity was quickly disappearing. How had his life been turned around so fast? The impact of a dragon, he reasoned.

"You believe that finding the dragons will stop this war?" the mage asked.

"Dragons are deeply magical beings," Adilandra said. "Their magic was essential in trapping Valanis in the Amber Spell. I believe that with their help, we can find a way to remove him from the face of Verda all together, ending the threat of his return."

"I've never heard of that spell."

Galanör, like every elf, had been taught the history of The Dark War. "It would normally freeze anything in a single moment, though it cannot be sustained indefinitely. That's why Garganafan, the oldest dragon of his time, lent his power to the spell. Unfortunately, we don't know if it will last forever or if it can be breached."

"If we can prevent Valanis from rising, my husband won't have a legitimate reason to invade Illian. But we need the dragons." Adilandra was compelling. Galanör could see why so many had followed her this far.

The mage paused before replying. "Then what are we waiting for?"

The question surprised Galanör profoundly. This was the same mage that had sworn to kill him, with no lack of rage in his eyes, only minutes earlier. It was the first time Galanör had been surprised by the actions of a human. For someone so young, the mage showed great wisdom in being able to set his feelings aside for the greater good.

"Your name, perhaps?" Adilandra replied softly.

The mage looked at Galanör again, his anger returning slightly. "My name is Gideon Thorn."

Galanör looked at the mage with new eyes, knowing that Gideon Thorn wasn't a man he would soon forget.

CHAPTER 39
HOMECOMING

Not long after dawn, the stone walls of West Fellion came into view as the hills levelled out into the flatter lands of the enchanted Moonlit Plains. The fortress home of the Graycoats sat on the northern edge of the plains, below the central forest of The Evermoore.

Nathaniel had spent many a night sitting atop West Fellion's turrets, looking out over the glowing fields on the horizon, which separated the four fiefdoms from the kingdom of Karath, in The Arid Lands further south still. It was exhilarating to think that the very race that enchanted The Moonlit Plains was riding alongside him.

"That is where you grew up?" Reyna asked, her beautiful green eyes taking in every detail.

Nathaniel looked back at West Fellion and thought about the elf's question. He had certainly been trained to do a great many things inside those walls, but he didn't grow up there and he certainly didn't think of it as home. The young knight had discovered the true depths of his character on the road, travelling through the wilds of Illian. He felt more welcome there than he did inside West Fellion.

"It isn't much, but..." The Graycoat couldn't find the words to describe it.

Every three months he would have to return and fill out a report of his work on the roads and wait to see if any specific mission would be assigned to him. It never was. The order never chose Nathaniel to represent the Graycoats, instead preferring to leave him to slay beasts and hunt fugitives across the land.

Every now and then he would be given a student to take out into the world, though it spoke more of the order's feelings toward the student than him. Nathaniel hadn't said anything to Elaith, but the fact that she had been paired with him suggested that the masters didn't expect much from her.

Elaith was riding up front with Asher but, from his angle, Nathaniel could see the hard stare she was giving the distant walls. The next time she walked out through those gates, she would be a Graycoat. Seeing her now, it seemed too young an age to be sent out into the land and run headlong into danger.

Nathaniel had also been eighteen when he graduated, twelve years earlier, but it didn't change his feelings on the age of graduation now. He felt confident, however, that the young knight would flourish in her work and go on to do a great many things in the service of Illian and its people.

"You believe that West Fellion can protect us?" Faylen asked loud enough to be heard by everyone.

Darius Devale turned in his saddle. "I assure you, Lady Faylen, those walls have never been breached. The stone was enchanted centuries ago by the mages of Korkanath, reinforcing them against ballista or magical attack. Though circular, it cannot be attacked from all sides, due to the trench that surrounds the high walls. Death upon a sharp pike awaits any who would fall in."

Nathaniel knew well enough of the fort's outer defences. Before graduating he had spent many months cutting down and fashioning logs into fresh pikes, that then had to be dug into the trench. It was back-breaking work, but the masters said it was the fastest way to hone their bodies into the physical shape required of a Graycoat.

"The main gate is similarly enchanted," Darius continued. "And should it be breached, there is an enclosed courtyard that has another set of warded doors."

"A kill box..." Asher observed.

"Indeed, Ranger. Any attacker would soon fall under our arrows and hot oil. And, of course, all eight turrets are mounted with two giant ballista that launch arrows the size of a spear. We have regular patrols that can see any threat from miles around, giving us plenty of warning. You will be safe here." Darius looked at Nathaniel and Reyna together.

A pit opened inside Nathaniel's stomach. He hadn't thought about the details of this particular return and the scorning he would receive. He had been occupied with thoughts of what would happen to Asher, but it was clear that Darius knew there was more between Reyna and him and would, no doubt, report Nathaniel to the Lord Marshal. Very soon he would be faced with a decision that was as clear as black and white.

Helping Asher and being with Reyna in any way could only lead to expulsion from the order, but being a Graycoat was the only thing he had ever known.

Could he leave it all behind? And for what, to be a ranger like Asher?

In his heart, he knew the truth of his relationship with Reyna. The princess of the elven nation could never be with a human, let alone one that wasn't even royalty. There was a good chance that he was nothing but the plaything of an elven princess. Their urges and desires were stronger than that of humans, after all.

～

Within the hour, the group was passing through the small courtyard between both sets of double doors, each large enough for a Mountain Troll to walk through.

The hundreds of sharpened logs, which stood erected at varying angles inside the trench, appeared new, having been placed in the weeks since Nathaniel left with Elaith.

As the group trotted inside, Nathaniel looked up at the walls of the small courtyard and saw dozens of faces looking back at him. The elves were a spectacle wherever they journeyed.

Asher had pulled back and allowed Darius and the other Graycoats to enter first. Credit to the ranger, he kept both of his hands on Hector's reins rather than the hilt of his broadsword.

When the courtyard opened into a muddy corridor, between two stables, Nathaniel felt his every muscle tense at the sight of Lord Marshal Horvarth and a score of knights.

Despite being in his sixties, the Lord Marshal appeared a formidable man, with a short spiky white beard and matching hair. Parallel scars ran diagonally over his left cheekbone, the upper scar crossing over his eye and cutting through an eyebrow. His cold blue eyes roamed over Nathaniel and settled on the elves, his stony expression giving nothing away. It wasn't long before his gaze narrowed between the companions and focused on Asher.

Darius jumped down from his horse and clasped wrists with the Lord Marshall.

"Well met..." the older man said. Horvarth spoke like a soldier; direct and to the point.

"Lord Marshal Horvarth, I present Princess Reyna Sevari and Lady Faylen Haldör." Darius moved aside, as the elves dismounted and came to stand before Horvarth.

Reyna bowed her head and Faylen followed suit.

"Welcome to West Fellion," the Lord Marshal said. "I read Galfrey's letter. You were lucky to survive an attack from the Arakesh; they are killers of the highest order..." Horvarth eyed Asher with his last words.

"We would not have survived, were it not for the bravery and skill of Nathaniel and Asher," Reyna replied. The princess was just as aware as Nathaniel about how welcome the ranger was inside these walls.

"Rooms have been prepared for you both and the patrols have been doubled. If the assassins make another attempt on your life, we will be ready for them. For now, however, some breakfast has been prepared for us, if you would join me? I'm afraid we can't provide the same feast you enjoyed in King Rengar's court, but you might find the company a little more... honest." A rare smile crossed the Lord Marshal's face.

"We would be honoured, Lord Marshal Horvarth."

"Excellent." Horvarth gestured for them to follow him into the main keep.

Nathaniel wanted to remain close to Reyna, but the knight paused and his hand fell to his sword, the warrior's sixth sense controlling his actions. He was pleased to see that Elaith had that same sense, as she too had turned around to face Asher.

The Graycoats that had accompanied the Lord Marshal made no move to follow him and the elves but had instead surrounded the ranger. Each of the knights gave Asher a look of pure disgust while drawing their swords. Surprisingly, Darius stood to one side with Tick and Orvin, rather than joining their brothers and sisters in ambushing the old ranger. Darius gave an almost imperceptible shake of his blond head to Nathaniel, warning him not to get involved.

Asher slowly dismounted and came to stand before the group, matching their looks of disgust with a hard stare of his own, daring them to raise a sword against him.

"This isn't right..." Nathaniel said under his breath.

"What is the meaning of this?" Reyna asked, accentuating her concern.

Horvarth sighed, no doubt expecting the conversation, but also hoping it wouldn't have to be said. "This man is to be our prisoner.

He is a known affiliate of the Arakesh and is in possession of many secrets pertinent to the safety of the realm."

"He has saved my life more than once," Reyna stated at once. "You are to consider him an extension of me. A guest, if you will."

"Forgive me, Princess..." Horvarth paused for a moment. "This is not Velia or Lirian. West Fellion is not a fiefdom or representative of our race. The Graycoats are an order of knights independent of the six kingdoms and, as such, we do not need to... *please* you, as they do. Asher will be imprisoned here for as long as I deem. He has information on the very animals that are hunting you. With his help, we might be able to bring Nightfall down and finally end this shadowy war."

Besides cutting the Lord Marshal down, her protest was the extent of Reyna's powers. Her authority meant nothing inside West Fellion.

A broad-shouldered Graycoat, who Nathaniel recognised as Ned Fennick, stepped into the circle and squared up against Asher. The knight was second only to the Lord Marshal and the only Graycoat more senior than Darius Devale. In his mid-forties, the hardened knight was, in Nathaniel's eyes, a good match for Asher in a fight, but he had no doubts that the ex-assassin would emerge the victor.

"Relinquish your weapons... or don't," Fennick added with a tightening grip around his sword.

Nathaniel removed his sword an inch from its scabbard, though he still didn't know what he would do if Asher refused. The Graycoat's resolve weakened further when he noticed Horvarth watching him closely.

To all their surprise, and disappointment, Asher unbuckled his sword belt and let his broadsword fall to the ground. He went on to methodically remove every dagger and hidden blade, as well as the silvyr short-sword on his back. Many of the knights took an interest in the compact bow dropped alongside his quiver of arrows.

Ned Fennick sneered. "Take him below."

Had Nathaniel not seen Asher in battle, he would have considered all twenty knights escorting him to the cells as overkill but, perhaps, in this case, it was simply good sense.

He let his sword drop fully back into its scabbard as the ranger passed him by. Asher gave him a small nod that implied he wasn't worried and that Nathaniel shouldn't do anything stupid. The ranger was unusually calm for someone who was being escorted to a prison cell. In all likelihood, the cell he was being taken to was a lot nicer than anything he had been subjected to in Nightfall.

Nathaniel turned back to follow Reyna when Horvarth stepped in his way. "I'll expect your report by first light tomorrow, Galfrey." The Lord Marshall's stern expression was enough to tell Nathaniel that he wouldn't be accompanying them.

Reyna followed Horvarth, only looking back to give the Graycoat a sad smile. The princess would likely continue to bargain for Asher's release. In the meantime, Nathaniel would see to Elaith's graduation and make certain that Asher wasn't mistreated.

He made for the entrance to the cells, beneath the main keep, when Ned Fennick turned to face him at the back of the escort.

"And where are *you* going, Galfrey?" Fennick's appearance was as precise as Horvarth's, except his greying goatee was well trimmed like his hair.

Nathaniel looked past the broad man to see the back of Asher disappear into the depths of West Fellion. This sort of treatment from Fennick was the usual way of life for the knight inside the high walls. Here he was no more than a mark against his father's perfect record.

"The Marshal wants your report by tomorrow," Fennick continued. "You didn't write one before you left with your ward, which makes it twice as long. Not to mention this mess." The Graycoat nodded over his shoulder. "Better get writing." Fennick went after the ranger and his escort, leaving Nathaniel to grit his teeth.

Elaith came over, having seen to the horses. "What are we going to do?"

"*We* are doing nothing. *You* are going to clean everything you're wearing and sharpen your sword. My report's going on the Lord Marshal's desk tomorrow morning. Yours had better be ready as well."

Elaith's expression told of the conflict they both shared.

Nathaniel walked away, unsure what to do. Darius had already left with Horvarth and the elves, leaving Orvin and Tick to come up behind Nathaniel.

"Looks like your boyfriend's in for a rough night..." Tick remarked to Orvin's hilarity.

Nathaniel whipped around and pinched Tick's broken nose in a vice-like grip. The lanky man squirmed and howled in pain, but Nathaniel held him in place, practically growling at Orvin, who made no move to help Tick.

Nathaniel pulled him closer, eliciting more pain. "Did you say something?"

Tick tried to shake his head through the pain. With that, he pushed the Graycoat away, leaving him to nurse his bleeding nose.

Nathaniel walked away, muttering under his breath, "There's no place like home..."

Asher counted twenty Graycoats ushering him towards the empty cell at the end of the tunnel. It was no surprise that they had passed the regular cells in favour of this particular prison - this cell had been custom built to hold an Arakesh.

The single door at the end of the corridor was reinforced iron, with four thick bolts that slotted into the surrounding stone. There were already two Graycoats standing either side of the door, ready to greet their new guest.

"Welcome to your new home." It was the same knight who had ordered his weapons be left behind that now stood by his side.

The two guards had to work together to open the door, while

Asher turned to face his jailer and the twenty Graycoats that filled the tunnel behind him.

The part of his mind that calculated the outcome of every fight told the ranger that he wouldn't reach the other end of the tunnel without serious blood loss. It was never in question that every Graycoat between him and freedom would be put down, but how far he got beyond that was incalculable.

Let them lock him away now and figure the rest out later, he thought. The Graycoats were incredible fighters and not to be underestimated, but when it came to the art of torture and imprisonment, they were amateurs.

The guards came up from behind and roughly removed his green cloak, stripped him to the waist and pulled off his boots. Only then did the broad-shouldered man slam his meaty fist into Asher's face, cutting his cheek.

The punch launched the ranger into the cell, where the waiting guards came down on him fast, swinging clubs. Covering his head, Asher curled up into a ball and presented them with his back in the hope of protecting his vital organs. The ranger knew how easy it was to kill a man without piercing the skin.

Years of training in the darkness took over and Nasta Nal-Aket's words rang clear in his mind. In his fifth year of training at Nightfall, Asher had been subjected to horrendous beatings for nothing more than to make him familiar with pain.

"Through this pain, you will be reborn," Nasta had said. His old master always stood to the side and watched the other teachers lay into Asher. "Pain leads to anger, and anger never wins in combat. Only when pain feels like an old friend will you free yourself from the shackles that bind so many men.

"If you pass this test, pain will mean nothing to you. You will be capable of anything. Nothing will stop you. But you must find a place in your mind where you can let your body go. Allow it to endure while you retreat and wait for your moment to strike."

Asher had never been tied down during these beatings but was in fact encouraged to fight back. Only when he was able to fight back with control and use the techniques he had already been taught, was the test completed.

Lying on the cold floor now, Asher retreated into his mind and let his body take the punishment. The ranger thought of the house he planned on building by the shore, with the land he had procured from King Rengar. He could finally find some peace there, perhaps. The fields were rolling hills of lush green on The Shining Coast, a good place for any man to settle and make a new life for himself.

After what felt like hours, he was finally rolled over, where the broad-shouldered Graycoat stood over him, full of smug satisfaction. The guards who had beaten him checked over his trousers to search for any hidden weapons or tools of escape. Asher wanted to protest as they pulled off his silver ring with the black gem inside, but his beaten body refused to obey.

"You're a tough old bastard, I'll give you that..." The Graycoat reached down and removed Asher's tattered red blindfold. He examined the strip of cloth before putting it over his eyes. "Well, I don't see shit."

Asher collected the blood in his mouth and spat it over the knight's famous coat. "I would tell you to go screw yourself..." Every word was painful to say. "But since you're a Graycoat, I guess that's a given..."

The broad Graycoat looked down at him with new fury, but Asher could only laugh through his broken ribs, as the beating began anew.

"String him up!"

The knocks to the head made everything a little harder to understand. Still, Asher felt the manacles fasten around his wrists and ankles before the *rattling* of chains could be heard around the room. Seconds later, the ranger was suspended in mid-air, with each limb pulled in an opposite direction.

His head dropped to his chest limply and he caught sight of his bruised and battered torso. It was nothing that wouldn't heal - it was his mind that mattered the most. The ranger blinked hard in an effort to keep his senses sharp and his mind on task. He had to be ready for any opportunity.

The Graycoat threw the red cloth onto a nearby table, where it landed next to his ring. Asher tried not to show any attachment to the items, but couldn't help but feel naked without them, especially the gem, a trinket he had owned for as long as he could remember.

"The name's Ned Fennick, you killing-piece-of-shit." The Graycoat moved closer to Asher. "Let that name sear into your brain. You and I are going to get to know each other very well..."

Fennick stepped aside as a new man, much older than the rest, entered the cell. He wasn't a Graycoat if his sweeping robes and tall staff were anything to go by. The older man had a braided white beard with a perfectly bald head and two narrow eyes that focused on Asher.

"Meister Kalantez, thank you for your time." Fennick harboured a wicked grin. "The Meister here is a caster, a mage that is, from Vangarth. He arrived not long ago at the Lord Marshal's request. He's here to add the finishing touches to your new decor." Fennick waved the mage on.

Meister Kalantez stepped closer and released his hold on the tall staff, which continued to stand perfectly without aid. The mage reached into his robes and pulled out a slender wand that zigzagged from end-to-end. Kalantez touched his wand to each of the four manacles and began to chant with a low guttural tone. When the old man had finished, the iron bands surrounding Asher's limbs were lined with ancient glyphs.

"Is it done?" Fennick asked. Meister Kalantez simply nodded, never even glancing at Asher. "Excellent! Your locks cannot be picked and the manacles cannot be broken by any blade. You're not going anywhere..."

CHAPTER 40
RECLAMATION

Alidyr flexed his fingers over the armrest of Nightfall's throne, feeling the cool wood under his sensitive elven fingers.

The transition to ruling over the Arakesh was not as satisfying as he had imagined for so many years. The elf chalked it up to the fact that he lived only to serve Valanis, and commanding an army of human assassins was simply another tool for his master's will.

The halls were quiet now. Adellum had taken the five hundred Arakesh in the dead of night, leaving the rest to keep watch over Nightfall.

With their unparalleled speed, the Arakesh would reach West Fellion in a couple of days. Woe betide any who came across the marching force as they swept across The Arid Lands and onto The Moonlit Plains.

"DID YOU THINK I WOULDN'T FIND OUT?" The echoing question roared from beyond The Cradle, but Alidyr recognised the voice.

Thallan...

Six hidden assassins dropped from the surrounding balcony and drew their twin blades, ready for battle. The sound of clashing swords rang out in the dark before Alidyr's keen ears heard the splatter of blood against the walls. He remained seated on the throne and rolled his eyes at Thallan's dramatics.

The body of a dead Arakesh exploded through the doors in a shower of wooden splinters and flailing limbs. Thallan stormed into The Cradle with his imposing jewelled sword and a face of thunder, not bothering to conceal his appearance with his hood and half-mask.

Still, Alidyr remained seated while his assassins charged the enraged elf.

"You betray me!" Thallan cried, as the first two warriors closed in.

The pitch black was instantly illuminated by a light brighter than the sun, penetrating the fabric of their blindfolds. The Arakesh were momentarily disoriented, their senses in shock. Alidyr blinked hard, casting a spell to adjust his eyes.

His vision returned, Alidyr discovered The Cradle's decorative pyres were blazing. Striding up the middle, Thallan was brandishing his onyx scimitar...

The Arakesh shook their heads and rose to the challenge. It was all for naught, Alidyr reasoned. Thallan would kill a hundred Arakesh if they stood between him and the cause of his wrath.

Thallan used his elven speed to dash past the first attacker and whipped his sword horizontally, removing the head from another. Now in the thick of it, and surrounded by three assassins, Thallan was in his element. He dodged one sword and parried the other two before balancing on the ball of his foot and kicking the first Arakesh he had evaded. The woman was launched into the pillar behind her, passing partially through the old stone in a shower of rock and dust.

Alidyr heard her spine and skull shatter upon impact...

The green blade flashed in the firelight and cut the second-to-last assassin from shoulder to waist, separating the two halves completely. The last surviving Arakesh attacked Thallan from behind, but the nimble elf dropped to one knee and spun on the spot, evading the twin blades, so he could twist his magical sword around and plunge it into the man's back.

Without taking his eyes off Alidyr, Thallan slowly stood up and slid his blade from the dead man's body.

"Feel better?"

"Did you really think you could march a make-shift army across Illian and I wouldn't know about it?" Thallan's deep blue eyes narrowed.

"Does it enrage you more that I have an army at my disposal, or that I have Adellum leading them?" Alidyr adjusted his seating and gritted his teeth in an effort to hide the pain that bit into his leg and shoulder. He had applied several ointments and taken multiple healing elixirs since the Father had wounded him with the deadly Reaver, but none had succeeded in combatting the pain and sealing the wound.

"Adellum will answer for his insubordination when I see to it. You should be more concerned with your own betrayal, brother."

"You would speak to me of betrayal?" Alidyr abruptly stood up, clenching his fists against the pain in his leg. "You betray the Master every day by abandoning the search for the gem!"

"Always the gem with you," Thallan replied, exasperated. He began to pace in front of the throne. "It is *lost*, Alidyr! You know the legends as well as I! It was most likely taken by some Outlander into the depths of The Wild Moores and lost again! I am seeing Valanis's plan for Verda fulfilled until he returns to power. A plan you are compromising by attacking West Fellion so openly."

Alidyr purposefully walked down the throne steps towards Thallan, his hands threateningly resting on his twin-blades. "Valanis will never return to power without Paldora's Gem. If you can't grasp that simple fact, brother, then you are of no use to our Master."

"*I* am the head of the Hand, Alidyr." Thallan pointed his onyx sword at his elven brother. "You failed in that role. It is my time now!"

Alidyr could hear the crack in his voice, the doubt that lingered in the back of Thallan's mind. If Alidyr took the position back by force, there would be nothing Thallan could do to prevent it.

"I have found it..." Alidyr couldn't help himself. The look of confusion on Thallan's face was worth giving away the upper hand.

"You *lie*. You'd say anything to..." Thallan looked long and hard at Alidyr's serious expression, the truth slowly dawning on him. "Where is it?"

"West Fellion of course. Why else would I send so many to ensure its retrieval?" Alidyr remained a step higher to physically match his superiority over Thallan.

The bald elf lowered his green blade and looked away, his eyes darting from left to right. This changed everything. Alidyr was counting on it to put Thallan off balance and lower his guard.

"You would let Adellum claim the gem?" he finally asked.

"Are we not equal in our service to Valanis?" Alidyr countered, slyly. "Return to Kaliban, brother, you need to *heal*."

Thallan looked confused. "My burns are gone, I require no healing."

Alidyr struck with the ferocity of a king cobra and plunged his short-sword into Thallan's shoulder, driving him to one knee in agony. The elf looked up at him, stricken with equal amounts of fear and pain.

"Return to Kaliban, heal your wounds and await my return. As the head of the Hand, I *command* you..."

Alidyr's self-proclamation stunned Thallan, even through the pain of the blade in his shoulder. The bald elf fell to the floor after Alidyr pulled his sword free, but the master assassin continued on, walking between the recently fallen Arakesh and ignoring the groans from Thallan.

"You won't... get away with this." Thallan managed to stand while gripping his wounded shoulder.

"I already have." Alidyr sheathed his blade and whipped his white robes behind as he turned to face the bald elf. "Return to Kaliban. I will see to our master's ascension."

Thallan opened his mouth to protest, but he wasn't given the chance. With the short throw of a crystal, Alidyr opened a portal beneath the other elf and watched him drop into the abyss.

Alidyr didn't have the power to transport Thallan all the way to Kaliban and so he left him somewhere between The Arid Lands and The Ice Vales, in the north - he hadn't been too picky when conjuring the portal.

CHAPTER 41
A LESSON IN HISTORY

It had been a long day and slow progress for Gideon and the elves, cautiously moving through Malaysai unseen.

The young mage had been forced to enact a spell across the palms and fingers of his hands, creating rough calluses to help him grip the numerous walls, as the three climbed over every rooftop. Galanör and Adilandra scaled every obstacle with ease, ascending the building tops with incredible speed.

Often had they been forced to hide or cast enchantments to conceal themselves from the many inhabitants.

The first of the Darkakin armies continued to pour into the city. Galanör pointed out that their tattoos differed greatly, indicating the presence of another army having arrived. Gideon's human eyes couldn't easily make the distinction, but he was inclined to agree if the many fights that broke out were anything to go by.

As the sun was setting, the three companions finally made it to the last building in the street, which sat at the base of the pyramid. The elves stayed low, catching their breath, while Gideon moved to the edge, curious about the spectacle taking place below.

A long wooden platform stood by the side of the road,

surrounded by hundreds of screaming Darkakin, who were pointing at a line of men and women displayed on the stage. The mage couldn't believe what he was seeing. Gideon had heard of the slave markets in The Arid Lands, back in Illian, but it was frowned upon by the rest of the kingdoms.

Seeing it so openly and among such savages was an entirely different experience to hearing about it in a land far away.

A fat Darkakin, with a stomach resembling that of a barrel, strode up and down the platform with a cane in one hand. Every now and then he would point at one of the slaves and command one of his men to accept the payment offered. The slave would then be shoved off the stage, into the hands of their new owner. It seemed to Gideon that the women sold first and much faster. The thought sickened him.

"Slaves are just another form of currency here." Adilandra was beside him, her movements undetectable. "The women will become playthings and the men forced to serve in one of the armies or used for hard labour. Only the strong survive here."

"It's not right..." Gideon could only watch as a slave girl was thrown over a man's shoulder and taken away, into the baying mob.

His hand dropped to Abigail's wand on his thigh, before Adilandra rested her own hand on top of his and shook her head.

"It would be folly to fight so many," Galanör commented from behind.

Gideon's sense of right and wrong had always steered him in life, along with a dangerous sense of adventure, and the mage knew that helping Adilandra was the right thing to do, but working alongside Galanör felt so very wrong. The elf's continued existence was an offence to the memory of Abigail. He couldn't deny, however, the other voice in his mind that told him it would be wrong to take Galanör's life. A smaller voice.

"A pity you didn't have such reservations when you and your lot attacked Korkanath." Gideon couldn't hide the venom in his remark.

Galanör looked away, an expression of shame staining his angelic features.

"Enough," Adilandra commanded with a queen's tone. "Let the Darkakin enslave and kill each other. They aren't worth our time."

It was a harsh statement that Gideon felt was hard to agree with. The Darkakin were a cruel people indeed, but it didn't feel right to give up on anyone that needed help, even Darkakin slaves. If only Abigail was here, he thought. She would know the right thing to do; she always gave him the confidence and the encouragement to be brave.

"Stay here and rest, both of you." Galanör looked over the adjacent roof as if measuring the gap. "I will scout the perimeter of the pyramid and search for a way inside."

"We should stay together," Gideon replied. He hated being with Galanör, but they were alone and vulnerable - having more blades and magic was simply the best way to protect themselves.

"The quicker we find Lörvana and Fallön, the quicker we can leave this wretched place. It'll be easier if I go alone." With that, the elf was gone, vanishing over the lip of the building with the grace of a cat.

It wasn't long before night fell and the slave market was replaced with Malaysai's other forms of entertainment. The armies collided with contests of strength, often ending in bloodshed and arguments that led to more bloodshed.

Drunks wandered the streets before passing out in alleyways where they were stripped of their belongings. Numerous brothels opened across the neighbourhood, a staple business in every city, apparently. Malaysai was louder at night than it was in the day.

"You know him... Galanör?" Gideon asked Adilandra. She had remained cross-legged and silent since the warrior-elf had left.

"He is betrothed to my daughter, Reyna, though I believe that neither of them wishes it so." The queen studied Gideon for a moment, a moment that made the mage uncomfortable in his skin. "There is more to him than just a blade, Mr. Thorn."

"Do you know what he did to my home?" Gideon replied sharply.

"I was privy to all of my husband's plans before I left. I believe Galanör was charged with bringing Malliath the voiceless to Ayda. I imagine he didn't ask for Malliath's company politely."

"They killed innocent people, most of them children!" Gideon stopped himself before his voice carried too far.

"Galanör cannot be blamed entirely; he is the product of his ambitious father. As a child, I remember Galanör being a delicate and sensitive boy. Unfortunately, his father had sights on being at my husband's right hand and sought to accomplish that through his son. His father had him taken away as a young elf and trained in the Shalarian forests, not an easy place to survive. It is certainly no Korkanath."

"Do you think any of that excuses him?"

"I think none feel the pain of his actions more than he. But I should warn you, if you challenge him on behalf of your friend, Galanör will kill you. Maybe you wish to add to his pain, with your death..."

Gideon remained silent and thought on Adilandra's warning. He knew that challenging the elf wouldn't be what Abigail wanted; it wasn't even Galanör's blade that took her life.

The mage sought to change the conversation. "What is the dragon wall? You said Malliath had to open it."

Adilandra looked at him before resting her head back against the wall and gazing at the starry field above. "Tell me what you know of The Dragon War, Gideon."

Gideon hated his questions being answered with questions. "It took place around the same time your people left Illian. Malliath started a war with man for our riches, believing that the elves wouldn't help us since you were leaving. King Gal Tion rallied the..." He trailed off seeing the queen shake her head.

"King Tion had history re-written in his favour, young mage. It was Gal Tion and his lapdog, Tyberius Gray, who started the war by convincing the other regions to stand behind them in attacking The Lifeless Isles. Only the *Dragorn* stood with the dragons, but even they fell in the end..."

"Dragorn?" Gideon knew well of the island nation and the Dragornians that inhabited it, but what did they have to do with The Dragon War?

"It's not surprising that your history books don't speak of them. Man never understood the Dragorn. They were a group of a chosen few who had the ability to communicate with the dragons, and were allowed to live with them on their island. It was your people who named the island after them, once they conquered it and The Lifeless Isles beneath."

"Communicate? With the dragons?" Gideon had heard Malliath's roar and couldn't imagine how anyone might talk to them.

"They are creatures of pure empathy." It was the first time Gideon had seen Adilandra smile. "To you or me they can reflect their feelings in our emotions. If you were to anger them, *you* would feel angry, if you made them happy, *you* would feel happy and so on. Dragorn had the ability to discern individual words from the dragons and carry entire conversations. They were the best of us all. When the first dragons fell, my people made the wrong choice to leave for Ayda, abandoning Illian to war and the dragons to near-extinction."

"Why did you leave?" Gideon asked.

"We were still reeling from The Dark War. We have long memories and elven blood still stained the ground. Fighting another war was simply too much, though our inaction is greatly regretted now. Man's defeat over the dragons was unexpected, but victory was only claimed when the surviving dragons fled The Lifeless Isles, leaving man to his *greed*."

"They fled to Ayda as well? To Mount Garganafan?"

"It wasn't so named until we arrived, but yes. It is the biggest mountain in all of Verda. Rainael the emerald star led the last of her kind to the base of the mountain, where they stored the remaining dragon eggs to keep them safe from mankind.

"To ensure that man didn't follow them to the mountain, they left for the south. It was Galandavax who unleashed his breath upon the mountainside, sealing the entrance with fire and magic. It can only be opened with dragons' breath."

"That's why you need Malliath..." Gideon couldn't believe the history of the world that was being imparted to him. The real history. Abigail would have loved to hear it.

"That's why my *husband* wants Malliath," Adilandra was quick to correct.

"You don't speak fondly of him, your husband I mean."

"We have a stark difference of opinion. Now, I require rest *and* silence. Galanör will be back soon and I need to gather my energy for what comes next." Adilandra closed her eyes again and turned away from Gideon.

What a strange life the mage had been thrown into. Gideon adjusted the leather jacket around his neck, unaccustomed to the heat of the south. How could everything have changed so much in so little time?

How could it all have gone so wrong?

Galanör crouched on the corner of the tallest building. Beside the pyramid he was able to get the lay of the land, savage as it was. It felt good to be out of the mage's gaze and the shame that came with it. It would be an uneasy alliance between them, but Galanör didn't fear for his own life, rather that he would be forced to kill Gideon.

Having almost circled it completely, he knew that the structure had four entrances, one at the base of each side. The number of Darkakin guarding the rectangular openings varied, an indication of their disorganisation.

The scimitar resting on his hip filled him the confidence that no single group of guards could keep him out. He still longed for a second sword, as he had since embarking on the king's mission. The elf had spent centuries training and fighting with two scimitars, learning the techniques required to handle both at once. Most fumbled and struggled to coordinate their hands and body while wielding twin swords, but never Galanör.

Still, one sword would be enough to cut through the Darkakin.

It would be impossible to enter the pyramid at night. There was too much activity on the streets and more than a few fighters, with the added army filling every gap in Malaysai.

Pre-dawn would be the best time to infiltrate, by Galanör's reasoning. The guards would be tired or drunk and the city's inhabitants would be sleeping. Of course, getting in was going to be easy. Getting out would be a different matter...

CHAPTER 42
A HEAVY CONSCIENCE

Not long after dawn and a modest breakfast, Reyna walked along West Fellion's outer wall, accompanied by Faylen, Lord Marshall Horvarth and a small company of Graycoats. Nathaniel was notably absent, as well as his ward Elaith and, of course, the ranger.

The princess felt uncomfortable without them and oddly vulnerable. Faylen and herself were more than capable of defending themselves, probably more so than any of the knights that surrounded them, but it didn't change the way she felt.

Thunder rumbled in the distance. The great storm that had steered them north on their crossing to Illian had invaded the land and continued to hunt them ever westward.

Somewhere beyond that storm, her father was preparing their army and building ships for the inevitable attack. If his plan for the dragon eggs was anything to go by, however, they had several years before they would go to war.

The Lord of Elves would expect a report from them soon, wanting to know everything Reyna had learned. The princess was to gather as much information about the various armies of Illian and who held what alliances. It would be her information that told the elven army where to strike and how many would be needed. Faylen was in possession of the diviner but had yet to communicate with anyone in Ayda and inform them of the Arakesh's involvement.

They would find it troubling to know that the head of Valanis's Hand was behind the attacks. Reyna's father had suspected that there were forces opposing them, but none could have guessed that it would be any remnant of the dark elf's forces. If Alidyr and the other dark elves had been in Illian for a thousand years, it stood to reason that they would have contingencies in place for the elves' return.

The princess could see the folly in their announced arrival now. They stood against an enemy that had been planning this war long before her father had even decided to take back the country.

"You seem troubled, Princess." Horvarth walked beside her with his hands clasped behind his back.

For the most part, the Lord Marshal had been a gracious host. The man had an air of honesty about him that came across as refreshing after meeting the royal families. The respect his knights gave him was easy to see and even easier to understand.

"I fear that we have placed your home in peril, Lord Marshal." Reyna stopped at the edge and looked down.

A team of sweaty and hardened Graycoats was busy removing and replacing the giant pikes with fresh ones, while a separate group of topless knights ran around West Fellion's perimeter, keeping fit.

"We have dealt with the Arakesh before," Horvarth replied. "If they come for you it will be a single assassin or a small group. Stealth and darkness are their weapons, Princess, but here we will expose them to the light."

Reyna followed his gaze and noted the extra fire-pits being fitted to the top of the wall, as well as the many torches being nailed into the stone. Farther out from West Fellion's perimeter, Graycoats were already erecting giant pyres that could be lit at night to illuminate the surrounding land.

"Have you ever encountered one yourself, Lord Marshal?" Faylen asked.

"As a younger man, I had the displeasure, yes. I was escorting a dignitary from Skystead to Palios. To save time we cut through The White Vale and on through The Vrost Mountains. I regret allowing the head of the guard to make that decision now; we should have stuck to The Selk Road. I have no doubt that the assassin trailed us the entire way, but she didn't strike until we made camp in the mountains..."

"Did she succeed in assassinating the dignitary?" Reyna asked.

"Sadly, yes. She killed everyone but myself and another guard, lucky enough to survive having only his hand removed. I struck a wound across her back that would rightly kill any man, but she slipped into the night and vanished. I hunted her for many days but never found a body."

Darius Devale chipped in, "They are more monster than man."

"Asher is no *monster*," Reyna fired back. "He has turned his back on their order and made a new life for himself."

"A life of killing still," Darius replied just as quick.

"Enough." Horvarth held up his hand to silence the knight. "New life or not, Princess Reyna, the ranger is in possession of vital information, information we have sought after for centuries. We cannot pass up the opportunity to question him."

"But how many *words* are being exchanged?" Faylen whispered into Reyna's ear.

They continued to walk around the grounds, as the Lord Marshal pointed out the different defences they had in place. All the while, Reyna scanned the face of every Graycoat in search of Nathaniel.

In the courtyard below, students and knights trained side-by-side with practice swords in light armour. Some honed their technique against straw-filled dummies, while others fought one another under the supervision of a trainer. Younger recruits, who looked to be children in Reyna's eyes, assisted the much older Gray-coats in the stables.

New knights appeared on horseback, having received the Lord Marshal's call to return. For all their numbers, training and preparation, Reyna felt no safer than she did with Nathaniel and Asher by her side.

"If I might ask, Princess." Horvarth clasped his hands behind his back. "Why did you choose Velia to liaise with? Rengar is a good king, but Alborn is not the richest or most powerful region. I would have thought King Merkaris in Namdhor would be a better choice."

"Why do you say that?" Reyna asked.

"Well, he's a descendant of Gal Tion for a start, the first king of Illian."

"Not the first..." Faylen muttered under her breath so that only Reyna could hear.

"That alone commands a certain level of respect from the people," Horvarth continued. "But he also rules over the north. All of Orith is his to command, and a wealthy region it is too. It is rumoured that he even trades with the dwarves in Dhenaheim."

"My father didn't want to upset the balance and tip the scales too far in one king's direction. Velia was the closest kingdom with the mildest climate; though we hadn't foreseen the storm that over-shadowed our arrival." Reyna lied all too easily now, and she hated it.

Velia had been chosen because they could give Galanör the signal when permission had been granted for elves to enter Korkanath.

"Elves are truly as wise as the legends say." Horvarth smiled warmly.

Reyna returned the smile, but it didn't reach her eyes. There didn't seem to be any wisdom in going to war, even to justify ending the threat of Valanis's return.

~

Later that evening, before they were expected at the Lord Marshal's table, Reyna paced in their shared quarters, staring at the diviner that lay dormant on the table.

Faylen sat cross-legged on the bed, failing to meditate while the princess was so restless. She looked at the black orb and shared Reyna's concern. Very soon they would be expected to contact the Lord of Elves, or whoever Mörygan spoke with in Elandril, and inform them of their progress.

Ölli flapped his wings by the narrow window, eager to fly away and hunt. The owl only served to remind Faylen of Reyna's mother, Adilandra. She missed her oldest friend and their long talks into the night. They could walk through The Amara for hours, discussing the gods in private and talking about their hopes and dreams for Reyna.

Those walks and conversations soon became more secretive as the Lord of Elves made his plans for Illian and the future of the dragon race. Adilandra had commanded her to keep Reyna safe in her absence, a command she needn't have given; the princess was as much a daughter to Faylen as Adilandra was a sister.

Faylen looked back to the diviner, wishing there was some way to communicate with her old friend and make certain she was safe, or even alive. No elf had journeyed into the south of Ayda before.

No, she thought. Such worries were unfounded, especially when the gods themselves were in support of her pilgrimage. Faylen truly believed, as Adilandra did, that the queen was the one Nalana spoke of in her prophecy.

That knowledge gave her sour feelings towards her own part in all of this. Faylen was doing the bidding of her king, playing a crucial role in a plan that wasn't in line with the will of the gods. Mörygan had already been taken from the mission, a possible indication that the gods desired a different course for Reyna and herself. The princess clearly had doubts about her father's plan and voiced them all too willingly. Her mother's daughter, indeed.

The weight of right and wrong hung heavy on Faylen's shoulders. The elf had been in service to the royal family her entire life. Serving was all she knew, and going against the Lord of Elves was the worst crime she could commit, yet every fibre of her being and faith told her that it was right.

Valanis was the real threat, not mankind.

Despite their many flaws, humanity could not be blamed for their nature and the need to take and expand. Faylen knew in her heart that the king wanted to take back Illian and wipe out humanity for the land and some twisted sense of justice.

But, they were firmly set on their course now. Eventually, the army would invade and march on Elethiah and destroy Valanis, but not before decimating every town and city between there and The Shining Coast.

Unless...

Faylen looked at Reyna, pacing endlessly. If Elethiah could be breached with elven magic, perhaps there was a chance she could infiltrate the old citadel and find the frozen remains of Valanis. Faylen couldn't imagine that killing Valanis was any harder than removing his head from his shoulders while he remained frozen in place.

If she could report that Valanis was truly dead, then the king wouldn't have just cause to invade. Reyna would be safe in West Fellion while she journeyed to Elethiah, but travelling alone was never a good idea when so much rested on an individual. But who? She couldn't risk Reyna's life and the Graycoat would be of no use to her. The magical wards that surrounded the city were designed to keep all at bay.

That conundrum sparked a new idea. She had already seen a man stand up against one of the most powerful elves who ever lived, though she knew not how. Asher's resilience to magic must have been something gifted to him during his training at Nightfall. There was no telling what Alidyr Yalathanil had done to him and the other Arakesh.

Could she do that? Did she have the courage to help Asher escape and travel to Elethiah, accomplishing what so many had failed to do a thousand years ago?

Could she truly leave Reyna?

Faylen wouldn't be going anywhere safe, but at least she would be able to keep her eye on the princess if she stayed. The thought of Adilandra's bravery bolstered her own. If her queen could have the courage to journey into lands unknown then Faylen could make it to Elethiah.

Now she just needed to help the ranger.

Nathaniel waited in the shadow of the stone arch, hidden from Ned Fennick as he entered the courtyard. The veteran Graycoat walked out into the moonlight, wiping his knuckles with a bloody white cloth. He had been with Asher for several hours. There was no telling what would be left of Asher.

"Get me cold water, boy!" Fennick barked at the young Graycoat that followed him about.

Once out of sight, Nathaniel entered the cells beneath the keep. Already prepared, he retrieved a small pitcher of water and a handful of dry bread, holding them both out to be seen clearly. The two guards stiffened slightly at the sight of him, but kept their swords sheathed, seeing no threat from one of their own.

"What are you doin' 'ere, Galfrey?"

Nathaniel recognised the knight's look of disgust, as well as his first name: Talbot.

"Fennick ordered me to—"

"High Commander Fennick," Talbot quickly corrected.

Nathaniel blinked slowly to stop himself from rolling his eyes. "*High Commander* Fennick ordered me to make sure the prisoner is fed and watered."

"An' why would he do that, eh?" Talbot had always been slow minded: an exceptional fighter, but slow all the same.

"Because if he dies from dehydration, thirst that is, then the High Commander won't be able to question him anymore." Nathaniel explained it as simply as he could.

Talbot shared a look with the other guard, whose name Nathaniel had forgotten. A non-committal shake of the head and a subtle shrug later, the guards went to work on opening the heavy door.

Talbot sneered as Nathaniel walked past him. "At least they've finally found a job worthy of the great Nathaniel Galfrey..."

Nathaniel let the door close behind him without a rebuttal.

The Graycoat lost his breath at the sight before him. Asher hung suspended by four chains to keep him off the floor, a floor now heavily stained with blood.

The ranger's head hung low over his chest and his greying hair plastered his face. His torso was bruised, cut and even burnt in some places. Nathaniel looked to the black pokers left at the ranger's feet, their ends still radiating intense heat.

The room was lined with a gutter that burned with fire, keeping the room in constant light.

"Back for more, Fen-dick?" Asher's words were surprisingly strong for a man in his condition.

"It's me," Nathaniel replied, crossing the room.

Asher looked up with no sign of relief on his battered face. His left cheekbone was surely broken, along with his nose. Both of his eyes were black and his right eye was almost entirely red. His lips were dry and split in more than one place.

Nathaniel immediately put the pitcher to Asher's mouth and helped to tilt his head back while the ranger drank his fill. He groaned in pain as the water washed over his cuts and ran down his chest, its transparency quickly turning red before it touched the floor.

"Why did you come here?" Nathaniel asked, frustrated. "I told you they would do this. Now they have you they'll never let you go, even if you tell them everything."

Asher choked for a moment before replying, "It seemed like a good idea at the time..."

"Have you told them anything?" Nathaniel asked, inspecting some of the more serious wounds to Asher's body.

"He hasn't asked anything yet." Asher's head dropped to his chest once more.

Nathaniel didn't know what to say to that. Ned Fennick was a bastard, but to beat a man senseless and ask no questions was something else.

"Have you really been calling him Fen-dick?" the Graycoat asked with a forced smirk.

"Yep." Asher looked up again and managed a half-smile before the two shared a short laugh together. "I think it's starting to grow on him..."

"I'm going to help you." Nathaniel didn't know how yet, but he knew he had to try.

"Forget about me. The Arakesh will be coming; you need to prepare."

Nathaniel gave him more water. "The guard and patrols have been tripled. New pyres are being erected everywhere and the black-smiths in Vangarth are sending more supplies every day. We have enough arrows to block out the sky now."

"It'll be different this time," Asher explained. "They sent a team and failed, they sent their best assassin and he failed. They won't make that mistake again. You need to prepare for several teams to strike at once, each from a different angle. You need to expect them to breach the walls and be ready for that fight.

They'll watch you for days and attack when they know your every move. It'll be in the darkest hour when the moon is low and the current guard is coming to an end and they're tired as hell."

"We need you out there, advising us." Nathaniel couldn't see any way that the Lord Marshal would allow an ex-assassin to walk freely among West Fellion's walls.

"You *need* to keep her safe." Asher looked him in the eye with more intensity than he was used to seeing in the detached ranger. "If they're right about Valanis, then there's a lot more at stake than just a few lives. Elves are powerful; they might just be the only ones who can stop this war from ever happening."

"You realise there's no payout for all of this." Nathaniel couldn't quite figure out why Asher had so much concern for the welfare of the country. There was a very good chance that the ranger would die inside this cell, be it at the hands of the Graycoats or the Arakesh.

"I've already made the deal of a lifetime. It would be nice to retire knowing I did something good for once..."

Nathaniel could see the shame that hung over the ranger. His deeds as an assassin would haunt him for ever, no matter how much good he did.

"What did the Father ask you to do, all those years ago? What finally broke the cycle?" Nathaniel had wanted to know ever since he met Asher.

The ranger hesitated. "Have you ever been to Dunwich?"

"Many times. I grew up in Longdale, remember? Dunwich is just south of there."

"Then you know of the lord that presides over the town. You know that he has a daughter, Esabelle and a son, Thomas." Asher clamped his jaw in what looked to be an effort to control his emotions.

"I actually met Esabelle once; a fine young lady, much loved by the townsfolk, but the lord of Dunwich doesn't have a son..." Nathaniel could see where the ranger was going and lost his words.

"Fourteen years ago, when Esabelle was only six years old, she had a brother. Thomas was only four..." A single tear streaked down Asher's bloodied face. "I wasn't alone. I was mentoring a new Arakesh, eager to kill for the Father. I didn't even hesitate when I put the dagger in Thomas's heart." More tears ran from his eyes. "He awoke only a moment before I killed him. I saw the shock and pain fade from his eyes, as his life ebbed away. I had never killed a child before, in all my years..."

Asher was looking past Nathaniel now, as if he was there again, inside the lord's house. "The other Arakesh deliberately woke Esabelle up, just so he could see her terrified look before he murdered her. Before he could strike I put my blade through his eye, killing him instantly."

Nathaniel was speechless again. He knew the ranger had to have done terrible things in service to Nightfall, but hearing the details was hard to swallow. It was only a shame that it took the death of a boy to free Asher of his shackles.

"Who would wish for such a thing?" the Graycoat asked.

"Lord Tarn, of Skystead." The tears stopped flowing now and the ranger's face was that of resolve. "He was the first person I killed as a free man. I couldn't return to Nightfall after Dunwich, but I could look Lord Tarn in the eye when I slide my blade between his ribs.

"Apparently, he was in contest with the Lord of Dunwich for a higher place in King Merkaris's court. Tarn thought that the death of his children would cripple his opponent, paving the way for himself."

"Death does not atone for death, Asher." Nathaniel knew all too well that revenge was futile. "When I earned this coat, the first thing I did was take a patrol on the border of The Wild Moores. I wanted to kill every Outlander beyond those trees for the death of my father.

"I stayed longer than I should but, eventually, I came across a small band preparing to raid the town of Bleak. I put them all down, even the ones that tried to escape. Killing every one of them didn't make me feel better, it didn't make me feel more of a man, and it certainly didn't bring back my father."

"It's all I know," Asher replied solemnly. "When Nightfall's finished with you, killing is all that's left. I just put my talents to better use. There are plenty of monsters out there that don't walk on two feet. Helping the elves is the right thing to do. Maybe now I can save a few children, rather than..."

"We'll find a way through this, Asher, together."

Nathaniel wanted to help the ranger become the man he desperately craved to be. There was honour and courage inside Asher that few would ever see, or even expect, but the Graycoat knew it was there.

CHAPTER 43
PROMISES, PROMISES

Another day and night had gone by while Adilandra gathered her strength and the three of them rested, ate and drank. Gideon had been quiet during the reprieve, however. The journey across Verda had been taxing for the young mage, holding on to Malliath for so long without sleep or sustenance.

Another army had arrived at dusk, filling the city with more savages, eager for a fight. Galanör and Gideon had taken it in turns to sneak down to street level, disguised in stolen rags, to acquire the supplies needed for their eventual escape from Malaysai.

Their trek to the east would be all the more difficult with Lörvana and Fallön, injured as they were. The enchantment on Gideon's satchel was perfect for storing all their goods without weighing them down further.

Dawn was a couple of hours away and the three companions readied themselves at the edge of the building top. The streets were quieter now, but far from empty with the added army.

"You are sure it was Alidyr Yalathanil?" Galanör asked for a third time that day.

Adilandra had informed them both of what she had seen upon

her arrival in Malaysai. Though Galanör had never seen the dark elf, he, like every other elf, knew well of Valanis's chief general and head of the Hand.

"I will never forget that face," Adilandra explained. "The fact that he is still alive is shocking enough without the thought of what he's doing with the Darkakin. He made a blood oath with The Goddess, but I know not why."

"It must have something to do with the arrival of the armies," Galanör reasoned. "What the head of the Hand wants with a Darkakin army is beyond me."

"It can't be for anything good, but it proves that my husband is wrong to move ahead with his plan."

"How so?" Galanör asked.

"The Echoes of Fate." Adilandra could see Galanör already losing interest in her theory. "The gods are *real* Galanör. Just because our people lost their faith doesn't make that fact any less so. Through Nalana they told us that the dragon eggs offer great promise, but they will not win the war against Valanis.

Alidyr's presence here is proof that Valanis's forces are gathering. They're clearly preparing for war, securing allies. And for what?" the queen asked rhetorically. "Because Valanis will rise soon and lead them against the free people of Illian." Galanör looked to be seriously considering her words. "You know this to be true. You saw it yourself when Lyra Valarkin turned on you at Korkanath and proclaimed her true master. We don't have long before The Dark War is renewed."

Gideon shuffled beside them. "Before we start fighting any wars, why don't we free your friends?"

Adilandra was growing to like the mage. There was real good in the young man and a heart that only felt for others, if a little tainted by his anger for Galanör. Gideon showed a need to do what was right, whatever the cost and despite his personal feelings - a trait that many an elf could learn from.

"Dawn will soon be upon us." Galanör looked up at the starry sky, where a faint glow had already begun to appear in the east. "Follow me in and keep your wits about you."

Adilandra put a hand out to stop the younger elf. "I know a better way in." With her other hand, the queen presented them with a pair of shining crystals.

"Hey!" Gideon protested. "Those are mine!" The mage opened his satchel and looked inside, as if the infinite space within would reveal the theft.

"Forgive my deception," Adilandra said. "I took them while you slept. I have been storing energy inside them and now they're ready."

Galanör reached out and closed her hand around the crystals, using his own to keep it shut. "I know what you would intend, but you're not thinking clearly. Using a portal would drain you of much-needed strength, even with the crystals."

"A portal?" Gideon sounded just as excited as he did nervous. "You can use portals?"

Adilandra looked back at Galanör. "It will ensure that we get inside without alerting anyone. Freeing Lörvana and Fallön is going to be hard enough with the Darkakin already inside the pyramid, let alone having them follow us in. Trust me Galanör; I have over a thousand years of experience with magic. Two crystals; one to get us inside and one to get us out."

"You're not even going to use them both to open a portal?" Galanör's grip tightened around Adilandra's hand. The magic stored inside the gems hummed against her skin, ready to be unleashed.

There was no time to argue for the sun would be up soon and the Darkakin with it. Adilandra was unaccustomed to being challenged, especially by another elf, and continued the only way she ever had - her way.

The queen pulled away from Galanör and flicked her wrist across the top of the building, throwing the crystal into the air. Before the gem vanished beyond the roof, Adilandra called on the magic inside herself and the crystal, willing the energy therein to rip open a hole in reality.

The space in front of the companions was encompassed in darkness, as the portal's inky abyss formed a rough circular shape. The edges of the hole sparked with lightning, that licked the rooftop in silence.

Gideon's eyes couldn't have stretched any wider, but Adilandra contained her smile, all too aware of what was on the other side of that portal. Galanör didn't look happy, but the elf was too smart to argue now. It had been done and their only course was to move forward before the magic drained Adilandra.

As one, they stood up and rushed through the portal, though the queen had to grip Gideon's arm to ensure he came with them. The dark veil passed over them like water, before the world was remade.

Adilandra quickly scanned the dimly-lit throne room and Galanör removed his scimitar, pivoting in every direction. Gideon stood amazed, staring at the portal, which had already begun to collapse on itself.

"Incredible..." the mage whispered with the hint of a smile.

"Focus, Gideon," Galanör instructed, much to Gideon's obvious disdain.

The young mage removed his staff from the sheath on his back and the wood grew, as if from nothing, in both directions. Adilandra had seen Gideon fight with them to escape the arena and was confident that he could be of great help.

That thought was suddenly crushed, when the weight of responsibility fell upon the queen. She had already brought a company of her kin into these badlands and watched as they were all cut down or taken by savages. Now, here she was, doing the same thing.

Galanör was four hundred years old, with so much experience and wisdom already, and Gideon was a young mortal with so much promise. Adilandra had potentially doomed them both with her quest.

The queen took Galanör's advice and focused on their new surroundings. The throne room was empty at this early hour, with four single fire-pits illuminating the corners. The long balcony offered a spectacular view of the night sky between the translucent drapes that blew in the warm breeze.

Adilandra was drawn to the spot where Ederön had been beaten by Krenorak, the elf's blood staining the floor, before he was thrown from the balcony. Some Darkakin slave had scrubbed the floor well, but Adilandra's keen eyes could still see the dark blood between the flagstones.

"How do we know where to go now?" Gideon asked.

"I was kept prisoner here before they took me to the arena." Adilandra's anger bubbled to the surface when she thought of the nights chained to the wall in The Goddess's bedchambers. The things she had been forced to watch...

"Fallön is being kept a few floors above here, in the apex of the pyramid. I confess that Lörvana's whereabouts are unknown to me. Krenorak took her as a trophy, but I never saw his chambers." Adilandra thanked the gods for that small mercy.

"Perhaps we should split up?" Gideon responded.

"Shh..." Galanör had heard the voices at the same time as Adilandra. The younger elf put a finger to his lips and indicated to Gideon, with his hands, that they had heard something afar.

The three companions followed the growing voices until Gideon could hear them too. A set of stairs had been built into the floor on the other side of the throne room, the source of the foreign tongue.

Without a sound, they crept down the stairs and huddled beside an open doorway. The room beyond opened into a circular balcony that overlooked what Adilandra assumed was a council chamber of sorts.

The queen went for her sword when she saw The Goddess, sitting on another throne below. Before her was a semicircular table with two heavily tattooed and pierced Darkakin men. Their harsh language made no sense to the elves or the mage, but it was clearly a heated discussion.

Gideon held his finger aloft, as if an idea had suddenly struck him. Adilandra watched curiously when the mage rummaged through his deep satchel, though more curious was the face made by the human during his search. With typical human elegance, Gideon's tongue stuck out and his brow furrowed under the concentration. Had their situation not been so dire, the queen might have found it amusing.

From within the bag, Gideon removed a small, delicate spinning top, etched with the tiniest of ancient runes. He quickly placed it on the floor, pinched between his thumb and finger, and flicked the spinning top into motion. As it spun between their crouched bodies, the Darkakin language came to life in their ears.

"How dare you make blood oaths with an elf!" The dark-skinned warrior, with small dragons' teeth fused into his bald skull, roared and slammed the table. "You speak for Malaysai and Dovosai, *not* Gravosai! Why should my people fight for some elf a thousand miles away? Let Illian rot I say!"

"Do the people of Gravosai not crave the fight?" the Darkakin on the other side of the curved table fired back. His skin was as white as milk and half of his head was completely bald. The other half had hair that flowed down to his shoulder in scraggy, pale blond knots. Deep red tattoos covered his bare chest and arms, while a thick red line that ran across his forehead and eyes.

The horned Darkakin spat on the floor in disgust. "Overlord Kett... Typical Dovosai. You have your head so far up this bitch's arse you can't see what's right in front of you!" The Goddess remained perfectly still, despite the insult. "We now know that elves live on this very land. We should march north and sack their cities in Ayda. The elves will offer a greater fight than the prissy little shits in Illian. Our ancestors left that place for a reason."

"They did not leave, Overlord Balgora." The Goddess spoke from her tiered throne. "The world of man and elf alike cast us out. Alidyr Yalathanil assures me that the elves will be invading Illian soon. Imagine the war to be waged when we march beyond Syla's Gate. In the bloody fight between their two people, we will wade in and show them what real war looks like."

The spinning top wobbled and stopped altogether. Their next words became garbled, as unknown words replaced the language the companions understood. Galanör beat Gideon to the spinning top and flicked it with more strength and precision than any human could achieve.

"No Darkakin has stepped through Syla's Gate since the elves built the damn thing!" Overlord Balgora spat.

"It was abandoned when the elves left Illian," The Goddess replied calmly. "I have more than one elven source..." Adilandra's stomach flipped at the thought of how The Goddess was extracting information from Fallön and Lörvana.

"How do you know its defences haven't been taken up by the Illians?" Balgora sat back in his chair.

"Alidyr assures—"

"You trust an elf?" Balgora cut her off.

Overlord Kett stood from his chair with enough force to launch it across the room. "And you question The Goddess too much! Your choices are simple Balgora. Join my army and those of Malaysai, disprove your cowardice and march on Illian - or return to Gravosai in several small boxes."

"You would take my army by force, right here in the streets of Malaysai?" Balgora looked back to The Goddess, disbelieving. "My people would resist. There would be more blood in the streets than you could handle, and your armies would be depleted, securing your demise in Illian." The horned Darkakin laughed with great mirth. "Do not think I am stupid enough to mistake your need for me. I hold the maps of our ancestors that ensure safe passage across Drowners Run. If your forces were to make camp on the wrong island, The Adean would claim their lives while they slept, or better yet, the beasts of black would drag them to the depths."

The Goddess held out her hand and the Darkakin Adilandra recognised as Hyvark appeared from the gloom. The skinny man handed The Goddess a bound scroll and bowed, before scuttling back into the shadows.

"Do you mean these maps?" She held the scroll aloft so that Balgora could see them better.

The expression on his face turned suddenly from surprise to anger. "You bitch!"

"Goddess-bitch!" The queen of the Darkakin stood from her throne. "There are those in your camp, Overlord Balgora, who would see our three cities join together, under one banner. *My* banner. For years you have denied this alliance, but I would see its conclusion here and now. The Darkakin must be strong if we are to emerge victorious in Illian."

"You speak of alliance but you mean servitude." Balgora stood up as well now. "You would have me bend the knee and offer you Gravosai with the bow of the head."

"Bow your head, or lose it..." Kett puffed out his chest.

Balgora bared his filed teeth and removed the semicircular sword from his belt.

The Goddess sighed. "I will take that as your final answer. Hyvark, bring in Overlord Balzal."

Balgora's face dropped, when the truth of his situation became obvious. "Balzal..."

Hyvark opened a set of doors that Adilandra couldn't see. A younger man strode into the chamber with every confidence. Like Balgora, the Darkakin had two rows of dragon teeth fused into his bald head.

"Traitor!" Balgora yelled at the other man. "You are my blood!"

"You should be proud of your son, Balgora," The Goddess continued. "He has secured his position as ruler of Gravosai; he will earn a place in history when he leads my armies into battle. He will sit at my right hand when Illian lies at our feet. He is wiser than you ever were."

Balgora almost growled. "But he's not stronger!" The heavy man flung his chair away and flipped the semicircular table out of the way, ready to kill his own son.

The Goddess rolled her eyes. "If strength is all you recognise... Krenorak?"

Thunderous footsteps preceded the Darkakin's entrance. The largest human Adilandra had ever seen entered the chamber from behind Balgora. The giant had hunted the queen and her kin for miles across The Flat Wastes and through the thick jungle of The Great Maw surrounding Malaysai. His dark skin rippled with thick muscle, though his face was forever hidden beneath his skull-mask.

Balgora swivelled on the spot with his curved blade held out in front of him. Adilandra detected the slight tremor in the man's grip, but he did an excellent job of concealing his fears.

"Balgora has insulted your Goddess." The queen possessed a wicked smile.

The horned Darkakin didn't wait for the man-mountain to attack. His curved sword whipped into the air and came down towards Krenorak's neck. With more speed than a man of that size should rightly possess, Krenorak caught Balgora's sword arm with an iron grip, halting the attack mid-swing.

Adilandra heard the bones snap in his wrist, before Balgora's screams filled the circular chamber. The curved sword fell to the floor and Krenorak launched his free hand into the helpless man's face, burrowing his strong fingers through his flesh and eyes. Once his grip was secure, the big man squeezed his hand, tightening his grip on Balgora's skull. Through the agonised screams and The Goddess's laughter, the man's skull audibly caved in on itself.

Once the pain had become too much, Balgora passed out with blood pouring down his face. Krenorak removed his hand from the deformed skull and gripped Balgora's jaw in a vice. One quick twist broke the neck, ending the Overlord's life once and for all.

"I suggest Overlord Balzal that you present your people with your father's body and inform them of your challenge for his title." The Goddess circled the new ruler of Gravosai seductively. She handed him the scroll with the maps of Verda's southlands, where Illian and Ayda met. "Lead my army across Drowners Run and reap your rewards." She turned to address Overlord Kett as well. "You leave for the Hook of the World at first light. You may camp there before crossing Drowners Run, but I want you in Illian before Paldora's Star crosses the night sky."

The Goddess made for the door as everyone bowed. Krenorak dragged Balgora's dead body across the floor and dumped it unceremoniously at Balzal's feet. The beast grunted and continued to follow The Goddess out of the chamber.

Gideon picked up the spinning top and replaced it in his satchel. They sat back from the balcony rail and looked at one another with revelation in their eyes.

The Darkakin were going to war with Illian.

Adilandra tried to take comfort in the fact that Balgora was right; no Darkakin had stepped foot beyond Syla's Gate in a thousand years. Even if it wasn't being fortified by elf or man, the impenetrable gate and its high walls would keep them out of Illian.

"We need to warn the six kingdoms," Gideon said. "We need to get word to Karath, in The Arid Lands. They can send soldiers to hold Syla's Gate."

"One problem at a time," Adilandra replied calmly.

"I suggest we follow the big one back to his chambers and find Lörvana," Galanör offered. "We can always find our way back to The Goddess's chambers, but we might never find Lörvana in this maze."

"Agreed." Adilandra motioned for them to follow her, as she climbed down into the meeting room. She noted Gideon taking the spare Darkakin map of Verda off the floor and folding it into his satchel.

Following Krenorak's heavy footsteps was easy enough in the quiet of the pyramid. Security inside the palace was more rigid than the milling around that took place outside. Guards were posted along the straight corridors, often at corners to offer a vantage.

More than once, Gideon was forced to use magic to lure the guards away, until Galanör and Adilandra could strike from the shadows. Opening the first portal had been taxing, but nothing the queen couldn't handle. Planning for their escape, however, Adilandra refrained from using magic and relied on her physical talents.

Ultimately, it proved to be her nose that found Krenorak's place of slumber. His unique smell of death and shit was impossible to miss after they descended to the next level of the pyramid.

Had she had the time, Adilandra would have blamed that particular smell on the reason why she didn't take note of the Darkakin warrior, rounding the corner behind them. Luckily, it was Gideon who reacted first, whipping out Abigail's wand and hitting the man with a spell strong enough to render him immediately unconscious. Showing even more ingenuity, the mage had cast an enchantment that stopped the Darkakin from flying into the wall and giving their position away. Instead, the warrior flew silently and slowly backward, through the air, until Gideon crept over and carefully placed the body on the cold floor.

Galanör approached Krenorak's door and, leaning forwards, used his keen senses to detect any movement inside. Adilandra knew that the elf could discern vibrations in the wood and use them to pinpoint the giant's location.

A dreaded realisation erupted across Galanör's face, but it was too late, even for his reactions. Adilandra jumped back, seeing the impending danger, as the wooden door exploded into splinters. Two arms, as thick and tough as any tree, shot through the door first and picked Galanör up.

Adilandra could only watch, when the rest of the hulking Darkakin followed his arms and continued to charge Galanör into the room opposite his own. The door to that room didn't hold under their impact and caved in with Krenorak coming down on top of the elf.

Adilandra moved to help when a faint whimper rang out from within Krenorak's room. The queen couldn't help but be drawn to that sound. Lörvana, who had been by her side for so long, Lörvana who had faith in her, Lörvana who had been promised she would see home again... Adilandra had to help her.

"Go!" Gideon instructed. "I'll help Galanör."

And help the elf would need. Adilandra could already hear the angry voices coming from inside the room they had entered, though barracks would be a better word.

Inside Krenorak's room, the queen quickly scanned every corner in search of possible threats. The sight of Lörvana gave her pause. The poor elf hung limply in the arch between the giant's bedchamber and living quarters. Her hands were roughly bound and looped over a thick hook screwed into the sandstone. There wasn't an inch of her body that hadn't been beaten, cut or burnt by Krenorak. Pools of blood had collected across the floor beneath the elf, some old, some fresh.

"What have they done to you?" Adilandra whispered.

The queen placed a delicate hand on Lörvana's swollen cheek and poured her magic into the broken bone, her own reserves be damned. Lörvana opened her eyes as her mouth took shape again and the swelling disappeared. Tears formed in both of their eyes, relief mixed with disbelief in Lörvana's, anger and deep sadness in Adilandra's.

"My queen..." The words barely left her dry lips.

"Hush now." Adilandra drew her scimitar and expertly cut the binding rope. Lörvana fell into her arms as dead weight, her bare feet slipping in the blood. "I'm taking you home. You're safe now." Adilandra repeated the words over and over again, taking Lörvana's arm and hooking a hand around her ribs.

"Fallön..." Lörvana said from beneath her matted hair.

"We're going to find him too. We're all going home now." Adilandra stopped when she saw Lörvana's elven sword mounted on the wall - another trophy for Krenorak.

∾

Galanör had lost his sense of what was up and what was down. Krenorak threw the elf around the room like a ragdoll, smashing him into other Darkakin, tables, chairs, hammocks, walls and even the ceiling.

All the while, Galanör continued to beat the big man around the head, knocking off his skull-mask and laying into his deformed face. The hulking beast had no nose and no upper lip, torn off by the looks of the ragged skin left behind.

Elven strength did nothing to persuade the giant Darkakin to release Galanör. Every now and then he was forced to kick out with a leg, however, and push back an attacking guard, determined to stab him in the back.

The barracks were a mess now, littered with bodies brought down by the rampaging Krenorak and Gideon's staff. The mage waded in without a hint of fear, though Galanör was only partially aware of the human's actions.

The sound of magic being discharged in every direction punctuated the air. Lightning, fire and ice exploded from Gideon's staff, striking the Darkakin before they could reach Galanör. It wasn't enough to stop Krenorak, who had been hit twice in the back by fireballs.

Smoke poured off the big man as he pushed Galanör through the external wall and back into the corridor. Krenorak shifted his hold on the elf and locked his hands together, behind Galanör's back.

Then he squeezed.

The elven warrior couldn't even shout out, as the man's mighty arms coiled around his ribs, a python ensnaring its prey. Galanör couldn't decide what pained him more, the air being forced from his lungs or his ribs slowly cracking. The elf decided to strike Krenorak with a more concise attack, giving up on trying to prise himself free.

Galanör arched his back as much as possible, bringing his arms out as wide as he did. Krenorak snarled and growled, the veins in his arms protruding like worms. The elf brought his hands back together with enough force to break the skull of an ordinary human. The palms of his hands clapped around the giant's ears, discombobulating him instantly.

Galanör dropped to the floor in a spluttering mess, his legs unable to hold him, while he regained his breath. Krenorak stumbled and wobbled on the spot, before he fell into the wall and dropped to one knee, utterly dazed.

"Get up!" Gideon shouted through the hole in the wall.

With blurry eyes, Galanör looked on as the mage whipped his staff around, cracking skulls and breaking bones with every blow. Every two strikes were followed by a spell that wrought devastation amongst the ranks of the Darkakin.

As his senses returned, Galanör heard the unmistakable sound of bare feet running through the pyramid's halls.

More were coming.

Adilandra emerged from Krenorak's chamber with Lörvana limping by her side. The elf had clearly been tortured for many days. Galanör had never met Lörvana before, but seeing her broken body still infuriated him. He staggered to his feet, keeping one eye on Krenorak, and glanced back inside the barracks.

"Gideon?" Adilandra asked with concern.

"He's on top of it."

At that moment, two Darkakin warriors flew out of the jagged hole and into the hallway behind them. One was partially on fire, while the other looked to have been beaten with a large stick.

The running footsteps were now accompanied by angry shouting. The pyramid's entire complement of warriors was rushing up to meet the intruders.

"Run," Galanör quickly instructed. "Find Fallön and kill that venomous bitch."

Gideon strode out of the barracks with his staff in hand, blood staining both ends. The mage had received his fair share of blows and wore his cuts and bruises with pride. In truth, Galanör was impressed. Gideon gave Krenorak a wide berth, the battered giant was still holding his meaty head in his hands.

"Go with them and rescue Fallön," Galanör said to Gideon. The elf kept his eyes on the corridor behind them and the growing noise of the approaching mob.

"They have a better chance if this lot don't catch up with them," Gideon replied stubbornly. "I'll stay with you, if it's all the same."

There was no time to argue and Galanör knew it was the mage's decision to make. "So be it." He turned back to Adilandra and Lörvana. "Go, now! If we all survive, then we'll meet at the eastern edge of the city." He could see Adilandra hesitate to leave them behind, even the human. "Whether you like it or not, you *are* my queen. I will be damned if I let you die in this gods-forsaken place. Go now, Adilandra, or this will all be for naught."

The group of Darkakin rounded the corner and filled the hallway from wall to wall. The sounds they made were closer to animals than human. Krenorak was starting to crawl up the wall again now, regaining his sight and hearing.

"Take this." Adilandra handed Galanör an elven scimitar, one-handed like his own. "Give them a reason to fear elven steel..." The queen cupped his cheek affectionately and met his eyes one last time, before taking Lörvana away from the mob.

Galanör didn't watch them leave but instead turned to face the Darkakin. He rotated the scimitars in his hands, feeling for their unique weight and balance together. They were more than enough for what needed to be done. Gideon pulled tight on his fingerless gloves and stood his staff on-end by his side. His dark curly hair was matted to his skin and dripping with sweat.

The Darkakin halted their charge halfway down the corridor and formed a rough line, as they bared their teeth and raised their swords, spears and clubs.

"Are you ready for this, boy?" Galanör asked the mage.

"*My* count's higher than *yours*." Gideon indicated the fallen Darkakin strewn across the floor between them and the mob. "And don't call me *boy*."

Galanör smiled wickedly. Cocky was better than afraid, though he suspected some of it was a mask to conceal his true feelings.

"Never stand still." Galanör called on his own training. "Keep moving and use the reach of the staff to your advantage."

"You want to see the reach of my staff?" Gideon exploded into movement and launched his staff out in front of him.

The Darkakin charged at the same time the mage unleashed an icicle the size of a spear. The needle-tipped icicle cut through the middle of their ranks and continued along its trajectory, until it had sliced through six warriors and finally impaled a seventh to the wall.

The shock was enough to slow their charge and allow Galanör a moment to leap into the fray, unscathed. His dark cloak billowed behind him when both scimitars came down hard, with unstoppable speed, and killed a Darkakin each by splitting their torsos open.

The elf immediately crouched low and, avoiding the inevitable slashing of swords, angled his blades out wide as he came back up. Adding a spin to his efforts, Galanör decapitated two more Darkakin and severed the arm of another.

Gideon's staff swung around the mage in a blur and both elf and man worked in tandem with one hacking and slashing, the other firing spell after spell into the crowd.

Galanör jumped off the wall with grace and agility honed over four centuries and cut four Darkakin down, one after another. More often than not, his elven blades sliced right through their parry, breaking their weapon, and diving deep into their bodies.

Fire erupted along the far wall when Gideon let loose a torrent of flames. The hall broke out in agonised screams and chaos. Galanör was forced to cut several warriors down before their burning bodies touched him. Their numbers continued to swell with more Darkakin joining the fight, but it made no difference to the elf, for as long as he wielded two blades of such fine make, there was not an army that could stand against him.

An alarm rang out in Galanör's mind when he realised Krenorak was no longer in the corridor. His hulking form was hard to miss, even amid the chaos of so many combatants. Galanör's alarm soon turned to fear when he thought of where the giant might go in favour of such a fight.

~

Adilandra approached The Goddess's chamber with caution. There were no guards blocking her way and the double doors were open.

Lörvana did her best to keep up. However, the elf was unable to conceal her footsteps as the queen did. Adilandra had given her a knife but knew that she was in no state to use it.

The chamber was as she remembered it. The large, square bed lay on the far side of the room, decorated in drapes. Torches lined the walls, casting stark shadows around the low tables and padded cushions.

Adilandra looked at the wall where she had been chained for several nights. She wanted to set the entire chamber on fire and watch it burn.

"Tread lightly, elven queen." The Goddess emerged from the shadows by her bed. "You have entered the dragon's lair now." Beside her was the Overlord known as Kett and her skinny servant Hyvark. "What were you going to do little elf? Walk in here and take back your friend?"

As she spoke, Fallön stepped out of the shadows beside her. He wore nothing but loose clothes around his waist, displaying his pale and malnourished body. His once beautiful eyes were dark pits against his prominent cheekbones. He made no attempt to escape or fight for his friends but stood obediently by The Goddess. The potions he had been forced to ingest had left him nothing but a slave.

Lörvana gained some life at the sight of Fallön. Like Adilandra, she wanted to free him from The Goddess and kill them all. The queen felt the weight of her and knew she would be the only one fighting. Lörvana was too weak to even hold herself up. She gently placed her on the floor and stood between them.

"I *was* going to free them and escape, continue my quest and find the dragons. Save Illian if I can, maybe all of Verda." Adilandra squeezed the hilt of her glistening blade. "But *now*, I'm going to bring them here first. This city will burn whether we stop Valanis or not..."

"Kett, stop her from talking now." The Goddess sounded bored.

Overlord Kett produced a smile of sharpened teeth and pulled free the double-handed meat cleaver from his back.

Adilandra didn't wait for the cleaver, but instead leaped across the room in a single powerful bound and brought her sword to bear.

Kett moved as a snake, evading the strike with spinning acrobatics. It would be foolish to assume that he hadn't achieved his position without some prowess. The queen deflected his blade and hammered his face with the pommel of her scimitar. The hilt broke his nose and sent him reeling into the wall, where his back caught a torch and burnt him.

That was when she missed it.

Krenorak had entered the chamber and picked Lörvana up from behind. His grip constricted her throat, turning her face from red to purple, as he lifted the elf off her feet.

Kett took advantage of the distraction and lashed out with his cleaver. Adilandra's elven reflexes saved her hand but weren't fast enough to prevent the wide blade from cutting her wrist, causing her to drop the scimitar. The Overlord followed up his attack with a swift fist to her face. The queen of elves fell into the middle of the chamber, helpless between her friends and their captors.

Lörvana screamed with rage, unleashing all the injustice done to her by the giant. With the knife in hand, she swung her arm up and back, into Krenorak's face, driving the blade into his left eye until the hilt jammed. The giant Darkakin went stiff and his expression dropped, lifeless as the rest of his body.

Lörvana shrugged the beast off and dropped on top of him in a fit of rage. She retrieved her knife and plunged the blade into his chest again and again, until Krenorak's torso was a ragged hole.

Adilandra lay sprawled on the cold floor when a sharp pain dug into her shoulder. Impaled deep into her shoulder was a green, feathered dart, fired from the blowpipe in The Goddess's possession. The toxin worked fast. The Goddess and Fallön were already becoming blurry and her muscles refused to move with any coordination.

All the while, Lörvana continued to stab Krenorak's dead body, oblivious to everything.

"Overlord, if you please..." The Goddess looked from him to Lörvana.

"No..." Adilandra's plea sounded more a moan than a discernible word.

Kett strolled over to Lörvana with his cleaver resting over his shoulders and a wicked smile displayed across his pale face. The elf didn't even look back when the Darkakin Overlord swung his deadly blade.

Lörvana's head flew from her body and rolled over the floor, stopping before Adilandra's poisoned body. Tears flowed from the elven queen's eyes, faced with the decapitated head of her friend. She had just enough strength to stand up, despite the soles of her feet slowly becoming numb.

"Fallön dearest," The Goddess's seductive voice called to the elf. "Take this and cut your throat." The evil queen handed him a fine curved blade with jagged edges.

"No!" Adilandra had managed to use a small amount of magic to rid herself of the toxins that coursed through her veins, but it was not enough to save Fallön.

Without hesitation, the elf took the knife and in one smooth motion, cut his throat. Adilandra cried out and fell back to her knees, watching his blood pour onto the floor.

The Goddess walked through it, allowing the blood to wash over her bare feet. "Mmm... it's warm." The Goddess appeared to take comfort from the feeling.

Adilandra felt the poison spreading once more through her body, threatening to surround her in darkness.

"Don't worry little elf, it won't kill you. I have so much more in mind for you."

"Adilandra!" Galanör was racing down the hallway with Gideon at his side.

The queen could see the future laid out before her. The three of them would never make it out of the pyramid, let alone out of Malaysai. They were surrounded by enemies and she would only slow them down now. The *three* of them would never make it out...

"Find them Galanör! Find the dragons!" Adilandra used all the strength that remained to throw the last crystal.

Galanör and Gideon sprinted into the room, as she opened a portal from within the crystal, swallowing their running forms whole. She needn't have closed it quickly, ensuring the one-way trip, as the magic drained the elf of any energy the poison had yet to take from her.

The Goddess's bloody feet slowly approaching was the last thing she saw, before the darkness consumed her.

Galanör and Gideon ran into the rising sun and skidded across hard desert. The portal closed behind them and with it any chance of returning to the pyramid, or even Malaysai.

The elf turned around, only to be greeted by a wall of jungle. Adilandra had teleported them beyond The Great Maw, placing them somewhere between the jungle that encompassed Malaysai and the mountains to the east.

"No!" Galanör shouted into the air.

It wasn't fair. They had cut their way through a hundred Darkakin, only to be foiled at the end. He had failed his queen, his people and his oath to the crown. The elf felt as if he did nothing but fail in his duties. All he wanted was to be free of it, and yet he constantly found himself in a position of great need to others.

"We're going back!" Galanör glanced at Gideon, before marching towards The Great Maw.

"We can't!" Gideon gripped Galanör's arm, but the elf shrugged him off.

"Come with me or don't, but I am going to find her and I—"

"There are three armies amassing inside that city!" Gideon cut him off in a bid to talk some sense into him. "We couldn't get back in if we wanted to! You heard her, you heard them. All of Verda is about to collide. The east marches against the west and the south rises up to swallow them both. We need to ally the two and push back the Darkakin, Galanör. I don't know about you, but I have no idea how to do that! Adilandra was convinced that the dragons would be the deciding factor in this war and I'm inclined to believe her."

"You would have me abandon her to those savages?" Galanör knew that the mage spoke the truth, but it didn't make it any easier.

"*Adilandra* would have you find the dragons..." Gideon produced the map he had scooped off the table.

Galanör looked to the east and the red mountains that rose up to meet the sky. The dragons flew east, the queen had said. Somewhere inside those mountains was the key to saving Verda, the key to saving Adilandra.

"Have you ever walked across a desert before, Gideon?" The barren land shimmered before them in the heat.

"No. Have you?"

"No..." Galanör sheathed the elven blades and covered his head with the hood of his cloak. They had a long walk ahead of them.

CHAPTER 44
THE BEGINNING OF THE END

Faylen opened the door to their chamber before Nathaniel or Elaith could knock. The elf ushered them in without a word and closed the door softly behind them.

The elves hadn't long finished lunch with the Lord Marshal where Faylen had made the excuse that meditation was required before they do anything else. What the Lord Marshal didn't know was that Faylen had crept around West Fellion during the night and left hidden messages for the only Graycoats she trusted.

"What's going on?" Nathaniel asked, looking to Reyna.

Faylen took the measure of the man and could see Reyna's attraction. As humans went, the Graycoat was striking in appearance, with elven symmetry to his facial features. The princess's attraction notwithstanding, Faylen was sure there were no feelings yet harboured by the young elf, though that particular future wasn't hard to foresee, with the Graycoat possessing some of the finer qualities man wasn't remembered for.

"She won't say," Reyna replied. "She's being awfully secretive..."

"I'm going to Elethiah," Faylen announced, "and I'm taking the ranger with me." Of them all, she knew that Reyna would be the most shocked. The young elf knew more about the ancient citadel than the Graycoats.

"You mean *we're* taking the ranger?" the princess corrected.

"War is coming to Illian," Faylen explained as simply as she could. "But, there are those in Ayda who think it folly to fight the humans. If Valanis can be destroyed, your father will have no justification to invade. He will lose allies in the ruling houses, and a diminished army will force him to rethink his strategy."

"*War*? Who's going to war?" Elaith looked to each of them for answers.

"That's a good question." Nathaniel turned to Reyna with evident concern.

"We're not here just to destroy Valanis," Reyna said hesitantly.

Faylen remained silent, knowing that there was no avoiding the truth now.

"I'm really confused," Elaith chirped in.

"I'll explain later." Nathaniel put a hand up to silence her. "What else are you here to do?"

"We were sent by my father to gather as much information as possible about Illian's defences. Learn which kingdoms posed the greatest threat before we invade. My people want to take this land back, and many still blame the humans for The Dragon War. I'm sorry I didn't tell you. We couldn't. Mörygan was a great supporter of my father's plan."

"Reyna..." Faylen wanted to caution the princess, but the elf was just as stubborn as her mother.

"No. They need to know." Reyna turned back to Nathaniel with glistening eyes. "We were part of a plan to lower Korkanath's defences. Another group of elves has attacked the school so they could... So they could take the dragon. I don't know if they succeeded, but if they have, then Malliath the voiceless has already reached Ayda's shores. He will be used to release the dragon eggs stored inside Mount Garganafan."

"*Dragons...*" Nathaniel's eyes glazed over.

"My father will have an army of them when he invades. I'm sorry." Reyna turned back to Faylen. "You know my father as well as I. With the threat of Valanis or not, he will take back Illian from the humans. You know how much he hates them, Faylen."

"Whether he will or not, Valanis poses a serious threat. Besides the benefits of taking him out of the equation, it will weaken your father's position." Faylen was going to Elethiah, no matter what the argument.

"How will you even destroy Valanis?" Reyna persisted.

Nathaniel appeared to be mulling the new information over, though what he made of it, Faylen couldn't say.

"The Amber Spell has frozen him in place. Removing his head will be easy. Getting through Elethiah's wards will be harder. Asher has shown great resilience to magic, and I don't entirely agree with his treatment here. His company will benefit us both."

"I will *not* stay here." Reyna intoned her authority. As the princess, she technically had the last word on anything they did, but not this time.

"You have an army of knights to protect you here. If I take you with me I will be putting you in harm's way and, believe me, Elethiah will offer more challenges than a few Arakesh." Faylen opened her chest of infinite depth and removed her scimitar and travelling clothes.

"How will you free Asher?" Elaith asked.

"Leave that to me. I am charging the two of *you* with protecting Princess Reyna of house Sevari, heir to the throne of Elandril." Faylen stepped very close to the Graycoats. "And you will not fail me."

"We will protect her with our lives," Nathaniel stated boldly, if a little distracted.

"You're not listening to me!" Reyna stormed over. "You're not going to Elethiah without me. It's too dangerous, even for you and Asher. You will need elven magic. It makes sense if we both go."

Faylen cupped Reyna's face in both of her hands. "The only thing that makes sense to me, is keeping you safe. Stay with Nathaniel.

Protect each other. When the ranger and I return, we will see to setting things right." The elf placed an affectionate kiss on the princess's forehead. "Now go. I would meditate a while and prepare. I will free the ranger this very night. I suggest you continue to keep up appearances." Faylen's playful smile was not mirrored in Reyna or Nathaniel.

The princess knew that Faylen wouldn't budge, that much was clear from her expression, but the older elf knew it was for the better. The three of them left together without a word, leaving Faylen to gather her strength.

Nathaniel watched Reyna fire arrow after arrow with graceful ease into the head of a straw mannequin. The elf barely used any concentration or strength to pull back the string and release the arrow with deadly precision. The Graycoat was uncanny with a bow, but he wasn't in the same league as Reyna.

"She *will* succeed." Nathaniel could see what was really driving Reyna's constant barrage of arrows.

"You can't know that," the princess shot back. "My people placed powerful enchantments around Elethiah for a reason: to keep people out. She's going to need all the elven magic she can get."

Nathaniel looked around and tried to ignore the curious looks the other Graycoats gave him. The pair were unaccompanied and the only ones in the archery range. No doubt his familiarity with Reyna would only add to everyone's dislike of him.

"You think we should go with them..." It was more a statement than a question.

"Do you *not?*" Reyna quickly replied. "Faylen's cause is more honourable and just than any quest in all of Verda. I think she should have an army behind her, but there is none in all of Illian who could break through Elethiah's enchantments. She needs me..."

"I would gladly join them if it weren't for the threat that hung over you. The Arakesh will come for you. I have no control outside these walls, Reyna."

"I can't stay here forever." Reyna let fly another arrow, this time striking the mannequin's crotch. "I *won't* stay here for ever."

Nathaniel nocked an arrow in his own bow. "I'm not asking you to stay here for ever." The arrow launched from his bow and split Reyna's arrow down the middle. "I'm asking you to be safe."

Reyna turned away and sighed, frustrated. Nathaniel wanted for nothing more than to please the elf, free Asher and take the entire complement of Graycoats to Elethiah. But he needed to keep Reyna safe.

"Do you have nothing to say?" Reyna glanced at him.

The Graycoat knew what she was talking about. "Your father and a great many of your people would like to go to war with us," Nathaniel said warmly, "but even a blind man could see that you do not, nor Faylen. What matters now is trying to make things right. And that's what you're doing."

Reyna smiled in that way that made him forget the troubles of the world. He desperately wanted to kiss her and comfort her, to tell her that together they would make things right, but beyond her physical attraction to him, the knight wasn't sure the princess shared his deeper feelings.

"The dragon part's a little scary," Nathaniel added with mock fear. Reyna smiled, but her melodic laugh was interrupted.

"Galfrey!" Darius Devale shouted his name from atop the wall. "The Lord Marshal wishes to see you in his office, *now*." Darius walked away without waiting for a reply.

Elaith emerged from the armoury with a new bow more suited to her size and strength. "Prepare to be awed!" The young Ameeraskan smiled with the carefree attitude that accompanied youth.

Nathaniel, however, was in no mood to entertain her. "Stay with Reyna." The Graycoat strode away sullenly, his mood matching the dark clouds that now hung overhead, threatening rain.

The Lord Marshal had never wanted him for anything good.

High inside the main keep, Nathaniel entered Horvarth's office, a room handed down through the generations of Lord Marshals from the time of Tyberius Gray.

Horvarth sat at the far end of the room, behind an ornate desk said to have been gifted to Tyberius by the first king, Gal Tion, himself. Horvarth continued to scribble across scroll after scroll, his eyes firmly fixed on the parchment and not Nathaniel.

An obedient Graycoat, Nathaniel stood before the desk with his hands clasped behind his back, silent until spoken to. He took the moment of invisibility to cast an eye around the room. Growing up in West Fellion, there wasn't a boy or girl who didn't dream of sitting in this office and holding the highest title a Graycoat could achieve.

As a warrior by nature, Nathaniel looked past the books, ornaments and tapestries, his eyes, instead, resting on the mounted sword behind the Lord Marshal. The pommel of the one-handed hilt shone a beautiful gold with the features of a lion, the symbol for house Tion.

"Magnificent isn't it?" Horvarth had stopped writing and was staring at Nathaniel. "The sword of Tyberius Gray. For many years it was handed down to the next Lord Marshal and worn with pride. It can be nothing but an ornament now..." Horvarth rose from his desk and removed the sword from its mount. "Feel the weight." He handed the blade to Nathaniel, who gripped it firmly with one hand, admiring the ancient craftsmanship. "Do you know why I cannot wear it, Galfrey?"

Nathaniel pointed the sword down to better examine the *lion's* head. There in lay the answer to his question.

"Very good. The Graycoats protect the realm, not a single kingdom. Back then there was only the one kingdom and it was ruled by the lions. It would be very rude for the Lord Marshal of West Fellion to be seen favouring any one kingdom over the rest. We would not survive without their charity." Horvarth took the sword back and replaced it on the wall.

"You wanted to see me, Sir," Nathaniel said at last.

"As a knight of this order I don't expect you to overly concern yourself with the upkeep of West Fellion, that job is mine and mine alone. With the exception of Dragorn, the five kingdoms pay us to keep their lands safe, so that they don't have to fear jurisdiction and clashes over borders. They pay for an order of knights, disciplined and skilled.

Right now, every king, queen and lord has their sights squarely set on those elves. Should we prove to be the knights we claim to be, the Arakesh will fail and the realm will see the benefit in our continued presence." Horvarth paused dramatically. "What makes West Fellion appear undisciplined, and not what it claims to be, is when members of its order go around screwing the princess of a foreign nation!"

Nathaniel felt dizzy for just a moment. No doubt Darius Devale had told the Lord Marshal of his suspicions. "Sir, I—"

"I don't want to hear it!" Horvarth moved away and walked around his office. "If I punished and exiled every Graycoat having sex there wouldn't be enough knights to open West Fellion's gate. Anyone stupid enough to get pregnant or get caught has the decency to never return."

"My father returned..."

Horvarth's mouth twisted. "Yes, he did. He returned a happier man for his newest creation. If you think I'm hard on them you should have met the Lord Marshal at the time. He wanted to have your father executed in the courtyard. Not only had he broken his vow but he wanted to have a family *and* remain a Graycoat. But your father was already famous across Illian by then, his deeds remembered by the people. The Lord Marshal was powerless to act." Nathaniel didn't like the way Horvarth looked at him then. "Are *your* deeds remembered across Illian?"

Nathaniel didn't know what to say. He had broken his vow and failed to hide his affection for Reyna, but surely he couldn't be executed for it. The knight opened his mouth to make his argument, but couldn't find the words he thought might save his life. When it came to saving his life he was better making the argument with a sword or a bow.

"Don't look so worried," Horvarth continued. "I'm not having you executed for your lapse in discipline. I'm *promoting* you." Nathaniel knew it to be a trap; he just couldn't see it yet. "Your skill with a bow has long been noted, so I'm making you master of the bow. You will be given a permanent room in the keep and your instruction of the knights-in-training will begin immediately. Congratulations," Horvarth added dryly.

"You're imprisoning me," Nathaniel countered.

"You consider West Fellion a prison? Scores of your brothers and sisters would be honoured by such a title. A room of your own, the safety of the keep and a master of the order! I fail to see the bars on your door."

"I am a *knight*. I belong out there, serving the realm—"

"You are indeed a knight of this order, and *I* am the Lord Marshal. You will do as I command and nothing more." Horvarth wasn't backing down.

"Am I that much of a disgrace that you would keep me hidden from the world?" Nathaniel softened his tone.

"*You* are the bastard of Tobin Galfrey. Everywhere you go you sully his name and deeds and bring this order down in the eyes of the realm. You should be on your knees, thanking me that I didn't instantly exile you the moment I was given this title." The tension was palpable between the two men, and it hung there in the silence that followed.

"Is that why you sent me to apprehend Asher alone? You hoped I would fail and the assassin would get the better of me." Nathaniel just wanted to hear the admission.

"I don't send my knights out to die, even the bastards. Despite your heritage, you are your father's son and every bit as capable as he was in his youth. I had no doubt that you would bring Asher to

Darius Devale, but you were supposed to fade back into anonymity, not entangle yourself in Illian's current events. You certainly weren't supposed to ally yourself with an Arakesh."

Horvarth took a breath and straightened his floor-length coat. "We're done talking of this. You're dismissed. Oh, and don't let me catch you with the princess or you'll find that your new room *does* have bars."

"Sir..." Nathaniel bowed his head and stormed out of the office.

Without stopping to think about it, Nathaniel marched across the courtyard to the firing range. Reyna was showing Elaith some of the finer points of using a bow when they noticed his expression of thunder.

"What's wrong?" Reyna asked.

"We're going to Elethiah, the four of us. Tonight, when Faylen frees Asher, we're going to be waiting."

"*Five* of us!" Elaith protested.

After Nathaniel had told her about the elves quest to destroy Valanis, the young Graycoat had been desperate to help in some way. He feared that it all sounded a grand adventure to Elaith.

"You can help us sneak out of West Fellion, but you're not coming with us."

"I want to help! Why can't I help?" Elaith's question was almost one word.

"If you come with us you won't be able to return. The Lord Marshal will exile you." Nathaniel saw the look on Reyna's face but said nothing. There was nothing to be said. He would gladly give up his title of Graycoat if it meant contributing to the aid of the realm, which he had just been told was no longer an option.

Elaith opened her mouth to protest, but Nathaniel cut her off. "You will make a fine knight, Elaith Nevandar. You may even be the best of us. But you have to keep that coat on." He meant every word though, in truth, he wanted to keep her safe from the horrors of Elethiah.

"As you say..." she replied begrudgingly.

Nathaniel looked from Reyna to the stone walls that surrounded them. His time as a Graycoat was over. When the sun rose tomorrow, he would be just a man, but perhaps that would be enough...

CHAPTER 45
THE RIGHT THING

Gideon looked out over The Flat Wastes with despair. They had been walking across the expanse since dawn. The sun was low in the sky now, setting over The Great Maw behind them, yet the heat remained.

The Red Mountains appeared no closer for their efforts, and even Galanör's elven strength was waning. The two staggered and slowed inevitably.

The ground was hard under their feet, unrelenting. This land wasn't meant to be traversed by man or elf, nor even beast apparently. The mage had yet to see a single creature of any size in the desert.

He had long taken off his leather jacket and folded it into his bottomless satchel, using, instead, a spare shirt to wrap around his head and neck to protect him from the sun.

The horizon rippled in the heat, threatening to go on forever. More than once, Gideon had thought about how they should have returned to Malaysai and searched for Adilandra, if only to get out of the wastes. The young mage kept such thoughts to himself since he had been the one who argued to find the dragons, as the queen of elves had demanded.

Galanör hadn't said a word since they set off. The silence suited Gideon. He wasn't sure yet how he felt about the elf. Fighting alongside another person had a way of changing one's perspective, and the mage felt his was shifting.

That thought took him back to the pyramid's halls. There had been so much blood... and the smell! Gideon had never killed anyone before, but killing to survive didn't feel like *killing*. He had done what was needed to keep breathing, nothing more. No glee was taken from the act, nor did he feel hunger for more.

In some way, the mage could empathise with the ones he had used magic against. The thought of them dying and how they died felt almost too real to Gideon, and he tried to forget the feeling immediately. Empathy could be a curse if he allowed it.

Now, they were in the wild, surrounded by an enemy that knew how to hunt them and a land that knew how to drive them to madness. Gideon had to be strong. He couldn't let his feelings get in the way of surviving, especially if his survival was tied to Illian's future.

Galanör stumbled but stayed on his feet in front of the mage. His dark cloak was tattered and covered in blood and sand. Gideon would never forget for the rest of his life seeing the elf fight the Darkakin. Like a man on fire, Galanör had cut through nearly a hundred warriors with his elven blades. More often than not, the elf had moved with such speed as to be a blur in Gideon's eyes.

The mage didn't know how many he had killed himself and he had no intention of ever keeping count, but it seemed to him that Galanör would never be able to keep count of so many.

"We will rest here for the night," Galanör's voice croaked, as the elf stopped walking and pulled down his hood.

"I haven't seen you drink for hours." Gideon brushed Galanör's cloak aside and grabbed the waterskin off the elf's belt, checking its contents.

Galanör pulled away from the intrusion, knocking free a small black orb from the back of his belt. Gideon watched it drop to the ground and roll for a metre before the elf scurried after it with haste. The mage recognised it immediately as a diviner.

The Magikar and some of the council members possessed one each, along with other mages across Illian, though most were in the court of some king or queen. Gideon knew that most diviners were paired with another in their binding spell, to make for more intimate conversations over a large distance.

Who was on the other end of that diviner? he thought.

"I don't need to drink as much as you do." Galanör tucked the orb away again.

"You still need to *drink*," Gideon quickly replied. It was a bemusing thought, to think that not long ago he would have gladly watched Galanör die from thirst. Now, he needed him to live.

"We need to rest. When that sun rises again we set off; we need to be ready. Do you have anything in that bag of yours to start a fire?" Galanör sat cross-legged on the ground, adjusting the scimitars on his hip as he did.

"Fire? I'm too hot to think about fire." Gideon placed himself on the ground, opposite the elf.

"It's going to get very cold soon. Either of us can start a fire, but it must be sustained while we sleep." There was no emotion in the elf, just simple facts. Leaving Adilandra weighed on him.

"I'll have a look…"

After the sun had set and the stars were displayed across the night sky, Gideon found himself not only wearing his red leather jacket again, but also wrapped up inside two blankets they had stolen from the Malaysai market.

The nights in the desert were as cold as the days were hot. Galanör sat with his knees to his chest and his dark hood drooped low over his head. They had eaten and drunk what they needed, being careful to ration what was left. There were more supplies now that only two of them remained. It had been a bittersweet revelation.

"Tell me about her..." Galanör said into the firelight. "Tell me about Abigail Rose."

Gideon felt his guard go up at the sound of her name, especially coming from the elf. The mage knew Galanör hadn't been the one to end her life, but his involvement complicated things.

"She was..." Gideon hesitated, unsure how to describe someone who meant so much to him. He had taken her for granted. So used to her presence was he, that it was only after she was gone that he realised how important Abigail had been.

"She was gentle but strong." Gideon felt the tears gathering at the edges of his eyes. "We had been friends since we were eleven, always in competition with each other, yet always supporting each other. So obsessed was I with the thought of adventure and a life on the road that I couldn't see what was right in front of me. I wish more than anything that I could..." Tears ran down his cheeks and he was glad of the shadows that concealed his face.

"I just want to see her again, talk to her. Abigail always knew what to say and when to say it. She kept me grounded. Without her, I would have been expelled from Korkanath years ago." A dark thought crept into his mind. "It's my fault she's dead. I didn't mislay the hex-traps; I just wanted a real challenge. The Hydra, however, was stronger than my ego. We were forced into your path and Abigail's fate was sealed."

"Abigail was killed by Lyra Valarkin," Galanör said. "You cannot blame yourself. Lyra was more skilled with magic and a blade before your great-grandparents were born. There was nothing you could have done."

"Perhaps I should blame you?" Gideon met Galanör's eyes across the fire.

"Perhaps..." The elf didn't look away.

"Do you feel no guilt for your part?"

"I have more than just Abigail Rose on my conscience. Pray that you never discover the true depths of *duty*. Men and elves alike are capable of great atrocities if they can do it in the name of another, be it gods or kings. Duty can give you courage and a sense of honour, but it can give you cause to act without thought.

"My future was sealed before I was your age. My skill with a blade could not be overlooked, especially by my father. I was killing for him long before I was killing for the king." The elf continued to stare into the fire.

Gideon didn't truly believe that the elf was being an obedient servant to his queen. "Are you bound by duty now, crossing The Flat Wastes and searching The Red Mountains for dragons? Has the word of your queen set you on this course, or is there more to the will that drives your feet onwards?"

It was clear to see that Galanör wanted to make a difference, to tip the scales, as it were.

"I'm doing the *right* thing. It's not what I want to do, but I'm not doing it out of duty anymore. It's taken me four hundred years, but I finally see that doing the right thing is all we can do."

"It's all we *should* do..." Gideon corrected. Though it was his voice, they were Abigail's words and it warmed him to use them.

The two sat in silence for a while, each contemplating the other's words.

"Won't the fire attract the Darkakin?" Gideon asked with a lighter tone than he had ever used with Galanör.

The elf studied the map for a moment. "Doubtful. We're a day's trek across The Flat Wastes, and Malaysai is in the heart of The Great Maw. They'd have to cross The Trident river before they broke through the jungle." Galanör pointed at the river that cut through the jungle and ran off in three different directions, to the south. "They won't be on our trail for a while. We'll be in The Red Mountains by the time they reach the edge of The Great Maw, providing this desert doesn't kill us first."

Neither was talking about what they'd do when they finally

found the dragons. That was a part of the plan that couldn't be prepared for.

"Have you ever seen a map like this?" Gideon asked, pointing to the parchment with his chin.

"I have never seen a map of anything south of Syla's Gate," Galanör replied. "The Darkakin must have mapped out the south over the centuries. Thankfully they never found a way to Elandril. From the looks of this," the elf said as he stretched out the map on the ground, "The Flat Wastes continue north for almost four hundred miles before it meets some kind of valley between the mountains. On the other side of that is another desert we call The Q'ol. They clearly believe an army cannot be exposed to such terrain."

Gideon moved closer to Galanör, shuffling around the small fire, to better see the map.

"This is where their armies are amassing." The mage pointed to the map where the land curved around in the shape of a crescent moon. "They called it The Hook of the World."

"And this is how they will enter Illian." Galanör pointed to an archipelago of nearly thirty islands that formed a bridge between the two continents. "Drowners Run."

"Do you think they could get past Syla's Gate?" Gideon asked, looking at the map. The great gate was situated in the middle of The Undying Mountains, the most southerly point on any map in Illian.

"My people left it when they sailed to Ayda. From what I read about it, the gate would be difficult to open even if it were undefended." Galanör pulled his cloak tighter around him. "Do any of the kingdoms man it?"

"The emperor of Karath had it manned for a couple of centuries after your people left, or at least that's what the history books say. Since meeting you and Adilandra I'm thinking the history books need re-writing. Syla's Gate hasn't been defended for nearly eight hundred years."

That would be the first thing he warned them of, Gideon

thought. The emperor of The Arid Lands needed to move his army there as soon as possible.

"There's a good chance they won't even make it across Drowners Run," Galanör added with little encouragement.

They sat in silence for a while longer. Gideon couldn't believe the war that was coming. Armies from the east and south were readying to fight the west, but Illian wasn't even allied. The six kingdoms had six armies and their own selfish reasons for guarding their land.

If they didn't see that all of Illian was under threat, and not just their own fiefdom, then there might be a chance that the allied kingdoms could repel the elves and the Darkakin or, better yet, ally with the elves.

Either way, finding the dragons was crucial.

CHAPTER 46
FIGHT OR FLIGHT

Asher spat blood on the floor after Ned Fennick had finished doling out his final beating of the night. The Graycoat seemed to take a few hours to sleep and eat in between his interrogation; a pattern the ranger had taken note of.

Pattern and routine were the worst things to have when trying to break a prisoner. In Nightfall he would never see his beatings coming and they never lasted the same length of time. They weren't even in the same place.

From the sound of it, he knew the guard outside his door changed shifts every five hours. The old assassin would continue to build his knowledge of his captors until he could use it against them.

"I fancy myself a little kip in a nice feather bed," Fennick began, as he unbound his hands from the blood-soaked cloth. "When the sun rises and I've had myself a hearty breakfast, maybe some bacon, I'll return to this shit-tip and we can start over.

"While I'm gone, I suggest you think really hard about the location of Nightfall. I want to know where they are, how many there are and how to make that Nightseye stuff." The grizzly knight knocked on the iron door and the guards opened it for him. "Sleep tight!" Fennick laughed all the way down the hall.

With his jailer gone, Asher lowered his guard and let his head drop, allowing the pain to be felt. His ribs burned and everything ached at the slightest movement. The fresh cuts stung as if Fennick had stuffed glass in the wounds.

He wanted to scream and rage but he refused to give in, to give the guards the satisfaction. Instead, the ranger hung there wondering if he was getting too old for this. Could he survive this? Would he ever be free?

Suddenly, his ears popped, as if the atmosphere had changed on a mountaintop. Asher looked up to see Faylen stepping out of a black hole that sat between him and the door.

The elf entered the room dressed as a warrior in a tight-fitted green coat, which hung to her knees, with a bow and quiver strapped to her back. The hilt of the elven scimitar, attached to her hip, glistened in the firelight. Faylen's dark hair was tied back and blended into the inky darkness of the portal behind her.

The elf stood there for a moment in silence, as the portal collapsed in on itself. Asher had never seen such magic before, but the concept wasn't beyond him and, if anyone would be using it, it would be the elves.

"Nice trick..." Asher's mouth ached to just form the words.

"Quiet, Ranger. I'm getting you out of here." Faylen began examining his manacles. "You and I are leaving West Fellion tonight."

Asher couldn't help his look of bemusement. "And where are we going?" He swallowed blood.

Faylen stopped and met his eyes. "We're going to Elethiah. You and I are going to find a way in and we're going to destroy Valanis. You have shown remarkable resilience to magic. I can only assume there's elven blood in you. Together we can breach the citadel's wards and stop our people from going to war."

"Sounds good..." Asher replied coolly.

Faylen went to speak, but no words came out for a moment. "Did you hear what I said? Our people are going to go to war. My king will use Valanis as an excuse to invade and..." The elf looked utterly perplexed.

"This is not a revelation," Asher explained in a bored tone.

"You already knew?"

"I've had a lot of time to put things together in here." Asher looked around his cell. "There's not much to do in between the torture." Faylen appeared to be finding his skills of deduction hard to believe. "I knew the two of you were hiding something. Reyna wears her emotions on her sleeve, and she's wearing *fear*. I've seen her fight and hunt and neither bother her one bit, but talking about her father's plans for our future *alliance* scares the hell out of her. She looks at the knight like she knows she's going to lose him."

"How very perceptive... for a ranger." Faylen looked him over.

"I thought I was an Outlander?" Asher tried to smile through the pain.

"How would you like to be a *hero*?" Faylen countered with a calculated expression.

"I'll be whatever you want if you get me out of these damn chains." Asher *rattled* his manacles.

Faylen examined the manacles around his wrists and ankles. Her nimble fingers ran over the runes and glyphs burned into the iron. The elf moved around the room to see the manacles from behind and gasped. Asher assumed she was looking at the whip marks that lined his back. The worst part had been the salt Fennick threw into the wounds.

A delicate finger touched his back. "It will take me too long to find a way around these enchantments."

Asher grunted as he adjusted his body to better see the table in the corner. "Over there. My ring is on the table, under the red cloth." Faylen moved to the table and lifted the cloth to see his black crystal ring. "Put it on my finger." The ranger wiggled his fingers.

Faylen picked up the ring with a curious glance at Asher. Without warning, the elf's hand went into spasm and clenched tightly around the gem. Her knees gave out. She cried out in pain, though her voice was deeper and unnatural.

The table and all of his belongings floated into the air at the same moment the fire in the gutters climbed the walls. As suddenly as it started, the phenomenon ended when Faylen managed to throw the ring away. The table dropped to the floor and the fire died down.

"What is that?" The elf sounded exhausted and yet full of energy all at once. It occurred to Asher that no one besides himself had ever actually touched the crystal before.

"Put it on my finger, quickly!" The noise had alerted the guards, who were now working on sliding the bolts out of the door.

Despite her obvious reservations, Faylen used magic to levitate the ring across the room and placed it over Asher's right index finger.

The ranger wasted no time.

He willed the ring's superior magic to freeze the manacles and chains until they were so weak he only had to tug at them to be free. If Meister Kalantez's enchantments offered any resistance he didn't feel it. What he did feel, however, was the floor as he fell to his hands and knees, his legs unable to support him.

Asher whipped his head back and sighed in relief as the black crystal went to work on healing his wounds. Bones cracked and popped back into place, while his cuts and bruises sealed up and faded. It was as if he was coming up for air after a long dive. The clarity of the room took on a sharpness it had been missing for a couple of days.

The heavy iron door swung open, just as Asher rose to his feet, his body remade. The two Graycoats stared at him with disbelief, their mouths ajar. They looked dumb-founded from him to the frozen chains that lay scattered across the floor.

"Guarantees are hard to come by in this life, fellas." Asher met their stunned faces with a menacing expression. "But I guarantee you, if either of you pulls a sword, I will break your goddamn neck." Asher meant every word. After what he'd been through, cracking a couple of necks was just what he needed.

The Graycoats hesitated, with their hands over their hilts, until good sense won the day, and they attacked Asher with their bare hands. The ranger batted their fists away with ease, twisting wrists and bending arms before he countered with a flurry of strikes that targeted the knights' nerve clusters. In seconds, both men were rendered unconscious.

Asher stood over them heaving as his newly healed muscles rippled in the firelight. It felt good to be strong again. He cracked his knuckles and rolled his shoulders and head, enjoying the freedom. That need to fight was always there, just under the surface.

Nightfall would never leave him, it seemed.

"Where did you get that ring?" Faylen managed to stand, though she was still massaging her sore hand.

Asher looked at the black crystal set into the silver ring. Nasta Nal-Aket had always taught him to keep his strengths a secret, but there would be no secrets kept from the elf now. Faylen was too old and wise to be lied to, especially after touching the ring.

"I've had it for as long as I can remember." Asher could see the featureless face of a woman giving him the black crystal as a child, but he couldn't remember why anymore.

"Let me see it." Faylen hesitantly gripped Asher's hand and raised it to her face for better inspection. "As black as night..." The elf appeared to be losing herself to the depthless facets of the crystal. "It cannot be..." Faylen manipulated his hand to see it from every angle. "There are many magical trinkets in the world, but none as powerful as this." Faylen met the ranger's eyes. "Except for one, and this cannot be it."

"Why not?" Asher had a feeling he already knew why.

"Because if this is what I think it is, it should be much bigger than a shard. It should be the size of a finger."

Asher gave the elf a hard look. "I cut this piece away years ago, from a black crystal the size of my finger."

Faylen gasped and stood back as if the ranger was plagued. The elf continued to look from him to the ring and back.

"You have Paldora's Gem..."

Asher didn't see how it could be possible that he would have such a legendary relic, but he knew her words to be true. In some way, he had always known that the crystal was of great importance, but he couldn't remember why. The situation in which he had been given the gem was long forgotten, thanks to Nightfall's vigorous teachings.

"Where is the rest of the gem?" Faylen asked with considerable concern.

"I threw it away after I crafted the ring. Arakesh don't have many possessions and the crystal caused many to become suspicious."

"Where? *Where* did you throw it away?" The elf was suddenly a lot closer.

"In a place where no one will ever find it..." Asher would have elaborated if it weren't for the ringing of bells in the distance.

They both looked around, fearing they had done something to sound an alarm, but no one knew of his freedom. The ranger wasted no time in fitting his leather armour to his chest and tying his bracers to his forearms. It felt good to have his sword on his hip again, its weight offering comfort. The spiked pommel was dull in the firelight and in need of a polish.

He prepared to strap the quiver on, attaching his folded bow to the side, before hanging both over the top of his green cloak for easy access. Finally, he admired the silvyr hour-glass blade, gifted to him by the dwarven smith Danagarr Bairnson. The ranger quickly sheathed the fine sword on his back.

All the while, Faylen paced the fire-lined room, as if the weight of Verda were on her shoulders.

"Time to go," the elf said, at last, pulling a small white crystal from a pouch on her belt.

"Wait." Asher held up a hand. "We need to see what the alarm is."

Faylen closed her hand around her crystal and looked past Asher. It was clear to see that she was concerned for Reyna. The two stepped over the Graycoats and ran down the corridor, the ranger more than happy to leave the cell behind.

As they rounded the final corner, the two came to a sudden stop when Reyna, Nathaniel and Elaith blocked their path. There was a moment of surprise on Nathaniel's face, as he looked over Asher's healed appearance.

"What are you doing here?" Faylen hissed.

"We're coming with you." Reyna looked at them both. The princess wasn't to be argued with.

"No you're—" Faylen was interrupted by Asher.

"What are the bells for?"

Nathaniel appeared distracted, looking up at the ceiling as if he could see the keep above. "They've never had need of them before…" The Graycoat's steely expression was all Asher needed to see to understand what was happening.

"They're here!" Elaith drew her sword.

"Then it's the perfect time to leave." Faylen pushed past them. "We can use the distraction."

Asher could see the conflict on Nathaniel's face. The knight wanted to stay and help his brothers and sisters in the fight against their oldest enemy.

"Stay if you must," Reyna said softly, with a comforting hand on his shoulder.

Nathaniel glanced at the ranger. "What we're doing is more important."

Faylen groaned in a very un-elf-like way. "Well come if you're coming!" she called over the sound of the bells.

A light rain covered the five, as they cautiously entered the court-yard, keeping close to the walls in the hope of avoiding detection. No one cared. Several Graycoats ran past them with abandon, heading for the steps up to the outer wall. Many looked at the five companions but none questioned them or tried to detain the ranger.

The knights shouted to each other from across the fort, rallying their forces to the main gate and the outer wall.

Asher had a very bad feeling.

"Nathaniel!" Reyna shouted to the Graycoat, who had made a dash for the steps. Faylen sighed when Reyna and Elaith followed him without hesitation.

Asher gripped the hilt of his broadsword, ready for the inevitable fight that would occur when he was noticed. The ranger wasn't entirely sure if he could stop himself from cutting Ned Fennick down if he saw him.

He climbed the stone steps and joined the others on the outer wall. The entire platform was lined with a thousand Graycoats, most of whom had been recalled. More were filing out of the keep and making for the main gate. Asher had never seen so many Graycoats in one place before.

The ranger found a gap between Faylen and Nathaniel at the edge of the wall. There were few things left in life that could shock the old assassin, but the sight before him now was nothing short of shocking. He couldn't get rid of the surprise that marred his face, as he looked out over a field of Arakesh.

The moon shone down over what Asher estimated to be around five hundred assassins. Never in the history of the Arakesh had so many been brought together for a single purpose.

Faylen was watching him. The elf looked from him to the ring, to the army at their gate. The Arakesh hadn't been amassed to kill one elf, royalty or not: they had been sent for Paldora's Gem.

At the head of the dark army, a figure stood alone, dressed in black and gold with a hood and mask that covered his mouth and nose. His cloak billowed about him as the storm gathered overhead and the rain picked up. Thunder rumbled about them with stray bolts of lightning striking the fields around the Arakesh.

The Graycoats were a mix of emotions, judging by their expressions. Some appeared eager for such a battle, while others looked to be on the verge of running for The Evermoore, to the north. The ranger might as well have been invisible.

The sound of a sword being unsheathed behind him forced Asher to turn away from the dark spectacle. Ned Fennick was crossing the small bridge, between the inner and outer walls, with four Graycoats at his back.

Nathaniel pulled himself away from the terrifying view and came to stand beside the ranger.

"You will suffer a great price for this, *traitor*." Fennick glared at Nathaniel before he had a closer look at Asher's unscathed features. The broad knight stared blankly at the ranger, examining him from head-to-toe.

"Ned!" The Lord Marshal came striding down the outer wall with a pair of knights either side. Horvarth paused to lock eyes with Asher, before looking past him to the Arakesh. "You have spent a long time trying to convince the world you're something else, *ranger*. Your actions thus far appear to support that claim." The leader of West Fellion looked over the elves and Nathaniel. "Do you swear by all the gods that you had no hand in this, and that you will lend your sword this day?"

Asher looked at Faylen, who now wanted to take Reyna away from West Fellion, even if it meant heading towards Elethiah.

"Lord Marshal?" Fennick pleaded.

"Perhaps you haven't seen what's at our door?" Horvarth snapped. "His blade will claim more Arakesh than your own." He looked back to Asher. "What say you?"

Nathaniel removed the bow from his back and Reyna notched an arrow, signifying their joint decision. Elaith nodded and hefted her sword, proud to be wearing her coat. Faylen sighed and looked back to the army with dismay.

"Don't let them breach the main gate," Asher replied. "If they get inside the walls we'll be overwhelmed." The ranger lifted his head to the moon. "If we can hold out until daybreak we might have a chance of repelling them; the dark is their greatest ally." The sound of the rain drowned out almost everything, as it bounced off the multitude of leather coats and swords.

"He speaks nonsense, Lord Marshal," Ned flustered. "We outnumber the Arakesh two-to-one!"

"Your numbers count for nothing in the dark," Asher countered.

"As you say." Horvarth stepped onto the turreted wall. "LIGHT EM' UP!"

As ordered, torches were taken out of the fire-pits and dropped into the moat of pikes below. The fire climbed the walls when the oil poured into the moat was set alight. In seconds, West Fellion was encircled in a fire that could be seen for miles.

Hidden deep in the canyons of The Arid Lands, Alidyr sat cross-legged on the floor of his private chambers. The elf was surrounded by a circle of ancient runes and elven glyphs.

He had prepared this particular spell days ago before the army had even left Nightfall. Twenty of his best warriors had volunteered their bodies to be branded with a spell of the ancients that allowed the Father to see through their eyes. At least that's what he had told them. In truth, once Alidyr had enacted the spell, he would be able to control any one of them.

His eyes glazed over with a milky white, as his consciousness traversed Illian in the blink of an eye. The elf was now looking through the eyes of Jai Hadrok, a young and talented assassin who had proven himself on many missions.

Beside the young killer was the older, more experienced warrior, Ro Dosarn. The five hundred strong stood in the cold rain with hardened discipline. They didn't complain, they didn't ache, and they didn't even shiver. This weapon he had created for his master would bear fruit once they retrieved Paldora's Gem for him.

Standing as a wall in front of them all was Adellum. His magnificent bow was in hand; ready to carve a path through the Graycoats until he found Asher.

Everything was about to change.

CHAPTER 47
A LITTLE RUCKUS

Galanör awoke with a start. He had fallen asleep while it was his turn to keep watch as Gideon slept by the fire. The familiar sound of large feet padding across the desert floor, however, had found the elf's sensitive ears. The last time he had heard that particular sound was back in Malaysai, when the guards had patrolled the streets astride giant lizards.

Using magic, Galanör waved his hand quickly over the fire and stole the oxygen from the hungry flames.

Darkness consumed them, as the only light filtered down from the stars. The moon was distant now and low on the horizon, offering little illumination to the elf's fears. He reached out and nudged the mage vigorously, since the human wasn't easily roused, even in the dangerous Flat Wastes.

"What's wrong?" Gideon called out, alarm creeping into his croaky voice.

Galanör clamped a hand over his mouth. "Shh..." The elf continued to stare into the distance, desperate for his vision to adjust in the dark.

The mage joined him on his knees and followed Galanör's gaze across the desert. Gideon's expression told of his blunt human senses. Only Galanör could hear the approaching feet. The elf slowed his breathing and closed his eyes, trying to focus his efforts on hearing.

"I don't see anything," Gideon whispered.

"Shh!" Galanör gripped the mage's leather jacket around his shoulder.

His keen ears caught the familiar sound of a spear whistling through the air. The elf pushed Gideon away, while he dived the other way. The spear flew between the two and drove into the hard ground. The padding feet picked up speed until Galanör could hear the guttural breathing of a large beast.

"Gideon!"

The mage responded by rolling to his knees and bringing up his staff. A fireball exploded from the end of his staff and streaked through the dark, lighting up the desert ground before it finally struck the meaty leg of a giant lizard. The lumbering beast toppled over its own momentum, sending its Darkakin rider sprawling out in front. His cries of surprise were cut short when the bulk of the lizard rolled over him.

The charging feet of more lizards could be heard over the injured creature's panting. Galanör couldn't discern their number but guessed it to be at least a dozen. The elf conjured a ball of light and launched it high into the air. He quickly counted nine more riders making their way across the wastes, each wielding a spear or a bow. Without thinking, he retrieved both scimitars and braced himself for their attack.

Gideon, apparently, had no intention of waiting.

The mage ran ahead as if to meet them, before he dropped to one knee and brought his staff down hard into the ground. Galanör wasn't sure which spell Gideon used, but the mage certainly filled it with enormous will.

The ground cracked outwards from the end of the staff, replicating a spider's web. When the giant lizards crossed into the broken ground, the land exploded, as if it were built upon geysers. One lizard was fired high enough into the air to take all four of its feet off the ground. Another had its head taken clean off by the heavy slab of rock that shot up through its neck. The fallen beasts created havoc for the others and caused collisions that crushed their riders.

Two Darkakin were able to let loose a pair of arrows into the gloom. Galanör held his breath, seeing that both arrows were flying true, aimed at Gideon.

The young mage stood up and whipped his staff aside; creating a wall of magical energy that swept the arrows away. Gideon followed up his defence with a lightning spell. The burst of energy closed the gap and caught the Darkakin in the chest, launching him back into the night.

Only two riders remained, and both charged at Galanör. As skilled hunters, the Darkakin didn't even shout out when they found their prey, always trained to remain silent.

The elf met their charge with a flat-out sprint of his own. With incredible precision, Galanör flicked his right scimitar towards the furthest rider, while at the same time launching himself into the air, using the nearest lizard's head as a stepping stone. As the flying scimitar plunged into the farthest Darkakin's chest, Galanör flipped his body over the closest rider and landed behind the saddle. A horizontal swipe removed the Darkakin's head.

Galanör pushed the rest of the rider's body from the saddle and took control of the lizard for himself.

Gideon waved his arms to slow down the last lizard, with a dead Darkakin still sitting in its saddle and a scimitar stuck in his sternum. The mage calmed the lizard with a slow hand and patted the beast across its flat maw.

"Easy..." When the lizard appeared calm again, Gideon moved around and pushed the rider to the ground, retrieving the sword as he fell. "Yours, I believe."

Galanör rode up to his side and happily took back his scimitar. The starlight spell continued to glow overhead, illuminating the miniature earthquake that had devastated the ground. Bodies littered the desert between the giant lizards and fallen boulders.

"That was impressive," Galanör remarked, looking at the staff in Gideon's hand.

"As were you." Gideon looked at the lizard the elf sat astride.

"They were scouts. I didn't think they'd mobilise so fast. There will be more out there, and they no doubt heard our little ruckus." Galanör glanced at the new landscape created by the mage. "The lizards will get us to The Red Mountains before dawn, but we ride all night."

"Agreed." Gideon pulled himself into the saddle, picked up the reins, and dug his heels into the beast's sides. It didn't move. "I have no idea what I'm doing..."

Galanör almost laughed, almost...

CHAPTER 48
THE BATTLE OF WEST FELLION

Horvarth strode up and down West Fellion's outer wall with authority. The Lord Marshal was in the middle of what Asher assumed was a rousing speech for the knights. The ranger hadn't taken anything in past the first sentence. He didn't need words of encouragement or reminding of his honour to help him kill a man.

Instead, Asher looked to Elaith, feeling concerned for her life. The young woman wasn't ready for this kind of fight but, then again, neither were half of the Graycoats on the wall.

Asher looked around and saw too many young faces. Some hadn't even been made Graycoats yet and were just unfortunate enough to be here.

Elaith had shown great promise in their sparring sessions on the road, but this battle would more than test her. Asher was beyond questioning why he was so concerned with these people's lives and simply resigned himself to this new way of life.

"They were never meant to fight like this," the ranger offered. "Their armour is lightweight: it won't hold up to an arrow. If your aim is true they will fall."

All nodded their understanding except for Elaith, who continued to stare at the fields of black-clad assassins.

"In the light, they're just as human as you are. Remember your advantages." Asher looked at her sword, reminding the young knight of its superior length. It was hard to tell whether it was tears or rain that ran down her cheeks. "Just stay close to us." Asher reached for the pouches on the side of his belt and searched with his fingers for the Talo spices he kept in neat little bags. "Damn..." he cursed.

"What is it?" Elaith asked, fearing the worst.

"I left the Talo spices with Hector." Asher considered going back down to the stables and retrieving them from his saddlebags.

"I remember using them when I lived in Ameeraska," the young knight replied. "We used them to start campfires on the rooftops at night, to keep warm."

The ranger made to leave when Nathaniel nudged his arm. "Why aren't they attacking us?"

"Fear..." Asher reasoned. "They want it to sink in before they attack."

"At least they can't breach the walls," the Graycoat continued. "They have no war machines, no ballista, not even a few mountain giants."

Asher noticed the elves talking frantically in hushed tones and looking out over the Arakesh.

"What is it?"

"The hooded figure in the middle," Faylen said. "Do you recognise him?"

Asher examined the distant figure as best he could with his human eyes. Through the rain, he was just able to discern the gold lining that formed patterns across his dark armour.

"The one who attacked us at The Unmar... Thallan Tassariön."

"He *is* one of the Hand, but that is not Thallan." Faylen spoke in grave tones. "See his bow? That is Adellum Bövö..."

"He's too far away to worry about his bow," Nathaniel ignorantly replied.

"That bow was gifted to him by Valanis," Reyna explained. "It is no ordinary bow. In the histories of The Dark War, it is written that Adellum fired but one arrow from his bow and the gates of Elethiah were breached."

"He is Valanis's battering ram." Faylen slowly removed an arrow from her quiver.

Asher looked back to the shadowy figure and then down to the main gate, where forty or more Graycoats had taken up position behind the second, inner door, between the stables.

"Get them back!" Asher roared, cutting off Horvarth's speech. "Get them back from the gate, NOW!" The ranger was already running down the outer wall, until he was standing over the main gate.

Horvarth just looked at him bewildered. "They are fortifying the gate! You will fight with us but will not—" The Lord Marshal never finished his sentence.

A lone arrow streaked across the empty field between Adellum and West Fellion. Defying the pull of the earth, the arrow continued straight, until it struck the main outer gate.

The arrow blew through both outer and inner doors with all the subtlety of a Troll. The fort was physically rocked and giant splinters of wood were launched into the air in every direction.

Asher was hit by the concussive wave and knocked into the square courtyard, between the inner and outer gates. Before landing, the ranger was slammed into the wall, which saved his life having taken some of the distance out of the drop.

He lifted his head in a daze to see the forty odd Graycoats, who had been standing behind the inner door, lying dead on the ground. Adellum's arrow had reduced both doors to pieces and was now stuck in the stone of the main keep, a hundred feet away.

The ranger blinked hard in an attempt to regain his senses. There was a loud pitch humming in his ears, causing the nearby cries of alarm to sound distant. A sharp pain stabbed at his ribs with every

463

breath - the knock against the wall had bruised at least two ribs on the left side of his chest.

Blood annoyingly trickled down his forehead and into his left eye, until he wiped it away with the back of his fingerless gloves. The black crystal crossed his vision, reminding Asher of the magic he had available. With a tentative hand over his bruised ribs, the ranger willed the crystal to heal him. The bones ached, causing some discomfort and a groan from the ranger.

"Asher!" Nathaniel cried from atop the wall. The Graycoat was above the remnants of the main gate now, eyes wide with concern. "They're coming! Get out of there!"

Adellum strode across the field, while the army of Arakesh charged for the exact place Asher was now standing. All of them were blindfolded behind their red cloth, twin short-swords in hand. There were no torches in the small courtyard, no light to remove their advantage.

"Hold that gate, assassin!" Ned Fennick screamed beside Nathaniel. The broad knight was dragging the limp body of the Lord Marshal, though Asher couldn't tell if he was dead or alive. "Hold that gate!"

"He can't hold them all!" Nathaniel protested. "We need more men down there!"

Fennick ignored him. "Archers!" Every Graycoat still standing on the wall notched an arrow in their bow. Fennick, however, continued to drag Horvarth away from the wall.

"I'm coming down!" Nathaniel shouted.

"No!" Asher shouted back. It was hard to look up at the knight through the pouring rain. "Stay with the elves and Elaith!" The ranger pulled out his broadsword and plunged it into the dirt, where it wobbled, upright. "I'll be fine," he whispered to himself, the red cloth soaking in his freezing hands.

Asher tied the cloth around his head, covering his eyes. The Nightseye elixir, which would be forever in Asher's veins, came to life in the darkness. The ranger could now hear everything. He could hear the individual raindrops across his shoulders and the smaller droplets they formed that coursed down his cloak. The rough, dragging of arrows from their quivers atop the wall roared in his ears before a thousand *twangs* rippled like a tidal wave.

Asher could smell mud and grass being kicked up into the air by the rain and the charging Arakesh. A young boy, no older than fifteen, had pissed himself in the stables, where he cowered beneath the hay.

The ranger's heart boomed in his chest and he worked to steady it, falling into the rhythm. He removed the green cloak from his back and flexed his muscles in anticipation.

Over a thousand arrows whistled through the air, arcing through the night's sky and descending on the charging assassins. Asher felt as if he could discern every individual arrow, allowing him to judge the gap between the projectiles.

If he could sense all that, then so could they.

The arrows rained down amid the hundreds of Arakesh. Asher observed it all through his excited senses in dismay. The older, more experienced assassins flew, twirled and twisted their bodies out of the way of the arrows, while those unsure of their extra senses fell under the barrage. Thankfully there were many who couldn't avoid them, due to their close proximity. The Arakesh just weren't trained to fight in such numbers.

There was no time to think of anything else. The Arakesh poured into the courtyard as a river of death, their numbers funnelled by the narrow entrance.

Asher decided to use the only other weapon he had that gave him the advantage against such numbers. With their blades only feet away, the ranger extended his hand and willed the assassins to be pushed back. A wave of magic energy surged from his palm and battered the horde, breaking bones and tearing muscles.

Those on the fringes of the mob managed to stay on their feet and continue their charge towards Asher.

Just as he had taught Elaith about the advantage of having the longer sword, Asher now took his own advice and swiped his broadsword horizontally. The long blade sliced open the bellies of two Arakesh and parried the blade of a third. The ranger went on the attack and smashed the spiked pommel into the assassin's face repeatedly. They didn't get back up.

His keen senses detected the multitude of blades coming for him, as well as the angles at which they were pointed. Asher's actions became hard to follow when he contorted his body in every direction to avoid the strikes, while simultaneously parrying others and cutting through those too slow to parry him.

Arakesh fell all around him, their bodies piling up. A metallic scent filled his nostrils, as the pools of blood collected at his feet. The ranger was more than aware that some of that blood was his own. He had already been cut on almost every limb.

Asher dodged, ducked and evaded blades from all around him, always calculating his counter attacks. A dozen of the assassins had run past him in the melee and headed into West Fellion in search of easier prey.

Still, the ranger remained.

Nathaniel fired arrow after arrow into the charging mass of assassins below. With only one way inside the keep, they were funnelled into a neat line that was easy to target. Reyna put him to shame with her speed and accuracy - for every arrow he let fly, the elf loosed two.

"Oh no..." Faylen's words could just be heard through the rain.

The Graycoat followed her gaze to Adellum Bövö, who was standing in the middle of the running assassins. The dark elf raised both of his hands towards West Fellion and created two black holes in the middle of the charging army.

Faylen placed her bow on her back and unsheathed her elven scimitar. Nathaniel didn't understand until he saw the Arakesh run through the black holes and disappear. Before he saw them, the knight heard his fellow Graycoats screaming and roaring, as they drew their swords farther down the wall on each side.

"He's opening portals!" Reyna moved away from the edge and jumped the gap between the inner and outer walls with a single bound - a jump that Nathaniel could not make.

The princess fired a series of arrows down the line, where the Arakesh were emerging atop the wall. Dozens ran out of the dark portals and fell between the gap in the walls, each a victim of the elf's deadly precision.

"Stay with Reyna!" Faylen dashed between the scurrying knights, sword in hand. The elf was soon past the Graycoats and face-to-face with the Arakesh.

Nathaniel ordered Elaith to follow him farther up the wall, to reach the bridge. Reyna continued to pick off the assassins, while Faylen weaved between them, dancing with her sword.

As the knights crossed the small bridge, Nathaniel dared to look to his right, where Asher was somehow stemming the flow of assassins. The old ranger moved in a way the Graycoat had never seen before. The red cloth that covered his eyes did little to conceal the fury that clouded his face. Limbs and heads flew all around him, yet the ranger defied the odds and continued to fight. Nathaniel wanted to be down there with him, but Reyna was just as big a target for the Arakesh since she was felling them with every arrow.

By the time they reached the princess, new portals had been opened inside the keep and assassins with bows began to pick off Graycoats fighting atop the walls.

"Cover me!" Reyna pointed at the Arakesh climbing the inner wall and charging up the steps towards them. The elf pulled another arrow from her quiver and shot an assassin in the eye before his blade could touch Faylen on the other side.

"Form two tiers," Nathaniel said to Elaith. "Any that get past me don't get past you, understand?"

Elaith hefted her sword and stood defiantly in front of Reyna.

The clash of steel and cries of death echoed across the entire fort.

Adellum's arrows were easy to spot since any soul unlucky enough to be struck by them was flung into the distance, as if hit by a giant's club.

Nathaniel let fly another arrow before dropping the bow to the floor in favour of his sword. He roared, preparing himself mentally for battle. These were no ordinary warriors he was about to face. There was something terrifying about an enemy that clearly couldn't see him and yet had uncanny sight, as it were.

His fear triggered a memory of his father and one of the last conversations they had before his final departure from Longdale. With such little time together, Nathaniel's father had always tried to impart any wisdom he might have.

"*Fear can be a powerful tool, son,*" Tobin Galfrey had said. "*Respect it. Listen to it. Fear will keep your wits about you while others run headlong into peril. But I tell you this...*" His father had leaned down and gripped his son by the arm. "*When you're surrounded by enemies and the only option left to you is fight or die, fear becomes irrelevant - it has no use. You give it all you have and you live or give it all and you die. If that day should ever come, just make certain that you have more to give than they do.*"

"*How do I do that, Pa?*"

"*It always helps to have something to fight for, son.*" Tobin had ruffled his son's hair affectionately.

Nathaniel looked back, with a second to spare, and locked eyes with Reyna. He finally had something to fight for besides his own life.

The first Arakesh made the mistake of trying to confuse Nathaniel with a flip through the air. It was a classic misdirection technique, designed to make the opponent wonder whether they were about to be kicked, punched or stabbed.

The Graycoat knew the assassin would immediately go for the stabbing option and stepped into the jump, without fear of being kicked. The Arakesh had clearly never seen his victim move so boldly and was unable to bring his blades about quickly enough. Nathaniel performed a single clean swipe of his sword and cut the assassin across the abdomen and chest. The man was dead before he hit the floor.

The second attacker was propelled from the wall by an arrow from Reyna's bow. The princess was obviously finding it hard to choose between the Arakesh attacking the knight and her mentor. Faylen, however, was cutting her way towards the portal, flipping and jumping over the assassins with graceful ease. Those that didn't suffer her blade were kicked from the wall or beaten back by a strong elven fist.

Nathaniel waded into his own group of attackers, stepping over the two dead bodies as he did. The next pair came for him at the same time, with four blades diving towards him from different directions.

The knight didn't calculate his actions, he simply reacted to survive. A swift kick knocked the closest fire-pit towards the Arakesh, spilling the hot coals across the wet stone. The fire blazed at their feet and penetrated the darkness of their blindfolds. Like before, the transition for their senses was disorientating and caused the assassins to swing their swords blindly.

Nathaniel speared the assassin to his left, driving his sword through the man's sternum until his hilt could go no further, and continued to drive the man from the wall, allowing the Arakesh to slide from his blade. Nathaniel spun on the spot and swiped his blade across the next assassin's neck, decapitating her with one blow.

The Graycoat didn't see men and women before him, only Arakesh - killers who would take Reyna from him and murder Elaith without thought.

There was no reprieve. Another assassin was already moving to take their place and had his blade held high, ready to come down hard on Nathaniel's head. The knight misjudged his footing, however, and slipped on the wet stone, falling to one knee. At the last second, he was able to hold his sword over his head and block the downward strike.

In such close proximity, the assassin now had the advantage, for while Nathaniel parried the heavy attack from above, the Arakesh had the perfect opening to impale the Graycoat with his second blade.

The thrust never came.

Instead, the assassin toppled backwards with a West Fellion sword sliding out of his chest. Elaith pulled her sword free, letting the assassin fall, before dropping back to cover the gap between Nathaniel and Reyna. The two knights shared a nod, Nathaniel's one of thanks.

The Graycoat shook the rain from his eyes and turned back to the steps. More were coming.

Nathaniel paused, seeing Ro Dosarn on the outer wall in the distance. The assassin who had impaled him was now cutting through other Graycoats with ease. The knight started for the bridge until he caught himself. He couldn't leave Reyna so vulnerable and Elaith alone to defend her. Allowing his rage to grow, he directed it towards the oncoming Arakesh. Ro Dosarn would just have to wait.

Jai Hadrok ran through the portal and emerged inside a large courtyard, inside West Fellion. Through his eyes, Alidyr could see the smaller courtyard beyond the stables, where the main gates used to be. What a sight that was...

Asher, a single man and older than most of the Arakesh sent to West Fellion, stood defiantly between both entrances, his sword swinging about him with incredible precision.

Every now and then the ranger would unleash a fireball or a wave of magical energy that would push the horde back. Between Paldora's Gem and the red cloth around his eyes, Asher was a force to be reckoned with.

Alidyr thought about entering the fray and cutting down the ranger, leaving the ring to be taken from his dead body. But, the elf looked at the hands of the human body he possessed and thought twice about it. He would be slower than if he were fighting himself. There was a good chance that Asher would best him by the number of bodies he was quickly piling up, and Alidyr only possessed the Arakesh so that he might better observe the battle.

The elf hadn't become Valanis's general by wading into every battle he came across. Besides, he thought, the ranger couldn't sustain that level of energy indefinitely. He would soon fall and Adellum would recover the gem.

"Asher! Get out of there!" The cry came from a blonde elf standing on the inner wall, above the main gate.

Princess Reyna Sevari...

The elf was firing arrows into the small courtyard, thinning the masses that poured in to fight the ranger. Across from her were two Graycoats that appeared to be protecting the elf from the advancing Arakesh. Perhaps there was a little fun to be had after all.

Alidyr ran to the stables and used what agility Jai Hadrok had to run up the corner pole and onto the wooden roof. Directly in front of him was a small jump up to the inner wall, where a young female Graycoat stood, ready for battle. Alidyr could see the inexperience in the girl and knew killing her would be easy. Then, a blade into the back of the older Graycoat would leave the princess vulnerable.

"Nathaniel!" The younger knight had spotted Jai Hadrok to her right.

"Stop him!" the older knight shouted back, as he fended off two assassins.

The young knight found her courage and jumped down onto the stables roof. Through Jai's mouth, Alidyr smiled menacingly. Victory was assured and the gem would soon be his to gift to his master, freeing Valanis once and for all. The elf was in a playful mood and decided to take his time with the girl.

The young Graycoat approached him with caution and her sword pointed out in front of her. Alidyr slowly circled her, his swords lowered, showing no signs of concern. Even with a human body he could easily best this child.

The girl dashed towards him, but the elf could see the feint and simply moved aside, not bothering to raise his blades for a blow that would never come. Surprisingly, the knight tucked into a roll and slid from the edge of the roof, using her hand to hang off the lip for a second, before dropping into the stables below.

Alidyr frowned and looked over the edge, but the girl was gone, off to cower in some hole somewhere, no doubt.

The sound of Arakesh dying on the wall brought his attention around. The older knight, Nathaniel, was managing to hold back the assassins from reaching the princess. The human showed great skill for, well, a human. The Graycoat displayed more than one injury and still continued to hold his own, much like the traitorous Asher.

Alidyr ran along the roof and jumped onto the inner wall. First, he would fell the knight, then he would cut the princess's throat. The Graycoat didn't even know there was an enemy at his back, so busy was he fighting the others.

Hot coals and licking flames littered the ground between him and Nathaniel, where a fire-pit had been knocked over. Alidyr stalked behind his prey, walking over the coals, already visualising the short-sword slipping between the man's vertebrae.

"Oi!"

Alidyr spun around, cursing his own arrogance. The young Graycoat had climbed back up the stables and onto the wall, flanking him. In her hand was a small pouch, tightly bound. Now it was *she* who wore the menacing smile.

The elf raised his swords to end the silly little girl's life when the Graycoat flicked her wrist holding the pouch. The bag dropped into the flames and exploded with a brilliant flash of light. Jai's senses were exceeded beyond their limit, blinding him in every way.

Flames clung to his legs and licked at his belt, as the man floundered in pain. Alidyr found the air sucked from his lungs, when the girl drove her sword through his chest, dropping him to his knees.

Hundreds of miles away, Alidyr's real body was flung from the circle of runes, leaving the reeling elf to clutch at his chest with the memory of the pain. He panted and wheezed in the dim glow of his chamber, thankful for the privacy.

Alidyr crawled back to the enchanted circle and reached out for one of the remaining nineteen that he could possess.

There appeared to be an unlimited supply of Arakesh charging forth from the portal. Faylen did her best to keep the Graycoats alive but, for the most part, the elf continued to fight her way towards the portal.

She parried a blow to her right, while extending her hand to the left and conjuring a fireball to knock another from the wall. A quick duck and a spin on one knee brought her up beside the Arakesh, where Faylen quickly slashed across the woman's abdomen, cutting through the armour with ease before whipping her scimitar out the other side.

The elf slid on her knees across the wet stone and popped up amid three unsuspecting Arakesh. Their extra senses allowed them to react quicker than Faylen would have liked, but it did them no good. The elf parried all three assassins with her scimitar, before spinning like a fallen leaf on the wind. Her blade slashed and hacked, as her feet kicked out to the left and right. By the time her feet touched the floor again, all three were dead. The surrounding Graycoats stared at her, awestruck.

"We have to close that portal! With me!" Her call rallied the knights behind her.

They ran as a single battering ram, towards the emerging assassins. At the last second, Faylen skipped and hopped along the buttress of the wall, gaining height over her adversaries. She came to land behind the first line of Arakesh, her actions distracting the front line long enough for the Graycoats to hammer through and cut them down.

The elf took note of several cuts and bruises that continued to appear on her body, but she never stopped to check their severity.

When at last Faylen was standing before the abyss-like portal, she fired a static burst of lightning at the Arakesh running through the barrier. The man was flung back into the field below, out of sight.

The elf immediately dropped her scimitar and raised both of her hands towards the portal, calling on her innate magic to close the doorway. A Graycoat dashed to her side and plunged his sword into another assassin trying to pass through. The magic that had opened the portal was powerful, that much she could feel from her efforts.

A final scream accompanied her desperate efforts to seal the portal. Faylen's shoulders sagged as blood trickled out of her nose, exhausted as she was. The cheers of triumph behind her were barely audible over the ringing in her ears.

A man and woman helped her up and handed the scimitar back. From her vantage, she could see another portal within the keep - Arakesh funnelled out of the inky abyss on the far side of the main gate. She would close it... if her legs would move.

Reyna danced between flying arrows, as she continued to rain down her own on the Arakesh that charged through the main gate. Her efforts made Asher's battle just manageable, thinning their numbers enough to keep the ranger on his feet.

Never before had she been so impressed with another's fighting ability. The princess had seen some of the best fighters her kind had to offer in Elandril, but none could stand against so many and never waver. The ranger fought as a man possessed by Krayt, the god of war, himself and all with a blindfold over his eyes.

Nathaniel and Elaith fought valiantly behind her, keeping the assassins at bay. But her support of Asher had gained her the attention of others on the outer wall. Six Arakesh broke away from the battle and made for the bridge that connected the two walls.

Reyna notched arrow after arrow and let loose with deadly accuracy. With the help of their, so-called, Nightseye elixir, five of the assassins were able to evade the barrage of arrows, flipping and twisting their bodies as they ran. The man at the back, however, came out of his roll too soon and caught an arrow in the throat, halting his charge indefinitely.

Reyna strode towards them and crossed the wall. She stole a glance at Asher below. The ranger flew about like a wild man, jumping off the walls and diving into the fray. If he could hold so many, then an elf could certainly defeat five Arakesh. The princess kept her stride fluid and her sight fixed on the distance, never giving away her intentions.

Her hand tightened around the grip of the bow, moments before the first of the assassins came at her with his blades. Reyna swayed her body to the left by just a few inches and avoided the slice of the steel.

The elf continued to walk into the group of killers, paying no heed to the first attacker. Now, she was surrounded by the five and felt that familiar calmness that filled her body in battle. Her body knew what to do; she simply had to listen to it.

Reyna flipped her bow with incredible dexterity and battered aside two of her attackers' swords while bending her torso downwards to bring her leg out behind her. The first attacker was not only forced back but lifted from his feet when Reyna's foot slammed into his chest. The elf felt the man's ribs cave in before he fell into the courtyard that Asher was turning into a mass grave.

Without stopping, the princess snapped her body back and brought her powerful leg out in front of her, push-kicking another Arakesh off the other side of the wall and through the roof, into the stables.

Her bow came up, again and again, to deflect and parry their short-swords, often following them up with a swift punch to knock them back and give her room.

Using a technique her mother had shown her, Reyna twisted the bow allowing her to hook the string over the back of an assassin's head. The princess pulled the bow back, bringing the man's head with it, where she then thrust her fist into his nose. The assassin's head snapped back and he fell into the closest fire-pit, tipping the bowl over with him. He screamed and rolled around in an attempt to douse the flames, only to accidentally roll off the wall.

The remaining two didn't appear deterred by her fighting prowess and came for her still. Reyna drew her scimitar at the last moment and twisted her body between the two assassins, narrowly missing both of their attacks.

Once on the other side, the elf dropped down low and spun around with her sword out-stretched. The two Arakesh were helpless to stop her from cutting out their legs and forcing them to their knees, leaving them vulnerable to a deadly slash of elven steel.

The breaking of wood to the left caught her attention, as the Arakesh who had fallen through the stables clambered back out. Reyna sheathed her scimitar and reached for another arrow when the Arakesh was killed by another's.

Nathaniel stood above the main gate with his bow in hand.

He cast an eye over the dead assassins at her feet with an impressed look. Elaith fought on behind him, making short work of the Arakesh with her Talo spices.

"Don't just stand there. Keep moving!" Faylen called from the outer wall. Reyna's mentor and a gathering of Graycoats were charging through the assassins and heading for the portal on the far side.

"We need to help Asher!" Nathaniel looked down at the court-yard with disbelief. "Elaith!" The young knight turned from her victory and followed him down the steps.

Reyna was torn between helping them and offering her magical assistance to Faylen. She was like a mother to her, and the need to protect her mentor was natural, but Faylen's talents with a sword were also undeniable. The elf would no doubt succeed in closing the portal as well as killing any who stood between her and it. Her friends, on the other hand, were about to face unfavourable odds, odds she could help tip with her bow.

The princess dropped onto the stables roof and deftly flipped onto the muddy ground. At least forty dead Graycoats littered the ground where Adellum's arrow had devastated the gates.

Nathaniel and Elaith were quick to join her, only stopping briefly to bring down a single Arakesh foolish enough to challenge them.

"Don't you ever run out of arrows?" Nathaniel glanced over her full quiver.

"No. It's enchanted." Had she not been so cold and exhausted in the downpour, Reyna might have laughed at the Graycoat's surprised expression.

"By all the gods..." Nathaniel's attention was then wholly captured by the events inside the small courtyard.

The number of Arakesh bodies that had piled up was becoming a hindrance to those still trying to fight the ranger. The rainwater that ran between the stables was red with all the blood that poured from the courtyard.

Reyna was unsure whether to help or simply stand and watch the ranger. Asher moved with implausible speed, a testament to his endurance and lifetime of training. His broadsword thrust, cut, stabbed, sliced and hacked at anything that moved within those walls.

Through blood and rain, Asher's blindfold was plastered to his eyes. The ranger had to be light on his feet now, to avoid tripping over the bodies that piled around him.

As the fight wore on, he became more and more aware of the injuries he had sustained. A particular slash across his back had made certain manoeuvres hard to pull off and had forced him to adjust his fighting style. A cut across his left thigh had stopped him from using that leg to kick or jump.

The key to surviving, he had found, was to ensure that every swipe of his sword killed more than one Arakesh at once. The ranger was sure his spiked pommel would be blunt by the time the fight was over. He had lost count of how many faces and bones he had broken with it.

He was only partially aware of the dagger protruding from his shoulder...

As suddenly as it started, the barrage of attacks came to an end and Asher found himself with no one trying to kill him. The surrounding Arakesh slowly backed off, as if the pack of hyenas had realised they couldn't bring down the lion.

"Come on!" Asher screamed, his bloodlust at its apex.

Still, the Arakesh continued to back off and part down the middle. Asher's extra senses discovered the reason before any ordinary senses would have. Striding through the centre of the horde was Adellum Bövö and his magnificent bow.

The fire from the moat cast the general in a malevolent light as he passed into the courtyard, his vibrant eyes, shining from within his black hood, fixed on Asher.

Without warning, the elf raised a hand and let loose spell after spell of fire, ice and lightning. Every spell dissipated or deflected around Asher's body, protected as he was by Paldora's Gem.

"You are the ranger!" Adellum announced. The elf looked down at the stacks of bodies around them, but any expression was concealed behind his mask.

Asher sized up the dark figure and knew he was outmatched. The fight thus far had exhausted him to a point he was only now starting to feel since he had stopped. The injuries he had sustained would only slow him down and the elf would be sure to inflict more.

Of course, all that was moot if Adellum decided to use his bow.

Asher had deflected arrows before with his sword, but an arrow from that bow would cut him and his sword in half.

Asher's heightened senses could hear the elf's heart beating beneath his chest. It was slow and steady, and easily the loudest beating of any heart he had ever heard. The ranger likened it to thunder. The magic that surrounded and penetrated the dark elf gave off a static charge that Asher could feel against his skin.

The battle continued to rage across the walls and deeper within West Fellion's keep. Only those within the courtyard had stopped to watch these two warriors collide. Asher could sense Reyna, Nathaniel and Elaith behind him, standing between the stables. More than that, he could hear the tension in all three of their bows, ready to let fly their arrows at Adellum.

"Give me the gem and your death will be swift," Adellum continued.

"The dead have no need for trinkets..." Asher raised his sword with a grimace to match his threat.

"As you wish." Adellum almost sounded entertained.

Both man and elf made for one another, Asher with his sword raised high and Adellum with his bow kept low. The ranger predicted how the elf would attack him, but was simply too slow to do anything about it. Adellum jumped and turned in mid-air, bringing his outstretched leg up behind him, and slammed into Asher's chest.

The ranger didn't know at which point he had dropped his sword, but by the time he had stopped rolling backward and come to a stop, it was no longer in his hand.

Through the sodden ground, his body had created a trail on his journey out of the courtyard. Somewhere along the way his red blindfold had come off his head and been left behind, along with the dagger protruding from his shoulder. Now the cold rain pelted his face, as he lay in the mud on his back.

"Asher!" Reyna cried. The princess, along with a helping hand from Nathaniel, picked the ranger up and steadied him on his feet.

Seeing Adellum with his human eyes only worked to make the shadowy figure appear more menacing. The dark elf strode through the entrance and stepped over his previous victims with little care.

Asher could now see the ornate recurve bow up close and wasn't thankful for it. The ends of each limb were adorned with fine blades, making the bow perfect for close melee, as well as a projectile weapon.

While the ranger had been mid-flight, the other three had fired their arrows at the dark elf, only to see their projectiles batted away with the wave of a hand. With that in mind, Asher left his own bow where it was; Adellum wasn't going to be beaten by an arrow.

Perhaps more troubling, Adellum continued to march towards them and Asher had no idea what his plan of action should be.

"I will have that ring, Ranger."

Asher ignored his friends' curious looks and focused on the approaching problem. His sword glistened in the rain, some feet behind the dark elf. The ranger pulled free his rune-sword from its sheath on his back, but the moon was low in the sky now, leaving the shining silvyr to appear as any other steel.

Though shorter than his broadsword, the weight of the rune-covered blade felt more familiar in his hand. He had trained and fought for decades with short-swords, though none as deadly and strong as the one he now wielded.

Never one for words or banter before a fight, Asher dived into a flat-out sprint for the elf. Before they could collide, the ranger used his momentum to spring into a leap, while raising his sword high to come down in the fashion of a scorpion's tail.

Adellum swayed to the side at the last possible second, leaving Asher to cut through nothing but air. The dark elf was quick to follow with his own attack and swiped his magnificent bow, to remove the ranger's head using one of the limb-blades.

Anticipating this counterattack, Asher had already dropped into a roll and come up with his back to the fort's entrance. He could only hope that the Arakesh would spectate rather than get involved.

The dark elf spun to face Asher, leaving his own back exposed to Reyna, Nathaniel and Elaith. The four quickly surrounded Adellum and attacked as one. Unfortunately, Adellum had the mind of a tactician and, not just any tactician, but one who had coordinated battles ten times the size of West Fellion's siege.

Before any could touch him with a blade, the dark elf lashed out with a swift side-kick that sent Elaith flying towards the central courtyard, in front of the main keep. Adellum had clearly decided that the young knight would be a hindrance and that a simple kick would remove the potential thorn. This, of course, made Nathaniel hesitate and look back to check on his ward. That slight lapse gave Adellum all the time he needed to parry both Asher's and Reyna's attack before spinning around to back-hand Nathaniel. The Graycoat flipped around in the air and flew through a stable door, into the mud.

In only a few seconds, Adellum had gone from being attacked by four adversaries to two. As if he was wielding a spear, the dark elf used his bow to deflect their blades, as well as using it to counterattack. The limb-blades cut through the rain with a speed that Asher was finding hard to track without his blindfold.

Reyna danced around the ancient elf, with her scimitar slashing at every opening she could find, only to be evaded and parried by Adellum's bow.

Asher used his free hand to grip the mighty bow and force it down at the same moment Reyna whipped her scimitar across Adellum's shoulder plate. The blade failed to find skin, but the blow was strong enough to push the dark elf back, allowing Asher the room to jump and bring his head down into Adellum's nose.

The dark elf's head snapped back and the ranger kicked him in the stomach. Asher gave no quarter and chased the elf, as he rolled back towards the larger courtyard. Beyond him, Elaith was starting to stir with her arms propping her up.

Adellum shot up from the ground with his hood swept from his head and his mask pulled down. The General was as pale as a ghost underlaid with dark veins beneath the skin. His bald head was laced with tattoos, in the ancient script, that curled around his pointed ears. With a gloved hand, he mopped the trickle of blood that ran from his nose and observed the red liquid as if he hadn't seen it for an age.

Supernatural eyes bored into Asher before his next attack. Adellum snarled and knocked Asher's sword aside, following through to slice his right leg. The ranger would have yelled in pain had the dark elf not punched him in the jaw, forcing him to the ground.

The night was illuminated with a blinding flash when purple lightning streaked across the courtyard and slammed into Adellum with enough power to push him back. The elf's feet skidded across the ground until he lifted his hand to form a magical barrier.

Reyna screamed with fury, her arms outstretched, as she unleashed her magic on the general. The lightning began to spark around Adellum as his barrier grew stronger. With slow footsteps, the dark elf ploughed towards the princess, his black cloak pushed out behind him.

"Silly little princess!" Adellum roared over the rain and lightning spell. "You are throwing a stone at a mountain!"

The dark elf expelled a blast of energy that ran through the current of Reyna's spell and struck her entire body. The princess was flung into the archway behind her, where her head slammed into the stone with enough force to knock her out.

"Reyna!" Nathaniel came running out of the stables and dropped to the ground at her side.

Asher got to his feet and stood between them and Adellum. Smoke and steam rose from the general's armour, but still he stood, his gaze flitting from the princess to the ranger.

"Why protect them?" Adellum asked. "The elf is nothing to you. The Graycoat would see you dead. You could have led the Arakesh to countless victories. Instead, you live like filth, standing between that which cannot be beaten..." The dark elf looked past

Asher, to Reyna and Nathaniel. "...and that which was born to be beaten."

"Why don't you come over here and I'll show you what beaten looks like?" Asher defied his aches and pains and straightened his back, broadening his shoulders.

"Fool..." Adellum came at the ranger with his bow high.

The limb-blade was halted mid-air, only a foot from Asher's face, by an elven scimitar. Faylen delivered a swift kick to the general's midriff, knocking him farther into the courtyard.

"That's twice I've saved you from a falling blade." Faylen smirked through the rain.

Asher had just enough energy to smile back before they attacked the dark elf as one.

Alidyr had taken to the shadows on a high beam, in the corner of the courtyard. He now possessed a female assassin whose name escaped him. They were all tools for Valanis, nothing more.

He looked on as the Graycoats put up a valiant effort to defend their home against insurmountable odds. Many had fled or taken up hiding within the keep now, their fate more obvious to them than others. It didn't matter. Wiping out the Graycoats was a side-note compared to their true cause for attacking.

Paldora's Gem was only feet away.

Asher and the elf known as Faylen attacked Adellum from all sides, seeking a gap in his defences. It was his counterattacks they had to watch for. The blades attached to his bow could tear through any armour.

The fact that Adellum hadn't used any arrows was testament to the fun he was having. The dark elf was enjoying the thrill of a real fight for a change. For too long they had stuck to the shadows and operated in secret. Now the Hand of Valanis would show Illian what the power of Naius could really do.

In the far corner of the courtyard, he could see the princess was coming to. The over-familiarity between her and knight was clear to see.

The Arakesh began to gather in the archways and atop the walls to watch the fight. The heroes were completely boxed into the court-yard with one of the deadliest warriors in all of Verda.

Alidyr observed the ranger land several blows as well as a significant cut across Adellum's hip. The ranger's prowess gave the head of the Hand pause, wondering if they weren't the ones who were trapped in West Fellion with him...

Nathaniel cupped Reyna's face in his hands and thanked the gods when her eyes opened. He kissed her tenderly before she sat up and looked at him, dazed.

"Stay here." Nathaniel put the scimitar in her hands and only stood up once her grip tightened.

The Graycoat hesitated when he saw the dozens of Arakesh gathering at the edges of the yard. They filled the walls above them and blocked the archways. All were watching Asher and Faylen battle the dark elf.

He would be damned if he didn't lend his own sword to the fray. They would deal with the Arakesh when the time came. Nathaniel jumped into the opening between Asher and Faylen with his sword pulled back. The knight's thrust was parried by the elf and sent dangerously close to Asher's head.

For every blow they landed, Adellum struck them twice, often drawing blood. More than one fist found its way into Nathaniel's face or chest, knocking him back.

Exhaustion was setting in. The Graycoat had no idea how Asher had maintained such stamina, especially with twenty years on Nathaniel. Faylen, however, appeared as if she could keep fighting for hours.

"Give me the ring, Ranger," Adellum commanded between attacks, "and I promise your friends will be granted a quick death."

Nathaniel didn't have time to think about Adellum's strange request, and continued to search for an opening.

Elaith found it first.

The young knight appeared from nowhere and jumped onto Adellum's back, hooking her legs around his waist and clinging to him like a leech. The dark elf struggled under her added weight and became off-balance. Elaith pulled an arrow free from the general's quiver and jammed it into his neck until half of the shaft was buried beneath his flesh.

Adellum roared and dropped his bow to the ground. Asher didn't hesitate to kick the weapon away, before turning his sword against the elf. Elaith was thrown from his back when the ranger thrust his short-sword into Adellum's gut, penetrating the gap between his armoured plates.

Faylen came in at another angle and plunged her scimitar between the armour around his chest. The dark elf dropped to his knees when Nathaniel brought his own sword to bear. The Graycoat drove his blade with both hands down into Adellum's chest so that it cut into his gut.

All was silent, but for the pouring rain.

Adellum became very still, resting on his knees with three swords skewered through his body and an arrow in his neck. Nathaniel dared to hope that they had defeated the dark elf.

That was when Adellum began to laugh.

It wasn't the laugh of a man about to die, delirium setting in, or even the laugh of a man with three blades stuck in his body. It was the laugh of a person who knew they had already won...

The dark elf looked up at them. "Did you think it would be that easy? I have been granted power by Valanis, the herald of the gods themselves! You possess no weapon capable of killing me!" Adellum's roar was infused with enough magic to create a bubble of energy that exploded from his core, slamming into Nathaniel and the others.

They were each flung, along with their weapons, across the courtyard. Adellum rose to his feet, laughing as he did. It was his laugh that disguised the sound of a bow string being pulled taut. Nathaniel looked up from the ground to see Reyna wielding Adellum's bow.

The princess's aim was trained on the elf. "How about this weapon?"

The arrow flew through the air, cutting the raindrops, until it found its mark in the centre of Adellum's chest. The dark elf was launched into the wall of the main keep, where he remained, pinned to the stone. If the general roared, it was drowned out by the expulsion of energy that rocked the very foundations of West Fellion.

A mighty crack shot up the keep's wall, breaking the stone.

Waves of energy continued to pour out of Adellum, who clawed at the arrow in his chest. His movements began to slow in proportion to the waves of energy, which increased in intensity. More cracks appeared along the walls, each stretching out from the epicentre where Adellum was pinned.

Reyna was by Nathaniel's side in moments, helping him up, as the others gathered around them. The giant crack grew up the side of the keep and along the central tower. The Arakesh ran for the main entrance, sensing the same doom as Nathaniel.

"He's going to explode!" the Graycoat shouted over the humming waves of energy that pulsed from Adellum.

The archway between them and the main gate collapsed under a ton of stone and flailing Arakesh bodies. If they sought shelter inside the keep, it would surely fall on them. There was no way out.

"I'm too weak to create another portal..." Faylen said with dismay.

They could only look on as West Fellion continued to crumble around them. Soon the tower would collapse on top of them, or Adellum would unleash all of his magic and wipe them out.

"Asher..." Faylen gripped the ranger's arm.

"I don't know how to do that." Asher replaced the silvyr blade on his back.

"Just think about where you want to go! We need to reach Elethiah! Think about it and command the world to take you there!"

Giant slabs of stone were already coming loose and falling into the yard. The group was forced to huddle together to avoid the debris.

"Do it now!"

Adellum's screams could no longer be heard amid the waves of energy. His body hung limply against the keep wall and the veins beneath his skin glowed hot red.

Asher raised his hand and closed his eyes. Paldora's Gem knew no bounds, its power expelling the rain from the black hole that opened in front of the group. Lightning sparked from the edges of the abyss and the rain continued to fall as it should.

Nathaniel had never seen anything like it before, but if Faylen's words were anything to go by, Elethiah was on the other side of it. He didn't want Elaith to go to that place, but anywhere had to be better than this courtyard.

"Run!" Faylen grabbed Reyna's arm and rushed her through the portal, followed by Elaith and Asher.

Nathaniel took one last look at the place where he had grown up. West Fellion had given him the tools and skills he needed to survive, to be a knight of worth... But it had never been his home.

The Graycoat ran through the portal only a moment before Adellum's body exploded with the magic of Naius, the shockwave taking all of West Fellion with it.

Alidyr pulled back from his acolyte's body as Adellum's death brought the entire fort down. The elf leaped to his feet and turned his table over in rage, spilling the water and sending scrolls flying into the air.

Adellum's death was significant, and the Hand would surely suffer for it, not to mention his bow was now in the hands of the princess. But, his death aside, Alidyr was furious that Paldora's Gem had escaped his grasp.

Still, there remained hope for his master's salvation. Faylen, the princess's mentor had instructed the ranger to open a portal to Elethiah. They meant to destroy Valanis. Alidyr had been studying magic for over a thousand years and knew better than most that, even with the gem providing Asher power, he would be too inexperienced to open a portal to Elethiah. No one ever opened their first portal and found themselves where they wanted to be.

There was still time.

CHAPTER 49
DRAGON'S REACH

Gideon looked up, between the canyon walls, to see the orange sky of dawn give way to a brilliant blue. There was nothing but cloudless skies in the south. The young mage found himself missing the cool winds and grey clouds that drifted over The Adean. He missed Korkanath.

The mage shook his head and brought his mind back to the present, not wanting to dwell on other things he missed, other people he missed.

The Red Mountains consumed the entire landscape for miles around them. There was little vegetation dotted around the canyon floor, but it could be considered lush in comparison to The Flat Wastes.

Gideon was just thankful for the shade. It would be midday before the light of the sun found his skin again. His usually pale skin had turned a shade of olive he had never experienced before.

"I can't feel my legs anymore." Gideon adjusted his position on the lizard's saddle, but it made no difference.

Galanör drained the last of his waterskin, squeezing the hide to get every last drop. The supplies attached to the scouts had provided them with more than enough food and water to see them through The Flat Wastes.

"When the midday sun graces the sky, we'll find shelter and rest for a while." Galanör appeared rejuvenated after finishing their trip across the desert with mounts and a good supply of water and food.

The canyon soon opened up to a valley as vast as an ocean, with rolling hills of desert sand and dusky red rock. The landscape's colour certainly earned its name.

Gideon noticed the falling stones to his right but failed to see what had caused the disturbance, thanks to the sweat that ran into his eyes. Whatever it was, his lizard began to express great concern. The beast reared its flat head and bellowed to its companion, who suddenly tried to turn around, against Galanör's wishes. Gideon fought with the reins to keep the animal under control until he saw what had spooked them.

"Sandstalkers!" the mage shouted.

Galanör turned in his saddle and pulled free one of his scimitars when he too saw the hideous creatures.

Gideon had seen Sandstalkers before, but they had been lighter in colour to blend in with the sand of The Arid Lands in Illian. These monsters were a dirty shade of red to allow for better camouflage.

Standing on six pincer-like legs, at eight-feet, the creatures' bodies were that of a spider until it formed up into a torso, not dissimilar from a man's. Two thin, but well muscled, arms extended from the vertical torso and ended in five long fingers, as razor sharp as any blade. The head was a grotesque amalgamation of man and spider, with two meaty fangs hiding a smaller mouth of serrated teeth.

Unfortunately, Sandstalkers were as fast as they were hideous.

Gideon counted fourteen standing on the ridge of the nearest dune, each stomping their sharp legs in anticipation of the meal to come. The lizards took no heed of their riders' directions and ran blindly into the valley.

The Sandstalkers needed no further assessment, seeing them

only as prey. Like a spell fired from a wand, all fourteen of the monsters belted across the dunes, kicking up clouds of sand behind them.

The two lizards panicked and collided into each other with enough force to knock Gideon and Galanör from their saddles. The mage rolled again and again through the sand until he landed awkwardly on a small rock.

"I really hate this place…" Gideon remarked through laboured breaths.

The ground shook under the thunderous footsteps of their lizards, who charged back towards the valley entrance. The line of Sandstalkers began to fill out with dozens more arriving from beyond the distant rises. Both man and elf were soon looking out over two hundred hungry Sandstalkers.

Gideon was adept at magic and Galanör skilled with a blade, but these monsters didn't fight like men. The elf's blades and his staff would not be enough to defeat an entire horde of Sandstalkers. Running, however, wasn't an option.

"We have to cross this valley," Galanör said with a determination that didn't match his expression.

"That's going to be a little difficult when I'm being digested in the bellies of a dozen Sandstalkers…" Gideon held his staff tight in his hands. The horde was charging up the rise towards them. "Maybe we could run a little bit?"

Galanör replied with a curt nod and turned to run with the mage. The two ran as fast as they could, though Gideon suspected Galanör was going deliberately slower.

Suddenly, shadows both swift and large crossed over the desert. Gideon looked up to see the underbellies of the two dragons that flew overhead. The mage recognised the light blue scales and the gold-speckled green hide of the younger dragons from the Malaysai arena.

"Look!" he exclaimed.

The dragons glided low to the ground and picked up both giant lizards between their two front claws. The reptilian mounts shrieked, but their cries were soon lost in the distance covered by the ascending dragons.

The dragons arced through the air and glided back towards them, at least a thousand feet high. As they followed their flight path, Gideon and Galanör realised that while the dragons were leaving, the Sandstalkers were fast approaching.

Though the horde had been given pause at the sight of two superior predators, they continued to charge for their prey while the dragons flew away, heading deeper into The Red Mountains.

The dragons had taken the lizards and left them for the Sandstalkers. The mage was left with a sinking feeling in his gut.

The beating of heavy wings preceded the stream of fire that rained down across the Sandstalkers' frontline. A shadow, as big as the two younger dragons combined, passed overhead before the ground shook beneath Gideon and Galanör.

The mage felt waves of confidence overwhelm him, feelings that he knew could not be his own. He was speechless in the shadow of the giant emerald dragon that came to land before them.

The dragon roared and reared up on its hind legs, its wings spread out, casting the entire horde in shadow. The Sandstalkers quickly turned around and ran for the safety of their underground nests, scattering across the valley.

The ground shook once more when the front legs dropped back to the ground. Galanör dug both of his scimitars into the ground and immediately bowed on one knee before the mightiest of creatures. Gideon continued to stand there, dumbstruck as two beautiful blue eyes took him in. A series of small horns ran along its head from its eyes, and one curving horn adorned the centre of its head.

"Kneel..." Galanör hissed beside him.

Before the mage could even collect his thoughts, the green dragon exploded into action and picked both of them up in its front claws. Galanör was just quick enough to retrieve his blades before they were swept away. They quickly gained height, leaving the valley and the mountains far below.

"Not this again!" Gideon clung to the green scales as tightly as he could, despite the dragon's already considerable grip.

They weren't flying very long before the dragon tucked in its wings and dived. Gideon was forced to take shallow breaths on the way down, though he spent most of his energy trying to ignore the ground that was rushing up to meet them.

As death looked sure to claim them, the dragon banked to the left and glided for several miles over the tops of pointed trees. Gideon could see from their height that The Red Mountains surrounded what could only be described as an oasis. A circle of grassland and forestry occupied a massive crater. In the distance, he could even see a river that crossed the expanse.

The dragon banked right and flapped its huge wings to gain more height, heading towards the centre of the oasis. The land was only feet below them now and Gideon began to worry about the speed at which the dragon continued to travel.

At the last second, great wings filled the air and the dragon arched back to slow down. The leathery wings rippled and became taut, similar to the sails of a boat in the wind.

The two back legs thundered into the ground and the dragon released them. Galanör's elven agility allowed him to gracefully turn his momentum into a roll until he found his feet. Gideon, on the other hand, tumbled over his own weight until he hit a particularly blunt rock.

It took a minute for the mage to gather his senses and find his footing, but Galanör appeared at his side and helped him up with a strong hand and a warm smile. Gideon could feel the same thing as the elf. Wherever they were, the feeling of being safe and satisfied filled his mind. The very air tingled with magic and, upon simple observation, Gideon could see why.

In the centre of the oasis, between the trees and boulders, giant hunks of rock the size of houses floated in the air. Thick roots grew over them and down into the mossy ground, but the rocks remained elevated. Even the trees appeared larger and healthier than any forest Gideon had ever seen or heard of.

A sharp expulsion of air behind them reminded the two companions that they weren't alone. They both turned to see the colossal emerald dragon that had brought them there. Despite its blood-stained teeth, Gideon at no point felt as if his life was in danger. Instead, the feeling of curiosity overcame him, and he could no longer tell whether his emotions were actually his or the dragon's.

"We did it, we found them..." He knew he sounded like a dazed idiot, but he didn't care; he was standing in front of a dragon!

"Welcome to Dragons' Reach." They were startled by the new voice that came from behind them. "I hope you weren't too attached to those lizards." A tall man of handsome features, in long blue robes, appeared from behind a tree. "I'm afraid Bravog and Ilargo are learning to hunt. Your mounts were easy prey." The man's waist-length blond hair moved in the breeze as he approached, revealing two pointed ears.

Galanör's mouth opened, but no words came out. Both elves stared at each other before the stranger took a moment to look over Gideon.

"Who are you?" the mage asked.

The stranger smiled and simply glanced at the enormous green dragon, who snorted and strode off into the clearing.

Gideon gasped when at least eight more dragons appeared from within the forest and the skies. The two dragons known as Bravog and Ilargo landed in front of the one who had saved them, with their dead lizards.

"What's wrong with it? Why's it leaving?" Gideon was easily distracted by the magnificent creatures.

The stranger smiled again. "What's wrong with *her*," he corrected. "That is Rainael the emerald star."

Both Gideon and Galanör turned to stare at the green dragon, who was now inspecting the dead lizards. Gideon thought he might burst with excitement.

"In the hierarchy that you understand, she would be considered queen." The stranger walked slowly to the edge of the clearing, before turning back to them.

It was hard to focus on him with a dozen dragons lounging in the distance.

"How is any of this possible?" Gideon gestured to the floating mountains of rock.

Galanör continued to simply stare blankly at the dragons and the stranger.

"Dragons are magical beings. They exude magic with their every heartbeat. When they gather in such numbers, their natural magic begins to affect the world physically."

As his explanation finished, at least three dozen dragons descended from the sky and landed in the clearing or on the floating rocks. Gideon looked up to see more flying in circles across the sky.

"There's so many..." the mage remarked.

"Yes, and one more recently..." The elf looked to the highest floating boulder, where a familiar black dragon lay curled up, alone. "Malliath heard the call of the younglings. When in distress they can hear each other across thousands of miles. Incredible beings. Unfortunately, I feel Malliath will require more time before we address his *unique* situation."

Galanör held out a hand to stop Gideon from continuing the conversation. "Who *are* you?"

The stranger smiled again. "Forgive me; it has been an age since I have conversed with another elf or human. My name is Adriel. I am the last Dragorn..."

CHAPTER 50
ECHOES OF THE PAST

The cool water washed over Asher's face and body, as he broke the surface of the lake. The water around him had turned red with all the blood running off him. It was impossible to say whose blood it all was, but a fair portion had certainly been his own.

While under the water, the ranger had taken the time to use the gem to heal his wounds once again. He walked up the bank and began to untie the knots that kept his various pieces of armour in place, leaving them where they fell. When he was left wearing only his trousers, Asher flexed his muscles, testing the power of the ring. He felt whole again.

When they emerged from the portal, the group had collapsed on the ground and slept right there, under the oak tree, until dawn. They had all been beyond the point of exhaustion after the battle at West Fellion.

Even now, Elaith sat with her back to the tree and her eyes closed. Nathaniel had removed many of his clothes to inspect the fresh wounds that marred his back and torso, while Reyna used clean rags, from Faylen's infinite sack, to mop up the blood, before she used her magic to heal the knight.

The elves had already healed each other, but even they appeared haggard around the edges. Reyna's spirits had been lifted when her owl arrived, though how it could always find the princess was a mystery to Asher. It made the ranger think of Hector and he wondered if he would ever see the horse again. If there was anything that cowardly beast of burden could do, it was run away.

The ranger looked past the trees, to the rise in the west. Elethiah was another two days' walk from the lake. As impressive as his ability was to open a portal, he had failed to get them all the way. The group was somewhere in The Moonlit Plains, between West Fellion and Elethiah.

"Wait." Nathaniel grabbed Reyna's wrists to stop her dabbing his ribs. "I have to know what's going on. How are you healed, *twice*? You walked into that lake with more injuries than all of us. Now, you look as good as new!"

Asher's glance at Faylen was noticed by Reyna. "What aren't you telling us?" the princess asked.

"I have Paldora's Gem." Asher replied simply, holding up the back of his hand to show them the crystal.

Reyna's mouth dropped and she stammered and stumbled over her words.

"How is that possible?" Nathaniel managed on her behalf.

Reyna strode across the grass and grabbed the ranger's hand to examine the gem closer.

"Don't touch it!" Faylen warned. "I believe the gem is firmly attached to Asher, though I know not why."

"It's smaller than I thought it would be," Reyna observed.

Faylen looked at Asher with a cocked eyebrow and a questioning expression.

"It's only a piece of the gem. I cut this part away before I even passed the trials at Nightfall." Asher took his hand back.

"Where's the rest?" the princess asked desperately.

"Lost," Faylen answered for him, though her disappointment wasn't hard to miss.

"I can't believe you've had Paldora's Gem this whole time and you didn't tell us!" Reyna exclaimed.

"Just as you kept it from us that the elves are planning to invade Illian?" Asher's counter-argument was enough to silence the princess, who only looked to Faylen in return.

"If the ring can heal you," Elaith said, "then why are you covered in scars?"

Asher looked down at the patchwork that marred his torso and arms. "I wasn't always in a position to use the ring, at least not without bringing attention to myself. That's why I got rid of the larger gem years ago; it was gaining me too much attention."

"How did you come by it?" Nathaniel asked again.

"I've had it since before I arrived at Nightfall. Everything before then is a haze of jumbled memories."

"This changes *everything*." Reyna was pacing now. "This changes everything. Don't you see?" the princess asked the group. "We have Paldora's Gem, or at least enough of it to make a difference. We can use it to enter Elethiah, past its wards."

Faylen nodded her head as if she had already come to that conclusion. "The ring and the bow will be of great use inside those walls," the older elf replied.

Adellum's powerful bow stood propped up against the oak tree, beside Elaith.

Asher suddenly felt very vulnerable without his broadsword. The blade was irretrievable now, buried under several tons of West Fellion's stone. As was his blindfold. He had always been loath to use it, but having it around his belt had offered comfort, like that of a child's blanket.

The ranger had already cleaned his silvyr sword, washing it in the lake to ensure no blood gathered in the runes. The hour-glass blade didn't look as ferocious as his broadsword, but it was just as deadly in his hands.

"Without horses, it's a two-day trek across The Moonlit Plains to Elethiah," Nathaniel offered. "We should leave soon."

"Agreed," Asher replied.

The group spent the morning preparing their gear and inspecting their weapons. It seemed Reyna had claimed the magical bow as her own after delivering the killing blow to Adellum. Asher made a fire to cook up some breakfast since he planned on walking until nightfall with no intentions of lingering on the plains.

The Moonlit Plains didn't belong to man.

"Here..." Faylen presented the ranger with a new cloak from within her enchanted chest. "It's not green like your old one, but it's clean and it'll keep you warm. I'm afraid I don't have any broadswords in my bag." The elf added the latter with a playful smile. So enjoyable was it that Asher couldn't help but smile back at her.

"Thank you." The ranger clipped the grey cloak over his leather shoulder plates and hung his quiver and sword over the top.

After eating, the group left the peaceful lakeside and headed south-west. They had a lot of ground to cover.

The companions walked across the plains unfettered, enjoying the sun that broke through the grey clouds. They walked in silence for most of the day, still somewhat in shock from the battle.

Elaith finally broke the tension with amusing stories from her time in Ameeraska. This eventually prompted the others to share stories of their own. Asher kept his tales to those that had taken place after leaving the Arakesh. The ranger wasn't too keen to dwell on those darker days.

The sun had begun to cast an orange glow over Illian when a gasp from Reyna caught the instant attention of her companions. Asher quickly joined them on the rise of the nearest hillock, where the princess crouched low.

"Look! Centaurs..." Reyna whispered, even though the creatures were far away.

Asher crouched low next to Nathaniel and instinctively reached out to pull Elaith down from her knees. The ranger could see from Nathaniel's expression that the knight understood the danger of being so close to a team of Centaurs. The elves simply looked on in wonder, showing a clear desire to interact with them.

"There are no Centaurs in Ayda," Reyna explained. "My mother spoke of them in the tales of old. Half-elf, half-horse..."

Asher had never thought of them being half-elf before, but it was known that Centaurs had pointed ears. The ranger cast the random thought aside and pulled back from the hillock. The Graycoats willingly joined him, but the elves remained fixed on the rise.

"We can't stay here," Nathaniel said. "It isn't safe."

"Why?" Faylen asked, struggling to take her eyes away from the galloping team.

Asher explained, "I don't know what creatures your stories tell of, but these Centaurs are not what you think they are. When your kind left Illian, they were hunted for years by man. Some still consider them to be the ultimate prize. These Centaurs are hunters now; they use bows and spears as we do. Anyone travelling on The Selk Road through The Moonlit Plains does so at their own peril. Most pay for an escort in Tregaran, on the edge of The Arid Lands, or Vangarth if they're travelling south."

"Our elders speak of a gentle race," Faylen replied solemnly. "Our people would commune with them often."

"They'd put an arrow through you before they realised you were an elf. That's if they even remember what an elf is..." Asher reached over his shoulder and absently checked the number of arrows he had left. Reyna, thankfully, had restocked all of their quivers from her own enchanted quiver before they left the lake.

"Come," the ranger bade. "I want us to reach The Unmar before we lose the sun."

The elves took a lasting look at the roaming Centaurs, before joining the humans on a longer path that would take them away from the creatures.

It was a cold night on the plains. The clouds had moved north and left the stars and a crescent moon in their place. Asher was grateful for his new cloak, which he pulled tight around him.

As usual, Elaith was the first to find sleep, nestled close to the fire. Faylen sat close to the ranger but said very little, wrapped up in her own cloak and blanket.

"It's happening!" Reyna exclaimed.

The princess sat inside the same blanket as Nathaniel and both watched The Moonlit Plains come to life with a fluorescent green glow.

"I've always wanted to see it," Reyna said with excitement.

Asher looked out at the glowing plains though, in truth, he was searching for any more teams of Centaurs. The illuminated fields made it much easier to spot anything moving through the grass.

"It was a gift for the Centaurs, from my ancestors," Reyna continued. "Under the light of the moon, the grass literally glows..." Nathaniel smiled and chuckled to himself. "Are you laughing at me?" Reyna asked playfully.

"It's just a nice change to have you explain something that I already know about," the knight replied with a coy smile. The elf poked him under the blanket and the two laughed some more.

There was clearly something building between the two, though whether it was beyond the physical, the ranger was yet to see. Asher was waiting for Faylen to intervene and separate the two, but her chastising never came. Instead, the elf stared into the flames of the fire with a grave look, a look the ranger had learned not to take for granted.

"What's wrong?" he asked.

"We are not the only ones trying to find a peaceful solution to this war." Faylen lowered her voice. "I worry about those that we cannot see, far from here. Every day I see ways in which Nalana's prophecy speaks the truth. With that in mind, I fear for Adilandra,

Reyna's mother. If she can rally the last of the dragons before the king does, and we can defeat Valanis in his frozen state, we can save so many."

"Tell me of this prophecy," Asher said a little too loudly, causing Nathaniel and Reyna to turn around in their blanket and observe the conversation.

Faylen looked at Reyna. "The Princess knows it better than I."

Reyna looked into the fire. "We call it the Echoes of Fate." The princess cleared her throat. "*These favoured elves fall and lose their way, as man's anger devours all dragons' fire. The immortal man is set to rise, bringing the dark one closer to his most dangerous desire.*

Paldora's celestial gem graces daylight sky, and in its beauty ordains calamity. Only alliance and trust between two shores offers an intimation of hope and a glimpse of eternity.

Children of fire and flame offer great promise, but only one perceives the time we will fall. As the gods recast their fortune and power, one will suffer the burden of destiny for all."

Asher took a deep breath and raised his eyebrows. To the ranger, prophecies were like old history tomes: lengthy and full of shit. He had met many folks who peddled such skills, and all turned out to be con-artists.

"You don't believe in prophecies?" Reyna asked, having seen his sceptical expression.

"You have to believe in the gods to believe in prophecies," Asher replied dryly.

"You sound like my father..." The princess didn't sound happy about that fact.

"He doesn't believe in it either?" Asher asked.

"No, which is even more ridiculous since it was his sister who spoke the words to him no less!" Reyna's anger was quick to rise, like so many of her elvish emotions.

"Nalana was his *sister*?" Asher felt his mind fighting through years of training and torment in Nightfall, trying to find the hazy memory that tugged at those words. "What's your father's name?"

"Elym... Elym Sevari," Reyna replied with curiosity in her voice.

Asher ignored the princess's look and continued to focus on the memory slowly rising to the surface.

"But you can use magic." Nathaniel returned the conversation to the ranger's lack of faith, completely oblivious to Asher's faraway look.

The memory gone, the ranger replied, "So? Magic is just another part of this world like this blade of grass." Asher plucked a piece of grass from beside him and held it up. "It doesn't mean the gods put it there."

"But her words have come true!" Reyna sat forward. "Nalana gave her prophecy *before* The Dragon War. *These favoured elves fall and lose their way, as man's anger devours all dragons' fire.* She told of how man would go to war with the dragons, and that our people would leave instead of staying and making things right."

Asher shrugged, unable to dispute the events surrounding The Dragon War prediction. "Well I hate to inform you, but there is no immortal man. We're lucky if we see seventy."

"It's probably not meant to be taken literally. Nalana's probably referring to the immortal reign of man in these lands, and that their presence here will bring Valanis back to power."

"*Only alliance and trust between two shores offers an intimation of hope...*" Faylen interjected. "Ayda... Illian." The elf put her fist to her breast before placing it against Asher's. "We might not understand every word of the Echoes, but some words are clearer than others. Only together can we free the world of Valanis's evil."

Asher couldn't argue with the sentiment, even if he didn't understand the concept of fate. The country would be crippled if the elves and men went to war, leaving the remains to be easily picked off by Valanis's forces.

The ranger sighed, tired of arguing the points of something he knew to be ridiculous. "Let's just get some sleep. We breach Elethiah tomorrow."

The next day, the companions crossed The Unmar at its shallowest and continued south-west, until the marshes of Elethiah were in sight.

Asher turned back to observe the lush green fields of The Moonlit Plains, before looking over the land that surrounded the ancient citadel. The surrounding fields had once been a part of The Moonlit Plains, and no doubt been under to the same enchantment that made the grass glow, but now there was nothing but swamp. The grass had grown long in the stagnant water, its healthy green now a pale yellow.

The city itself was a ruin. There was barely a tower that hadn't been damaged or brought down in the last battle of The Dark War. Giant roots and monstrous weeds crept up the stained walls like the tentacles of a great squid.

Buried under a thousand years of swamp growth, Asher could see various siege machines abandoned, before the Amber Spell took hold. The sound of clashing steel and roaring beasts filled his mind once again, but he couldn't place the memory.

Take this...

The ranger's mind worked furiously to place the memories that fought their way to the surface. He could hear a woman's voice.

Hide it deep in the forest...

The picture of his child-sized hand holding Paldora's Gem filled his vision.

Faylen's voice cut through his reverie. "I have seen many paintings of Elethiah, but none like this. It was the jewel of Illian, they said. The greatest elven minds in the land came here to learn from each other."

Ölli, the white owl, suddenly squawked behind Asher and flew away. Elaith and Nathaniel were slowly walking backwards, away from the citadel, taking no notice of the distressed owl. Their faces bore expressions of confusion with a hint of terror. The ranger looked at Reyna and saw that she too was taking a step back, her face contorted in disgust.

"What's wrong?" he asked, concerned.

Faylen whipped around with him. "It's the enchantments we placed over the land after the battle. The spells were designed to keep people away, through *fear*." The elf dashed over and grabbed Reyna by the arm. "You can feel the magic in the air, yes? You can feel the spell worming into your mind. Fight it, Reyna!" The princess couldn't take her eyes off Elethiah. "I should have prepared her for this."

The ranger walked over and put a strong hand on Nathaniel's shoulder. Before he could say anything, the knight's face dropped and he shook his head as if waking from a dream.

"What's happening?" the Graycoat asked.

Asher looked from Nathaniel to his hand on the knight's shoulder. Paldora's Gem peered out from his fingerless gloves. The ranger quickly put his hand on Elaith's shoulder and she too came back to her senses with a confused expression.

"It's the ring!" Faylen cried. "Help Reyna." The princess was starting to shake Faylen's hands off in a desperate attempt to run away from Elethiah.

Asher walked over and touched the princess on the arm. The reaction was instantaneous and identical to the Graycoats, but its duration clearly didn't last. As Reyna came to her senses, both Nathaniel and Elaith became slaves to the powerful enchantment again. Faylen and Reyna grabbed them both, holding them still with strong elven arms.

"Cast a spell over us, Asher." Faylen struggled to contain Nathaniel. "Think of a shield, or a bubble, and cast it over us!" Reyna's grip loosened on Elaith as the enchantment began to take effect on the elf again. "Quickly!"

Asher used Faylen's simplified idea and thought of a protective shield covering all of them. He pictured the invisible spells attacking them and being repelled by the field he erected. When he opened his eyes, all four of his companions appeared to have regained their senses. Nathaniel looked to be embarrassed more than anything.

"As tombs go, it's a damn good one," Nathaniel commented.

They gathered at the edge of the swamp and judged the distance between them and Elethiah's main gate. To Asher, there looked to be about a half mile of swampland between them.

"Let's take his head and be done with the place." Asher set off first, leading the way.

The group trudged through thick mud and a foot of cold water traversing the swamps. The ranger had an uneasy feeling. He had spent a lifetime learning to listen to that extra sense, a sense that had saved his life more than once. The feeling of being watched came over him and he slowly reached behind his back for the folded bow. Behind him, he saw every one of his companions had similarly rested a hand on their weapon of choice.

The only sound came from the parting water - even the breeze had disappeared. Everything went still, too still. They had only covered half of the distance and still had a way to go.

Someone drew their sword behind him, having seen the threat before the ranger did. Asher didn't need to turn around, however, to see what had caused the alarm. The water broke gently all around them, as ancient elven warriors rose slowly out of the swamp.

Some wore dark armour and ragged black cloaks, while others wore faded white armour with blue cloaks. Whatever their armour, they all had the same bloated pale faces, covered in dark veins. Some had terrible scars across their faces, while others were missing entire limbs. The dead continued to rise as if a stone had been thrown into the swamp and created a ripple in the water. Asher watched as hundreds more rose from the dirty water in the distance.

The dead elves stared at the companions with blank faces and white eyes while drawing their scimitars. The ranger had already flipped the switch on his bow and notched an arrow. Everyone but Elaith, who drew her sword, had done the same.

"We cannot take on so many," Faylen said with an edge of fear creeping into her voice.

The companions took several steps back and observed the dead halt their stride. Asher frowned, unsure if he had seen the reaction. The ranger took one step forward and the dead continued their approach.

"Step back!" Faylen warned. "The spell only works if we're walking towards Elethiah."

"Well, we can't kill Valanis out here," Nathaniel replied through gritted teeth.

"Run..." Asher whispered. The dead began to wade through the swamp towards them again. "RUN!"

The ranger burst into the quickest run he could manage in the swampy waters. The others had no choice but to follow him towards the city.

The five ran across the swamp with all haste, firing arrows in every direction. The dead warriors ploughed through the water with a steady rhythm. Almost every arrow found its mark, often striking the ancient elves in the head. If they were forced to the ground, they didn't stay there long. With arrows protruding from eyes and necks, the dead continued to rise and stride towards the group.

Asher fired an arrow into the head of a white plated warrior, causing the elf to fall back into the water. As they charged past, the elf sat up in the swamp with Asher's arrow still in its head. Elaith swiped her sword with a back-hand and decapitated the already dead elf. Still, it rose from the water behind them.

"Keep running!" Asher cried.

The dead, elven warriors started to pick up speed as they got closer to the citadel. Asher noticed several to his left were starting to run through the swamp instead of walking.

Elethiah's gates were nowhere to be seen, hidden beneath the swamp or blown to pieces by Adellum's bow a thousand years ago. The giant archway was guarded by two sixty-foot stone elves, clad in armour. Over the years their details had decayed and one of them was missing its head, most likely destroyed during the siege.

The companions ignored the exhaustion that clawed at their muscles and lungs, and ran between the two statues, into the shadow of Elethiah's halls.

"They're still coming!" Reyna shouted from the back of the group.

Faylen pulled everyone behind her so that she stood between them and the approaching horde of undead. The elf raised both of her hands to the arched ceiling and unleashed a barrage of brilliant blue lightning. The stone cracked and fissures spread out across the arch in the style of a pane of glass. As she clenched her fists, Faylen pulled her arms down with dramatic effort and brought the entire ceiling down with the gesture. Large slabs of stone quickly filled the entrance and continued to build, until a new wall of debris barred the way.

They were dropped into darkness.

A minute passed while the companions waited to see if the wall of rock would hold the ancient elves at bay. Only the sound of their heavy breathing could be heard in the dark tunnel.

Asher's senses exploded to life in the inky abyss. He could hear his companions' heart beats and the individual drops of water falling from their bodies. There was no smell of fresh blood, offering relief that his friends hadn't been hurt by any of the dead warriors.

What he could smell surprised him.

The ranger had expected to smell the decay of rotting bodies inside the citadel, but he could only smell the damp moss. It wasn't long before he found the reason for the lack of decay.

The ranger lifted his hand and conjured a ball of light, which floated above them, illuminating the tunnel. Faylen and Reyna did the same and offered more light to their situation. Asher walked over to the body he had discovered with his heightened senses, commanding the orb to follow him. The others gathered behind him to marvel at the scene.

"The Amber Spell..." Faylen whispered.

An elf in black armour and cloak stood before them, perfectly preserved in a running stance and with a face filled with despair. His blond hair was thrown out behind him but frozen in place, along with his flowing cloak. It looked to Asher as if the elf was simply staying very still. The warrior had no markings or an aura about him to suggest why he wasn't moving.

"He was running away," Elaith observed.

"They all were..." Nathaniel was looking farther down the tunnel, where dozens of elves were similarly frozen. It didn't matter what colour their armour, all were fleeing.

"They've been stuck like this for a thousand years." Reyna walked around the elf.

Asher removed his silvyr sword in a flash and cut the elf's head from his body. The elf launched himself forward as if continuing the run he had started a millennium ago, before his body collapsed to the ground and his head rolled away. Fresh blood poured from his gaping neck, suggesting he had never been frozen in time.

"Killing Valanis is going to be easier than I thought." Asher sheathed his blade and turned for the tunnel, ignoring the looks of shock he was receiving.

"Follow me." Faylen overtook Asher. "Elandril, in Ayda, was built in the same style as Elethiah, and all accounts from the battle state that Valanis was in the Hall of Life when the Amber Spell was cast. If that's the case, then we need to head into the centre of the city."

Moving through the ancient city, it became clear that the Amber Spell had kept everything inside the walls frozen in time, leaving the exterior to decay. Hundreds of elves dotted the interior, some frozen mid-battle, while others were left fleeing. Asher saw more than one child looking lost and distressed, as well as parents frozen in place, cowering in the corners with their child in their arms.

The ranger was forced to walk around a frozen stream of blood that was spurting forth from the chest of a white armoured elf, after having just been attacked by one of Valanis's soldiers. The elf's expression of pain and surprise had remained on his face for a millennium.

They climbed many stairs, as they passed between the different buildings and towers. The ranger was more than aware of the moving shadows that appeared to be following them. He had no doubt that the city was haunted by some creature that had been conjured up to keep people out. The silvyr sword never left his hand.

Faylen pushed open a pair of wooden doors, which creaked loudly in the empty halls. Asher stopped when he entered the new room, his legs refusing to go any further. They had entered a grand library with a tall ceiling and spiral staircases either side. Thousands of books and scrolls lined the bookshelves in the oval-shaped room. A long wooden table ran the length of the library, connecting both sides of the room, where another set of double doors lay.

"What is it?" Nathaniel asked.

Asher looked at the four dead elves, each in black armour and cloaks. Three lay dead on the table and another lay dead on the floor, with a heavy book next to his body. Drops of blood remained frozen in mid-air, as they had dropped off the table edge.

The ranger didn't know what to say...

He had been in this room before. He had seen these four elves and the book. Asher knew that the book had hit the elf and distracted him long enough for another to kill him.

They all saw the distortion in the air at the same time. On the far side of the table, a visible ball of rippling air hovered over the floor. Thankfully, it distracted them from Asher's reverie.

"What is that?" Reyna asked.

Asher bent down to collect the book and threw it into the distortion. Elaith gasped when the book passed into the ball and froze in mid-air. The rippling distortion disappeared but the book remained frozen in time.

"It must be the Amber Spell," Faylen said. "It looks as if it's *fractured... Strange.*"

The feeling of being watched overcame the ranger again. He

looked up to see his companions observing him curiously. "Let's keep going." Asher walked ahead, happy to leave the disturbingly familiar scene behind.

It was almost another thirty minutes before Faylen brought them before a set of ornate, wide double-doors. The white oak had been crafted with two trees on each door that met and entwined in the middle. A dozen elves in white armour lay scattered in the hall, each of them long dead. Their blood decorated the walls and most wore expressions of pure horror and agony.

Faylen stopped at the door. "This is the Hall of Life." She gripped her scimitar tightly.

The heavy doors *creaked* as the elf parted them. The companions cautiously entered the large chamber, circular in shape and lined with thick pillars. The ceiling was high and domed, with shafts of lights poking through the windows and jagged holes.

On the far side of the hall was an open balcony, as wide as the chamber, with an archway big enough to fit the tallest of giants through. Asher looked up, though his mouth remained ajar when he realised what the giant entrance and balcony were really for.

Curling around the circular hall was a dragon of tremendous size, covered in stone. Its mammoth head wrapped around one of the pillars and hung over the centre of the hall, where an empty podium sat. Surrounding the podium were six elven statues, each pointing a staff towards nothing.

"Garganafan..." Reyna looked up at the dragon with tears in her eyes.

Faylen was not so concerned with the stone dragon. "Where is Valanis?" She ran into the centre of the hall and rapidly circled the stone elves.

Asher felt a pit open in his stomach as her words sank in. He tore his gaze from the dragon and strode into the middle of the hall. Faylen was right. The six elves were clearly aiming at something that had been in front of the podium, but there was nothing there now.

Bar the statues, the entire Hall of Life was... lifeless.

"He's not here..." Reyna whispered, wide-eyed.

"It cannot be!" Faylen cried. "Every account has him right here! The elders and Garganafan were turned to stone in their effort to enact the Amber Spell. They wouldn't have sacrificed so much if he wasn't right here!"

"Maybe he's in another room?" Nathaniel offered.

A familiar, yet menacing, voice echoed from behind one of the pillars. "You could look in every room in every tower." Alidyr stepped into view, dressed in his white robes. "But you would never find Valanis in this wretched tomb."

The dark elf smiled arrogantly, but Asher's experienced eyes immediately found that the elf was favouring one leg over the other.

"What have you done with him, *snake*?" Faylen crouched into an attacking stance, like an animal ready to pounce.

"For a *thousand* years, he stood right there." Alidyr looked to the spot by the podium. "Freeing him became hopeless when the years turned into decades, and the decades turned into centuries... I knew that without Paldora's Gem, he would never be free to serve the gods, for only the gem could break through the Amber Spell. I blame myself for having missed it all those years, under my nose." Alidyr looked at Asher. "But the gods act in mysterious ways do they not? And their timescale is not our own. While I scoured the land and did my best to see the master's plans fulfilled, the gods were already seeing to his freedom."

"Speak plainly Alidyr, or lose your head!" Faylen was filling with rage.

"Did you not see it?" Alidyr gestured to the white doors behind them, but Asher noticed the flicker of pain that crossed the elf's face.

How had Alidyr come by so many injuries?

"The Amber Spell has been ruptured," he continued. "It took a thousand years but Paldora's Gem found a way." The dark elf turned to Asher and flashed a grin of brilliant, white teeth. "In the hands of a small human child, it pushed against the Amber Spell for a millennium, until the spell *cracked*. Of course, by that point, the world had changed and the boy was a stranger in his own lands. How does it feel to be over a thousand years old?" Alidyr tilted his head, still smiling. "The immortal man, as it were..."

Asher fought against the world that tried to spin out of his control. The memory of being found by Nasta Nal-Aket outside Elethiah came rushing back. He had been chased by Gobbers after fleeing Elethiah...

Nalana!

The ranger remembered the beautiful elf and his lessons in the tower. She had given him the gem after her brother Elym, now the Lord of the Elves had retrieved it from this very hall.

He had been born over a thousand years ago in The Wild Moores...

His clan had been hunters...

The faces of his family were still featureless in his mind, but he remembered them running from the citadel with him. They must have abandoned him when they saw that he was frozen in the doorway.

Frozen for a millennium.

"Of course," Alidyr continued, "when the spell was fractured it didn't just release *you*. Pockets appeared throughout the city. The spell began to break down. My master had already started to repel the Amber Spell before it was cast, but when the spell weakened... he broke free. How long have you been free, Asher? Ah yes, *forty* years..."

A lone tear streaked down Faylen's cheek. "Valanis has been free... for forty years?"

"Do you see now? Your plans and schemes are worthless. Valanis has been a step ahead of you since before you even decided to invade." Alidyr laughed. "Who do you think had the idea planted in your king's mind in the first place? The Dark War saw our forces depleted, but your army will suffice, *and* that of man's."

Faylen's eyes widened with revelation. The entire elven nation had been manipulated and was going to be used as fodder. In one strike, Valanis would weaken both man and elf. Faylen's shoulders visibly sagged.

"Now," Alidyr continued, full of confidence, "give me the ring and tell me what you did with the rest of it. If your answer pleases me, I will consider letting you all leave this place."

Asher clenched his jaw and squeezed the hilt of his silvyr blade. The ranger wanted for nothing more than to wipe that smug grin off his old mentor's face.

"Hmm, I've seen that look before," the dark elf said. "Nasta Nal-Aket had it, right before I pushed him into the *pit*."

Asher's resolve faltered. He hated and loved Nasta like a father. The man had been hard on him and disciplined him severely, but he had also been the only friend Asher had. Nasta had not only saved him but made him strong, giving him the skills to survive.

The thought of him dead stirred the ranger in ways he hadn't expected. A lot had been left unsaid between the men, and now it would remain so. Not that Asher expected to live should he ever meet Nasta again. Despite everything between them, Asher was still a traitor.

"Kill him." Asher's words were meant for Reyna, who had slowly slunk around the pillars until she had a clear shot with Adellum's bow.

The arrow flew from the weapon with magically enhanced speed. But it still wasn't enough. Alidyr twisted his body and deflected the arrow with one of his short-swords, a weapon equally as powerful as Adellum's bow.

The arrow drove into the nearest pillar with the force of a hurricane. The marble column exploded near the base and spread devastating cracks that reached the ceiling.

Asher and Nathaniel managed to dive and roll out of the way before the pillar flattened them. The ground shook and the elven statues were shattered into a thousand pieces, as well as a large portion of Garganafan's tail.

A thick fog of dust and debris quickly settled over the large chamber, creating the perfect screen for Alidyr to slip away. Faylen dashed to the spot where he had been standing, but the elf was already gone.

Asher came up from his dive with his blade out, ready for the next attack. Nathaniel swivelled on the ball of his foot, his sword out in front of him.

"Where is he?" Elaith shouted.

Asher cursed, but it was too late. Elaith had given away her position in the dust cloud, and Alidyr's blade found her before Asher could react. The short-sword spun through the air, inches from his face, and continued past him, into Elaith's chest.

The young knight experienced a single moment of shock, with tears filling her eyes and a faint gasp escaping her lips. In the next moment, Elaith fell to the floor, dead.

"NO!" Nathaniel ran to her.

Asher never saw him reach Elaith's body. A fist, as strong as any hammer, slammed into the ranger's face and dropped him to the floor.

Asher tried to make sense of his surroundings only to find the Hall of Life a hazy mess. Reyna and Faylen screamed somewhere in the distance. Lightning erupted between the pillars, blinding Asher momentarily. Steel clashed and spells exploded against stone and marble.

The ranger was on his hands and knees, blinking hard to regain and sharpen his vision. Elaith was dead and lying several feet to his left and Nathaniel was rolling around on the floor next to her, fresh blood dripping from his shoulder and head. Reyna slid to the floor, at his side, and the two crouched over Elaith. The elf removed the powerful short-sword from her chest and dropped it to the floor in disgust.

As Asher rose to his feet, Faylen was thrown across the hall, until her body collapsed in a heap at Nathaniel's feet.

Asher was too slow. Alidyr was already in front of him.

He managed to bring his silvyr sword up, however, before the elf could cut him in half. The ranger twisted and spun to avoid Alidyr's blade, always making the dark elf turn on his injured leg and swing with his wounded arm.

The elf's pain gave Asher the precious moments he needed to evade a death delivering blow. Their short-swords rang out in the hall, but only for a minute. Even with his apparent injuries, it seemed that Alidyr was only playing with Asher. A swift open-palm attack caught the ranger across the throat, stopping the air from reaching his lungs. The elf followed up his attack with a gut punch and an elbow to Asher's chest.

All three attacks pushed him back until Alidyr caught his right wrist in an iron grip. Slender fingers wrapped around the silver ring and pulled the gem free of his hand. A quick push-kick sent Asher flying into his friends, creating a tangled mess of limbs.

Alidyr laughed with the backdrop of the balcony behind him. The dust settled and the dark elf turned on them, Asher's ring on his finger. The ranger waited for the violent reaction upon touching the crystal, but the elf stood proud, unaffected.

"Where is the rest of it?" Alidyr asked with shining gold eyes.

Asher spat blood on the floor between them. "I threw it into The Adean!" he lied. The ranger had abandoned the gem in a far worse place than the ocean.

Alidyr snarled and swept his hand across the fallen pillar. With his powers amplified, the marble column flew into the air and snapped in half, sending more debris in every direction.

"Fool!" Alidyr's anger subsided quickly and he turned on them with a wicked smile. "An especially *big* fool if you think the depths of The Adean are beyond my master's grasp." The dark elf surveyed the broken companions, sheltering Elaith's dead body. "It seems to me that this city has stood for too long as a monument to Valanis's defeat. I think it's time to move on. After all, a new age is upon us..." Alidyr raised his hands dramatically and unleashed his magic.

The dome cracked and the city's very foundations shook. Giant slabs of stone fell all around, threatening to crush them. The pillars split and wobbled and dust rained down in the great hall. Alidyr laughed throughout it all before he stepped into a portal and vanished from sight.

Asher cursed the elf and turned to his friends with a new look of determination. They wouldn't die in here! Nathaniel and Reyna had tears running down their faces and Faylen looked a broken elf. Elaith lay between them all, so very still.

"Follow me!" Asher picked up Alidyr's short-sword and hooked an arm under Faylen to bring her with him.

With his life in the balance, Asher's mind found it easier to recall the memories he needed to save his friends. They ran through the corridors and halls without saying a word. Nathaniel followed behind them all with Elaith in his arms.

The city crumbled around them, as pillars fell and staircases split down the middle. Those frozen in the Amber Spell were buried under the rubble. Asher kicked the door to the kitchens open and charged in, searching the floor for the hidden trap. His heart thundered in his chest when the hatch opened into a darkened tunnel.

"This way!" The ranger bundled them all down the hatch until he took Elaith from Nathaniel's arms. Once the knight was down, Asher carefully lowered her body.

The ground shook, knocking the ranger aside while he climbed down. Faylen picked him up and offered her own expression of resolve. The companions ran down the tunnel, where a familiar wooden door with a small window at the top waited for them. Reyna kicked the door off its hinges and they ran into the swamp.

"Quickly!" the princess urged.

The four of them ran for what felt like an age until they found hard ground on the edge of The Wild Moores.

Exhausted and out of breath, Nathaniel dropped to his knees with Elaith still in his arms. Through laboured breaths, they looked back, witnessing the destruction of Elethiah, as it was razed to the ground in a cloud of dust and rubble.

Asher hefted Alidyr's hour-glass blade and stared at the blood that stained the steel. Elaith's blood.

"He's alive... Valanis is alive," Reyna said in disbelief.

"And he has the gem..." Faylen added in dismay.

Asher threw the sword into the ground and continued to watch Elethiah fall into the earth in a great plume of smoke and dust. If Alidyr was capable of collapsing an entire city with the gem, what was Valanis capable of?

EPILOGUE

The dark halls of Kaliban were frozen and covered in thick sheets of ice. Snow blew through most of the corridors, having breached the shattered windows and broken doors.

Set high in The Vengoran Mountains, to the north, the fortress was virtually inaccessible to any who weren't masters in the art of magic, though Alidyr was confident that even Korkanath's Magikar would struggle to find a way inside.

The stone and masonry soon gave way to jagged rock, as the dark elf entered the depths of his master's home. It wasn't long before he left Kaliban far behind and entered a series of cave networks that would confuse any human.

The magic that ebbed within these caves distorted Verda's pull, making up become down. To untrained eyes, it would appear as if the elf was walking up the walls and along the roof of the caves.

A sweet smell found his nostrils and Alidyr knew he was home. A cavern the size of the Hall of Life lay before him, shimmering with the thirteen pools of Naius. The water looked to be made from the purest of crystals, setting the cavern alight. The pools surrounded him, with some on the roof of the cavern and others climbing the walls.

Thallan stepped out from behind a glittering stalagmite, his shoulder healed. The dark elf said nothing but simply stared at Alidyr and his clenched fist, sensing what was within his grasp.

Samandriel and Nakir appeared from behind another stalagmite, on the other side of the central and largest pool. The three of them had offered their power to Valanis, helping to fuel the mighty storm that they had dragged across the land, guiding their enemies.

Seeing his brothers and sister only reminded him of the blade he had lost. The twin to his gifted set now lay under the rubble of Elethiah. In his joy to wield the power of the gem, he had simply forgotten to retrieve the short-sword: an oversight he now greatly regretted. It had felt satisfying, however, to kill the young knight who had stabbed him at West Fellion.

The Hand bowed their heads out of respect for their leader, finally restored to his rightful position after Valanis had stripped him of it, upon his return to the living. The master had been upset with Alidyr for his failure to find the gem in his absence, but that was about to change.

Alidyr strode to the edge of the shimmering pool and took a knee, with his head bowed low. The pain in his leg was beginning to fade, as Reaver's magic finally lost its bite. He offered out his hand and revealed the ranger's silver ring.

"I have returned it, as promised, Master. Paldora's Gem is finally yours..."

The pool of pure magic rippled, giving way to the greatest elf who had ever lived. His naked body sparkled and hummed with the magic that he contained. Flowing blond hair fell over his muscled back, as he lifted his head and trained two brilliant purple eyes on Alidyr, before shifting to the ring.

Without any sign of gratitude, as none was required, Valanis held out his hand and commanded the ring to jump from the general's hand and onto his finger. The master clenched his fist and marvelled at the black crystal. The constant hum surrounding his body died down, while his skin lost its glow and returned to its normal shade.

Alidyr quickly backed away, as Valanis took his first step outside of the pool in forty years. The Hand dropped to their knees and bowed their heads in awe.

For the first time in over a thousand years, Alidyr saw his master's wicked smile.

PHILIP C. QUAINTRELL

Hear more from Philip C. Quaintrell including book releases and exclusive content:

 PHILIPCQUAINTRELL.COM

 FACEBOOK.COM/PHILIPCQUAINTRELL

 @PHILIPCQUAINTRELL.AUTHOR

 @PCQUAINTRELL

AUTHOR NOTES

I can't tell you how much I loved writing this book! Actually... I'm probably about to ramble on and tell you as much, so never mind.

I had never planned on writing a fantasy genre novel, with my primary interests being sci-fi, but I'm also a huge fan of Lord of the Rings, Game of Thrones, Eragon and anything written by R.A. Salvatore etc.

I remember distinctly being away with friends at the time, staying in a cottage somewhere in the country (the perfect setting!). I was probably a boring so and so, tucked away in a comfy spot with my notepad and headphones in, but when I get the spark of an idea, I HAVE to do something.

I was getting up earlier than everyone and staying up later to make pages of notes and imagine what this new world would look like. In other words, I looked like a giant nerd to my friends. By this point I hadn't even released Intrinsic, my first foray into the writing world, so I was just a nerdy guy who liked writing stories for himself.

Unlike sci-fi, a fantasy book can actually be mapped out with accurate distances and landscapes in one, single image. The map in question came after I detailed the six kingdoms of Illian and their general locations started to form in my mind. I definitely went through 4 or 5 versions of the map, each one increasing in size. I think I enjoyed making the map just as much as I did writing the story, to be honest.

In the same way that I wrote Intrinsic, Rise of the Ranger was entirely spontaneous in its creation. Asher, Nathaniel and Reyna were the only characters that I had fleshed out in my notes (and Valanis – obviously!), though even their story went in directions I hadn't planned. I had scenes and specific plot points throughout the entire story arc, which I knew I wanted, but every chapter from beginning to end was thought of as I arrived at it. This also led to the creation of some new characters, that I now realise the book could never had been made without. I was on holiday in Majorca when I thought up the story arc with Galanör on the Mediterranean-like island of Dragorn – the hot weather really helped! Gideon was thought up because I really wanted a younger character... and a mage... and I liked the name Gideon! It can be that simple. But looking back, I don't know how the story would have looked without either of them.

One of my favourite characters was also a spontaneous creation; Adilandra, the queen of elves. Hopefully the day will come when female characters won't need to be described as strong and independent, but simply as a woman, and all will understand the intricacies, depth and strength that accompany that title. I love Adilandra because she's a mother, and boy does that make her fierce! As well as being the queen of a nation, with whom she can no longer identify, Adilandra is a woman of faith, and this faith keeps her steadfast to her mission. Now I could go on and on about faith and equality, but I have to keep this to my notes, otherwise it could turn into another book!

I knew from the start that I didn't want Valanis to actually be in the story. I really like the idea of a villain that everyone talks about and bigs up, but you never actually see them. Obviously if you're reading this, you've already seen the prologue to book 2, and you know that Valanis is going to play a much bigger role, now that he has a shard of Paldora's Gem. Having planned out book 2 and 3 of the planned 9, I can tell you that Valanis is going to be a badass! I really enjoyed writing from his perspective. I'll ramble on about Valanis in my notes at the back of book 2 so I don't give any spoilers.

As with my other series, The Terran Cycle, this is self-published on Amazon. If you enjoyed the book, please leave a review, I read every one, and they mean so much. I also have a Facebook page, Philip C. Quaintrell, and you can follow me for updates and cool things on Instagram - philipcquaintrell.author. If you want to check out the map in HD quality then head over to my website www. philipcquintrell.com and dive right in. I hope you've enjoyed my notes or they at least helped you to fall asleep.

Until the next time...

APPENDICES

Kingdoms of Illian:

1. ***Alborn*** (eastern region) - Ruled by King Rengar of house Marek. Capital city: *Velia*. Other Towns and Cities: Palios, Galosha, and Barossh.

2. ***The Arid Lands*** (southern region) - Ruled by Emperor Faros. Capital city: *Karath*. Other Towns and Cities: Ameeraska, Calmardra and Tregaran.

3. ***The Ice Vales*** (western region) - Ruled by King Gregorn of house Orvish. Capital city: *Grey Stone*. Other Towns and Cities: Bleak, Kelp Town and Snowfell.

4. ***Orith*** (northern region) - Ruled by King Merkaris of house Tion. Capital city: *Namdhor*. Other Towns and Cities: Skystead, Dunwich, Darkwell and Longdale.

5. *Felgarn* (central region) - Ruled by Queen Isabella of house Harg. Capital city: *Lirian*. Other Towns and Cities: Vangarth, Wood Vale and Whistle Town.

6. *Dragorn* (island nation off The Shining Coast to the east) - Ruled by the four crime families; the Trigorns, Fenrigs, Yarls, and the Danathors.

〜

Significant Wars: Chronologically

The Great War - Fought during the First Age, around 5,000 years ago. The only recorded time in history that elves and dwarves have united. They fought against the orcs with the help of the Dragorn, the first elvish dragon riders. This war ended the First age.

The Dark War - Fought during the Second Age, around 1,000 years ago. Considered the elvish civil war. Valanis, the dark elf, tried to take over Illian in the name of the gods. This war ended the Second Age.

The Dragon War - Fought in the beginning of the Third Age, only a few years after The Dark War. The surviving elves left Illian for Ayda's shores, fleeing any more violence. Having emerged from The Wild Moores, the humans, under King Gal Tion's rule, went to war with the dragons over their treasure. This saw the exile of the surviving dragons and the beginning of human dominance over Illian.